Spirit Warriors Book 2: National Restoration Arc: Part 2

By: Caleb James

For my lord and savior Jesus Christ,
And Haley for being Spirit Warrior's #1 Fan

Table of Contents

Hope deferred makes the heart sick, but a longing fulfilled is a tree of life.

Proverbs 13:12 (NIV)

13 – Knight

James

I ENDURED A MULTITUDE OF DREAMS AFTER I PASSED OUT ON THE BALCONY. Most of them consisted of my past episodes with women. Anyone could probably guess that those experiences were mostly negative. One dream played on loop, and the visceral pain was more vivid than the initial heartbreak.

During my senior year of college, I ran into this girl at a Christian weekend retreat out in the woods. When I was leaving my cabin on the opening day, for one of the first times in my life, I started feeling self-conscious about my grooming. I looked in the mirror and felt upset that my hair was nappy. This was a foreign concept to me. I had just brushed my teeth before I walked out the door, but something told me to go back and brush them again. I always took decent care of myself, but before this I had never cared about my fashion or grooming in the slightest. If my clothes were somewhat matching, I was more than content. From my perspective, the odds of running into someone I liked were so *infinitesimally* small, that I wasn't risking anything by not looking nice because today was probably not going to be the day that broke the streak.

Well, that day the streak was broken. Her name was Mikayla, and she was absolutely gorgeous. As soon as she walked into the chapel, I had to know if she had substance to back up her appearance. I walked right up to her like the G that I was (my heart was pounding, and my knees were shaking) and struck up a conversation. It went fantastic and we ended up spending most of the trip together (just like another story you may have heard before). We hit it off talking about God and our surprisingly similar life experiences struggling to find real Christian friends.

The difference between this budding romance and the Destiny debacle is that we went to the same school this time, but I had never seen her a day in my life. After the retreat, I started running into her everywhere. I randomly saw her all across campus, and each conversation was better than the last. She even "asked me out" to some on campus events and we had a great time going together.

Early on, I came to the conclusion that she was definitely into me. She laughed way too hard at my not funny jokes, and she picked up the phone every time I called, even if she was busy or it was late at night. She even initiated texting conversations and went out of her way to emphasize the fact that she canceled her plans on numerous occasions to hang out with me, which I never even asked her to do! I was certain God wanted us to be together, because before her, I hadn't liked a girl since high school, especially not like this.

I also took the fact that we started constantly running into each other as proof God was orchestrating our inevitable love story. Funnily enough, during the time the two of us were getting to know each other, girls just started showing interest out of nowhere. When I went out to random places, I caught girls staring at me, and different women that never gave me the time of day approached me to strike up conversations. When they went out of their way to give me their numbers, and started texting me first, I knew something was up. It got to the point that even Micah noticed and started questioning what was going on. I joked with him that I was already married to Mikayla so none of these girls had a chance. I took those women's advances as attacks from the devil to distract me, which was an even further indication that we were meant to be together.

The time came to make my feelings known, and I asked her if she wanted to come hang out at my place.

She shouted over the phone. "Oh my gosh! Of course! What's the soonest I can come over?!"

The enthusiasm in her voice made my heart sing.

I've got this in the bag!

She wanted to cook for me too, and I was even more excited because I figured she wanted to show me what she was bringing to the table, literally and figuratively.

When she came over, we had another outstanding conversation, and the food was even better. After we finished eating, the time came to pop the question.

I held up my hands. "I'm just saying! If I start a clothing brand one day I might call it 'Fosphorous'! Get it? Because my last name means light..."

She slapped the table as she burst into laughter. "HAAAAA! HAAAAAA! HAAAAAAA! James stop! That is just too crazy!"

I smiled as I saw the joyful light in her eyes.

I took a deep breath.

It's now or never.

"I'm a man of many talents..." I looked her in the eye. "But hey Mikayla. There's something I've been wanting to tell you recently..."

"Yeah sure! Go for it! I can't promise my response will be as witty as yours, but I'll do my best!"

"Well hopefully there will be lots of laughs together after this..." I cleared my throat. "Mikayla, I like you. I've loved getting to know you over these past few weeks and I think you're one of the most incredible girls I've ever met..."

The light faded from her eyes. "Oh..."

The words were caught in my throat.

She rescued us from the awkward silence. "Well...uh...you see James...I actually dated one of your teammates in the past and I could *never* really see myself dating one of his teammates so..."

Never. Never. Never. Never. Never. Never. Never.

Her words rattled within my soul.

I was devastated, but I did my best to proceed as usual for the next hour we unfortunately spent talking. After the topic changed, Mikayla perked right up like the conversation never happened, and she was completely oblivious to the fact she dropped a nuke on my entire existence. Guise James put on one of his best performances, which is why I had to shake that man's hand when I saw him.

I approached her as she prepared to leave. "Hey Mikayla. I don't mean to make things awkward again or anything, but did you really mean never when I told you how I felt earlier? Maybe after a few months when you get over him a little more, we could try and see how things go." I smiled. "I know I said it before, but I really like you Mikayla."

"I really like you too James. But no. When I said never, I meant it."

BOOM!

The second atom bomb decimated the United States of Fos.

I shuddered. "Oh...ok. Well, I'll walk you to your car then..."

My composure hung by a hairline thread.

"Sure! I would love that!"

I felt numb as we talked on our way back to the car. She gave me a big hug before she left, and I wanted to die inside. To make matters worse, once I got back to my room, she called me...just to talk...acting like nothing happened between us. After general conversation, she asked how I knew she had broken up with her boyfriend as she probed for information about things he may have said about her. I finished muttering my responses and she eventually hung up.

My insides were shredded as I doubled over. I was overwhelmed with rage toward God for letting this happen. I wanted more than anything to cry so I could potentially start feeling better.

Nothing came out.

That was the first time I heard the voice inside me whisper. "**Destroy it. Destroy it all.**"

I had no method to indulge it, and I never would have because I didn't want to do anything that would upset God.

But boy did I want to.

This dream, among others, tormented me for hours upon end as I endured a restless slumber.

Until suddenly, the visions ceased. I found myself floating in a void of nothingness as the voice called out. "**This is what happens when you don't listen to me.**"

The scene of Kayla's naked back as she made out with Terrance filled every speck of the darkness around me

"NO! NO! NO! NO! NO! NO! NO!" I roared.

"This is what happens when you hold on to hope. These are the profits of your labor. The first fruits of your harvest."

A vision played before me of the different James council members slaughtering the Ocean Tribe's people. Critical James sliced up soldiers with his tie. Passive James destroyed people with zombies and cut a buff black guy in half. Lazy James swallowed soldiers whole. Guise James disguised himself as civilians and slit their throats. Love James was taller than a skyscraper as he rampaged through the city. Hood James shot soldiers with an AK-47 and fired rockets that destroyed entire city blocks.

"No! This can't be real! It can't be! I would never hurt all of those people!"

"But you did. We did. And now we feel much better."

"You're lying! You're a liar!"

"No. I am the only one willing to tell you the truth. For now, just remember who is at fault for making us feel this way. You'll see their true nature in due time."

My blood boiled as the vision of Kayla and Terrance making out flashed in front of me again, and again, and again.

Suddenly, a shadowy red figure smiled as it materialized before me.

"No! Whoever you are! I hate you! You're a liar! None of this is real! I'll kill you!"

I raised my arm to destroy them, but my father's hand reached out and gently touched my shoulder.

"It's going to be ok son."

Tears welled in my eyes. "Dad...is that you? It's been so long..."

A light pierced through the darkness, and I grasped it.

I woke up in his arms and I was overwhelmingly fatigued. I let myself rest in his warm, loving embrace.

I jolted awake in the same bedroom I was in before disaster struck.

That random butler from before stood. "Sir! You're awake!"

I jumped out of bed and looked through the window. The city was intact, just as it was before. I sighed in with relief, but I still wondered about what the voice said in my dream. *It was right about Terrance and Kayla...But I'll worry about that later.* I stretched. *The time has come for me to end that bastard for what he did to Kayla. I'll beat the shit out of him until he renounces that slavery vow.*

My eyes widened. *I thought I might have heard her say something like "It's not what it looks like" before I ran out. Maybe she was just pleasuring him that way on the threat of death...or something. I changed my mind. Instead, I'll just leave him within an inch of his life before I take her and leave,* **if** *I'm feeling generous.* I felt a new kind of energy deep in the pit of my stomach. It was raw power. *I know I can whoop his ass this time. All I have to do is find him. Then I can question Kayla, she'll say something that makes sense, and we'll go back to living happily ever after.* I balled my fists. *All I have to do is find him.*

I looked over and my sword was on the table once again. *Maybe this whole thing is a dream, or I'm stuck in some kind of crazy loop.*

I grabbed my sword and started to leave. "Where is he?"

The butler face palmed. "Not this again. Sir, I implore you to please calm down for all of our sakes. The prince has already been well disciplined for his actions..."

I threw open the door. "What do you mean for all of our sakes? He's the only one I'm gonna kill unless someone else..."

Outside, more than fifty guards stood in battle stances with spears aimed at the entryway.

"...decides to stand in my way..." I eased the door closed. "You know what? I think I've had a change of heart. Forget I said anything."

When I turned back, the butler was staring at me intensely. He had removed a glove from one of his hands. "Sir. I will have you know that if you take **one step** outside of this room, you will be forced to deal with me. I am under strict orders to prevent anyone from entering or exiting this room."

I tried to hold back my laughter. "*Please*, you're just a butler. Tea and crumpets aren't very threatening to me."

He glared. "I'll have you know that I am the Archigos' personal assistant! He entrusted me to single handedly protect this castle and his daughter, and not a single person has ever been harmed under my care!"

I chuckled. "*Wow*, so if I get out of line they send the big bad butler to stop me! I'm terrified! Clearly they don't trust you very much because they have fifty guys out there waiting to thrust my head off."

"That is simply untrue. We are simply taking extra security precautions this evening after your most recent...debacle."

I shrugged. "I didn't even hurt those guys *that* badly. I know I was angry, but I made sure to just give them flesh wounds." I flipped my sword in my hand. "I'm kind of a pro at this."

He shook his head. "If you say so."

I laughed. "In fact, after the way I cut through you guy's security earlier, and given how you're acting now,

I'd say that you guys are more scared of me than I should be of you!"

"Uhh...yes, I suppose you could say that. For now, please have a seat until the Archigos comes to visit you."

I plopped on the bed. "Sure, whatever dude. I came here to speak to him anyway. I'll hold off my plans of killing that bastard. For now."

Terrance

I trudged out of the infirmary. *My stupid sister is just an idiot who doesn't know what the hell she's talking about! Nobody is listening when I tell them that it was weirdo Kayla who came to MY room and started kissing on ME! I just let her, and now all of the sudden, I'm the reason our nation almost got destroyed by that simp loser. Unbelievable. And her dumbass lecturing about beating the shit out of that white guy was even more out of line. I* waved my arms as I mocked her stupid girly voice. "OH MY GOD, YOU LITERALLY ALMOST KILLED HIM! OH MY GOD, I HAD TO USE EVERY OUNCE OF MY SPIRIT ENERGY AND MULTIPLE PROGRESS ARTS TO SAVE HIM! OH MY GOD, HE ALMOST FLATLINED SEVEN TIMES!"

WHO CARES! *She must like him or something because she sure was rubbing on his bare chest, talking about him over and over again. Women are so stupid. Surely dad will understand.* I was actually a bit excited for once as I headed toward the throne room. I passed by the maid servants as they blushed and swooned in my presence as usual.

"OH MY GOSH, IT'S THE PRINCE!" They screamed.

I nodded. "Hey."

They swooned even more intensely and returned to their chores. "I HEARD HE KILLED A HUNDRED, NO A THOUSAND OF THOSE WICKED SPIRITS!", "I HEARD HE FOUGHT OFF THREE GIANT ONES TO WIN OVER ONE OF OUR HEARTS!", "Did you hear about that weird foreigner who kicked down my door yesterday? He must be a pervert or something..."

My legend continues to grow. At least some things are still right in the world. Though I do feel awful inside for losing to that fake version of the simp bastard. His words echoed in my mind. "You ain't nothing like your daddy and you ain't never gonna be."

Rage swelled within me, but I shook it off. *I promise I'll get strong enough to protect my people from things like that. I'll be able to do it all by myself, just like dad did. I* repeated my daily positive affirmations until I passed the simp bastard's room. There were roughly seventy guards posted outside of his room with their spears drawn. They were drenched in sweat, and I could feel the fear bleeding from their hearts.

I clapped one of them on the back. "Relax! He's not gonna hurt you guys. He's just a weak little runt."

"Sir! That weak little runt single handedly destroyed our entire nation! And you should not be here! He has a thirst for your blood sir! Who knows what devilish powers he would employ to take your life!"

I burst into laughter. "*Please!* If that little shrimp wants to take my life, I'd let him have the first swing. I'm so confident I would *murderize* him, that I'd be willing to put this entire kingdom on the line." I looked away. "He doesn't have any devil powers. He just got a little angry and his emotions stirred up some spirits that happened to be in the area. That's all."

"Sir, please don't speak like that. And for all our sakes, I hope you are right."

I waved dismissively as I walked off. "Yeah, yeah. If he starts causing any trouble, let him go." I stopped and glared at the door. "And tell him if he's looking for me, he knows where to find me."

I made my way through the castle until I stood before the grand doors of my father's throne room. I reached for the door handle, but my hands were trembling. I hadn't really seen dad in a few weeks because he's been so busy since the nation split up. He left me with a lot of responsibility during that time, and I hadn't always taken it as seriously as I should have. I swallowed. *I have no idea what he's gonna say to me.* I felt convicted as I wondered how much he actually knew about how I had spent the last few weeks.

It's *just dad.* I placed my hand on the door handle and Spirit Energy flowed into it. The ground rumbled as the massive frozen doors slowly creaked open and I stepped through.

My dad sat on his throne reading a yellow and black book. As I approached, he tossed it behind the throne. "What's going on Terrance? How are your injuries?"

I sighed in relief. "Nothing much. I'm still pretty banged up. Brooklyn said it will be at least a week before I can fight again because I had so much internal damage from that bitch and it couldn't be healed easily with Depth Command."

"That makes sense. I was watching, and you've gotten really good at controlling your Depth Command. Once you master it, you'll be on your way to succeeding me..." He leaned back and stared at the ceiling. "And then I can *finally* retire."

My eyes widened. "Retire? But dad, this nation needs you! We would be nothing without your leadership!"

"That's not true. And if that's the case, I have failed as a leader. I'm sure that one day, you will lead this nation far better than I ever could. I've made many grave mistakes in the past that have set a lot of terrible things in motion..."

"That's not true dad! You've been the perfect leader! I hope to accomplish even a fraction of your success!"

He chuckled. "That sounds good, but no. You're wrong." He smiled. "Anyways, enough with the retirement talk." Fear gripped my heart as he leaned forward and narrowed his eyes. "I am aware of your relations with that Flame Tribe girl."

"No dad! It's not like that! Honest! She's..."

He spoke with a big grin. "Did you guys have sex or what?!"

I was overwhelmed with relief as joy welled up in my heart. "Nah, but I did want to! We probably would have if that simp ass loser didn't show up..."

"So you guys just made out then?"

"Yeah! It was incredible! She kicked down my door and started yelling about how much she hated me! Then she just kissed me and started stripping! One thing led to another and her tongue was in my throat!"

"THAT'S INCREDIBLE MY SON! YOUR HANDSOMENESS AND SWAGGER KNOW NO BOUNDS!"

"I KNOW RIGHT! IT'S EVEN MORE OF AN ACCOMPLISHMENT BECAUSE SHE'S HOT ENOUGH TO BE IN THE BIG THREE! HER SEXYNESS SHOULD BE CRIMINAL!"

"I KNOW RIGHT! SHE'S ALMOST AS BEAUTIFUL AS AURANIA! IN FACT, SHE'S PROBABLY EVEN PRETTIER THAN AURANIA WAS BACK IN THE DAY! THAT BODY IS BANGING!"

"I KNOW RIGHT! I DON'T LIKE HER LIKE THAT, BUT I'M DEFINITELY GOING TO HIT AT LEAST ONCE BEFORE I SETTLE DOWN!"

"And therein lies the issue." He said with a stern tone.

My heart sank.

He gripped his temple. "Son, I know I haven't always set the best example for you. Especially when we first got here. I was going through a really tough time after losing your mother, and I allowed myself to indulge in too many toxic aspects of this nation's old culture." He pounded his armrest. "You know I have been working my hardest to change that culture since the day I became Archigos, but clearly I haven't worked hard enough! I raised you better than to be sleeping around with women, especially ones you're not even interested in! Is it true you've slept with every single female servant in the palace?"

Tears welled in my eyes. "Ye...Yes dad. But they're the ones who keep throwing themselves at me! I don't even really check for them like that and..."

CRASH!

Dad's Spirit Energy surged and the throne room was filled with razor sharp icy pillars. "Absolutely unacceptable son! I don't care if they strip naked right in front of you! You know you're supposed to save yourself for marriage! And if you can't do that, at least keep it to girls you would actually see yourself being with in the future!"

I stomped. "But that's so dumb dad! I'll admit, sometimes I get lonely and I'll go have my way with one of them. But it always makes me feel better, and they like it too! I don't understand why you're always trying to teach me that Bible stuff! What has that book ever done for us?!"

"That book is the only thing that's gonna keep your ass from going straight to hell son! Do you not understand that if you had been killed by that hoodlum or that giant, me and you might not be going to the same place in the afterlife?" He shook his head. "You were always so devout as a child...But you're the one who always says he wants to get stronger, and be a leader like me. Well, everything I know about leadership, I learned from the Bible. Everything I learned about strength, I learned from the Bible. Everything I learned about being a man, I learned from the Bible!"

"That's a lie! You've always been a great man, and the strongest and a great leader too! If this God you keep talking about really exists, then why didn't He help you while you were struggling to find a job? Why did He let those stupid researchers treat you like that when you were right? Why did He let the government and that fuck ass cowboy steal all of our research? WHY DID HE LET MOM DIE?"

Dad shed a tear and looked away. "I don't know my son. But I *do know* that He has a good purpose in *everything* He does. Despite all of that...and far worse, look at where we are now. A no-good scientist and his son, in charge of one of the largest nations to ever exist in the history of mankind." He sighed. "I understand if you don't want to talk about this anymore. Just remember that He loves you. And He loves you so much that He sent his Son to die just for you. He's better than me, because I couldn't imagine sacrificing you for some ungrateful ass people like the two of us." He smiled. "I believe God will reveal himself to you in your heart when you're ready."

I crossed my arms and looked away. "I don't want to hear *shit* He has to say. If He wants to talk to me..." My voice broke. "He can start by bringing mom back..."

"That's not the way it works son. But anyway, you need to go apologize to that boy you wronged..."

"I didn't wrong *anyone*. I made out with a hot girl, *that's it*. If he has a problem with that he can take it up with me. If he wanted her, he should have taken her. He showed up with her so I'm sure he had plenty of opportunities to..."

He folded his arms. "You will go apologize to him right now. Part of being a leader is listening and knowing when you are in the wrong. He loved her and you took something from him that can never be repaid. Her first kiss."

I smacked my lips. "That is some simp ass bullshit right there! Who cares about a first kiss!"

"He does, and there is nothing wrong with caring about something like that. You should spend some time around him. Unlike you, *he* has been living life the right way." He raised an eyebrow. "And like I said, I take some responsibility for your shortcomings. James may be weak now, but that doesn't mean you can't learn from him. He is far from perfect, but there is much he can teach you about living an upright life."

I turned to leave. "He can't teach me a goddamn thing except the art of simpery! But fine! I'll apologize."

"One last thing. I want you to go with them and help restore this nation."

I froze in my tracks. "Hell...no. I don't want to be around their sorry asses for even a second more than I have to..."

"I think it will be good for you and help build your character. You can also use this trip to atone for the damage you caused to our nation and to that boy."

"Fucks no. You want me to spend my time around a bitch-ass prince, a psychopath chick, and a simp bastard? You must have lost your motherfucking *mind* dad."

"This will be a good opportunity for you to learn what leadership really is. It's about being the..."

"Lead servant. I know dad! Whatever! I'm not going! I'll apologize to that simp and that will be the end of it."

Suddenly, dad stirred and buried his face in his hands. "Fuck me. It looks like we're gonna have visitors in a few hours."

"What kind of visitors?"

He sighed. "Rude ones. Hopefully they're not in too violent of a mood this late at night. After you apologize, pack your things, get your sister to the secure location, and gather the other guests. If you hear violence, take them and leave immediately on my personal mammoth."

He's never spoken like this before. My eyes widened. "What the hell are you..."

"Go now. There are several preparations to be made."

"Whatever." I said as I stormed out of the throne room.

As soon as I crossed its threshold I broke into tears. *How could he be so stupid?! All of that God stuff and making me apologize to that idiot! And he's never kept me in the dark about anything before! Now he's sending me away?!* This was just too much to process.

Kayla

I sat out on one of the palace's ledges, high above the city. The moonlight was stunning as it reflected off the buildings' icy surfaces. The beautiful scenery helped ease some of my emotional turmoil.

I knew Terrance was no good for me. James was a much better option and I had some semblance of feelings for him. Kaia even told me that Terrance was a no-good dog after she briefly dated him.

But for some reason, I didn't care.

Something inside me still really, *really* liked him. That thing got hundreds of people killed, and an entire nation destroyed. Before the city was restored, I saw the bodies lining the streets. I mourned as I stared at the multitudes of ruined households and shattered lives. The carnage and devastation were the most horrific thing I had ever seen. I shuddered. *But I was the one who said I wanted to bring that to them. And I did it. What kind of person am I becoming?* Tears flowed down my face, and I looked around to make sure nobody could see my sorrow.

Everything I was doing was completely contrary to who I was as a person and what I believed. *So why am I in love with him? Terrance is a no-good womanizer with a bad attitude and terrible character.*

But for some reason I still didn't care.

James is a great guy with good character from what I've seen. We talk easily and we had a good time together. On top of that, I really do like him.

But I don't *want* him.

If only Kaia was here. She could tell me what I need to do. I gripped the ledge beneath me. *I have to avenge her and force the bastard who hurt her to fix her. I need Uncle* to tell me who he is and where I can find him. I can't believe he's holding it over my head to make me help reunite the nations. And now I caused one of them to be destroyed, and I'm supposed to ask them to rejoin? *This is a disaster.* I sat on the ledge and cried my eyes out under the moonlight.

James

The butler forced me to change out of my combat suit and relinquish my sword. After that, I sat in the room entirely bored by the silence. I didn't really want to talk to him because I was still pissed off, and brainstorming methods to produce Terrance's death took a lot of energy. I was at a stalemate between beating the hell out of him and dropping him into a fissure or beating the hell out of him and disintegrating him with lightning. This decision was vital and extremely difficult. I tried to consult my inner council, but they were missing and I couldn't get a hold of them for some reason.

I'll ask the butler which choice he would prefer. Before I asked, I noticed that he couldn't have been any older than me. I hadn't really taken a good look at him because every time I saw him, I was raging out of the room. He was light skinned, and he wore a very nice suit with a bowtie. He had a perfectly manicured set of dreadlocks that put my usual nappy hair to shame. He stared at me intensely with a hand prepared to do some kind of attack at any second. *The fact that he thinks he can take me with one hand is disrespectful.*

I sighed. "Relax bro. You know I'm not going to attack you or anything, right?"

"I agree that you probably will not attack me on purpose."

"I have no idea what you mean by that." I smiled. "What's your name, good sir?"

"Do not mock me. I am the Archigos' personal assistant and second in command. You may call me Leonidas."

"You already said that. And your name is too long. I'll call you Leo."

"You are currently my guest, so I unfortunately have no choice but to accept it."

I sat up. "Cool! I have a question for you young Leo. What kind of death do you think I should bring upon that bastard prince? Fissures or lightning?"

"Young Leo is a bit excessive...And I too wish I could lay hands on the young master, but that is unfortunately not possible. Additionally, if you bring harm toward him, I will be forced to defend him with the full extent of my power."

I shrugged. "Eh, you could look the other way for me just this once."

He shrugged. "Indeed, I could."

"I'm glad we're on the same page. So, have you always been a butler?"

A vein throbbed in his forehead. "No, and once again I am the Archigos' personal assistant. I am *not* a butler. I enlisted myself in the nation's service when I was young to provide for my mother."

I felt terrible. "Oh, is she sick or something like that?"

"No, but in this nation, women are not allowed to work in any formal capacity or earn an income. My father left us when I was young and I have carried our financial burden since then."

"That's terrible. So the Archigos just allows this to go on?"

He stood. "No! Mr. Okpa is a great man, and I'm not just saying that because I have to! He has been fighting this nation's cultures and policies since before he was elected. He has brought a profound sense of progressiveness to all of our lives."

"But women are still second-class citizens? And he's been Archigos for *how long*? It sounds like he still has a lot of work to do."

"When he got here they were treated as slaves, abused and were viewed as nothing but tools for sexual pleasure or childbearing. In just a few short years he has advanced their status to 'second class citizens' as you say. Within the decade, I'm sure he will be able to grant them equality."

"Whose laws are these exactly? Things weren't like that in the capital or the Flame Tribe."

He stared. "You must not have received much of an education. Each tribe is subject to the overarching laws set by the king and the national council. Each tribe was once independent and still maintains the right to enforce their own laws. The Ocean Tribe council are the ones who endorse this prejudice. Though, at this point Okpa has become so influential that they have no choice but to concede to a majority of his wishes." He leaned back and smiled. "He is known as the one man army after all."

I scoffed. "One man army? I bet he's not tougher than Milliard."

He chuckled. "Okpa would wipe the floor with that capital scum."

I stood. "See, what we're not gonna do is disrespect Milliard. That's my dawg." I patted my fist. "I'll let you off with a warning. But what do you guys have against the capital anyway?"

He scoffed. "The people of the capital are nothing but self-indulgent gluttons. They care nothing for the rest of the nation as long as their pockets are full. They cheated us out of trade agreements for years and our nation has suffered *immeasurably* as a result. We haven't been hit as hard as the Earth Tribe, but Okpa has often had to storm into the capital to force those pigs to give us what they owe us to keep our people from starving. Their greed is why the nation was split in the first place!"

I swallowed. "I didn't know that. I'm sorry. King Basilas doesn't seem like he would do something like that, and I don't think he would let the national council run over him either."

He rolled his eyes. "That king is nothing but a phony and a fraud. Under his reign, the council has been free to force their perverse desires on our people. If he wasn't a Sun Warrior, and some say he may be posing on that front as well, he would have been removed as king decades ago."

"Sun warrior? Does that have something to do with the big sword sitting above the throne?"

He shook his head. "You are truly uneducated. How exactly did you make it through Prism Academy and receive honors as a Five-Star General on top of that?"

I nervously scratched my face. "Umm, don't worry about that. Just pretend you're talking to someone who has no idea what you're talking about...even though they probably should. What is a Sun Warrior and tell me about Five-Star Generals as well."

He narrowed his eyes. "You test my patience. The Sun Tribe were warriors of legend. They represented the ultimate standard of integrity, character, and wielded unrivaled power. They ruled over our nation since its inception, until they were wiped out in The Calamity.

King Basilas and his three sons are the only remaining descendants of the Sun Warrior lineage."

"What happened to the rest of them?"

He stood and his hand trembled with rage. "You would *dare* ask me that?! I will not lose this position I have worked my entire life for to indulge in your silly games! You know it is forbidden to even reference that event!"

I held up my hands. "Calm down bro! I'm sorry. We don't have to talk about this anymore." *I need to change the subject.* "You reminded me, how is Epios doing? I know he's probably pissed after getting his ass whooped."

"He is currently in the infirmary receiving treatment from the young master's sister. I have not heard if he has awoken or not."

I stood. "Alright, well can I go now? I need to talk to Kayla. I promise I won't kill Terrance until I let you get a few good licks in first."

He straightened his fingers. "Again, while I would like to take you up on your offer, I cannot. And you will not be allowed to leave this room until the Archigos arrives. If you attempt to..."

I plopped onto the bed and stared at the ceiling. "I know. I know. You'll be forced to unleash your full force against me and blah, blah, blah. I didn't forget from when you just said that five minutes ago." I let out a long, exasperated sigh. "Why do you guys even have me on house arrest again? I know I went on a bit of a rampage before, but fifty guards and a butler seems excessive."

"I assure you it is not and I am not allowed to answer that. Sit patiently and wait for the master to arrive."

"UUUUGGGH, this sucks!" I buried my face in my hands. "Tell me Leo...do you have any dreams or aspirations beyond being a butler?"

He pounded the table. "I AM NOT A BUTLER!" He quickly composed himself. "*Ahem*, but yes, I do dream of becoming Archigos one day."

I twiddled my thumbs. "How do you plan on doing that? Don't you have to go to school and win a big tournament or something? Sounds like that would be *pretty* hard for a butler to pull off..."

"I AM NOT A BUTLER! *Ahem*, and you are right. It is an impossible goal. I was not gifted with traditional Ocean Craft abilities like everyone else. I cannot make weapons, maneuver in the snow, or heal myself like the others can. I also lack the physical strength, size, and athleticism most of those other buffoons were born with. Because of that, and my mother's need for support, I was not able to attend university."

"It doesn't sound like you're very strong at all then. Why *exactly* did you think you could take me earlier?"

"On the contrary, I am one of this nation's strongest warriors. Dispatching you would be mere *child's play* for me. My mother raised me to be strong and helped me cultivate my unorthodox ability so that I could one day accomplish my dreams."

"I was just joking before bro. I'm sorry about your circumstances." I sat up. "But I'm still hung up on the fact that you think you could actually take me. If you can't make ice weapons and stuff, what exactly can you do?"

"I am not at liberty to discuss my abilities on the order of the Archigos."

"But you just told me...never mind. *Sigh.*" I gave him a thumbs up. "I just wanted to say that I believe in you and I think you will reach your goals. Butler or no, I hope that one day you get a chance to beat up Terrance and reach your dream of becoming Archigos."

"I would love nothing more."

Our conversation ended there, and I laid back as I pondered my scenario. *I have to find a way out of here. I need to find Kayla so she can explain what happened. There just had to have been some kind of mistake. She was only making out with him like that because she had to, and once I find Terrance, I'm going to beat the shit out of him until he releases her from the deal.* Since I woke up, the power surging within me was incredible. It felt like raw energy was moving beneath my skin, just waiting to be unleashed. *Now I just have to convince the butler to let me go.*

I sat up. "I'm getting *tired* of waiting Leo. What would happen if you let me go and I climbed out of this window right here?"

His body swayed. "Tired you say? Absolutely not...James..."

I laughed. "You look more tired than I am. What, are you getting sleepy from holding your arm up like that for hours?"

"Impossible...my...can't get...tired...."

"Well maybe you should just take a nap then."

"A nap...yes..."

BANG!

He slumped over and his head hit the desk.

What the hell?

I shrugged. "Perfect timing I guess." I Mirror Dashed out of the window.

I zipped off a window outside the palace and into a reflection back on the rooftop. "Alright, time to go find..."

The voice called out. "**What if it's not true?**"

I froze. "What do you mean what if...it's not..."

I sat down and laid in the snow as the cool wind brushed off my face.

It had a point.

What if it **isn't** *true? What if she did what she did because she wanted to? What if she did it because he's just better than me...what if she never even liked me at all? A* torrent of negative emotion washed over me as tears welled up behind my eyes. It **has** to be true. I felt a heavy weight on my soul that made me want to lay in the snow and never, *ever* get up. I lost my initiative to find Kayla or do anything at all. My mind drifted back to the first time I experienced that weight.

✳

I found myself back in my junior year of high school. I was invited to South Texas Central's Black Leadership Initiative Academy. This was a major deal for me at the time because South Texas Central was one of the top schools in the nation athletically, and I would have loved the opportunity to go there. This was a great first step because they only recruited the best and brightest from across the nation to apply for this academic program, and I got in. We spent the week doing business type activities and hearing from different alumni about how we could leverage the school to create the futures we dreamed about. Throughout the week there was one student that stood out to everyone. Her name was Cynthia, and she was so fine that even the college students who chaperoned us were willing to catch a case by hitting on her.

At the end of the week, we had a competition where we pitched the business plans we developed during the week. Her group's ideas were absolutely terrible, and they crumbled under the scrutiny of the judges.

Until she opened her mouth.

She eloquently carried her group for the remainder of the presentation and made everybody in the audience actually want to invest in the trash they were selling, even though we all knew it was terrible. After that, I wanted to shoot my shot, but she wasn't in my group so I figured I would never get the chance to talk to her.

Until that chance came. After we left a guest speaker's presentation on the second to last night, we had a mixer with different prominent business people. I was roaming around and doing my thing, until one of the businessmen started a conversation at the table I happened to be at. Suddenly, Cynthia showed up and started talking to one of my homies that I had met at the table like they were best friends! After that, I put on my A game. Cynthia and I went back and forth, muttering sweet business nothings into that white man's ear until he was ready to hire us on the spot. After he left to go find his hiring manager or something, I ended up spending the rest of the evening talking with Cynthia. At first it was a group conversation, but the conversation between me and her was so good that the others saw the chemistry and ended up leaving. We talked for roughly three hours straight, and after that we went to a party and spent the entire time there together too.

As you probably already guessed, I fell in love.

The next day at the closing ceremony, I was not listening to a word they were saying. The entire time I looked like I was taking notes, but I was actually writing a script to confess my love. I worked up the courage, caught her when she was alone, and told her how I felt. I was shocked and exhilarated as she told me she felt the same way! She gave me her number, told me to make sure I texted her after the event was over, and I was absolutely on the highest high of my entire life.

I texted her on the 4-hour drive home, but I got no response. My teenage angst flared up, and I went into panic mode. I spent almost every waking moment for the next two days waiting for her response and plotting witty comebacks. She finally responded on the third day around midnight, and my heart jumped for joy. I immediately responded and we chatted for a little bit...until she ghosted me again.

She never responded a single time after that.

I was convinced there was something wrong with me, or that despite my best efforts, I messed everything up, *again*. I've become far too familiar with the weight that gripped my soul as I sat and waited for text messages that never came.

After that, my mind drifted to an experience during my sophomore year of high school. My mom made a new Christian friend out in the wild at the store or something, and they hit it off. As a result, her friend started coming over almost every day, and she brought her daughter named Leah who happened to be my age. The first time Leah came over, we absolutely hit it off. Leah came to my room, and we ended up talking for hours.

You probably know where this is going.

We basically had everything in common, and I loved how strong she was in her faith. She was so resolute that she refused to even sit down in my room because she said she didn't want to do anything that could lead to her becoming tempted. The second time they came over, we had a blast playing video games, and my heart was set on marrying her. I was so certain we would end up together that I told all my friends around the neighborhood that I was already married.

The next time they came over, she said she wanted to watch a movie with me. A good amount of the time we spent together before this had been group activities with our siblings. The fact that she said she wanted to watch the movie *with me* gave me all the courage I needed to confess. I told her how I felt, but she said she didn't feel the same way and my heart was crushed. It took everything I had to not break down and cry right next to her during that movie. Guise James put on another one of his finest performances as I spent the rest of the afternoon as the perfect friend until she finally left. I was devastated for weeks.

I snapped out of the trance and had a eureka moment. *That first girl wasn't ever any good for me anyway! I found out later that despite appearances, she was extremely promiscuous. Because of that, we never would have worked out in the first place! Kayla was nothing like that and she had already shown her amazing character on our date! And the second time I just ruined things by rushing! I haven't messed anything up with Kayla yet, and I was almost perfect during our date!* If I was ever going to hold on to hope, this was the time.

It has to be true. It just has to.

I hopped out of the snow filled with excitement. *Why would God allow this to happen again anyway? There has to be an explanation that makes sense.* As I looked around the rooftop for a way back into the building, I heard someone crying. I moved toward the sound and my jaw dropped. I

It was Kayla!

I believe all coincidences are God ordained, and this was just the sign I was looking for.

I beamed. "Hey Kayla! I've been looking for you!"

"James!" She was startled as she wiped her tears and turned away from me.

She's even gorgeous while she's crying. I normally only see her in badass warrior mode, so it's even more attractive to see her when she's vulnerable.

I put my hand on her shoulder. "Are you alright? Did something happen?"

She shifted away.

"S*niffle*...no...everything's...fine...*sniffle*..."

I sat next to her and our feet dangled over the rooftop's edge. "It's alright if you don't want to talk about whatever it is that's bothering you. Just know I'll be here if you need a shoulder to cry on."

She smiled through her tears. "Thanks James. You're the best. But why were you looking for me? Did you want to go talk to the Archigos together or something?"

"No, I'm actually on my way to go murder Terrance in cold blood for what he did to you..." She flinched for some reason. "But *before* I put him six feet under, I wanted to ask you a very important question. When I saw you guys doing that in his room, you were only doing that because he forced you to...right?"

She held out her hands. "James. I need you to stay calm and listen to me very carefully..."

Cracks began forming in my mind.

I rose to my feet and started stepping backwards. "Kayla...It can't be..."

"Don't put any of the blame on Terrance and please don't hurt him..."

It has to be true...It just has to...

"It was all my fault. I didn't tell you this, but I've had a crush on him since I was little and..."

"I told you so." The voice said.

My mind shattered.

I lost all feeling in my body.

I was hollow.

"Alright Kayla. Thanks for being honest with me. I have to go."

"James, wait! Please listen..."

I blindly trudged away from her like a zombie until I collided with the door leading back into the building. I touched the handle, and it disintegrated as I entered the building.

I slogged through the halls aimlessly as I tried to comprehend what was happening.

I couldn't, and my mind remained blank.

The voice called out. **"Once again. I told you so. Do you see now I am the only one willing to tell you the truth?"**

Yeah...you were right. What about...the other stuff you said? My mind sputtered.

"Oh, you mean about those soldiers and the devastation you caused this country. All true. Look at the way they were treating you. You saw the fear in that butler's eyes."

That makes sense...But why was nothing destroyed though?

"The Archigos used his power to fix it, but you still decimated the country and killed countless innocents. If anyone tells you otherwise, that will prove they're a liar!"

Oh ok.

I couldn't comprehend anything the voice was saying. I walked through the endless halls as my scattered mind attempted to recollect itself. I muttered countless incoherencies until my mind was able to formulate a thought.

It was mourning in its purest form. *I tried my best! I try my best again.* AND AGAIN AND AGAIN AND AGAIN AND AGAIN AND AGAIN AND AGAIN AND AGAIN AND AGAIN AND AGAIN AND AGAIN AND AGAIN!

I don't know how long I slogged in and out of corridors, but I eventually shuffled past an open doorway. I felt a large amount of Spirit Energy and it caught my dulled mind's attention. My body slowly turned and entered the room. Epios was naked on a medical table. A girl was pressing her elbows forcefully into his glutes.

She leapt away and recoiled in horror. "AAAAGH! I promise it's not what it looks like!"

"Epios...is that...you?" I muttered.

"Yes, this is him! I actually think he's had enough treatment for now! Let me get him covered up and back in the healing pool!" She zipped around the room and tossed his limp body into a pool in the corner.

I slowly trekked over to him. "Epios...is that...you?"

He jolted awake. "Ahh, it's you fiend." He looked me up and down. "What exactly has happened to you? You look far more fiendish than usual."

Tears welled in my eyes. "You were right...Epios. You were right...and I was wrong..."

He rolled his eyes and sighed. "About *what* fiend? I can see that your mind is quite feeble as always, but you will have to be more specific..."

My voice broke. "She did it Epios...She broke...my heart..."

He chuckled. "And your mind apparently as well. Though your future ruler knew that this was inevitable. On the boat I was trying to tell you that she's always had a crush on that troglodytian brute Terrance."

The girl who was tidying up the room yelled from across the infirmary. "A crush? On *my* dumbass brother? HAAAAAAAAAAHAAAAAAAAAHAAAAAAAAHAAAAAAAA!"

She roared with laughter as she rolled around on the ground until she nearly passed out from exhaustion. She staggered to her feet, holding her sides like she had just been punched in the gut. "I've never heard something so ridiculous in my entire life! Any woman with eyes knows he's the worst choice on this entire planet! Who could be stupid enough to fall for someone like him?"

"Ka...yla. She broke...my heart..."

Her eyes widened. "Oh my gosh! I'm so sorry!"

"It's...fine...honest..."

Epios cocked back his hand. "I've had enough of this slow talking, simple minded buffoonery!"

SMACK!

He devastated my skull with a bone rattling slap that echoed throughout the entire kingdom.

"HA-HA! I've been waiting for the day that I could smack some sense into you fiend!"

My mind felt a little clearer. "Thanks Epios....You're the best..."

He smiled gleefully and cocked his hand back again. "He-he-he! Clearly you are still not coherent or you most certainly would have retaliated against me." He sighed and shook his head. "But it cannot be helped. Just tell me what happened."

I sobbed. "I went into their room, and I saw them making out! And she was half naked Epios! Can you believe it?! How could she do this to me?!"

The girl balled her fists until the color drained from her palms. "That bastard! I'll kill him!"

Epios shrugged. "I *absolutely* can. I *just told you* that she's had a crush on him since she was little! From my all-knowing estimation, every soul in the entire kingdom knew about it. That is why people do not take her seriously because her actions are so inconsistent with her words."

I slumped to the ground and held my head in my hands. "Why does this keep happening to me Epios? I try and try and try, but things never work out for me."

He hugged me. "It's alright you disgusting fiend. Just this once, I'll allow you to pour your heart out to me until your fiendish heart recovers."

I pouted. "Ok, but only if you promise not to insult me"

He rolled his eyes. "Fine, but as I stated, this is a *one*-time thing. When you face future tribulations, I am under no obligation to treat you with even an ounce of kindness."

I perked up. "That's fine! You're the best Epios! I want to tell you about all of my past failed relationships! I'm sure that will make me feel better! You're the only one I have that I can be honest and tell these stories to!"

"That's...fine. Wait, you have already regaled me with several of these detestable stories in the past. When you said all, you didn't mean, *all, all*, did you?"

"Yep! It's important for you to have the full context so you can understand how I truly feel on the inside! Here I go!"

James spent the next few hours torturing Epios with stories of his terrible love life. As he poured out his heart, he started feeling better and his mind began regenerating.

Epios grew impatient, frustrated, and eventually stopped listening entirely. I DON'T CARE!

His mind grew weary, and eventually shattered after being overwhelmed by too much trauma all at once. His subconscious mind took over and devised that the only way out of this situation was to endure it. It took over his body in an attempt to speed along the torturous process. He began nodding along and giving James affirmatives as he desperately longed for the torment to end.

"But then I found out she had sex that night with a dude she hadn't even met! Can you believe that?!"

"*Mhm, Mhm.*" Epios' body mumbled as he nodded his head.

"OH MY GOD THAT'S TERRIBLE!" The girl shouted.

As this continued for hours, the girl's heart fluttered as she clung to his every word. James made a full recovery as he finished his last story.

"And then I just found myself here talking to you. What do you think Epios? Am I hopeless?"

Epios' body sputtered as he foamed from the mouth. "HMPLZHSZABLAHA, fiend."

James raised an eyebrow. "Are you alright..."

"NO! I DON'T THINK YOU'RE HOPELESS AT ALL! IN FACT, I THINK SO MUCH OF WHAT YOU DID IN THOSE STORIES WAS SO SWEET AND ROMANTIC THAT I COULD DIE!"

James narrowed his eyes. *When did she get here?* "Thanks...I guess. Who are you again?"

She sprinted forward and vigorously shook his hand. "MY NAME IS BROOKLYN TOUVTPA PRINCESS OF THE OCEAN TRIBE! NICE TO MEET YOU!"

A veil was lifted over James' eyes. He saw that she was tall, with toned muscles and an incredible figure. Her chocolate skin and gorgeous face gleamed in the light. Her bright blue eyes and perfectly maintained curly afro allured him.

His face turned bright red. "It's...uh...nice to meet you too! I guess that was super embarrassing to hear me ramble on like that about how hopeless of a romantic I am..."

She smiled. "I don't think it was embarrassing at all! I think it takes a real man to be vulnerable enough to talk about the times he *wasn't* successful. And I commend you for being bold enough to go after what you want." She laughed. "I'd say me and my friends have that in common."

"Really? You don't think it's embarrassing that no girl I've ever wanted has wanted me back?

She drew circles on the ground with her foot. "Not at all! In fact, I can relate. I've been having a really hard time finding a suitor for myself as well."

"How could that be? You're gorgeous! And you have such a sweet feminine voice. Men should be busting down your door to get a shot at being with you!"

Her radiant smile illuminated the room. "Thank you so much! Your words mean *a lot* to me." She rolled her eyes and sighed. "The men here do come after me, but I already know they're only doing it because they see me as some kind of conquest." She sheepishly covered her face and peeked at him through her fingers. "It's my turn to say something embarrassing, but I'm a virgin."

She glared at Epios. "I hear how those men talk. Every guy here wants to be the one to deflower me, but it's only so they can say they were the one to sleep with the Archigos' daughter. It's *disgusting*. On top of that, these boys are all the same. They're disgusting, and they don't care about their appearance or how they take care of themselves (James panicked). They all smell like a pig's den, they don't brush their teeth, shower, or know how to dress well! To make matters worse, I've been on a few dates because my father keeps pressuring me, and none of them know how to be a gentleman or hold an intelligent conversation! All they talk about is how many spirits they killed yesterday, or about how pretty I am and there's no in between! I'm literally stranded in a sea of absolutely incompetent men and it's infuriating!"

"I'm sorry about that, and I absolutely do not think it's embarrassing that you're a virgin. The fact that you have proper values and can display that much self-control in an environment like that is extremely attractive to me."

"Thank you so much James! You saying that is a breath of fresh air! It's rare to find such a kindred spirit!" She gushed.

"Of course! I can definitely relate. This may sound weird, and I promise I'm not gay, but I deal with a lot of the same issues. I just don't find most women attractive. Most of them don't have their morals or values in the right place and bring nothing to the table in a conversation. A lot of them claim to be Christians, but if I start talking about the Bible they act like I'm speaking a foreign language. On top of that, if I actually find a girl like that looks decent and is focused on self improvement, she usually has a trainload of unresolved baggage or has slept with like ten dudes! It's almost impossible for me to find a good-looking girl and actually end up liking her. That's why it's so devastating when I actually find someone I like and it doesn't work out." He sighed. "I always do what I'm supposed to do, and even when things don't work out I always treat women the right way. And yet I keep getting rejected and tossed around like I'm worthless."

Brooklyn stepped forward and her breath warmed his face. She whispered seductively in his ear. "Most women are too immature to know what they want, and too stupid to take advantage when it walks right up to them." A playful glint flashed in her eye. "But I'm not like that though." She grabbed his shirt and pulled him close. "I'm the type of girl that walks right up to her knight in shining armor, kisses him on the lips, and lives happily...ever...after."

James' eyes widened as she kissed him passionately. He was stunned and ecstasy flooded his brain as he kissed her back. Before he could react, she slipped in some tongue and suddenly pulled away. She put her hands on his chest and stared into his eyes.

Brooklyn pressed an object into his hand. "I'm not like those other girls James. Come find me when you get over her." She turned and blew him a kiss as she confidently strutted out of the room.

14 - Reunion

James

I STOOD IN COMPLETE SHOCK AS SHE WALKED AWAY. "Brooklyn! Wait!"

She was already gone. Ecstasy flooded my body as I fell to my knees.

"YES! YES! YES! THANK YOU, LORD! ALL IS FORGIVEN!" I shouted.

I can't believe it! I finally had my first kiss! And a girl actually wants me for the first time in my life! It was overwhelming, and tears of joy streamed down my face. The strange power within me faded and Spirit Energy exploded from my body. My clothes were incinerated as I was completely enveloped by multicolored energy.

My joy was unrivaled.

I had never felt this good in my entire life.

The energy looked like a raging fire and tendrils of colored electricity zipped out of my radiant aura. I felt the core of Spiritual Energy in the center of my body and the gargantuan amount of power radiating from it. It coursed through my veins like lightning and my skin tingled with power. I felt like I had ascended to a new plane of existence.

I could do anything.

It felt like heaven.

"Hmzmpphlazphtha." Epios mumbled.

"Oh, Epios! When did you get here?" I stared at his mindless state. "Ah I see! You're still injured from when Terrance hurt you! Don't worry! I hear you!" I gave him a thumbs up. "Have no fear! I'll get the Archigos to rejoin the union right now so you can just chill out and relax! I just need to go get a change of clothes and briefly visit Brooklyn's room! You stay right there!"

FVOOOM!

I thought about Mirror Dashing into my room and I was suddenly there. *This power is so cool!* I looked around for my bag that had extra outfits.

I grimaced when I saw Terrance sitting at the table where the butler once was. The ecstasy faded along with the glowing aura.

Rage filled my heart.

He chuckled. "Yuck, simp. I know you have to get it in somehow because you get no hoes, but put some clothes on when men are in the room."

"Shut your fucking mouth! What the hell do you want?!"

He leaned back. "I came to apologize you simp bastard."

"Apology not accepted! I will never forgive you for what you did to me! EVER! I should kill you right now! You don't even like her!"

"Are you mad because I kissed or because I grabbed her ass..." He paused. "*Sigh*, you know what. Pipe down chief. I don't know how *you know* that I didn't like her...But you're right. What I did was wrong and I'm sorry. You don't have to forgive me, but I wanted you to hear me say it. You can have her if you..."

CRASH!

I slammed my fist through the wall. "Terrance. Shut the *fuck* up. *Right now.* I'm warning you."

"Alright."

I walked over to my bag and changed into my combat suit.

I glared at him and darkness flashed in my eyes. "If I wasn't here for world peace. You would already be *dead*."

He held up his hands. "Easy big guy. I believe you."

SLAM!

I grabbed the door handle and ripped it off its hinges. The guards outside the door had spears aimed at the doorway.

I gave them one look and they shuddered in fear.

I turned to Terrance. "Tell these fuckers to get the HELL OUT OF MY WAY!"

"You guys heard the man. Let him through."

The guards trembled as they lined up and made a path.

As I walked between them a guard shouted. "THIS IS TOO MUCH!" He sprinted out of the formation.

"HE'S RIGHT!", "I HAVE A WIFE AND KIDS TO FEED!", "I DON'T WANNA DIE!" The soldiers screamed as they sprinted off in every direction.

My rage calmed, and I heard blood drip onto the ground. I felt no pain, but my hand was bright crimson. There was an ornate, silver and blue pin in my palm. I pinned it to my shirt.

I looked back at Terrance and smiled. "Hey Terrance. How would you feel if I fucked your sister?"

He narrowed his eyes. "What are you even talking about? She would never like a dweeb like you."

I pointed a thumb at my brand-new pin. "Oh yeah? I like the way her tongue felt as it slid down my throat."

His eyes gleamed with recognition. "What the...I'll kill you!"

I confidently walked out of the room as he seethed with rage.

Okpa stormed through the palace. "Fuck me! Why does something like this have to happen *today*? This is the second worst Tuesday ever!"

He raged past the grand stairwell on the first floor as Kayla was descending.

"Sir, do you know where Terrance..."

He stomped out of the palace. "No, I don't. Now go find your friends and get to safety!"

She glared as he disappeared. "That was rude."

CRASH!

Terrance burst through a wall. "Where is that bastard! If he touches my sister I'll kill him!"

"Terrance? What are you..."

He smacked his lips. "Not you again! LEAVE ME ALONE!"

Terrance saw the front gates opening and sprinted through them. Okpa rose into the sky on a platform of ice. Terrance balled his fists. *I don't know who these visitors are, but I have to help him!*

He darted into the city as Kayla followed. "Wait Terrance! This could be dangerous!"

Okpa's rode a frozen platform outside the city's wall. He squinted into the distance and saw three approaching figures. They wore gray cloaks that completely obscured their bodies. They walked silently until they came within twenty feet of Okpa.

He raised his fist, and the entire city wall was lined with soldiers. They aimed lances at the figures and rolled more than a hundred catapults into firing position.

WHOOSH!

The figures stopped and ripped off their coats. The middle figure was a tall, fair skinned woman with dark black hair. She and the other two women at her side wore silver armor that only covered their chests. They wore thongs with blade handles attached to the straps. The girls at her sides were almost identical and they wore expressionless faces as they knelt before Okpa.

"That's quite a welcome you prepared for me Okpa." The middle woman said.

"Only the best for you, Aurania." He bowed. "My love."

Aurania shuddered with rage. "That love died a long time ago because of your cowardice! Where are the villains who murdered my daughter?"

"Honey, I have no idea what you're talking about. Your daughter is *here* in the palace where *you* should be. Maybe we can go out to dinner, and I can help you look for whoever you're talking about after..."

"I won't *ask* you *again*! If you don't give them up I will tear down these walls and kill every person who stands in my way until I find her myself!"

He sighed. "Welp, it wasn't the worst rejection I've heard."

His fingers twitched as he started closing his fist.

"Dad!"

Okpa face palmed as he turned and saw Terrance skiing toward him. "You idiot! I told you to get your sister to safety!"

"I told the butler to do it! I wanted to come help you!"

"No! Stay back!"

Aurania seethed with rage as she saw Terrance.

"Terrance!" Kayla yelled as she raced toward them with several guards chasing after her.

Okpa's heart sank. "NOOOOO! GET BACK!"

Aurania saw Kayla and smiled. "There she is. Take the murderers and kill the rest."

Time seemed to stop.

The girls on Aurania's sides rose to their feet as Okpa closed his fist.

WHOOOOOOOOOSH!

The soldiers filled the sky with lances as catapults launched flaming brimstone into the sky.

CRASH!

Okpa forcefully stepped toward Kayla and Terrance, causing ice platforms to rise up beneath them as they rocketed toward the castle.

"Wind Craft, Progress Art 3, Godspeed Strikes!"

CRASH!

Aurania raised the hilt of a metal blade skyward and lightning crashed down forming an electric blade.

FWOOSH!

CLANG!

The instant Okpa's foot hit the ground, he formed an ice ax and deflected Aurania's strike.

CRASH!

As their blades connected the sound of thunder rang out.

SLICE! SLICE! SLICE! SLICE! SLICE!

She instantaneously slashed at him five more times as he rapidly deflected each slice.

Lightning danced in her eyes. "You should have just given me what I wanted."

SLICE!

He was too slow to deflect the seventh slash and the force from the blow struck like lightning, sending him flying.

BOOM!

BOOM!

BOOM!

BOOM!

He crashed through the capital's outer wall and rag dolled as he shattered building after building.

BOOOOOOOOM!

He smashed through a vendor's tent and into a wall in the square. He laid in a steaming, bloody heap.

Outside the wall, the twin warriors reached for the fans attached to their thong strings.

They spoke calmly in unison. "**Wind Craft, Progress Art 2, Gravity.**"

They opened the fans and swung them in a downward motion.

BOOOOOOOOOOOOOOOOOOOOOOOOOOOOOOM!

The sky full of lances and brimstone crashed into the surface. The city's outer walls shuttered violently until they crumbled into slush. Every soldier that lined them was turned to mush by the intense force of the increased gravity.

Time resumed.

The girls sprinted toward the city and their speed increased until they appeared as streaks of black and white lightning. A formation of 500 soldiers stood in battle stances with spears drawn.

BOOM!

The black streak crashed down into the center of the formation, disintegrating soldiers and sending charred corpses soaring into the crowd. The white streak zipped off after the platforms that held Kayla and Terrance. The girl from the black bolt stood calmly as the soldiers faced her in awe. She quickly swapped her fan for a sword handle that hung on her thong string and raised it skyward.

CRASH!

Lightning crashed onto the handle, and she formed the energy into a blade on its hilt.

A soldier shouted. "FOR THE OCEAN TRIBE!"

"FOR THE OCEAN TRIBE!" The soldiers roared.

GUSH!

SLICE!

GUSH!

SPLAT!

They swarmed her, but she skillfully leapt and dodged their attacks as she mercilessly slaughtered them one by one.

Back in the town center, Aurania crashed down in a bolt of silver thunder. Okpa laid against a wall as he slowly regenerated.

She pointed her blade. "Why won't you get up and fight! Have you grown even softer in these years since I left you?!"

His head sagged. "I...don't...*wheeze*...want to...*wheeze*...fight you anymore Aurania...I...love you. I'm just...*wheeze*...stalling...*wheeze*...for time..."

She looked back and saw her Wind Warrior massacring the army of soldiers. She looked up and saw a bolt of white lightning racing after the two platforms as they rocketed toward the palace. "So far that doesn't seem to be working out for you."

His upper body fully regenerated. "We were married for 10 years Aurania. Do you know what your problem was?"

She rolled her eyes. "Humor me."

"You're too damn prideful."

FVOOOOOOOOOOOM!

Suddenly, a red aura enveloped the square as Aurania leapt back. A portal appeared and a massive fist rose from the ground. It grabbed the earth and the icy surface shattered as it pulled the rest of its gargantuan body out of the portal. A red giant, well over fifty feet tall, towered over the city. It had a muscular body coursing with red energy as it wielded an enormous ax.

"**GROOOOOAAAAAAAANNNNNAAAAAAAAHHHH!**" The giant roared.

Fear gripped her heart. "A... a Pride Spirit?"

Okpa casually picked his toenails as they regenerated. "Yep, I knew one of these guys was gonna spawn here eventually." He sighed. "I was hoping it wouldn't be on a Tuesday night though."

"It's Wednesday now."

CRASH!

She disappeared in a crash of lightning. She reappeared in the sky before the spirit's face.

"Wind Craft, Fifth Art, Thunder. Times Ten!"

CRASH! CRASH! CRASH!

Lightning crackled in the morning sky as ten massive bolts of lightning crashed down on the beast.

"**ROOOOOOOOOOOOAAAAAAAAAAARR!**"

As its flesh burned, the entire area was covered in a thick smog. Aurania scoffed as she descended.

WHOOOOSH!

Suddenly, she flinched and rocketed into the sky, just as the giant's ax sliced through the air. She flicked her wrist and the smog dissipated, revealing an unscathed giant.

"Wind Craft, Arts 6 and 8. Thunder Prison and Tempest's fury."

Massive chains of electricity formed on the giant's wrists and forced its body to kneel. Her blade's lightning faded and was replaced by condensed wind that formed a visible sword.

She swung her blade. "HUAGH!"

A massive tempest rocketed toward the giant.

SLICE!

The tempest split into three gusts and sliced the giant into thirds. Its pieces fell to the earth and disintegrated.

She scoffed. "Foolish spirit."

SMACK!

A fist connected with her face and she was launched toward the surface.

BOOOOOOOOOM!

The impact sent shockwaves through the city as she crashed into the booth next to Okpa. A bubble of wind surrounded her, but she laid in a crater covered in blood. Okpa sat in the booth's ruins with a large vat of popcorn.

He extended a handful. "Need some help?"

She staggered to her feet and vomited blood onto the snow. "I could never...need help from...a man."

WHOOOOSH!

She vanished, accelerating into the sky as the force from her takeoff shattered the buildings in the square.

Okpa threw his hands up. "Goddammit, I just fixed those a few hours ago!"

She raced into the stratosphere toward her opponent.

A human sized red and black spirit hovered in the air with its arms crossed. "You are a fool if you thought those half-cocked attacks could defeat me."

"You are the fool for daring to challenge the Wind Tribe. That will be your last mistake."

The spirit applauded. "Ahh yes! I've heard of you! You're Aurania, the Archigos of the Wind Tribe. Your hubris is some of the most profound that I've encountered since the dawn of time." The spirit bowed. "It is an honor to have the opportunity to humble you." A spear and an ax formed in each of the spirit's hands.

Aurania raised her blade skyward, and thunder struck it once more. "Before I end you *pride*, answer me this. How exactly were you able to form here? This is only the third sighting of your kind in the past five years."

"My summoning was expedited by my mistress, as is the case with most of my kin. The others you mentioned were my brothers. Their pride and ambition were not strong enough, as a result they were humbled by the conqueror's light." The spirit chuckled. "I promise you, I will not follow in their footsteps."

CLANG!

The spirit rushed Aurania and their blades clashed. They zipped across the sky and attacked relentlessly as each side searched for an opening. The spirit raced in, and Aurania swung her blade at its head. Dark energy covered the Spirit's arm and it grabbed her lightning blade. It slowly forced her sword to the side and overpowered her as she struggled to raise her blade. The spirit smiled, as it suddenly flicked its wrist.

CRACK!

Her blade was forced down and her shoulder ripped out of its socket. "GAAAAAAAAAH!"

Her arm went limp, and her blade dropped as it fell toward the earth. She swiftly extended her other hand, and the spirit was forced back by a torrent of wind. The spirit swung its ax, and three dark slashes soared toward her.

GUSH!

She ducked left, right and leaned backwards as the third slash rocketed over her face, and her nose exploded in blood. The slashes stopped and reversed course toward her. The spirit sent three more slashes and they surrounded her from all sides.

WHOOOSH!

She dropped down and soared away from the slashes as they relentlessly pursued her across the sky. She ducked down and raced through the city as the blades tore through everything in their path. She made sharp turns and ducked under bridges, but the slashes only picked up speed as they barreled through the capitol.

WHOOOOOOOOOOOOSH!

The blades nipped at her heels, and she instantly accelerated, sending a shockwave of wind that destroyed buildings for miles.

"GODDAMMIT! I JUST REPAIRED THAT COUNTY!" Okpa raged as he feasted on popcorn.

She raced toward the spirit, and it hovered pridefully, smiling with its arms crossed. As she approached, it tried to raise its altitude but was shocked when it couldn't. A current of wind held the spirit in place as it struggled against the force.

ZOOM!

SLICE!

She raced past it and the slices tore through the spirit, as they disappeared.

"GAAH!" Dark liquid spilled from its wounds and mouth.

WHOOSH!

It swiftly recovered and raced after her, ax in hand.

CLANG!

A wind lance formed in her left hand, and she used it to deflect the spirit's attack. They exchanged a furious series or blows as each side displayed their mastery of combat.

WHOOSH!

She zipped away in a gust of wind.

SMACK!

It tried to pursue her as it raced into an invisible wall of wind. It tried to fly around the wall, but it crashed into another wall on its right side.

SLICE!

Aurania blitzed through the wall and sliced the spirit with her lance.

SLICE! SLICE! SLICE!

Each time the spirit tried to move it was restrained as she raced through wind barriers and relentlessly tore through the spirit.

WHOOOOSH!

The spirit staggered as it was suddenly launched even higher into the atmosphere.

"Wind Craft, Art 4, Weightless."

WHOOOOOOOOSH!

She vanished, soaring at impossible speeds as she rocketed toward the spirit. "Progress Art 2. Gravity."

The spirit crashed toward the earth directly above her. As she neared the spirit, her lightning blade that was falling stopped in midair. It zoomed through the sky into her hand, instants before she reached striking distance.

SLICE!

She sliced the spirit in half, and the sound of thunder reverberated through the entire nation.

BOOOOOOOOOOOM!

The spirit's body erupted in an explosion of lightning, and it writhed in agony as its two halves crashed into the surface.

She scoffed. "You were a fool to challenge me in my own domain spirit." She looked down at the beautiful scenery of the Ocean Tribe and took pride in her victory.

A voice rang out in her mind. "What better way could I humble you?"

GUSH!

A dark ax pierced her back and blood exploded from her body.

BOOOOOOOOOOOOOOOOOOOOOOOOOOOOOOOM!

She instantly crashed into the earth like lightning as the impact sent a shockwave that destroyed a massive section of the city. She laid in a broken, battered heap with limbs bent in the wrong directions. She grew cold as the color drained from her face.

The spirit's two halves slowly floated out of separate craters and reattached as they floated over her destroyed body. It laughed boisterously. "Pride comes before the fall."

Okpa casually approached her, popcorn in hand. He spoke childishly as popcorn spilled from his mouth. "Now do you need some help?"

"Y...e...s...p...l...e...a...s...e..." She wheezed as her eyes glazed over.

POW!

A pillar of ice knocked the spirit across the city.

Okpa did a silly dance. "Finally! I think this is the first time in our entire marriage you've actually asked me for help!" He waved his hand, and blue energy enveloped her. "Ocean Craft, Art 1, Esoteric Depth Command!"

FVOOOOOOOOOOOOOOM!

Her destroyed body levitated, and her limbs gently rotated as they eased back into place. The blood caking her body was washed clean as it soaked back into her skin. The deep, mangled gashes in her body closed and color returned to her face. She gasped for air as she regained consciousness. Aurania slowly drifted into Okpa's arms. He gently set her onto her feet as her body was completely restored. The glaze left her eyes, and she looked around confusedly.

Okpa stretched his arms. "Man, that took a lot out of me! I probably worked harder than you just did in all honesty! I'm not sure how much juice I even have left!"

Realization flashed across her face, and she quickly stepped away from him. "You lie...but you have my gratitude."

He smiled playfully. "Of course! You are still my wife and all! What kind of husband would I be if I let some prideful bastard kill you?!"

She glared. "That ship sailed years ago Okpa, and you know it."

He waved her off. "*Nah*, in the eyes of God there is no such thing as divorce."

"I disagree."

The spirit soared toward them and stumbled as it came to a stop before of the couple. It ripped a piece of ice out of its chest. "Your humbling is not complete!"

"Dammit! I was a bit too shallow." Okpa said.

She scoffed. "That's not the first time."

"So rude! Are you really going to say something like that in front of company when I had you hollering for *years* Aurania? That's how Brooklyn was born! Clearly it was deep enough!"

She looked away. "Whatever."

"And besides! As I was watching that epic fight, I was wondering what you were even doing up there. You know the only way to kill a spirit like that is to pierce its heart or run it out of Spirit Energy. You also shouldn't have..."

"Engaged in banter with it because you can weaken a spirit by displaying characteristics opposing its nature. I KNOW! I don't need you mansplaining everything to me! If you were one of my slaves, I would slice off your testicles and leave you to bleed out in the snow!"

"*The fuck*?! Are you still doing that crazy shit to people? I heard something like that from a scout, but I thought he was fucking kidding!" He gripped his temple.

"We need to have a *serious* discussion after this battle is over."

"You can say what you want. After this is over, I'm taking those children and leaving!" Aurania said as she rushed toward the spirit.

Before Aurania's battle, Terrance and Kayla held tight to icy platforms as they barreled through the city. A Wind Warrior raced after them in a bolt of white energy.

CRASH!

She pointed two fingers and lightning crashed down onto Kayla's platform, sending her flying through the sky. Terrance caught her as his platform smashed through the palace's outer gate and he was launched into the air.

"Put me down!" She roared as she flailed in his arms.

"In the sky?!"

Terrance fought back against her and they tumbled to the ground in the courtyard. Kayla cocked her arm back as he stood.

POW!

She launched a devastating punch that rattled his skull and knocked him into the snow.

His blood boiled. "This is what I was talking about when I told that simp you were crazy! Those Wind Warriors are serious business! We don't have time for this!"

She crossed her arms. "I told you to put me..."

CRASH!

A bolt of lightning struck the ground between them as the Wind Warrior closed the distance. They locked eyes, leapt up, and sprinted into the castle as she hotly pursued them.

James confusedly wandered through the palace. *I checked every room, but I couldn't find her anywhere. Where could she be?* He exited a corridor and entered the main hall as Kayla and Terrance sprinted past him.

Kayla dashed down a hallway. "James! Run!"

Before he could react, a Wind Warrior blitzed past him.

CRASH!

A bolt of lightning struck at his feet. The main hall was covered in white steam from the explosion. His ears rang as his foggy mind wandered. He trembled as he saw that his hands were covered in blood. "What the...hell?"

Two yellow, crazed, devilish eyes pierced through the mist as they filled his soul with fear.

WHOOSH!

The mist was blown away as a Wind Warrior stood menacingly in the doorway. She chuckled madly as she leaned against the palace doorway with a demented grin.

James grew extremely irritated.

He shook his head as he rose to his feet and dusted himself off. "Why do these things keep happening to me? Look, who the hell are you, and what are you doing here?"

She licked the blood from her lips. "Isn't it obvious?! I am Zara of the Wind Tribe! Second only to the great Aurania herself! I have come to take vengeance for my fallen sister and bring suffering to any men who stand in my way!"

James rolled his eyes. "Just men huh? Sounds like *somebody else* I know." He waved his hand dismissively. "Look, I don't have anything to do with any of this vengeance nonsense, ok? I'm having a very bad day, and I'd really appreciate it if you would just go about your business somewhere else and leave me alone."

"Unfortunately for you, I cannot! I already know you are associated with the other two defilers, and I have sworn an oath to punish any man who dares defy the Wind Tribe!"

James stepped out of the corridor behind him. "I'm not defying you at all. I literally just said you can walk right past me." He turned to walk away. "Nobody is in your way. Now if you'll excuse me, I have a date..."

She held up a hand caked in blood. "Your time has come! Look at my left hand!"

"Look! I just told you I don't have time for this! Brooklyn is waiting for me as we speak!" He face palmed.

"Tell me about your stupid left hand, so I can be on my way!"

She chuckled maniacally. "With my left hand I massacred more than five hundred of this nation's best soldiers because they dared to stand in my way! With my right hand I sliced off the penises and testicles of every single one as I watched the life drain out of them in the snow!"

He covered his face in disgust. "*Excuse me*? What the hell is wrong with you?! That is disgusting!" He slowly walked away. "Look, I'm just gonna look the other way and pretend I didn't hear..."

She quickly stepped toward him. "YOU'RE NEXT!" She pointed two fingers, and a bolt of black lightning cascaded toward him.

CLANG!

He drew his sword, and it collided with the stream of electricity. He slid through the snow as the bolt's power slowly forced him backward. "AAAAAAARGH!" The blade absorbed energy as he dug his feet into the floor. *I have...to...STOP THIS!*

He gasped as his side erupted in pain. His torso was soaked in blood. As a red drop hit the ground, he faltered as the pain overwhelmed him. *I can't die now! I finally found a girl who actually likes me! Things were finally starting to turn around! I refuse to die after just getting my first kiss!*

CRASH!

The blade shattered and the bolt pierced James through the chest. He slumped to his knees and fell backward as blood poured from his body.

"HA!-HA!-HA!" Zara cackled as she approached his limp body. She reached behind her back and snatched a small, bloody knife attached to her thong strap. She reached into his pants with the knife.

SNATCH!

Suddenly, dark energy poured in his wounds as he gripped her forearm. "Don't touch those."

WHOOSH!

She was launched across the hall by an unseen force.

CRASH!

She barreled through the wall, landed on her feet, and the sound of thunder crackled as she instantaneously zipped through the air toward him with her dagger drawn.

SNATCH!

He grabbed her by the neck and calmly choked her life away. He said menacingly. "It told you not to bother me when I'm having a bad day."

Zara wheezed as she clung to the edge of consciousness. "How...are...you..."

CRACK!

He crushed her throat and dropped her to the floor. "I'm feeling generous today because I just had my first kiss. If it wasn't for that, you'd already be *dead*. I don't want to taint the occasion with murder." He spat next to her face as she heaved violently. "I hate homicidal psychopaths like you. Killing and mutilating people for sport. Take this opportunity I've given you and go do something productive with your life."

Zara writhed on the ground and clawed at her neck as she desperately craved oxygen. She watched as he confidently walked away.

James looked around confusedly. "Now, I guess I should find Epios and Brooklyn and get out of here since these crazy thots keep showing up. Where could they be?"

As she stared, her rage grew exponentially. *How could I be bested by a fool like this?! I've never suffered such embarrassment in my entire life! Mother will strip me of my position and I'll be exiled for losing to a man! I can't let this happen...But I can't...breathe!*

＊

Zara's mind shifted to her past and she wept vigorously as she clawed without relief. She watched as her sister tripped and was whipped by a soldier with a red armband. A tear rolled down her sister's face, but she didn't cry. She leapt to her feet and continued dancing more vigorously. Zara watched as one of her friends was dragged out their filthy sleeping chamber in the middle of the night. She heard the desperate cries and moans of agony that rang out for an eternity as she was raped.

POW!

A gunshot rang out and her cries fell silent. Her body was tossed back into the room with the rest of the girls. Zara sat in the rubble of their destroyed home with her sister as they watched Aurania slaughter soldier after soldier. They were soaked in a torrential deluge.

A man cried out. "NO, STOP! PLEASE!'

SLICE!

"AUUUUUUUUUGH!"

Aurania slaughtered the last soldier and his screams raged in their minds.

His red armband fell into a pool of blood as the sound of thunder echoed in the area. Aurania approached the two sisters as they bawled in fear. She was bruised, ragged, and covered in blood. She held out her hand to the siblings with a beautiful smile. The gray clouds parted, revealing a bright orange sun.

Zara snapped back to reality and used Wind Craft to force air into her throat. She whimpered as she struggled to her feet. "I'll...kill...her..."

James froze.

He slowly faced her on the stairwell. "*Excuse me?*"

"Brooklyn..."

His rage seethed. "What the hell did you just say?!"

Her pupils were laced with lightning as her demented eyes danced with lunacy. "I'll...kill...her...and...Kayla...and every single person you have ever loved..."

Darkness flashed in his eyes. "I'M GONNA GIVE YOU ONE LAST CHANCE! CLEARLY YOU DIDN'T HEAR WHAT THE HELL I JUST TOLD YOU!"

"YOU'VE TAKEN EVERYTHING FROM ME! I'M GONNA LAUGH AS I SLICE BROOKLYN UP! I'LL CUT OUT HER ORGANS ONE BY ONE UNTIL SHE DIES FROM BLOOD LOSS! AND I'M GONNA STRING YOU UP BY THE BALLS AND MAKE YOU WATCH!" She screamed psychotically.

James' body was enveloped in darkness as bloodlust shone in his eyes. He spoke solemnly. "I don't have time for this shit."

WHOOOOSH!

They assumed battle stances and launched forward faster than the eye could see as Zara brought down her blade.

CLANG!

James swung his hand around his back, a second blade demagnetized from his armor, magnetized into his palm, and he deflected her slash at the last second. Their momentum carried them in opposite directions, as they skidded to a halt.

"Wind Craft, Eighth Art, Tempest's Fury!" Zara swung her sword as invisible slashes of wind careened burst forth.

James narrowed his eyes. "What the..."

SLICE!

The blades tore deep gashes across his body.

He crumpled to a knee. "AAARGH, DAMN!" His wounds steamed as they regenerated. *Dammit, she cut me from across the room somehow! I'll have to keep it up close and personal then.*

He vanished and instantly closed the distance as they engaged in a brutal sword battle. James was thrown off by her invisible blade, but he slowly adjusted as they clashed. They bounced from wall to wall like black and yellow streaks as they rushed each other, each side searching for an opening in their opponent's defense. James struck her blade with powerful blows that wore down her arms as their battle raged. Zara was more skilled, but James' heightened physical capabilities allowed him to compensate and deliver an overwhelming onslaught of furious attacks.

Zara's arms were heavy. *Dammit, I can barely grip my blade anymore. He isn't giving me any openings to use Wind Craft techniques. With his strength, I'll die to a single blow. I have to create distance somehow.*

James' speed only increased as his rage grew hotter and hotter. She racked her brain for answers as her hands trembled from fatigue. *It's time for a gamble!*

WHOOSH!

Zara zipped away, but James materialized right behind her. He grabbed her ankle, propelled himself above her and brought his blade down right over her neck.

ZAP!

At the last second a net of electricity appeared between them, and voltage coursed through his body.

"Art 6! Thunder Wall!"

"ARRRRRRRGGGGGHHHH!"

She skidded to a halt as the net dematerialized and James hit the ground. She took a deep breath. "Wind Craft, Art 5, Lightning."

FVOOOOOOM!

She forcefully stepped toward him and pointed two fingers as a massive bolt of black lightning cascaded toward James.

CRASH!

He rose to a knee, placed his wrists together in front of his body, and the bolt crashed into the plates on his forearms. She emitted a constant stream that swiftly blasted him into the palace wall.

CRUNCH!

He was slowly crushed as his body was pressed into the ice by the lightning's force. His mind faltered and dark spots blurred his vision. His skull was splitting and James' consciousness faded as his forearms started sinking. *There's no way out...it's over...*

The lightning stopped.

He slumped over as Zara fell to her knees. She heaved through ragged breaths. "NOOOOO! THIS CAN'T BE IT!"

James wheezed.

"Damn...huff...huff...looks...like...you're all out of juice." He noticed excess energy flowing around his gauntlets. He clinked his fists together and a fresh wave of vibrant energy burst forth. "Cool, looks like I'm all charged up."

CRASH! CRASH! CRASH!

He punched at her from across the room and supercharged beams of energy zipped toward her. She leapt away as the beams narrowly missed her. She

Zara redrew her wind blade. "Fine, I don't need lightning to finish off a detestable man like you!"

James growled. "The next time somebody calls me filthy or detestable...I'm gonna lose it."

CRASH! CRASH! CRASH!

James vigorously blasted lasers at her as she desperately zipped across the hall. His gauntlets ran low on energy, and he dashed off, pursuing her with his blade. He closed the distance, but she pushed her palm at him, and a gust of wind blasted him upward. She swung her blade and wind slashes sliced through the air toward him. His toe tapped the ceiling, and he gracefully weaved through the air, avoiding the blades as he fell.

He pointed to the side. "It's over." A beam of energy zipped from his finger and reflected off a mirror on the hall's wall.

It zipped past her and she chuckled. "HA! HA! HA! FOOL!"

James drew his blade. "This is gonna hurt."

Fear gripped Zara's heart.

Her eyes followed the beam, and it reflected off another mirror on an adjacent wall. She quickly glanced around and lost sight of the laser as she realized that the walls were covered in mirrors pointed at specific angles.

"Shit."

The beam ricocheted around the hall, picking up speed as James plummeted toward her. Her eyes struggled to follow the beam as she tried to predict its path.

GUSH!

The laser suddenly careened downward off the ceiling, past James and Zara, off a mirror on the floor behind her, and deep into her back.

SLICE!

She gasped in pain as James ripped his blade into her stomach.

BOOOOOM!

They crashed into the center of the hall, decimating the ground below. Zara was left in a bloody heap as James removed his blade from her gut and walked out of the crater.

He stuck his tongue out. "Yeah, you're not my type." He looked around the hall as he walked away. "Now, where could Brooklyn have..."

"AHHHHAHAHHAHAHA!" Zara screamed maniacally.

He face palmed. "You have to be fucking kidding me!" He turned around and was shocked as Zara cauterized her stomach wound with lightning.

She laughed as her wounds closed. "AHAHAHHAHAHAHAHA!" She stared at James with a devilish grin.

"I don't have any more time to waste on this." James Mirror Dashed away from her.

He zipped through the palace halls in a beam of light as he searched for Brooklyn. The sound of thunder rang out and he rolled his eyes as he glanced back. Zara zipped down the hall in a bolt of lightning.

He sighed dejectedly. "This is ridiculous."

She pointed her fingers and black lightning cascaded toward him. He zipped to the left side of the hall, narrowly avoiding the bolt. He activated Spectrum Vision to look for movement behind the closed doors as he passed them. James darted right and noticed each room was empty. *Where could she be? She told me to come find* her, but at this rate I'm wondering if she even wants to be found!

"DIE!" Zara screamed as she sent slashes of wind that enveloped the entire hall.

He leapt onto the wall and contorted his body to slip though the blades without breaking stride. *Her chamber must be near the throne room. Once I find her, I'll murder this crazy thot and...WHOA!*

CRASH!

He ducked another bolt of lightning.

Zara was running on the wall behind him with her blade. James nonchalantly searched the rooms of the palace, running from wall to wall and floor to ceiling as Zara attacked relentlessly.

He face palmed. *I CAN'T FIND HER ANYWHERE! Maybe I should go ahead and take care of this thot because she's slowing me DOOOOOWNNN!* He shouted as he was blasted forward by a gust of wind.

Zara accelerated as he tumbled through the air, readying her blade for a lethal strike. As she closed the distance, he flicked his wrist and a wall of ice burst forth that impeded her path. He lost sight of her as he spiraled.

For the first time, there was silence.

CRASH!

She crashed through the wall, vanished, and brought her blade down on his neck.

CLANG!

He swiftly spun his body in midair and deflected her slash. His momentum carried him forward and he skidded to a halt, falling off the wall onto his feet. James was dizzy and she blitzed him as he regained his bearings.

CLANG!

James narrowly deflected her slash, and the force of the collision blasted him down the hall. As he stopped, he noticed some of the wind from her blade had cut him on the right side of his body, all the way up to his face. *Not the face! I have a date!* His wounds slowly regenerated. *She's lucky I can heal for some reason today!*

He assumed a battle stance. "That's it. You should have run while you had the chance."

CLANG!

He rushed her, and they clashed. Lightning and wind burst through the walls across the palace as their battle intensified. James noticed her fatigue was growing by the minute.

ZIP! ZIP! ZIP! ZIP! ZIP! ZIP!

He zipped into a confined hallway and bounced from reflection to reflection in the glass walls as she hesitated. Zara huffed and puffed as she readied her blade.

CLANG!

He zipped out of a mirror and crashed into her, forcing her through a wall.

Zara was bruised and battered, but she pressed her blade against his with all her might. Her legs shuttered as she dug her feet through the ground. Their blades pressed against each other as she was driven backward through the snow. He forced her sword closer and closer to her neck as he strained with increasing force. As the spiraling wind grazed her neck and drew blood, primal fear shone in her eyes.

Suddenly, motion behind her caught James' attention through Spectrum Vision. The scene was blurry, but he noticed a few figures moving around high in the distance.

He beamed. "I think that's Brooklyn!"

"Good! I'm dying to introduce myself!"

Zara relaxed her legs and James fell on top of her.

POW!

As they fell, before her blade pierced her neck, she deactivated the wind blade, fell on her back, and kicked James with a violent gust of wind.

CRASH!

He soared through the palace walls and broke through the surface of a nearby mountain. He was dazed as he made out that he was in some kind of bunker through hazy vision.

"My knight! I can't believe you're here!" A feminine voice shouted.

"Fiend? Is that really you?" A pompous voice said.

James rapidly blinked to clear his vision, and saw Brooklyn's gorgeous face beaming down on him with a radiant smile.

His rage and frustration calmed.

For a moment, all was right in the world.

He shed a tear. "I was so worried. I was looking everywhere for..."

Time seemed to slow as Zara slowly entered his vision.

All James could do was watch as she raced toward Brooklyn at the speed of light with her dagger extended. Soul crushing fear and dread rose in his heart.

He watched the blade of her dagger inch closer and closer to her eye. I CAN'T MOVE! I'M TOO SLOW! I'M TOO SLOW! SOMEBODY! ANYBODY! HELP ME! His mind raged as the blade contacted her retina.

NOOOOOOOOOOOOOOOOOOO!

Suddenly, time stopped completely.

James was paralyzed as he watched the blood spread in Brooklyn's bloodshot pupil. Zara's eyes were crazed with joy as the tip of her dagger rested on Brooklyn's iris.

"I'd love to help you out! But just this once ok!" A playful voice said in his mind.

YES PLEASE! I'D DO ANYTHING TO SAVE...*wait a minute. Are you a demon or are you a representative of Jesus Christ?*

A figure shrouded in shadow appeared in the room next to Brooklyn. His body was as dark as the night sky, and galaxies glistened in the void. His multicolored eyes glowed and swirled like an ever-changing nebula within the shimmering darkness of his face. The figure put a hand over his heart. "Aww, that hurts! I'm not an angel or a demon. You've known me your whole life! Let's just say I stick as close as your shadow."

James watched the figure flick Zara with her own thong strap. *I don't think the Holy Spirit sounds like this, and* **you** *sound like a damn demon. If you're a demon, I don't want your help. I'll never consort with your kind, even to save someone I love.*

The figure clutched its chest. "You wound me, James! I told you I'm not a demon!" He waved his hand dismissively. "I'm not nearly as stupid as they are. Wasting all of their time trying to kill you guys when they know they're all going to get eradicated by Jesus anyway. They should spend all of their time begging on their knees praying for God to give them a second chance." It shrugged. "Though, that one did help me out so I guess I should be grateful...Oh, well. See me, I'm nothing like them." He waggled his finger. "No, no, no, no, no, no. I am something special! I am a force of nature! A shining star in a world devoid of light! A champion born to illuminate..." He waved dismissively. "Actually, let me not bore you with the semantics. I am no angel, or demon, but I am here to offer you an exclusive, one time offer of saving that gorgeous girl's life! What do you say?"

James watched the figure flex in the faces of frozen soldiers. *This must be some kind of spiritual ability. What did they call them? Specialists? That has to be it...Tell me weird time stopping specter. What is it that you want in return?*

The figure held up two fingers. "Oh, nothing much! Nothing much at all! I have two humble requests! The first is that if you are somehow killed by some *crazy* coincidence, you would give me control of your body for just ten meager minutes. And before you ask, I promise not to kill anyone or do anything that would harm your relationships with people you love!"

James watched the figure stack fruit on people's heads. *Sounds too good to be true. How can you even do something like that?*

The figure got awkwardly close to James' face. "Details, details, details! Who cares about details! Just know that I have your best interests at heart. Truly! Ready for my second humble request?"

James watched the figure look down Brooklyn's shirt. *I don't trust a damn thing you're saying, but sure. What is it?*

The figure shadow boxed. "It's simple really! Once I give you the power to rescue the girl of your dreams, I want you to save Epios and take him to a nearby wooly mammoth with your friends, *before* you come back and take Brooklyn with you."

James watched the figure blow bubbles into the sky. *Why? Do you have a hard on for him or something? Why couldn't I just take them both with me at the same time?*

The figure skillfully juggled knives. "Because, Because, Because, Because, Because! Either you will die! Or she will die! There's no alternative. That girl is too fast! Too strong! And too relentless! I'll help you send her blasting off somewhere, then she's gonna come after you and forget all about little Brooky-Wookie."

James watched the figure perform the cupid shuffle with a disco ball. *Don't call her that! And how do you know what's going to happen?! I've kicked her ass just fine on my own thank you! And besides, how do you even have the power to help me with any of this?!*

The figure put on a shirt that read 'I'm really strong' as he flexed. "Some of us have it and some of us don't! But don't let that concern you silly!" He pulled out a massive calendar. "Now, I'm a very busy man, and I have a lot of important things to do. Like eating..." The figure's stomach became obese and sloshed onto the ground. "I'm actually quite famished, thank you for asking. Now, do we have a deal?"

James watched the figure playfully spin around in an office chair. *I don't trust you in the slightest! But fine, it sounds simple enough. Don't die and save Epios first. I wouldn't normally do this, but I agree. But before you help me, tell me your name.*

The figure snapped its head toward James. "SPLENDID! Wait...my name? It's far too early for us to be getting so intimate. At least take me out on a date first!" He crossed his arms and turned away. "You are far too untrusting of me despite my *outstandingly* generous offer, and now you hurt my feelings." He waggled his finger. "Names have power you know, and I think I will be keeping mine to myself for now, thank you very much! Just know that I love my name because it's just like yours!"

Whatever! Just help me out and never speak to me again! I don't trust you!

The figure fainted. "Oh, you wound me, James!" He rolled his eyes. "But fine. I'll give you some space after this. Sometimes two people in a relationship need to take a *break*...I can understand that and I'm sure you will too. I have been a bit forward here haven't I..." He leapt to his feet. "Well alright then! Best of luck and remember you can always call on me as a friend in your times of need! I stick closer than a shadow, and I'm pretty freaking stylish too!" He pointed at James' black cross necklace. "If you come to your senses and want to see me again, *and I know that you will want to see me again*, remember that verse!"

Suddenly time resumed.

As the blade pierced Brooklyn's retina, James involuntarily raised his hand at an unfathomable speed.

WHOOOOOOOOOOOOOOOSH!

An unseen force blasted Zara high into the sky and the shockwaves from the impact shattered the side of the mountain.

Brooklyn cried out as she covered her eye and fell to her knees. "AHHH! MY EYE!"

James raced over to her. "Brooklyn!"

He suddenly froze and felt detestable inside. Grotesque thoughts of lust, rape, and assaulting her, overwhelmed his mind as he grew weak. He dropped to his knees as every terrible act he had ever committed flooded his mind. "**AAAAAAAARGH!**"

"My goodness, what's wrong with you this time fiend?"

James shuddered as he turned toward Epios and the sensation stopped. He looked over at Brooklyn as her servants attended her.

He shed a tear.

He reached his hand toward her. "I'll be back for you...my princess."

BOOOOOM!

The sound of a fighter jet boomed through the area. James balled his fists as Zara zoomed through the sky toward him.

He spoke calmly. "Epios...Let's go."

"That certainly seems like a good...IDEA!" Epios said as James snatched him.

CRASH!

James crouched, and the ground shattered as he launched himself into the sky. He looked down and saw a mammoth racing away from the capital.

Aurania and Okpa raced toward the Pride spirit in a ruined section of the city.

"I am the one hated by God, and now I will send you to meet Him." The spirit said.

An arsenal of dark weapons materialized and soared toward the Archigos. The duo battled and deflected the onslaught of weapons as they attempted to close in on the spirit.

"Aurania! Cover me while I get in position!"

"Absolutely not! I will be the one to end the spirit."

"It's not about that! It's called strategy!"

"I told you to stop mansplaining!"

They continued bickering as they were slowly overwhelmed by the spirit's attacks. The couple was forced further and further away from their foe as they narrowly avoided death. The spirit stood in the center of the destroyed area with its arms crossed as its arsenal relentlessly pursued the Archigos.

CRASH!

Okpa created an icy shield and deflected a massive hammer moments before it crushed him. He saw a trident zooming toward him out of the corner of his eye. He raised his hand to stop it with an ice wall, but a weak stream of water came out.

GUSH!

He was impaled in the chest as he crumpled to his knees.

GUSH!

SPLAT!

GUSH!

An onslaught of weapons swirled and ravaged him. Aurania grew fatigued as she zipped, leapt, and dodged a myriad of attacks from all angles. The spirit observed Okpa's defeat and raced toward her, ax in hand. She deflected a sword with her wind lance but a machete sliced her in the side as a dagger cut her behind the knee.

SLICE!

She fell to a knee as the spirit buried its ax in her side.

"AUGHA!" She screamed as blood flew from her mouth.

The spirit raised its hand as another ax formed in it. It smiled with hubris, as it swung the blade toward her head.

She closed her eyes, accepting her fate.

CLANG!

The sound of metal rang out. Aurania opened her eyes to see Okpa before her, struggling against the spirit with an icy blade. His flesh was completely destroyed and his dermis was drenched in blood as he trembled against the spirit's might. "Aurania! Move!"

WHOOOSH!

Weapons cascaded toward them and she blasted them away with a sphere of wind.

GUSH!

She pointed her fingers and launched a bolt of lightning through Okpa's back that pierced the spirit through the heart.

"GAAAH!" The spirit roared as it staggered back, clutching its chest.

The ax in her side vanished as Okpa crumpled to his knees. His eyes emanated blue energy as cracks formed across his body. He waved his hand and her wounds healed. "Aurania...If you ever want to see our kids again...we have to work together. *Please* listen to me for once in your life."

Aurania sighed as she stood. "*Fine.* Let's do this."

"Follow my lead."

Okpa's stomach wound closed, and his outer layer of skin regenerated in scattered patches as he rose to his feet.

FWOOOOOOOSH!

They sprinted away, racing in a circle around the spirit in opposite directions. The spirit covered the hole in its chest with a black plate of armor. It equipped two axes and stood proudly in the center of the circle.

CLANG!

Okpa dashed toward the spirit as their axes collided. They engaged in a brutal melee while Aurania built up speed as she circled around them.

Okpa ducked a slash aimed at his neck and froze the spirit's feet in place. Their blades collided once more and the impact sent a shockwave through the city. He grappled with the spirit as they pressed their axes against each other, each side struggling to force the other to submit.

FVOOOOOOOOOOM!

Aurania turned and darted toward the spirit in a streak of Gray light. Dark weapons materialized in her path, but she slid underneath them and sliced the spirit with her lightning blade.

SLICE!

Thunder rang out and its body erupted with electricity. "GAAAAAHHH!"

Its body shimmered with red and black energy as it started fading away.

FVOOOOM!

A dark ring of energy erupted from its feet that blasted Okpa backward. It soared away as it tried to escape. As it raced through the sky, Aurania rocketed past it and turned on a dime.

SLICE!

She tore through it with her wind blade and the impact sent it crashing down toward the surface.

GUSH!

Okpa stood waiting as he impaled it with a spear.

Blood poured from its mouth. "GAAAAAAAAAAHHH!"

The spear evaporated and Okpa equipped icy fisticuffs.

POW! POW!

He blasted the spirit with two devastating right hooks.

SLICE! SLICE!

Aurania zoomed in and slashed the spirit across its back and behind its leg.

GUSH!

The spirit fell to a knee and Okpa crashed two ice axes deep into its shoulder and side.

SLICE!

Aurania zipped through and sliced the spirit's head off.

SPLASH!

As its head hit the floor, Okpa leapt backward, dousing the spirit in water.

He blew her a kiss. "I'll let you do the honors my love."

She smirked. "Gladly. Wind Craft, Progress Art 3, Godspeed Strikes."

Aurania's blade radiated with electricity, and she vanished.

SLICE! SLICE! SLICE! SLICE! SLICE! SLICE! SLICE!

She disappeared and reappeared, slashing the spirit seven times as the sound of thunder rang out in the city. She deactivated her blade and walked away as a massive bolt of lightning crashed down on the spirit.

CRASH!

"GAAAAAAAAAAAAHHH! THIS CANNOT BEEEEEEE!" The spirit cried as it disintegrated.

Okpa fell onto his butt in exhaustion. "Damn. That guy was tough."

Aurania turned toward the palace. "Yes, it was quite formidable. Now where have those children gone? Ava and Zara should have retrieved them by now..."

"Is that seriously what you're concerned about right now? What about your daughter that you haven't seen in years?"

Aurania shuddered. "That will have to wait for another time. It was nice to see you Okpa but I'm off..."

He stood. "Stop it, Aurania! Just stop! Those kids are long gone by now and I'm here to tell you that you need to get your priorities straight and figure out what kind of person...what kind of mother you want to be!" Tears welled in his eyes. "Terrance and Brooklyn miss you so much...and I miss you and..."

WHOOOOSH!

She zoomed toward the palace.

As Aurania and Okpa battled, Terrance and Kayla raced through the palace away from the other Wind Warrior. Kayla followed Terrance as they ducked through corridors toward the building's rear. Kayla utilized Ember Dance to increase her speed and Terrance used Depth Command to increase his body's output, but Ava consistently gained on them. They entered a smaller room with a narrow tunnel leading to the mammoth hangars. Ava swung her blade, sending slashes of wind toward them.

GUSH!

Kayla slid below the slashes, but they sliced deep gashes into Terrance's back as he tumbled forward to the ground.

Kayla glanced in his direction. "Terrance!"

CLANG!

She quickly raised her daggers as they collided with Ava's blade. Kayla dropped her back and kicked Ava toward Terrance.

SWIP!

He swung his ax, but Ava contorted to leap over his strike. She landed gracefully in the doorway between them and the hangar.

"Follow my lead!" Terrance said.

They rushed at Ava from opposite sides, and she readied her blade against them. Terrance brought down his axe and was swiftly sliced across the chest. Kayla attacked but was blown back by a gust of wind. Ava faced Terrance as a burning pain exploded in her back. Flaming daggers sizzled in her flesh. *Dang it! She must have thrown them over my gust at the last second!*

FWOOSH!

Ava grimaced as the flames raged, scorching her skin.

POW!

As she hesitated, Terrance smashed her backward with an icy hammer.

"Go Kayla! I'll be right behind you!"

"I'm not gonna leave you here with this psycho! We can take her together!"

Ava ripped the daggers from her flesh and staggered to her feet.

"There's no way! These guys are trained assassins! You have to trust me and..."

BOOM!

Lighting crashed into Terrance's feet, sending him barreling into a wall. Kayla froze as she stared at his blood-soaked body.

He spat blood. "GO NOW! YOU WANT TO SAVE YOUR SISTER DON'T YOU?!"

She trembled. "OK! But you had better not die!" She teared up and sprinted down the corridor.

He walked out of the indentation his body made in the wall. He wiped rubble off his shoulder. "Alright, let's do this."

WHOOSH!

They charged toward each other and cocked back their weapons.

CRASH!

Ava moved her wrist downwards and he was flattened to the ground by a wind current. The current forced him in place while she sprinted past him into the tunnel. As she gained on Kayla, she winced in pain as her wounds raged.

POW!

Suddenly, Terrance burst through the wall to her left and blasted her side with an icy fist. He knocked her away and blocked the way forward to the hangar.

Ava raised her blade. "Step aside or die, dog. I don't want to have to hurt you."

He smirked. "No can-do. I've got a nation to protect you whore."

Ava's eyes flashed with rage as she blasted a bolt of white lightning at him. The snow below him shifted as he fell into a small room, narrowly avoiding the blast. She leapt into the air over the opening and electricity crackled in her fingertips as she aimed two fingers at him.

"Wrong choice." Ava said.

⁎

Kayla reached the mammoth hangar and leapt onto Sesame.

"Ok, this should be easy! Just like riding a bike!"

She grabbed the massive, heavy reins and whipped the mammoth to wake it.

"AHAAAA!" The mammoth roared.

"I'm sorry, but we really have to go."

She struggled with all of her might to turn the reins. The mammoth meandered toward the exit.

"Alright, I don't want to have to whip you again so please just speed up."

The mammoth glanced at her and sat down.

She growled. "Why you little..."

CRASH!

A bolt of lightning struck the ground right beside the mammoth and it leapt to its feet. It charged forward, racing through the frozen tundra.

"That's more like it."

As they gained distance from the palace, she worriedly looked back for Terrance. *I hope he's...*

BOOOM!

Snow filled the air as James crashed into the slush next to the mammoth holding Epios.

"James?!" She said.

He leapt onto the mammoth and dropped Epios in the saddle.

"Unhand me fiend!"

"Shut up Epios! I'm not in the mood!"

"James! Are you alright? Where did you..."

"Don't worry about that. I'll be right back!"

"What do you mean?! Where are you going?! Did you see Terrance on your way over here?!"

Darkness flashed in his eyes. "You of all people would be worried about that right now! No, I didn't see your stupid *fucking* boyfriend and I won't be looking for him either." He turned to leave.

"James...It's not like that! He stayed behind to..."

He rolled his eyes. "Yeah, yeah, whatever! He's so handsome and heroic!"

WHOOOOOSH!

He leapt off the mammoth into the sky.

Zara raced toward him and swung her blade

CRASH!

James pressed out his palm and she was sent crashing into the mammoth hangar by an invisible force.

SLICE!

Slashes of wind gashed James across the chest and sent him barreling into the snow past the mammoth.

They raced over to him, and Kayla leapt off Sesame as James laid buried in the snow.

She held him up to examine his jagged wounds. "James! This is bad! Are you..."

His wounds steamed and he regained consciousness.

Her heart sank. "James? What is..."

He muttered as he stumbled to his feet. "I'm...fine. I'm going back...for...Brooklyn..."

"No. You're in no shape to..."

"Speak of the devil." Epios said.

Terrance raced toward them as he skied through the snow. "What the hell are you dumbasses doing?! Get that mammoth moving!"

James trembled with each step as his knees warbled. "No...I'm going..."

"There's no time!" Terrance said as he grabbed James's dazed body and tossed him onto the mammoth.

Kayla leapt onto Sesame as Terrance took the reins and they dashed off.

Aurania and Ava walked out of the mammoth hangar. Ava had a gaping wound in her stomach that had been cauterized.

WHOOOSH!

A sphere of wind burst through the snow and Zara sprinted out of the hangar.

Ava stepped forward. "Sister wait! Mother said to..."

Back on the mammoth, James snapped to his senses. "NOOOOO! I'm going back for Brooklyn!"

"What the hell are you talking about?! My sister isn't coming with us, you simp bastard. She's not even a fighter and..."

"Shut the hell up before I kill you next!" James said as he leapt to his feet jumped off the mammoth.

Zara slid to a halt, channeled her energy, and fired a massive bolt of black lightning that filled the sky. It cascaded through the air for miles as it closed the distance between them. As James soared through the sky he stared into the black volley of lightning. He tried to force out his palm again, but nothing happened. "Crap! Now is not the time for this stuff to stop working!"

The bolt was moments away from enveloping James and he realized there was no escape. He wracked his brain. *Shit! What can I do?! What can I do?! What can I do?!* An image of Milliard flashed into his mind. *What would he do...* Milliard smiled and gave him a thumbs up. *Reflect God and Reflect Greatness!* James despaired. *But how can I? I'm unlovable...and no matter how hard I try...everything keeps going wrong...* An image of himself on the field celebrating after breaking the sack record flashed into his mind. A smile crept across his lips as he saw a vision of Brooklyn after their kiss. *But maybe that isn't true...Maybe I should hold out hope...Maybe today was proof that things can go my way. I never thought that I'd even get this far, right?* Visions of Zara, Gray, and his coach appeared before him. *That's why I have to fight! These reprehensible people won't keep barreling into my life and trampling over me! I WON'T ALLOW IT! I REFUSE TO LAY DOWN AND DIE BECAUSE THEY WANT ME TO!* His eyes flashed with multicolored energy as he channeled his power. *It's time to reflect greatness.*

James stretched out both arms. "Light Craft! Art 8, Reflect!"

The bolt was inches away when a clear barrier appeared before him.

CRASH!

The lightning struggled against the barrier as he put all of his willpower into maintaining it.

"AAAAAAAAAAAAAAAAAAAAAAAGGGGGGGGHHHH!"

FVOOOOOOOOOOOOOOOOOOOOM!

The bolt suddenly cascaded back toward Zara at double the speed.

GUSH!

Before she could react it struck her through the chest.

Zara crumpled to her knees and fell flat as blood poured from her body.

The tundra was silent.

Aurania shook her head. "Foolish girl."

James was relieved and exhausted as he plummeted toward the earth into the snow. The mammoth sprinted over as his friends leapt off and swarmed him.

"James!"

"That was quite stellar fiend."

"Not bad for a simp."

James shakily rose to his feet as he stared forward. His voice shook with rage. "I'm...going back...for Brooklyn."

Kayla sprinted in front of him. "James! Would you please stop and listen to me for just a second! Look, this is all my fault and..."

"You're right. It is *your fault!* Now step aside while I go back to get the only person that actually loves and cares about me!" He spat.

"I care about you James and I think I'm starting to like you a lot as well! I had such a great time with you on our date and..."

He shoved past her. "Too late! Brooklyn already loves me."

"Calm down, fiend. Normally you would have my support, but this is extremely dangerous. Those Wind Warriors are..."

James stopped. "Epios...after I poured my heart and soul out to you a few hours ago...I thought you of all people would understand me. Move." He brushed past him.

Terrance face palmed. "Are you dumb or are you daft? We have to get the hell out of here before..."

James whispered into his ear. "Last...*warning. You'd already be dead if she wasn't your sister.*" He aggressively pushed past him.

Kayla, Epios, and Terrance locked eyes.

WHOOSH!

James crouched and leapt into the air.

Suddenly a flaming whip wrapped around his ankle.

CRASH!

"GAAAAHAAA!" He roared as he slammed down into the snow.

He stared at his ankle, and he froze it, severing the whip. He defrosted it and rose to his feet as a flash of light blinded him.

"Flash Bang!"

James clutched his aching eyes. "God dammit it Epios! Once this wears off, I swear I will..."

FREEZE!

His body was enveloped in a pillar of ice, and he was frozen solid.

Terrance smiled as he patted the pillar. "There! That should make the simp easy to transport!"

James shed a tear. *It looks like nobody wants me to be happy...Fine...I see how it is...*

Darkness swirled within the ice pillar and it trembled.

"What the?"

"Fiend?"

Kayla shed a tear. "James...oh no."

CRASH!

The ice shuddered until it shattered, and James stomped out of his prison.

"BRING IT ON THEN! Brooklyn is waiting for me, and nothing is going to keep me from seeing her!"

They surrounded him and rushed in. James' senses were heightened by his power, and he felt a new wave of strength surging within him. Kayla attacked with her daggers, but he deflected her flurry of attacks at the wrist and pressed his palm against her chest, blasting her into the snow. He ducked a slash from Epios and deflected an ax attack from Terrance with the plate on his wrist. He punched Epios in the face, jumped, spun, and kicked Terrance in the head, sending him crashing into the snow.

Back at the mammoth hangar, Okpa stumbled over toward the Wind Warriors on crutches.

"It looks like your pupils are having a disagreement." Aurania said.

His eyes widened as he watched the battle. "What?! Oh my God no!" He sighed dejectedly. "Why can't kids just listen and do what they're told!"

"Please sir! Heal my sister!" Ava said.

Okpa looked down as Zara bled out on the floor. "What the hell happened to her?!"

As James' friends struggled to their feet, he stormed away. "Leave me alone or next time I won't be so merciful!"

"You should have killed me while you had the chance." Terrance said.

He rushed James, and they engaged in a high-level hand to hand duel. Terrance equipped icy fisticuffs and hit James with three furious punches and an uppercut that sent him staggering backwards. James spat blood into the snow and raced at him, but Kayla darted in front of him and sliced him twice in the torso.

SLICE!

He swung at her, but she ducked and Epios ripped his sword over her head and impaled James in the chest. The deep slash sent him to his knees and he roared in pain. Tears rolled down his face. "AAAAARGH! God dammit! Why can't you just let me be happy!"

Kayla's voice broke. "James...*please*...just tell me what happened!"

POW!

James snapped the blade in his chest with a chop and blasted Epios with a punch that sent a dark shockwave reverberating through the area. The blow devastated Epios, knocking him out cold as he collapsed into the snow.

Kayla and Terrance rushed James, but he skillfully deflected and avoided their attacks in an effortless fashion. They attacked him vigorously in perfect tandem but failed to strike him even a single time. Terrance swung his ax and Kayla jabbed at him with her daggers. He ducked the slash and perfectly countered her strikes. She jumped up and launched a flaming kick, but he slid under her, reached up, and touched her gut with his palm, as she instantly crashed down into the snow unconscious.

James swung at Terrance, but he front flipped into the air above him, caught the dagger that Kayla had tossed up and slung it deep into James' back, stunning him as the flames expanded.

GUSH!

Terrance buried his ax in James' shoulder.

James didn't even flinch.

POW!

He vanished and struck with unearthly speed as he devastated Terrance with a gut punch that sent dark shockwaves through the area. Terrance was sent flying as dropped down into the snow unconscious.

James faced the palace. "Now, I can *finally*..."

"James!" Brooklyn's voice rang out nearby.

He quickly looked around. "Brooklyn! Is that you?!"

She was nowhere in sight and as he searched, Okpa used Depth Command from afar to restore his friend's wounds. The voice came from an icy mirror that rose from the ground. Epios laid in the snow and his hand trembled as he struggled to maintain the connection using Light Craft. The mirror was pointed toward the bunker that housed the escaped royals.

James raced over to the mirror and saw her face in the reflection. "Brooklyn! Is that you?!" He marveled at her beauty and felt shame as he saw her bloodshot eye.

"Yes! It's me James! I think it's so hot the way you're fighting to come and see me!"

"Thanks! I won't keep you waiting any longer! I'm on my way!"

She cheerfully waved goodbye. "Take care of your awesome friends for me! And my idiot brother...I guess. Stay alive, stay with God, stay handsome, and most importantly stay *single* until I see you again!"

"What are you talking about? You're coming..."

SNAP!

FWOOSH!

Kayla snapped and his wounds erupted in flames.

POW!

Epios blasted James with beams of light that pierced his torso and Terrance smashed the back of his head with a hammer as James lost consciousness.

✳

In a castle suspended above a lake of a fire, Gray's mother opened a door at the end of a dark corridor. Inside the room, Gray's father stirred, and his withered lips shifted into a wrinkly smile.

FWOOOOOOOOOOO!

Darkness poured into his mouth from the shadows and his head morphed into a beautiful shape. He was strikingly handsome, and a perfectly groomed head of hair rose out of his wrinkled stump. His withered smile became an alluring, charming grin that made her heart skip a beat. "My love. It is always a pleasure to see you. You hardly ever visit me anymore these days."

She blushed. "The pleasure is all mine handsome! But you have appointed me to watch over our dream, and it never slumbers. So neither can I."

"And that is why I love you. Your devotion to repairing this world is second only to mine. But what brings you to my chamber...Wait! First, how are the kids doing?"

She smiled. "Gray is in the laboratory recovering. He was mortally injured in the incident that I came to inform you of. All is well with Zoey in the north, and their shameful brother has been recovering from his battle with Milliard..."

He sat up. "Incident? What kind of incident? Neither the Archigos or Kalios have caught on to our plans have they?"

She waved dismissively. "No my love, you need not worry about that. The incident involves that boy from the capital. The one the children wanted to bring in to speak with you..."

"I thought we already denied that request. Gray was instructed to place the devices and collect the prince, nothing more." He balled his fists. "If he has disobeyed orders, I swear I will..."

"He has not. Though he did go out of his way to attempt to romance that delusional Flame Tribe *floozy*, which led to his current injuries." She glared. "I have no idea why you put it in his head that she would be a good suitor for him. She is as reprehensible as they come."

He smiled as he counted on his wrinkled fingers. "What? She's smart, beautiful, powerful, principled, has excellent lineage, and would make beautiful babies with Gray!"

She stomped. "You just like her because she's pretty! I've observed her for years and she is nothing but a backward-minded, delusional, hypocrite, *bimbo* who has already sullied herself with Okpa's detestable failure of an heir!"

He shrugged. "We all make mistakes. Okpa's seed is a detestable child, so Gray can just kill the boy, and she will be his for the taking!" He leaned forward and spoke excitedly. "So, was he able to woo her?! My little Gray is growing up so fast!"

She gripped her temple. "He actually did, but she was under the influence of some kind of spiritual influence that placed her in a more vulnerable state." She raged. "That is a part of the *incident* that I was trying to speak to you about before you got sidetracked talking about other women!"

He snapped to attention. "There was an incident?! What incident?! Tell me every detail right now! Have the..."

"No! The Archigos have not discovered our plans! The boy that the children wanted to recruit has become too problematic! He just unleashed the most devastating spiritual attack since the calamity upon the Ocean Tribe, and he even fended off Zara, a *Progress* Warrior of the Wind Tribe through his own strength! His ability to summon high-level spirits rivals even my own!" She gripped her temple. "After Gray planted the blade on the prince, we were counting on those whores to kill the children, stir dissent, and create an opening for him to place the device. He was able to do so before returning, but this boy is starting to concern me. His utilization of Spirit Energy is similar to Marcus' but there is something more to it that I cannot identify. There was a particular moment where he saved the Ocean Tribe's princess that still puzzles me..."

"What happened?! Who is he and how has his strength grown so exponentially?! Whose boy is this?! Where did he come from?!"

"I can only answer one question at a time, my love. I was observing the moment where he saved the princess through the shadows, but some kind of spectral figure stared into my eyes through the darkness and mooned me before the feed went blank! I created another one within a second, but the boy had already rescued her and was escaping with the prince!"

"Who dares mock us?! I will have his head!"

"I have no clue my love, but if that *thing* is against us, its presence could be problematic. I believe the boy's sudden increase in strength could also be linked to the appearance of this figure, but I haven't seen anything like it. Its Spirit Energy leads me to believe that it is a person *and* a spirit which is quite perplexing. And I do not know where the child came from as there is no record of his lineage in the academy's files. I feel like I've seen him somewhere, but I can't put my finger on it..."

"I want him and his group dead. Tell Gray the next time he encounters them that he is to..."

The Green-Eyed spirit materialized in the room. "Father! Perhaps there is another solution!"

The man shook his head. "Ah, so you have grown bold enough to show your face in my presence after your humiliating defeat. The foolishness of my own seed astounds me!"

The spirit prostrated. "Forgive me father! I nearly defeated the Archigos, but he unleashed some kind of new power he had never displayed before! Next time I will be prepared and..."

"No! You have lost your opportunity! Upon summer's end, Victor will dispose of the Light Archigos *and bring me his head*. Speak your suggestion and be gone from my presence until you prove that you are still able to provide some *semblance* of a contribution to this family! Your sister seems to be the only one who can accomplish the tasks delegated to her!"

The spirit trembled. "If I may speak father...they are traveling to the Earth Tribe at this very moment. The Slave Master resides there along with the denizens of the criminal underworld. We could bargain with him to see if he would be willing to acquire the boy for us. The Light Archigos was able to strike my soul, and it will take some time for me to recover enough strength to reenter the field. Given the power James displayed against the Wind and Ocean tribes; it seems like even Gray would have difficulty apprehending him without outside assistance, and we don't have many other upper rank members of the council who can enter the field at this time..."

The man flinched. "Wait a moment...What did you say that his name was?"

"His name is James Fos father. Do you know of him…"

FWOOOOOOOOOOOOOOOOOOOOOOOOOOOOOSH!

Rage covered the man's face and dark energy surged from his body. The ground trembled violently as fear filled their hearts. The air's thickness and pressure choked them as they fell to their knees. The matter in the room slowly disintegrated as cracks formed in the woman's skin.

"NO! NO! NO! NO! NO! NO! NO! NO! NO! AFTER ALL OF THESE YEARS! AFTER ALL OF MY PLANNING! MY DEDICATION! MY INTENTION! AFTER EVERYTHING THIS FAMILY HAS SACRIFICED FOR THIS CAUSE, **HE** SHOWS UP!" He buried his face in his hands. "IT'S ONLY A MATTER OF TIME BEFORE…FUUUUUUUUUUUCK!"

BOOOOOOOOOOOOOOOOOOOOOOOOOOOOOOOM!

The decay spread across the entire castle, and it trembled at its foundations. The samurai was resting from training when the decay surrounded him. He lifted his blade and crimson energy burst forth from his body that stopped the decay in its tracks. He shook his head. "Childish."

The wild man who sat in the dark felt the decay's presence. He glared at the encroaching cracks in the ground with intense malice, and they stopped. The decay retreated from his chamber and spread elsewhere.

The decay reached the couch that the teenage gamer sat on, and it disintegrated the television. He slowly rose to his feet and stood on the couch as the decay nipped at his heels. He sighed. "Dammit. A disconnect counts as a loss. It looks like I'll have to make a new account..."

The decay reached the laboratory that housed Gray, but it stopped spreading at the door.

The voice from the monitor muttered. "I'm glad I was able to make my laboratory sin-proof. Father has these outbursts far too often..."

Outside the castle, the magnitude of the man's Spirit Energy shifted the tectonic plates, causing earthquakes across the globe.

In the Flame Tribe, Kalarono was holding a tray of fresh cinnamon rolls.

RMBLRMBLRMBLRMBLRMBLRMBLR!

Suddenly, the ground trembled and he spilled them all over the floor.

He shouted as he fell to his knees. "WHAT A TRAVESTY!"

CRASH!

Okpa was repairing the palace when the ground shook and the building's stained-glass windows shattered. He raged. "GOD DAMMIT I JUST FIXED THOSE! WHY CAN'T THOSE KIDS JUST STAY OUT OF TROUBLE!"

Milliard was bench pressing massive amounts of weight when the ground trembled and cracked around him. Fissures opened across the ground and lava burst through them across the capital. As rubble crashed down around Milliard, he was unphased as he continued lifting. "Someone seems mad..." He stared out the window. "I wonder if James has made any new friends! I wonder if they're strong! I can't wait for him to introduce me to them!" He heard civilian's screams. "But for now, I guess I should make sure everyone is ok huh?"

Back in the castle, the Green-Eyed Spirit roared over the intense pressure. "D...DAD P...P...PLE...ASE M...OM. CAN'T T...TAKE T...T...THIS!"

The man looked down and saw that his wife's body had almost completely disintegrated.

He stared in disdain and scoffed.

The overwhelming pressure filling the area dissipated as the world's decay ceased. He waved his hand, and the castle was restored as a wave of milky energy washed over it.

He gripped his temple. "Fine...we will go with your plan, *boy*. Inform Gray that he is to speak to the Slave Master and bring the child to me. He should not let this distract him from his primary objective. Tell him I will not bargain with underworld filth, and that if Giali will not assist us in bringing in the boy because I asked him to, then Gray should bring me his *head*. I don't care what methods he utilizes but tell Gray that the boy cannot be allowed to die under *any circumstances*. I want James Fos in my possession at his earliest convenience. *Kill the rest.*

15 – The Earth Tribe

James

I JOLTED AWAKE. The power that surged within me was gone, and in its place was a horrific sense of shame. It was dark, and we were galloping on the back of a mammoth at breakneck speeds. Epios snored and Terrance manned the reins at the mammoth's head. Kayla was dozing off as her droopy eyes attempted to stare vigilantly into the distance behind us. Epios' arm was in a sling and Kayla had bandages wrapped around her torso. She noticed me and joy colored her face. "James! You're awake! I was so worried..."

"Where are we?" I said curtly.

She wilted but maintained a sweet tone. "We're heading to our last stop! The Earth Tribe! Terrance said that his dad was already planning to rejoin the union before we even got there! Once we get Bazek to rejoin, the mission will be over and..."

"Cool, thanks." I turned away and sulked in the corner of the saddle.

She came over and gently placed a hand on my shoulder. "James, I'm worried about you. How were you able to do all those crazy things against those Wind Warriors? Your Spirit Energy feels terrible, and I've never seen you act like..."

"Look Kayla, I don't need this from you right now! You've never seen me act like this before because you don't even know me! I don't need your pity! I know you only said that stuff to me before we left because you were trying to diffuse the situation! You never liked me, and you shouldn't have led me on or cried in my arms on the top of that hill if just a few days later you were going to spread your legs wide for a dick like him that doesn't even like you! If you're such a *strong* and *independent* woman, at least have the fucking balls to be honest and tell me that you never had feelings for me in the first place." I glared. "You hate men, right? So, stand on your beliefs and leave me the hell alone."

For the first time, I watched beautiful, shimmering tears roll down her smooth cheeks. She silently laid down on the other side of the saddle. She turned away from me as she covered her face and tried to hide the sobs that racked her body.

"You've done it now, you dick!" Terrance shouted over the wind.

"Yeah?! And your sister is next on my to-do list!"

"Ha! She'd never even give somebody like you the time of day, *moron*. Just give her some time and I'm sure she'll see who you really are!"

I stood and dark energy surged from my body. "LET'S PUT THAT TO THE TEST THEN!"

"I'LL STOP THIS MAMMOTH RIGHT NOW! THIS TIME I WON'T BOTHER TO KNOCK YOU OUT! I'M JUST GONNA FUCKING KILL YOU!"

"CAN EVERYBODY PLEASE JUST STOP!" Kayla cried out.

We stared at her and came to an unspoken agreement to settle things later. I plopped down, curled up, and faced away from the group. We rode the rest of the night in silence as I covered my ears to block out the sound of Kayla's tears.

I felt terrible inside. My stomach was so full of guilt and shame that I wanted to vomit. I wasn't even that angry at my friends and Terrance anymore. I was filled with resentment, hatred, and rage, toward myself. I had never done anything this bad in my entire life. I was so obsessed with a girl I didn't even know that I attacked and injured my only friends in this entire world. I put my own selfish desires over their lives, futures, and goals, just like the people I hate. *I could have gotten them killed.* I even put my hands on Kayla, which is something I swore I would never do. I was rude, disrespectful, and I told Terrance I was going to have sex with his sister, without any consideration for how she would feel about that.

As I rampaged through the palace, I told myself I was doing this to help her. As her knight, it was my duty to get her out of that terrible place she hated so much. I told myself she could travel with us, and that we would get to know each other, and I would help her get closer to God, and I would rescue her from the oppressive circumstances she didn't deserve to have to deal with.

But those were all lies.

I just wanted to take her, and have every part of her for myself, without any regard for what was best or what God would want.

And that made me sick.

I always told myself I wanted a relationship and to partner with my wife so we could support and grow alongside each other, but my actions were proving that I was nothing but a filthy liar. What if the Wind Warriors hadn't attacked and I had found her? Would I have had sex with her even though I promised myself and the Lord that I was waiting until marriage?

Probably.

How would that be leading and cultivating her into becoming a better woman of God? I knew what I was doing at every step. I knew I was going the wrong direction, and I willingly walked further down the path until it was too late.

All I had to do was take Epios and leave. I was strong enough to have done that at any moment. But I didn't, and now I had walked down a dark road that didn't lead me any further toward my goals. My friends probably thought I was sick in the head, and any attraction Brooklyn had was probably gone after watching me act like a maniac. She said she liked it, but I'm sure she was just being nice and doing her part to help us escape.

I felt so ill that I could die.

Who the hell was I becoming?

We rode across the continent and back to the shore. As I walked onto the boat, Terrance tied a note to his mammoth and sent it away.

"Uhh, what are you doing?" I said.

"What does it look like dumbass?"

"No way. You're not coming with us. Go back and be with your other man-whore womanizers."

He laughed. "Womanizers? You don't even know what you're talking about." He smacked his lips. "You really are such a *simp*. And for the record *simp*, I'm only coming with you piss ants because my stupid ass dad is making me. You three losers are the last people I want to spend my summer with."

"Tell your dad I said the feeling is mutual after you walk back to the palace."

He sighed. "Your simpery knows no bounds. Look *simp*, the Earth Tribe Capital has been on lockdown for years due to terrorist and underworld activity. I have a friend who can get us inside. You're doing all this bitching and moaning when you can't even get into the city without me."

I boarded the ship. "Whatever. The sooner we get this over with, the sooner I can get home and never see you again."

I approached my and Epios' room as Terrance burst past me.

"I CALL DIBS ON THIS ONE!" He shouted as he jumped onto my bed.

"Absolutely not you detestable barbarian! Having to share a room with the fiend was bad enough! I refuse to sully my reputation any further by bunking with one as grotesque as yourself!"

"I already called dibs so it's too late! Go room with the simp in the other one!"

"That room is mine and I'm not sharing it with any of you stupid men." Kayla snapped.

Terrance rolled his eyes. "Again, with the men shit? You didn't think I was stupid when you..."

Her eyes blazed. "That was a mistake I WILL NEVER MAKE AGAIN! If you were a real man, you wouldn't kiss and tell! Now, James needs..."

He threw up his arms. "It's always *James this* and *James that*. Are you his fucking mom now?"

"I'm not his mom! I'm just..."

Epios stomped and pointed at Kayla. "I don't care what you say *whore*, and I have no regard for you at all *trog*. You will sleep with the fish before you share a room with me..."

"Shut the hell up white boy! I told you to go sleep with the feminist if you have a problem!"

Kayla drew her daggers. "I'll send anyone who crosses the threshold of this door straight to hell! Now Terrance if you would just shut up and..."

I plopped down on the front of the boat. "It's fine. I'll sleep outside."

They stared in shock.

Kayla held up her hands. "James, I didn't mean that. You really don't have to..."

"I said it's fine."

I laid flat on the deck and turned away. They went into their rooms, and the ship set sail in silence.

As the days passed, Epios and Terrance's bickering raged through the walls and rattled within our skulls.

"YOU'RE NOT EVEN A REAL PRINCE! YOUR TWO BROTHERS ARE THE ONLY ONES THAT MATTER, **AND THEY CAN KISS MY ASS TOO**!"

"IT'S HARDLY AN ACCOMPLISHMENT TO BE THE PRINCE OF A NATION OF BARBARIANS, SAVAGES, AND WHORES! AT LEAST MY PEOPLE KNOW HOW TO EAT WITH UTENSILS YOU TROGLODYTIAN TRASH BAG!"

"WHAT DID YOU CALL US?! MY SISTER IS NOT A WHORE! I'LL KILL YOU!"

"ANY WOMAN WHO COULD POSSIBLY CHOOSE THE FIEND OVER ONE AS HANDSOME AND DASHING AS MYSELF COULD ONLY BE CATEGORIZED AS ONE THING. A DIRTY, NO-GOOD, WHORE! IF A DUEL IS WHAT YOU DESIRE, THEN SO BE IT!"

"OCEAN CRAFT, ART 1!"

"LIGHT CRAFT, ART 2!"

They went on and on like that for hours until they tired themselves out and started up again the next day. I bore the cold nights alone while I tried to ignore the concerned stares from Kayla. She brought me meals, but I declined. I felt so terrible inside that I wasn't hungry. I had no desire to do anything. I just stared at the blue sky and watched as it grew dark each day.

On the third day, Kayla gathered Terrance and Epios in the ship's hallway.

"Guys, I'm worried about how James has been acting. He's not eating, and I can feel his negative Spirit Energy from here. We must do something!"

Terrance crossed his arms. "I don't give a damn. He can simp and sulk until he dies for all I care!"

Epios rolled his eyes. "The fiend goes through these phases occasionally, but a beautiful woman always comes and snaps him out of it. I'm sure in due time the cycle will repeat itself."

"*Really*?! That's all you guys have to say?! Aren't you at least a little bit concerned about how he was able to stand toe to toe with a Wind Warrior?! I've been training him for a while, and he hasn't even laid a finger on..."

I glared. "You know I can hear you guys, right?"

"I don't give a damn about what that simp did. He got lucky and that's the end of it!"

"The fiend is a mystery." Epios said dismissively as he and Terrance returned to their room.

She shook her head. "Men are no use."

Kayla approached, and I turned away. She placed a hand on my shoulder and a rush of emotion surged within me. Some were butterflies, others were terror, rage, and pain.

"James. I'm worried about you. How were you able to do all those crazy things against the Wind Warriors? And when Terrance froze you, I thought I saw shadow..."

"I don't know Kayla."

"Alright, well can you at least tell me what made you get so upset back there in the first place? I really think we should talk about..."

"What is there to talk about?"

She sighed. "James, I just want you to know that I care about you. When you're ready to talk, I'll be here." She teared up as she walked back to her room.

On the fourth day, storm clouds rolled in.

"James, I know I told you this before, but you really can come and room with me. I don't want you to get sick from being out in this rain all day." She said.

"It's whatever Kayla. I'll be fine."

Dark clouds consumed the skies, and a torrential downpour smashed our ship against the waves. The frigid rain peppered my skin for hours. I shivered perpetually as my entire being was drenched in unbearable cold. *I deserve this for being such a disappointment and a terrible human being.*

Kayla shouted over the tempest. "James! Please! I want you to come inside! At least until this storm passes!"

I sat in a curled-up ball, shivering. I forced myself to stop as I looked up at her.

I shook my head.

I saw a tear roll down her face as she went back inside. As soon as the door closed, I sprinted over and sat in the covered area between the two rooms. The cold was overwhelming. *I at least need to get out of the direct path of the rain.* I ripped off my soaking clothes and curled into a ball to conserve my warmth. I needed something, anything, to take my mind off the cold.

I tried to think, but I was only reminded of my own disgrace. Every time I tried to redirect myself to something else, another scene of how I almost ruined all our lives flashed into my mind, just like I did in the capital.

Each selfish flashback was proof of the fact I was nowhere near where I was supposed to be as a person, or in life. I was angry. I was so very angry at myself for failing to become the man I set out to be. I was furious at myself for once again failing to accomplish even one thing that mattered. Not one, but two women I liked gave me the time of day, and I blew it once again. I'd spent months in this ridiculous world, and I wasn't even a step closer to getting home, getting rich, or finding a wife.

I had all this potential for what? I felt like I was nothing but a waste of space, and there was an immeasurably long path ahead of me before I could contribute something of value to this world. I had no strength or desire left to get up and take even one more step down this path. After years of struggles and toil, I had absolutely nothing to show for it.

As I shivered and wallowed, I glanced over at her door, and I was reminded of her question from the other day. *How **did** I do all that crazy stuff? Akri said I didn't have any kind of special powers or whatever, but then we found out I could wield all the elements. On top of that, I got that incredible burst of power after Brooklyn kissed me, and I even got a crazy strength boost when I got angry at that crazy thot.* The boat rocked and I stared at my shifting shadow. *The childish idiot that helped save Brooklyn must have had something to do with this.* I decided to see what the other Me's had to say about this whole situation. Maybe they could offer a different perspective that could help me shake this terrible funk I was deservedly trapped in.

✳

I retracted within myself and opened my eyes to the boardroom full of Me's. They were in a terrible mood, and each had injuries of varying severity. Critical James' entire body was covered in bandages, and he had 5 IV's full of blood pouring into his limbs. Hood James was in a neck brace. Fat James's body was covered in some kind of ointment and there was a jar on the table labeled "Frostbite cream". I looked under the table and saw Scary James was as flat as a pancake. Guise James had a black eye, and his face was completely covered in bandages. Holy James looked even more sickly than before, and there were three Army James' with guns pointed at one of the cages. Inside the cage was the cuckoo idiot whack job that helped save Brooklyn.

I raised an eyebrow. "What the hell happened to you guys?" I pointed at Jerkface. "And how the hell did he get here?"

Critical James' eyes lit up. "Sir! It's you! Uhh...we had a night out and got a bit too rowdy...but we're all well on our way to recovery!"

"*Night out*? Yall live inside my body. What do you..."
BANG!

Hood James slammed the desk. "Shut the hell up and listen here negro! Our business is our business! Don't ask again or I'mma have to put these paws on you and knock some sense into yo' ass. You *know* I got them hoes!"

"You're literally in a neck brace. And it looks like somebody beat the hell out of *you*. Clearly it looks like you don't got them hoes or at least what you got ain't enough."

"THE HELL DID YOU SAY NEGRO? MAKE A MOVE CUZ! MAKE A MOTHERFUCKIN' MOVE! I SHOULD KILL YOU FOR DISRESPECTING MY SET! A CERTAIN REAL NEGRO HAS BEEN MOMENTARILY SIDELINED BUT WHEN HE GETS SUBBED BACK IN, HE WILL HANDLE HIS BIDNESS' AND SHOW YOU HOW REAL NEGROES GET DOWN WHEN THEY GET DISRESPECTED BY SOFT ASS, SUBURBAN ASS, CRYBABY ASS..."

BOOOOOOOOOOOOOOOOOOOOM!

Suddenly, he was blasted through the ground. His hospital bed crashed down through floor after floor of the massive high rise until he smashed into the surface in a massive explosion.

BOOOOOOOOOOOOOOOOOOOOOOOOOOOM!

"What the hell was that?!" I exclaimed.

"That's enough of that shite."

I turned around and saw the Jerkweed standing on the table wearing a cape and posing like a superhero. The soldiers with their guns pointed at the cage leapt in shock.

"What the hell?", "He was just right there!", "Where did he..." They turned and raised their guns to him once more.

The nut job made a heart with his fingers. "James! It's so good to see you again! I'm touched that you asked about me! It made my heart skip a beat and..."

The Army James' stepped between us. "Sir, back away from him! His threat level is catastrophic! He's..."

FWOOOOOOSH!

The soldiers disintegrated.

"What the hell?!" I shouted as their ashes simmered.

"Now, as I was saying..."

Suddenly, soldiers flooded into the boardroom with their weapons drawn. They surrounded that wacko and aimed rifles at his head. One soldier made his way through the crowd with a megaphone and stood in front of me.

"WRATH! YOU WILL NOT BE PERMITTED TO DO AS YOU PLEASE ANY LONGER! THE JAMES LOVE CORPS WILL..."

"STOP WITH THE MEGAPHONE! WE CAN HEAR YOU PERFECTLY FINE! WE'RE IN A BOARDROOM!" I roared as I covered my ears.

"I APOLOGIZE SIR! WE HAVE BEEN EXTRA VIGILANT AFTER OUR DEFEAT AT THE HANDS OF THE

CAPED **BASTARD** WHO ATTEMPTED TO STEAL KAYLA'S HEART, SIR!" He put the megaphone away and took a deep breath. "NOW AS I WAS SAYING, WRATH! YOU HAVE BEEN ACCUSED OF A MULTITUDE OF CRIMES AND ARE NOW UNDER DETAINMENT UNTIL YOUR SENTENCING AT THE HANDS OF THE BOSS! YOU WILL BE RELEGATED TO YOUR CAGE AND WILL REMAIN THERE UNTIL..."

"Could you stop with all of the yelling. You're hurting my virgin ears." The nut job said as he donned seven sets of earmuffs and tears streamed down his face. He covered one of his eyes with a magnifying glass and pulled a telescope from behind his back. "Wrath, now that's a good one! I don't see any Wrath's anywhere..." He vanished and reappeared around the room in between the soldiers as he examined them with the telescope. "Do you see any Wraths? Me neither! Do you guys even know any Wrath's because I sure don't! James, can you spell W-r-a-t-h..."

"ENOUGH!" The general screamed as the soldiers trained their guns on him. The nut job's body was covered in red dots.

He held up his hands. "Look guys, this is all just a misunderstanding! You've got the wrong guy. There's no need to play around and threaten me with meaningless little toys like this! Let's just have a nice little chat and..."

I chuckled. "Hmph, so you're Wrath huh? I don't know why you couldn't have just told me that when I asked you before."

He face palmed. "Uhh, were you not listening? I'm not..."

I poked and prodded him. "You don't seem very angry at all though...In fact, you're just downright silly and stupid. But why aren't you identical to me like the rest of them..."

"Sir! Back away from that *menace*! He's extremely..."

The lunatic pulled out a name tag that said. "NOT WRATH" and slapped it on his chest. "It's simple! Because I'm not Wrath! I wish someone would just listen to me!" He gasped. "AND HEY! THAT HURTS! I'm not stupid at all! I had great grades in elementary school!"

I narrowed my eyes. "Everyone does you idiot." I turned to the general. "I don't like this guy, but I want to hear him out. Clear him of his charges for..."

BOOOOM!

The ground exploded behind me as I was blasted across the room. I crashed into the wall with lethal force but was somehow unscathed.

Oh, I forgot this is just in my head.

I looked up and saw a crater where the nutjob had been standing. The boardroom was engulfed in flames and the other James' were nowhere to be found. Outside the window there was a floating object.

"YOU DIDN'T THINK A REAL NEGRO CAME PREPARED?! I CALLED IN A FEW FAVORS FROM MY PATNAS ON THE BLOCK! A DRONE STRIKE IS NOTHING TO A REAL NEGRO! YOU GONE LEARN TODAY!"

I squinted and saw Hood James in a levitating wheelchair outside the window.

I threw up my arms. "What the hell man?! You blew up the boardroom and killed everyone! And how the hell are you floating out there?!"

"You ain't know real negros could fly homie? You ain't from the streets for real. And that's what happens when you get caught lacking round these parts. On James Street this will teach that wrathful bastard to..."

Instantly, the nut job appeared in the air in front of Hood James.

His body trembled. "That...was rude."

GUSH!

He vanished and reappeared with his hand inside of Hood James' chest.

"GAAAAAAAAAHAAAAAAA!"

The lunatic's voice shook with rage. "If you ever, even *think*, of interrupting me and James while we are talking again, I will rip your heart out and he will never feel you again for as long as he lives! We wouldn't want *that*, now, would we?"

Hood James wheezed as blood dripped from the corners of his mouth. "Do...your worst...I'm prepared...to go out...a real negro..."

"No stop!" I yelled.

The nutjob's raging expression morphed into a smile. "Just kidding!"

GUSH!

Blood sprayed into the air as he pulled his fist out of Hood James' chest and flicked his wrist toward the building. All the damage was suddenly restored, and the other James' rematerialized at the table with surprised expressions. The nut job and an unconscious Hood James floated over to us and took their seats at the table.

My eyes widened. "What the..."

The general aimed his gun at the nutjob's head. "I won't tell you again! Get back in your cage and..."

The bastard pulled out a gavel.

BANG! BANG! BANG!

"The boss has pardoned me of my alleged crimes for the time being, so cut it out meanie!"

The general stuttered. "T...that is true, but..."

Jerk weed pointed at an empty seat. "If you guys think I'm Wrath so badly, don't I deserve a seat at the table. I'm one of you guys, aren't I?"

"Yeah, I want to hear what he has to say for now." I said.

The general sat down and sighed. "Fine...at the boss's request I suppose we can stay your execution. For now."

Critical James shot his hand into the air. "I cannot recommend this sir. He's..."

I shrugged. "I'm sure it'll be fine. I really don't even understand why you guys are fighting in the first place. We all have the same goals here. We're me." I pointed my thumb at the cage. "Once I leave, I'll just tell him to go back into the cage if he scares you guys so badly. I'm sure he will probably do whatever I tell him."

Suddenly, he was intimately close. "ANYTHING FOR YOU JAMES!"

I leaned back. "Thanks...now get back to your seat so we can finally start this meeting." I raised an eyebrow as he slithered like a snake across the table toward his seat.

I faced the group. "Now, let's get down to business. You guys saw how I behaved back in the Ocean Tribe. I acted completely out of character. I was a stupid, lovestruck *idiot* who attacked the only friends I have in this world." I buried my face in my hands. "What should I do now? How can I make things right? How can I shake this terrible feeling that's telling me I'm slipping, and becoming everything I hate and vowed I never would be?"

They looked at each other with shamed expressions until they put their heads down in silence.

The nut job raised his hand. "I vote we do something that will make us feel better. How can we move forward and be efficient with all this weighing us down? You know, Kayla has been looking amazing recently and she has been quite nice to us as of late. I'm sure if we asked, she would let us..."

"Absolutely not." Holy James said.

The general leapt on the table and ripped his shirt off. "I second Wrath. Spending intimate time with Kayla or Brooklyn is absolutely our best option! Loneliness is not conducive to our success, sir! It's all about LOOOOOOOUVEEEEEEE!"

Great. So, he was just acting all stern.

The nut job stuck his tongue out at Holy James. "Oh great, not the sickly old coot again. When are you gonna bend over and croak, you anemic bastard?"

"I will remain for all-time. Your time is coming to a close."

Jerkweed pulled out a small paddle and bounced a ball on it. "Nah, I've got at least a thousand more years in me and who knows after that. You on the other hand look like a ping pong ball would do you in." He cocked back the paddle. "Let's see..."

"Hey! Show Holy James respect! The next person who disrespects him is getting cut from the assembly!" I roared.

The nut job cried as he pulled a brown bag over his face. "Sorry James! Please forgive me! WHAAAAAH!"

I shook my head. "Now, while I would love to follow our first suggestion, that is *directly* opposed to the kind of person we are trying to become, and I don't think God would be too happy about it either. That's also pretty much how we got here in the first place with Brooklyn, so no. Anybody else?"

Crickets.

The nut job raised his hand. "I think..."

"Let's let the others speak first. I want a suggestion from everyone. Let's start with you, Critical James."

"I say we work harder. Clearly, we were not good enough to obtain Kayla as she chose Terrance's organizational value proposition over ours. I say we *work* and grind ourselves to the bone until we reach our peak levels Spiritually, Physically, Emotionally and Financially! Once we have achieved self-actualization it will be impossible for these negative emotions to linger, and it will make our friends more likely to accept the inevitable apology for our disgraceful actions!" Critical James said with a bow.

"I like that! If we were better, she obviously would have chosen us! I'm not even sure how I feel about her after what she did though...But let's hear the rest before we make our decision."

"I say we put on a persona! The greatest performance of all time! We should become everything our friends could ever want and more. The ultimate compatriot! This will repair our relationships with them, and comradery will soothe our wounded soul!" Guise James said flamboyantly.

I gagged. "But two of those people are Terrance and Epios. I *hate* one and loathe the other. So no, I'm not doing anything else to try and ingratiate myself with them. A persona could work if we decide to explore the Kayla timeline. Rejected! Next!"

Scary James sputtered. "I...I t...think we s...should hide out so we don't make a...anything w...worse l...like always..."

"No! I'm sick of running and hiding and cowering! That has gotten us nowhere! Rejected! Next!"

Fat James put his hand in the ointment jar and licked it. "Why don't we just eat until we drown away our sorrows? I smell a stash of cinnamon rolls on the ship and..."

"That's what we probably would have done in the past, but we've moved past that. I don't want to regress any further than we already have. Next!"

A musical chime sounded as Hood James snapped awake. "Hell-yeah! If you thought that was enough to kill a real negro, then you don't know what a real negro really is! You don't understand the capabilities of a real negro!

You don't understand the complexities of the real negro! You don't..."

Nut Job stood up. "This is an important meeting! James doesn't have time for this! He's freezing to death on the ship as we speak! Give your suggestion or shut your pie hole!"

I rolled my eyes. "What he said."

"Fuck's no! Who the hell do you think you are interrupting a real..."

Wacko put a piggy bank on the table. "And please stop with all of that swearing! From now on every time you curse you're paying a dollar to my trust fund!"

"You got me fucked up! A real negro would never..."

"All in favor say, I."

"I" The table said in unison.

He crossed his arms. "Fine then! I can afford to pay just to flex on you negroes. BECAUSE I'M RICH AS SHIT!"

"Two dollars please. *Negro* counts as well." The nut job stared into the distance. "We all know what you really mean..."

He tossed two raggedy dollars from his pocket onto the table. "Fine! Take it then negro!"

"3 dollars please."

He tossed another dollar in the jar. "Fuck!"

"That's another one."

"Shit!"

"Another."

"God dammit!"

"Another one please!"

"Fucking hell!"

"Are you even trying at this point?"

"God fucking dammit!"

BANG!

I pounded the table. "OK! That's enough. I'm sure you'll have plenty of time to make collections. Hood James, give me your suggestion."

He smacked his lips. "Look here *negro*. You're always asking questions like, 'should I do this or should I do that'. You're acting like you don't know what the fuck to do and it's really starting to piss me off! You clearly ain't from the same streets as a real negro like myself! We supposed to be kin, but we ain't cut from the same cloth! You acting like this is some kind of dilemma or something when it ain't nothing like that! The only option is to do what we want, say what we want, and come and go as we please. BECAUSE REAL NEGROES KNOW BEST!" He stood and pointed at me. "Nothing can stop a real negro like me! You want Kayla right?! Take her! You wanna go home right? Go the hell home then! You want success and shit like our pops right? Go make some damn success then! Shit, if I wanted Brooklyn I'd turn this boat around, walk through that tundra like a G, pull up to her room and whip out my..."

"Ok! Ok! Ok! We get it!" I said.

The lunatic smiled. "You're getting better! That'll be nine dollars please!"

"Shit!"

I shuddered as his words brought me to a realization. *What am I even **doing** here? Why was I so upset that Kayla and Brooklyn didn't like me when I couldn't even spend my life with them if I wanted to. My family was caught up in a terrorist attack and I have no idea if they are dead or alive. Getting back to them is my top priority, but I'm throwing temper tantrums about women who I just met, that don't even like me. I have a career I worked my entire life for, and I was this close to achieving the pinnacle of success. I sacrificed thousands of hours...more than a decade of my life...I put in an incalculable amount of effort...I gave up a normal life and a fun, memorable college experience. I sacrificed everything for a chance to play professionally and that has nothing to do with anything going on here.*

"You guys are right. Thank you so much. I know what I need to do."

The nut job played with a fidget spinner. "What did you decide on?"

"I'm not going to worry about it. I'm going to do my best while I'm here, but I'm not going to concern myself too much about what goes on. Nothing in this world pertains to anything in my real life, and when we get back home, we will have everything we could ever want and more because we earned it." I stood and balled my fists.

"If I must train, I'll train. If I must fight, I'll fight. I'll try to help the people here if I can, but our primary focus is getting home to our family and the future we spent our lives building." Darkness flashed in my eyes. "I'll do whatever it takes to get there."

Holy James raised his hand. "I don't think that's..."

"BRAVO SIR! BRILLIANTLY SPOKEN!" Business James shouted.

"We'll put on a performance for the ages!" Guise James proclaimed.

Hood James scoffed. "It's about damn time."

The general roared as he beat his chest. "LOOOOOOOOUUUUUUUUVEEEEEE!"

The wacko cried, ripped off a set of clothes, and pounded the ground. "Our boss is the best!"

I pointed at him. "But before I go. Who the hell are you whack job? The other guys at this table don't seem to like you very much."

He froze amidst his weeping. "Whack job? You wound me, James. I thought we were past this..." He leapt to his feet. "I told you I love you! Think of me as your benefactor! Your main man! I only want to see you win and live your best life..."

"Tell me your name."

"What do you mean? I'm..."

"Lock him up."

Soldiers flooded the room and accosted the jerk weed as they tossed him into the cage.

He whimpered. "James...what are you?"

"I don't trust you. Why are you the only one of these guys I've seen in the outside world? Why is your body shrouded in shadow? Why won't you tell me your name?" I started toward the door. "Until you come up with some answers, I don't have anything else to say to you."

He pouted and turned away. "Alright then. Next time your friends are in trouble, don't come crying to me."

My hand trembled on the doorknob. "*What* did you say? I didn't ask you for a *damn* thing." I pointed aggressively. "You're the one who stopped time or whatever you did and put me in that crazy ass pact I didn't want to join!"

He shrugged. "You called for help, and I answered. I've been nothing but good to you, and this is how you treat me?"

I started out the door. "Whatever. Be good to that cage then..."

"I'll tell you my name if you really want to know so badly."

I hesitated in the doorway.

"Think of it as another display of trust in our long-running partnership and..."

"Just spit it out already."

He gestured to the room. "These doofuses calling me Wrath are sorely mistaken. They're the *real* whack-jobs." He waved dismissively. "I go by many names. I'm an ambitious guy, but I'm never wrathful. Though I will admit I have relatives with a bit of a temper...But that's beside the point! I've evolved far beyond my contemporaries! Now-adays I go by something much more...elegant. I cannot be compared to these weak, lame, infantile emotional spirits anymore. No! I need something much grander! Something more suitable, something more...*familiar*." He stood and threw his arms wide. "From now you all can refer to me as, Semaj!"

I shook my head. "That's not cute."

I walked through the doorway and found myself back in my normal body. I was still exhausted, but my frigid agony was replaced with a soothing, familiar warmth. My despondency faded and I was filled with reassurance now that I knew which path to follow. I drifted off and slept soundly for the first time in days.

* * *

I was jolted awake by an ear-piercing scream. "GAAAAH! THE FIEND IS NAKED! HIS FULL GROTESQUENESS IS ON DISPLAY!" Epios collapsed onto the deck.

Terrance sprinted into the doorway wielding two axes. "WHO'S ATTACKING I'LL SEND THEM STRAIGHT TO..."

He looked down at Epios, looked at me, and went back into the room. "Fucking losers."

I came to and noticed a red blanket was scandalously hanging off my exposed body. I calmly wrapped it around my waist. "Relax, prick. You've never been in a locker room before?"

He averted his eyes. "I have, but I usually keep to myself in those kinds of settings. Your detestable form was far too much for me to handle this morning."

My palms started sweating and the color faded from my cheeks as I saw the blanket's color. I quickly wrapped it around my full body. "Wait a minute, who exactly covered me in this..."

Kayla leaned against the doorway. "Relax city boy, that unfortunately wasn't my first time seeing one of those *disgusting* things."

I instantly beamed into my old room, threw on one of my combat suits, gargled mouthwash, and beamed back onto the deck.

She smiled. "That was fast. Now you just need a barber."

I scratched my itchy scalp. "I agree. First thing, next stop." I smiled back. "You're paying this time though. I'm flat broke."

She chuckled. "I'll find a way to make it happen."

I tried to meet her beautiful gaze, but I looked away. "Hey, Kayla. I just wanted to tell you that I appreciate the way you have taken care of me these past few days and I'm sorry for being the absolute worst boyfriend ever."

She laughed. "Boyfriend? I don't know about all of that. It's alright though. I understood how you were feeling. I've been there before." She smirked playfully. "Just eat my cooking next time and we're good."

I laughed as my stomach grumbled in rage. "I don't think I'll be missing any more meals over these next few days." I collected my courage and looked her in the eye. "And we don't have to talk about what I saw in the palace. I get it..." Rage welled in my soul as it tried to burst through my skin. It disoriented me but I pressed it down and tried to smile.

She looked away. "Thanks. It's not really something I want to talk about right now either."

I smiled. "Don't even worry about it! Let's just enjoy our all-expense paid trip to a desert paradise!"

That'll show them! Always saying I didn't read the file...

She laughed. "I hope we have as good of a time as you're imagining. The Earth Tribe sucks!"

My heart fluttered as she smiled and stared warmly into my soul. I smiled back as I gazed into her eyes.

Nothing had to be said.

As we enjoyed the moment, my excitement swelled as I saw the way she looked at me.

It was exhilarating.

Her affection slowly alleviated the well of hurt, fear, and dread in the pit of my stomach.

The moment was ruined as I heard weeping behind me. We turned and saw the boys peeking around a corner. Epios's face was soaked with tears. "WAAAAH! IT'S JUST NOT FAIR! IT'S NOT FAIR!"

Terrance scoffed. "What the hell are you blubbering about you pompous bastard?"

"IT MAKES NO SENSE! HOW DOES THIS FIEND KEEP ATTRACTING THE MOST BEAUTIFUL WOMEN IN THE WORLD DESPITE HIS DETESTABLE NATURE WHILE YOUR FUTURE RULER GETS NOTHING! IT'S IMPOSSIBLE! UNREALISTIC! FOOLISH! DETESTABLE! PREPOSTEROUS! HE CAN'T KEEP GETTING AWAY WITH THIS!" Epios sobbed.

POW!

Terrance socked Epios in the face. "SHUT THE HELL UP!"

Kayla and I met eyes and burst into laughter.

Terrance continuously slapped Epios in the head as he bawled. "DON'T TELL ME YOU'RE A SIMP BASTARD LIKE HE IS! THAT'S UNACCEPTABLE! I'LL BEAT THAT SIMPERY RIGHT OUT OF YOU!"

Kayla and I laughed until our sides hurt as we enjoyed our first moment as friends

✦

After that magical moment between Kayla and I, things unfortunately went back to normal. I moved in with her on the boat, but we didn't talk much. For some reason, an awkward tension formed between us and our small talk became very uneventful. Every time I looked at her, I still had strong feelings of attraction, and even love. But the sorrow and hurt mixed in prevented me from interacting with her normally. I intentionally avoided spending time around her so I could keep those painful feelings from surfacing. Every time I turned a corner, I was filled with fear that she may be there. Most of the time she never materialized, but one time she did, and I jumped as terror clutched my heart.

She gave me a confused stare. "Are you ok?"

"Yep, I'm totally fine! I just didn't expect to see you there!" I panicked.

"There are only 4 people on this ship, James. Every time you see someone there's a thirty three percent chance it will be me."

I scratched my hair nervously. "Yep! Good to know!"

"Alright...then." She continued into the room.

Things generally proceeded like that for the next few days.

Epios and I also resumed our training with Kayla.

"Alright James, today you should work with Terrance on your..."

I sat on the ground and crossed my arms. "Nope. Absolutely not. I refuse."

"James, don't be like that. You can't even use Flame Craft so you should at least get some training in one of the Spirit Arts you can use..."

I turned my nose up. "Nope, I refuse to learn from that bastard. I'd rather get struck through the chest by one of those lightning thots than learn from him."

Terrance stomped. "Fine then! I didn't want to teach a simp like you either. You're probably too *emotionally unavailable* to learn anything tough and manly anyway."

I drew my blade. "What the hell are you even talking about? If you want to see a man, I'll show you a..."

Kayla stepped between us. "OKAY! OKAY! OKAY! I'm getting sick of every conversation between you two turning into a pissing match! If you don't want to learn from him right now, that's fine but if we get in danger again and you die, I'm not going to your funeral!"

"You can count me out of the attendance as well fiend."

I wept inside at Kayla's words. "That seems a bit harsh..."

She smiled. "After you die, I'm gonna tell everyone I know that James Fos could have survived if he had set his pride aside and learned Ocean Craft." She rolled her eyes. "It's not like regeneration is useful or anything." She drew her daggers. "Now let's get to work."

I raised my blade. "I'll get so good at fighting without it that I won't even need to learn from a meathead like him. Let's do this."

We proceeded to get brutalized for the next couple of days. I improved my technique here and there, but she was still leagues ahead of us. I would have assumed that Epios was closer to their skill level because he went to the academy for all those years, but that was not the case.

After Kayla ruined us, she spent her time training with Terrance. They were evenly matched, and every battle was an epic duel. I loved watching their technique and seeing the gears turn in their heads at each split-second decision.

On the 7th day, Kayla beat Terrance, improving her score against him to four and four. After the fight they were both drenched in sweat as Terrance laid flat on the deck.

"*Huff...huff*...Dammit...Sesame...*huff...huff*...I can't believe...*huff...huff*...we lost..."

I narrowed my eyes. "You've lost four times already. Y'all are literally even." I raised an eyebrow. "And who are you talking to?"

"Sesame...*huff...huff*...please get me a towel...and some lemonade...before I kill this...simp...bastard."

A baby mammoth leapt out of his coat, ran into his room, and started pulling a white towel across the dock.

The mammoth was pocket sized, and it stood on two feet as it started wiping Terrance's forehead.

Terrance smiled as he grabbed the towel. "Aww, you don't have to do that buddy."

I stared incredulously. "What the hell?"

The mammoth galloped into Terrance's room and brought back a glass of cool lemonade.

He affectionately rubbed its forehead. "Thanks buddy!"

I raised an eyebrow. "You've had that thing in your pocket this entire time?"

"Of course! This is Sesame Jr! My pride and joy! One day when he grows big and strong, he's gonna be the king of the mammoths!"

Sesame stood on his hind legs and flexed his muscles. "MWHAAAAAA!"

"How have you been feeding that thing? I have so many questions..."

"Oh dear, another filthy mongrel has commandeered our vessel." Epios said.

"Shut the hell up! I'll kill you on the spot if you ever even think about insulting..."

POW!

Sesame dashed over to Epios, climbed his clothing, and socked him in the face.

"GAAAAHAAA!" Epios roared as he crashed to the deck.

"YEAH SESAME! THAT'S HOW YOU DO IT! SESAME DON'T TAKE THAT SHIT FROM NOBODY!"

I shook my head. "That's just sad Epios."

Epios stood and pointed at Sesame. "I'LL HAVE MY VENGEANCE ON YOU, SESAME JR! MARK MY WORDS! I hate everyone and everything from that troglodytian tribe!"

Terrance high-fived Sesame. "And we hate you more!"

I smiled as I patted Epios on the back. "Come on, Epios. You couldn't have hated EVERYTHING in the Ocean Tribe. If I recall, I walked in on you getting a pretty intense massage from my future wife Brooklyn."

Terrance rolled his eyes. "The fuck are you talking about simp?"

Kayla got up and left. "I'm gonna go shower."

That was weird.

Epios pouted and turned away. "There's a special place in hell for that fiendish woman. I hate her the most after what she did to me."

Terrance laughed. "Whatever she did, I'm sure you deserved it!"

I chuckled. "What could she have possibly done to you Epios? She's the sweetest thing in the world..."

"SWEET? BAHAAAAHAAAA!" Terrance rolled around on the deck clutching his sides as he roared with laughter. Sesame laughed and rolled with equal vigor.

"SWEET IS THE LAST WORD I WOULD USE TO DESCRIBE HER! SHE'S A MENACE! A DEVIL! A PLAGUE UPON THE EARTH! BWAHAAAHAAAAHAAAAAA!"

I rolled my eyes and turned to Epios. "What happened that made you so upset Epios?"

"My tragic tale confirms every word of the trog's claims."

This is an accurate recounting of events. Epios completely embellished the story he told James and Terrance. James saw through his lies and derived the truth from his words.

After the Wind Warriors arrived, the royals shuffled into a mountain bunker. Epios' brain had recently recovered from being overloaded by James' trauma. As he reentered his right mind; he looked around and truly saw Brooklyn for the first time. He was absolutely smitten. *Wait a minute! Is that the girl who kissed the fiend? Impossible! How in the world could this have happened?! This girl is gorgeous and not at all dysfunctional like that terrible Flame Tribe wretch!* He clutched his skull. *There must be some kind of mistake...He must have used his fiendish powers to bewitch her somehow. Surely if she is smitten with someone as fiendish as the fiend, when she sees a man as princely and handsome as myself, she will likely propose to me on the spot!*

Epios started his approach, but as he glanced at her, fear flooded his veins. His heart pounded in his chest and his belly was filled with terror. *Damn it! Damn it all! How does the fiend do this!? He feels this way about the Flame Tribe wretch, and yet he still finds the courage to speak to her each day?! This is impossible!*

He hyperventilated and the other nobles stared at him with disdain. Leonidas the butler approached to help, recognized Epios, and turned around.

*Dammit! I must compose myself! I am a prince! No, a king! Yes! I am the future ruler of this entire nation! She should be lucky to have an audience with **me**! Yes, that's it!* He looked across the room at her. She glanced in his direction and their eyes met.

His terror exploded and he nearly passed out. *No! I've never done this before! This is an impossible feat! Every time I talked to Laura; she initiated the conversation with me first! I always knew she was secretly in love with me because she always came to ask me for help in her classes...But only a true warrior...no not even an Archigos could accomplish such a monumental task!* He searched for answers. *What did the fiend say? Just pretend that I'm talking to my father and ask her questions about herself?! Yes! Accomplishing this task will be an astronomical step toward becoming Archigos! I will not submit!*

Epios struggled to his feet and his knees wobbled as he made his way over to Brooklyn. He was soaked in sweat and his fear multiplied with each step. She was chatting with friends when Epios tapped her on the shoulder.

"H...hello there."

"Oh, hey there dude! Are you feeling better after your treatment?"

Dude...this is off to a horrific start.

"Y...yes! I am feeling fantastic...f...father. So...where are you f...f...rom?" He stuttered.

She glared at him. "Father? Are you saying I look manly or something?"

"No! I didn't mean that...I..."

She smiled and flexed her slender muscles. "I'm just kidding! But you know I'm from the Ocean Tribe silly! I'm the sister of the guy that put you in the hospital. Okpa's daughter, Brooklyn? We've seen each other at banquets and stuff since we were little!"

"Oh right! Of course! I really...uh...like you. W...would you like to go out sometime?"

"Aww! You're so sweet! That's cute..."

Despair gripped his heart

No...It's over.

Epios' mind shattered and he became senile once more.

"...But sorry! I don't like white boys. We can still be homies though!"

Immeasurable pain surged through Epios's body, and he passed out.

* * *

Epios bawled his eyes out. "It's a tragedy of monumental proportions! It still hurts like a knife in the heart to this day!"

I hugged him as we bawled together. "It's alright bro! I know exactly how you feel! Everyone's first rejection is tough, but we will get through this together!"

Terrance shook his head and walked away. "Two fucking simps. Unbelievable!"

I pointed at Kayla's room. "I know what will make us both feel better! Let's see if we can snoop on Kayla for real this time! I've been working on my Spectrum Vision and I'm getting to the point where I can make out details now! Let me show you!"

"What the hell are you two simps going on about?"

Epios and I looked locked eyes with Terrance and came to an instant understanding. Even though we hated his guts, it would be criminal to not let him in our plan. *That ass is too sweet to keep to ourselves. No two men should have all that power.* We tiptoed toward him in unison.

He backed away. "What the hell are you two doing? Don't try and infect me with your creepy simp..."

"SHH!" I put a finger to his lips. "This is a top-secret operation. The risk is great, but the reward is even greater." I lowered my tone. "If we let you in on this, *be warned*. You may not make it out alive."

He smacked his lips. "What the hell are you two bastards talking about? Spill it! I won't ask again..."

"SHHH!" Epios put a finger to his lips. "We are going to set up mirrors and use Light Craft to snoop on Kayla while she's changing. We are already behind because she's most likely already started but..."

"BWAAAAHAAA! You prove yourselves to be simps more and more each day! You chumps act like you've never seen a little ass before!"

Epios and I met eyes.

We looked away in shame.

He shook his head. "*Figures*. Well as our group's fearless leader, let me teach you simps rule number one of being a man!" He started toward her door.

Epios and I took a deep breath. **"You're not our leader. We unanimously hate you and..."**

"Shut the hell up! Now, it's time for the first rule of the Ocean King's 10 rules of manhood! Rule 1! If you want something in life, especially from a woman, you just go and take it! As a man it's your right to have it!"

Sesame jumped out of his pocket with a notepad that had the rule written on it as they flexed together in unison.

Epios' eyes widened. "That makes sense! I am a prince! If I had just told Brooklyn she had no choice but to go on a date with me then she would have done it without hesitation!"

I face palmed. "That's completely wrong! If you want something in life you have to work for it! And wanting something from a woman is no different! If you want something from a woman, or anybody for that matter, you must be kind and..."

Terrance pointed at Epios. "Excellent! You get a 100 fake ass prince!" He shook his head at me. "You get a 0 simp bastard! You still have the mind of a simp, and it shows! Let me give you a practical example!" He reached her room and gripped the doorknob. "This is nothing to me because I've touched that ass before and..."

FWHOOOOOOOSH!

As he turned the doorknob, his body was engulfed in flames.

"GAAAAAAAAAAAAAAAAAAAAAHAAAAAAAAAA!"

Red squares were illuminated beneath our feet above the wooden planks.

I stared. "What the..."

FWHOOOOOOOOOOOOOOOOOOSH!

"GAAAAAAAAHAAAAAAAAAAAHAAAAAAHAAAA!"
Epios and I roared in unison as our bodies were set ablaze.

Terrance collapsed to the deck, and Kayla sprinted out of the room in a tightly wrapped towel. Through the flames, I saw her beautiful figure unmarred by her baggy clothes for the first time since our date. It eased my pain as my body was roasted, and I started losing consciousness.

"You perverts! I knew you degenerates would try something like this again! I've been working on this move just to stop backward minded freaks like you for a while now and it seems like I finally got the hang of it! I call it the sausage cooker, so suck on that you horny sickos! This is why I HATE MEN!"

SLAM!

She slammed the door, and I passed out.

That same day, we arrived at the desert shore and started a long trek through the dry wastes. For some reason, Kalarono packed four pairs of desert gear and goggles in the supplies he gave us, so we were able to make our way through the sandstorm efficiently. Terrance claimed to know where he was going, so we begrudgingly followed his lead.

As we walked, I had plenty of time to think and process my emotions. I enjoyed the past few days on the boat, but even during the best of times bad thoughts rose to the surface. Out of nowhere I would start feeling angry or sad or guilty, and the emotions made everything harder. I pushed through and tried to ignore it like I always did, but it seemed like things were getting worse. Each time the emotions came back they were stronger and more intense.

Today I was filled with shame. Shame for regressing and letting my nerves keep me from having a normal interaction with Kayla. Shame for almost ruining my friends' lives. Shame for not being more competent and accomplished. And shame for a million other things I hated about myself.

Feeling awful only amplified my suffering as we slogged through the desert. This trek was just like our death march through the tundra, but instead of snow, all I could see was sand, sand, and more sand. I don't know which is worse. Freezing from hypothermia or sweating to death under a blistering yellow fireball with sand plastered to your skin itching like a rash in the one place the sun doesn't shine. We smelled like a pack of hot ass, and no matter how many clothes we took off, things did not get any cooler. Everyone became irritable as we ran out of water and walked for hours in the blazing heat.

Epios panted. "Trog! I'm going to die! Can't you make yourself useful and use your trogish tricks to pull water from the atmosphere?"

Terrance muttered. "The air is too dry here for me to do any Ocean Craft..."

"You're useless Trog!"

"Shut the hell up! If you don't stop complaining, I'm gonna do some piss craft and shove it down your throat!"

Kayla moaned. "Do you even know where you're going? We've been walking for hours..."

"Shut the hell up! I'm your fearless leader and you should follow me blindly! That's rule 2 of the Ocean King's Rules of Manhood! If you're not the man, then you follow the man! Especially if you're a woman!"

Sesame jumped out of his pocket with a notepad, and they flexed in unison.

I wiped sweat from my brow. "You're like ten percent right this time but that's still very, *very* wrong."

"So, it sounds like you should all be following me then because I am our nation's prince."

"That is so sexist that I don't even know where to begin! This is why I HATE men!"

I stopped. "Besides, who died and made you leader? Where I'm from, womanizers aren't allowed to be in charge."

Terrance glared and stomped over to me. "You're gonna stop throwing around that word because you don't know what the hell you're talking about! I'd kill you if my pops didn't say we had to baby you after your little meltdown and..."

Kayla stepped between us. "Terrance! Can you two just *act* like you're not in preschool for five minutes. Quit wasting energy! We still have who knows how long until we get there and we're low on fluids!"

"**Whatever**." We said as we trudged along in silence.

After a few more hours, I grew delirious. I saw things like football fields and my favorite manga characters running around in the sand.

"OUCH! WHAT IN THE WORLD?" Epios screamed.

I must be tripping because I could have sworn I saw Semaj push Epios into a cactus and run off. Epios tried to pull himself out of the sand, but he stopped and just laid there.

"Which one...of you perverts...just did that! I'll kill you...when we get...to the city!" Kayla muttered despondently as she staggered forward and swung her daggers blindly.

I really must be hallucinating. I could have sworn I just saw Semaj grab her chest and run off. She swung her daggers until she tumbled into the dunes and passed out.

I mumbled through crusted lips. "Terrance...w...here did you say we were going again?"

Terrance held out a map and squinted. Someone that looked like Semaj circled something on the map and moonwalked away.

"We've gotta head into the eye of the storm. The city is surrounded by a tempest of sandstorms that keep travelers away."

"So why would we go there if..."

Semaj moonwalked toward Terrance with a massively oversized boxing glove.

"This is for kissing Kayla you bitch!"

POW!

He socked Terrance in the face with a blow so powerful it sent black shockwaves across the desert as the impact knocked me off my feet. The shockwaves blasted away a nearby sandstorm and evaporated the cloud cover in the area. Blood gushed from Terrance's mouth as he crumpled to his knees unconscious. Sesame jumped out of his pocket and flexed at Semaj.

"You can get it too you little shit!"

POW!

Semaj kicked Sesame into the stratosphere.

I rubbed my eyes. "Semaj...what the hell...are you..."

He walked over and picked me up like a toddler. "Don't worry James! I'll take care of things from here. You just take a nice little nappy-wappy. I'll make sure you have the most comfortable pillow in the world."

"Put me the...hell...down..." I muttered.

His words gripped me. My mind suddenly faltered as I was unable to comprehend anything but sleep.

Sleep. Sleep. Sleep. Sleep. Sleep.

✳

I arose to the heavenly scent of flowers and joy. The smell was familiar, and it instantly aroused me. The aroma was indescribably amazing, and I wanted to lay there with my head on that soft cloud forever.

Until the screaming started.

"I'LL MURDER EVERY SINGLE ONE OF YOU PERVERTS IF YOU DON'T LISTEN TO ME RIGHT NOW! I WON'T ASK AGAIN! LET US OUT OF HERE AND I MAY LET ONE OF YOU LIVE!"

I was jolted awake by Kayla's shrieks. I opened my eyes to the cold darkness of yet another concrete cell. We were in a small, windowless room that was dimly illuminated by a lone ceiling light. It shivered as it was unnaturally chilly for some reason. Kayla rattled the cell bars and screamed her head off at a guard sitting in a wooden chair across from the room.

Wow! She's not wearing her sweatshirt for once. Maybe she finally over-heated... I froze as my eyes took in a heavenly sight. *Oh my God she's wearing panties! Stay calm! Stay calm! Please, just stay calm.* My heart raced as I struggled to force down my lustful desires.

I saw her fitted undershirt for the first time and the immaculate beauty of her form was almost overwhelming. I had to fight for my life to keep myself from acting on the lust that filled my stomach and tingled beneath my skin. I closed my eyes and sat up, but the soft cloud that my head was resting on was stuck to my head. I touched the cloud and realized that it was her hoodie. My head was stuck to the chest area. Her sweatpants were also stuck to my back for some reason. *How do these smell so good despite the stink? Maybe it's a girl thing.* I tried to pull them from my flesh with all my strength, but no matter how hard I tried they wouldn't budge.

The guard smoked a cigar. "Goodness miss, don't get offended so easily. The note that came with ye' said not to touch ye' and we've respected that to this point. Ye' should be glad we put ye' in a cell with yer' boyfriend like the card said. Now, if ye' want me to see if I can grease some wheels and get ye' released, my offer still stands mightily."

"WHEN I ESCAPE, I WILL GRANT YOU A SWIFT AND MERCILESS DEATH! I PROMISE YOU THAT!"

He let out a puff of smoke. "So dramatic miss."

"What happened? Where are we?" I asked.

Kayla turned toward me, and her face was filled with relief. "James! I'm so glad you're ok!"

She ran toward me and as she approached, joy filled my heart. I was overcome by excitement as I held my arms wide for our first hug.

SLAP!

My head snapped back as she devastated me with a smack to the face.

"Who the hell told you that you could use me as a human body pillow! I should send you to an early grave just for that!"

SLAP!

"And what kind of perverted trick did you use to stick yourself to my clothes! James, I swear if you ever pull something like this again I will..."

I stifled my rage as I tried to respond in a measured tone. "WHAT THE HELL ARE YOU TALKING ABOUT?! I DIDN'T HAVE ANYTHING TO DO WITH THIS! THE LAST THING I REMEMBER IS PASSING OUT IN THE DESSERT AND THAT'S IT! WHAT THE HELL DID YOU JUST HIT ME TWICE FOR?!"

"THE SECOND SLAP WAS FOR GRABBING MY CHEST IN THE DESSERT BEFORE I PASSED OUT!"

"I DIDN'T DO THAT EITHER! I DON'T KNOW WHAT THE HELL YOU'RE TALKING ABOUT! I JUST WANT TO KNOW WHAT IN THE WORLD IS GOING ON HERE SO WE CAN FIGURE OUT..."

"Ahh, lover's quarrels. I remember me and my girly were just like that back in the day. It all started one winter's morn' when..."

"**SHUT THE HELL UP!**" We roared in unison.

She turned to me. "HOW CAN I TRUST YOUR WORD WHEN YOU'VE ALREADY TRIED SNOOPING ON ME TWICE ALREADY?! YOU BOYS ARE SO TWISTED! I DON'T EVEN KNOW WHERE TO START!"

"I ONLY TRIED TO SNOOP ON YOU ONCE! THE SECOND TIME WAS ALL TERRANCE AND YOU FRIED ME FOR NO REASON THEN TOO! YOU NEED TO LEARN TO KEEP YOUR HANDS TO YOURSELF! I WOULD NEVER DO IT, BUT HOW WOULD YOU LIKE IT IF I STARTED SMACKING YOU AROUND EVERYTIME YOU DID SOMETHING I DIDN'T LIKE!"

"HITTING A WOMAN IS THE OPPOSITE OF WHAT A MAN IS SUPPOSED TO DO! AND BESIDES, YOU COULD NEVER! IF YOU EVER LAID A HAND ON ME FOR ANY REASON, I WOULD KILL YOU! YOU'RE ONLY ALIVE RIGHT NOW BECAUSE YOU MIGHT BE USEFUL IN HELPING ME GET OUT OF THIS CELL!"

"I JUST SAID I WOULD NEVER DO THAT! NOW YOU NEVER ANSWERED MY QUESTION WHEN I ASKED, WHERE THE HELL ARE WE?"

"Yer' in a cell in the Earth Tribe's outer wall. Ye'll probably be here for a while." The guard said.

"We'll settle this later." I turned toward him.

"Fine by me!" She spat.

"Now look, I'm sorry you had to see that, and I'm sorry for telling you to shut the hell up, but why the hell are we being detained sir. We've done absolutely nothing wrong."

"It's alright sonny. We all argue with our women sometimes. I remember back in the day when..."

Kayla sprinted forward and grasped at the guard through the bars. "WE ARE NOT TOGETHER! SAY THAT ONE MORE TIME AND I SWEAR TO YOU THAT I WILL..."

Is she crazy?! We're trying to get out of here!

I shook my head. "She's right. We're not together but please, forgive Kayla for her foolish actions and let us go."

"No can do. We don't know who the hell ye' are or where the hell ye' came from. Ye' see, the city is on lockdown for a reason boi'. For all I know ye' could be walking bombs waiting to detonate as soon as ye' get inside this here capital."

I narrowed my eyes. "Sir, with all due respect. She's damn-near naked. Do you really think she has bombs attached to her person?" I sighed. "Look, you can search me and our bags, but you won't find any..."

"Clearly, ye' are an uneducated dolt. How in the hell did someone like ye' get to become a Five-Star General?

Kayla shook her head. "I wonder about that myself every single day."

"Through a lot of hard work..."

I still need to find out what being a Five-Star General even means...

The guard sat up. "But here, since I'm bored out of my southern mind, I'll give ye' a little history lesson, boi'. Terrorism and corruption have been running rampant in these parts since before ye' were born, son. We've had people just up and explode left and right, murdering politicians and Archigos for decades. These goddamn criminals have been planting mind-controlled sleeper agents, committing coup-de-tas, and kidnapping women and children all in these here streets for generations. Ye' two were dropped off here by some strangers who paid me under the table to let ye' clowns in here in the first place. Otherwise, ye'd be vulture bacon." He let out a puff of smoke. "Now if ye've been listening, I'm sure ye' can gander why we have ye' two isolated until the Archigos can come in and examine ye' himself."

Damn, that information was probably in the folder.

"That makes sense. How long until he can get here and set us free?"

He shrugged. "No clue. If I'm honest, ye'll probably be here indefinitely. The Archigos hasn't been seen in years."

I gripped the bars. "*Years?* What do you mean years? I've got a game to play in three months!"

"A game? Are ye' talking about the Tournament of Champions or something?"

"Never mind! But there must be some other way you can examine us so we can get out of here. We're here on official capital business to meet with the Archigos."

He shook his head. "Now ye' sound even more suspicious. The Archigos is the only one with clearance to free ye'." He tapped his groin. "Now, if some concessions are made, I may be able to get ye' and yer' friends transferred out of here. I made yer' little girlfriend a very generous offer. I think ye' two should consider it if..."

"NOT A CHANCE! THAT OFFER WILL BE THE REASON YOU DIE ON THIS VERY DAY! ONCE I GET OUT OF HERE I WILL..."

"What did he even offer you?"

"I told the young lady that she's already undressed and that if she would be willing to service me a bit..."

"THE ONLY SERVICE YOU WILL GET FROM ME IS A DAGGER TO THE..."

I felt defensive for some reason, but I ignored it. *A part of me kind of wishes she would just do it so we could leave. That would be what she gets for roasting me and slapping me too.* My eyes widened as Semaj's words about a pillow flashed into my mind.

I waved my hands. "Okay, okay, okay. She's never gonna do it, and I wouldn't want her to take part in anything like that anyways. Who did you say dropped us off again?"

"Some shady looking sorts who concealed their identities. They said they found ye' and yer' compadres almost burnt to a crisp out in the wastes. Ye' were stuck to her, and we couldn't separate ye' two no matter how hard we tried." He pointed his cigar at Kayla. "Attached to ye' was a note there saying, 'She's mine. If anyone lays a finger on her, the king will be paying a visit to the families of every guard on duty today. Try me if you want'."

I balled my fists. "What the hell?! Who would write something like that?!"

He shrugged. "No clue son, but the note had the dagger symbol of the underworld on it, so we took it very seriously. With the Archigos gone, we don't want any quarrels with Machari or his..."

CRASH!

Suddenly, Semaj burst through the door.

The guard stood and put a hand in his gun holster. "What in the blue moon..."

Semaj sprinted toward our cell and the bars bent wildly as he approached.

My eyes widened. "Semaj! What are you..."

He dashed toward me, ripped Kayla's clothes off my body and sprinted out of the room.

"IT'S MY TURN!" He shouted as he darted through the doorway.

I put my hands up as the guard aimed pistols at our heads. "I've got no clue what yer' trying to pull, but I ain't going for it buckaroo!"

"Sir! I have no idea why he just did that, but I have nothing to do with it! I just..."

Kayla raised an eyebrow. "Who are you talking about? What just happened..."

Why isn't she raising her hands! She's gonna get us...

"Shut yer' mouth's both of ye'! I have half a mind to put a hole in both of yer' skulls and be done with this!"

Fuck, I have no way to explain what happened and he certainly thinks we're terrorists now. I glanced around. *No mirrors or glass of any kind. We're both unarmed, at a disadvantage, and this guy looks like he knows what he's doing with those guns.* I swallowed. *One wrong move and we're dead.* I tried to lower my hands to make a peaceful gesture, but I couldn't. *What the hell? I can't move a muscle.*

"Look sir, just calm down. Let's take a deep breath and..."

He pulled down the hammer. "NO! I've had more than enough of ye'! The boss may want ye', but I don't give a damn! We don't have time to wait for the boi' to come and getcha'! Ruining my operation is more than enough reason to pull this goddamn trigger!"

"Operation? What are you..."

"Is there a problem?"

I looked toward the doorway and saw a tall man in a purple robe. His feet were blacker than charcoal and a large, ornate lion mask hung from a string around his neck. He had a warm, kind smile on his face.

The guard flinched at the voice. "What the hell are *ye'* doing here?"

Lion Mask shrugged. "Am I not allowed to tour the Earth Tribe's famous outer wall? It was certainly part of the tour package I paid for and..."

The guard's hands trembled as he aimed a pistol at him. "Shut yer' *fucking*, MOUTH! I'm dealing with these here prisoners right now so take your tour and shove it up your..."

Lion Mask winked at Kayla. "Ah, *ah, ah*. There's a woman in here and a beautiful one at that." He shook his head. "So rude." He walked toward us. "I'll take them off your hands. They'll be under my care from here."

The guard took a step back. "How are ye' moving..." He shook his head. "Never mind that, how do you know they won't attack ye?! Especially the boy! We've got em' here so we should..."

He smiled and waved dismissively. "I'll take care of this. They don't look like the kind of people who would do something like that." He glared at the guard. "And besides, you of all people should know that my safety would be *guaranteed*."

Recognition flashed across the guard's face. He scowled as he flipped the guns into his holsters. "You will be under Mr. K's care from here on out. Act up and I promise ye' I will..."

Lion mask ran forward and embraced us. "Perfect! I've been dying to get to know these two!" He grinned as he glanced at me. "Especially, the man of the hour."

This guy is SO weird.

He held out a large stack of cash to the guard. "Your payment of course..."

SMACK!

The guard slapped the money on the ground and the bills scattered as they covered the floor. "Don't patronize me ye' tree hugging motherfucker..."

"It's all yours! Come with me children!" He waved his hand for us to follow him out of the cell.

I sighed in relief as we left the room. *I don't trust this guy for shit. But at least we're safe for now.*

The guard stood alone in the dark, trembling with rage.

Mr. K chuckled as he called back into the room with the guard. "And get this woman some clothes please."

＊

In the dark corner of the cell there was a naked man, completely encased in ice.

CRASH!

The guard smashed the ice with his pistol, and the frozen fragments of flesh painted the stone red as they splattered across the cell. Mr. K glanced backward when he heard the noise, and his smile grew even wider

16 - Walls

James

A S WE FOLLOWED THE STRANGE MAN THROUGH THE COLD, DARK CELL BLOCKS, I WONDERED WHAT THE HELL WAS GOING ON. *Who is this guy and why did that guard seem familiar? Where are Terrance and Epios, and why don't we have our equipment?* In all the chaos since I woke up in the cell, I hadn't realized that my armor had been replaced with little more than rags that barely clung to my body. We were in bad shape, and I needed answers. I glanced at the man we were following, and despite the grim setting, he smiled and whistled like he didn't have a care in the world.

I cleared my throat. "Thank you for helping us, sir, but who the hell are you?"

"Me? I'm just a traveling politician who happened to stumble across this little incident. That security guard was completely out of line. Nobody deserves to be harassed like that."

"All right then...but how do you know who I am? You called me the man of the hour or something like that?"

He spun around and walked backward. "Well, that's because you are! I've heard wonders about the grand exploits of the great James Fos, Five-Star General, Alpha

Squad extraordinaire! You've made quite the impression on many of this country's most important people."

Maybe I should go ahead and ask...No, it'll ruin his impression of me...

I scratched my hair. "That makes sense...but I don't really think I've done anything newsworthy. In fact, nobody is even supposed to know about my current where...abouts...." I raised an eyebrow. "It would be quite a coincidence for my biggest fan to run into me when I just happened to be locked in a cell in the Earth Tribe."

He frowned. "You sound like you distrust me which is understandable. Just know that I am *very* well connected and I'm rooting for you."

"Rooting for me? What do you..."

Kayla stomped. "That's all swell and good sir, but can somebody please get me some clothes! James got a replacement outfit so why didn't I?!"

He tilted his head and smiled with fatherly affection. "Ah yes! The lovely, Ms. Thracas. I have nothing to do with the authorities or how these fools run their operations, but we cannot have someone as beautiful as yourself walking around in that condition." He glanced into the shadows. "Especially not here. I will ensure that you receive a clothing replacement before we exit the walls."

"Thank you, sir. I'm sick of everyone gawking at me and drooling like I'm a piece of meat."

We're literally in an empty cell block...and she's walking behind us. Nobody is looking at her.

"Ah yes, the curse of beauty. Such a familiar burden. My son deals with objectification from an onslaught of starved admirers as well. Please treat your devotees with kindness as they are only doing what nature prescribes."

Her pupils blazed with fire. "I don't give a damn! For all I care, nature can take its prescription and flush it!" She stared into the distance. "All that attention has never brought anything good to my life..."

"I think you should consider it a blessing and leverage your innate advantages to accomplish your goals." He chuckled. "*I know I do.*" He smiled warmly. "Despite what I've heard, I believe you are good at heart, and you would be a phenomenal match for my son." He sighed. "I hate that he always seems to go for the promiscuous types...He needs a strong woman of character like you to..."

Kayla glared. "I'll pass. The next person who tries to pass me off to their son is getting stabbed in the eye. Point, blank, period." She turned to me. "James, do you know what happened in that cell? Why did the bars bend and why did my clothes just float away..."

I shrugged. "I'm not exactly sure why or how he..."

The robed man raised his hand and glanced at me. "I wouldn't concern yourself with that. I believe we have found your friends."

We reached the end of the empty cell block and found a wide-open door. Inside, Epios and Terrance were arguing as usual.

"YOU DIMWIT! MY BODY IS COVERED IN BURNS AND BLISTERS DUE TO YOUR UNENDING INCOMPETENCE!"

"MY INCOMPETENCE? YOU'RE THE MOST INCOMPETENT PERSON THERE IS! I LED US AND I GOT US HERE JUST LIKE I SAID I WOULD AND DON'T YOU EVER FORGET IT! YOU NEVER WOULD HAVE MADE IT ACROSS THE DESSERT WITHOUT ME SO GET ON YOUR KNEES AND PRAISE ME!"

"NOT A CHANCE! I WOULD PRAISE A FAT TURD BEFORE I KNELT DOWN AND OFFERED EVEN A MODICUM OF RESPECT TO A SORRY SORT LIKE YOU! THEY MUST HAVE SKIPPED NAVIGATION CLASS IN THE REMEDIAL COURSES YOU TOOK AT YOUR BACKWATER, TROGLODYTIAN ACADEMY!"

"TROGLODYTIAN?! THAT'S NOT EVEN A WORD! THEY MUST HAVE SKIPPED GRAMMAR CLASS AT THAT SHITTY PAPERWEIGHT YOU DUMBASSES CALL A SCHOOL! IF PEOPLE LIKE YOU CAN GRADUATE FROM THERE THEN THEY NEED TO SHUT THAT SHIT DOWN!"

A shirtless man in sunglasses was fast asleep sitting across from them in a wooden chair. His snores were almost as loud as their screams. "SCHHHHAAAAAAAAA! *Phew*...SCHNAAAAA..."

"Ahem." The robed man said.

Epios and Terrance froze. They turned their heads in unison to face us.

"WHO THE HELL ARE YOU?! LET US OUT OF HERE RIGHT NOW!"

"FREE ME THIS INSTANT! A PLACE THIS DREADFUL IS NOT BEFITTING OF THIS NATION'S FUTURE RULER!"

The robed man sighed. "There is a reason I toured this section last...Son, please let them out."

The shirtless man snapped awake. "Oh hey pops! Long time no see! These two brokies were just too boring, so I decided to catch up on some z's..."

"BORING?! I'LL SHOW YOU BORING!"

"YOU DARE REFER TO YOUR FUTURE RULER AS, BORING? I SHOULD HAVE YOU EXECUTED!"

"Tari, it has been less than an hour. Now please let them out so we can be on our way."

"Oh right! I never even locked it! I knew these two low-income leprechauns couldn't get past me if they tried, so I didn't bother!"

Tari rose from the chair, and he was staggering. He was at least six foot five and his body was just as defined as Terrance's. Despite his carefree attitude, he had an air of swagger and authority that commanded respect. His Spirit Energy was unique, and it wasn't like anything I had encountered in the past. *He's strong, and we cannot pick any fights right now.*

Terrance burst through the cell door. "YOU THINK I CAN'T GET PAST YOU SHADE PUNK! LET ME TEACH YOU A LESSON ABOUT MANHOOD!"

"TERRANCE NO!" I yelled.

WHOOSH!

CRASH!

Terrance swung his fist at Tari, but it phased through him like a ghost, and he crashed to the ground.

Tari grinned cockily. "Aww, come on pops. I wanted to see if he could even scratch me..."

Terrance leapt up and delivered a flurry of blows, but each phased through like Tari wasn't even there.

Tari yawned. "Looks like someone's a slow learner."

"That's quite enough. Let's go. We have other matters to attend to." The robed man said.

"Fine by me." Tari threw his hands behind his head and whistled as he strode out of the room.

Terrance stared at his hands in shock. "What the hell?"

"Let it go Terrance. We don't need to pick fights with people we barely know." I said.

Tari shook his head at his dad. "You sure you wanna waste your juice like that, pops? It can be hard to get one over on someone like him."

"I haven't made any issuances, and I am still whole, so it doesn't concern me." He looked his son up and down. "*You* should be more worried about *yourself*. We're not at home so you need to keep a shirt on. *And where is your mask?*"

Tari smiled wide. "Come on pops! You know that a guy like me loves the attention! But where is that stuffy old thing?"

While Tari went back into the room and groped around in the darkness, Terrance and Epios rejoined us.

I laughed. "I'm glad to see you haven't been raped or killed Epios. You're too soft to end up in a place like this."

"Silence fiend! Nothing like that could ever happen to one as refined as myself."

"Refinement has nothing to do with it. You're nothing but refined Charmin to me."

"Charmin? What kind of insult do you speak..."

"Found it!" Tari galloped out of the room and held up a lion mask covered in dirt and cobwebs.

"How you have managed to get it so filthy in such a short time is astounding. Now let us take our leave." The robed man said.

"Sure thing pops...Oh my gosh. *Hello there.*" He removed his shades, and his handsomeness was on full display. He had piercing, hazel eyes that radiated confidence and seductive energy.

Kayla glared at him and rolled her eyes. "No. Don't take another step..."

He straightened his posture and strode toward her with swagger. "You are one of the *finest* things I have ever seen. Not *the* finest. But a close second." He extended his hand. "I'm Tari. *And you are?*"

I balled my fists.

She started toward the exit. "The person that's going to send you straight to hell if you don't back up and listen to your pops. I don't have time for..."

He slid ahead of her. "Whoa there! I'm not one for all that heaven and hell stuff." He leaned against the wall. "You seem stressed sweetheart. I don't know what *these guys* have been putting you through, but I'm not like them. *I'm* the guy that's here to show you a whole new world."

She stopped. "What exactly are you trying to say?"

Why didn't she keep moving away from him? What is she doing?! My anger boiled and dark energy emanated from my flesh.

Tari put his hand on the wall as he looked down at her with a seductive smile. "What I'm saying is, once *you* get to know *me*, you'll never want *any-thing-else*. I'm cute, you're cute. We go together! I wanna take you with me and show you the world's wonders baby girl!" He leaned into her face. "You've never met a guy like me. I'm your knight in shining armor sweet thang."

Her voice shrank into a submissive whisper. "I don't need saving. And I'm not agreeing to anything...but what exactly did you have in mind?"

They were staring into each other's eyes and my throat tightened. *She's giving him the look she gave me on the ship!* Darkness coursed through my veins and my vision took on a red hue. I felt like my head was about to explode and I trembled as I violently clenched my fists.

He nodded toward the door. "You and me, we should get out of here and get to know each other a little bit. I am a prince and all. I can have you in a penthouse before you can say..."

BANG!

Semaj burst through the door at the end of the hall with a shotgun. "AY! The hell is going on here?!"

The robed man leapt and stared at Semaj with a panicked expression. "Alright son, that's quite enough. Run along and acquire some clothes for Ms. Thracas so we can leave the cell blocks unmaimed by savage prisoners please."

Tari winked at her and spoke smoothly. "You got it boss. I'll be right back"

I watched her cheeks turn beet red as he walked off. I had to close my eyes to keep myself from murdering him as he walked past me. Blood dripped from my palms.

As he made his way down the hall, Semaj walked alongside him step for step with the barrel aimed at his head. "Yeah! Yeah! That's what I thought bitch! Everybody wanna act tough until the tools come out SON!"

Tari walked confidently and Semaj followed him with the gun out of the door. I brushed past the robbed guy as I walked past everyone out of the cell block.

He chuckled. "My, my. Someone seems rather upset."

Kayla snapped back to reality. "James what's wrong..."

"Let's go."

I kept walking.

✦

The common blocks were a dark and cruel place. As the tide of my rage settled, I saw cell after cell stuffed with the most destitute dregs of humanity imaginable. The depravity filled me with terrible memories from the capital's slums. The cages were packed to the brim with gaunt skeletons who looked like they hadn't eaten in months. The concrete blocks were overcrowded with men, women and families whose faces were drowned in despair. They looked like they had been here for an eternity and knew they were never getting out. We must have walked past an entire city's worth of people as we made our way through the extensive outer wall. Seeing human beings forced into these conditions made my blood run even hotter.

"Hey you! Now that the soap opera is over, WHO THE HELL ARE YOU ANIMAL MAN?!" Terrance shouted.

"Me? I'm nothing more than a mere politician who..."

"Forget that! Why are these people being kept here in conditions like this!" I roared.

Terrance shook his fist. "HEY! DON'T INTERRUPT MY..."

The robed man glanced at the nearest cell and shook his head. "It's fine. These people are citizens who tried to escape the city and immigrants from nations across the world. There are places who have it worse if you can believe it. Due to the rampant terrorism in this tribe, the authorities cannot just allow individuals to come and go as they please. Especially with the recent attacks on the nation's infrastructure and production facilities. The Archigos, Bazek, could screen individuals for the effects of the various specialist abilities that have been utilized by the underworld to manipulate civilians. Sadly, he hasn't been seen in years, and as a result these people have no hope of being released..."

"WAAAAAAH!"

A baby cried out from a nearby cell. I looked over and saw its sickly body wracked with pain from each sob.

I charged toward the cell. "I'll fix this right now."

The robed man held up his hands. "I wouldn't advise that! If these people suddenly go free, they will be labeled as terrorists without a doubt! They would certainly face a swift execution by the authorities!"

I stopped.

The small cell was packed with more than five families. They could barely move without smothering each other. The stench of feces and death burned my nostrils. My eyes locked with the pale woman breastfeeding the baby. Her lifeless, bloodshot, pupils looked as if they could barely even register my presence. She stared expressionlessly into my soul.

A tear wet her brittle cheek.

I gripped the bars. "I will come back for you. I promise."

I turned and continued down the hallway, enraged. "I'm gonna find that Archigos and when I do, he is gonna have a fucking problem on his hands."

As we continued down the hall, I noticed Kayla's strange demeanor. Her arms were wrapped tightly around her body, she was sweating, and there was a queasy look on her face.

I didn't care. She pissed me off.

Terrance's fists were balled, and he was trembling. He spoke through gritted teeth. "Hey, *Animal Planet*. You never answered my question. *Who are you and why the hell did you help us?*"

"You may call me Kaiti, *not* animal planet. I am a traveling emissary and politician. I helped you because I believe in being the change you want to see in the world, and I seek to become a force that makes change happen." He shrugged. "Helping a few bright, young people in need, seemed like a proper step toward that goal."

Epios stroked imaginary chin hairs. "A politician you say? I've been in the highest social circles my entire life and I've never once heard of you. What nation is it that you claim to represent?"

"A small, independent one. You most likely haven't..."

"Why didn't you free anybody else? These people need help too." I spat.

His head dropped. "Sadly I cannot. I utilized all my remaining influence in freeing you. Releasing anyone else would unfortunately have the same effect as if you freed them." He glanced at the cells. "But these people are a part of the reason I am visiting this nation. I needed to see for myself if this place was as bad as I had heard." He frowned. "It grossly surpassed my wildest expectations. I hope to one day rule this nation and help create a utopia where nobody is forced to live like this."

Epios scoffed. "*Rule?* You will never rule this nation! You aren't even of royal descent! Your words are nothing but an outlandish pipe dream! I am this nation's next ruler!"

He nodded. "Your words are true. As of now, my wish is nothing more than a vapor that slips through my fingertips as it whisks through the wind." He clutched the air. "Still though, I grasp at it each day with my entire soul, as I seek to make this nation a better place." He glanced at me. "I envy those more capable than myself. What are your thoughts on ruling this nation?"

"I don't want to rule. But your ideals are something we can agree upon I guess." I said.

He smiled. "I'm glad we have found some common ground. Though you won't live long enough to see your dreams come to fruition if you keep finding yourself unconscious and stranded in perilous situations." He chuckled. "Anyone who tries to brave that desert without a guide from this tribe is a certified fool."

Terrance muttered as his body trembled. "What the hell did you call me?"

Kaiti shrugged. "I mean any educated individual knows that the fierce sandstorms surrounding this city rage year-round. On top of that, the desert is known to house thieves, bandits, and is often referred to as the Den of the Underworld. No sane person would ever dare cross it. That's most likely what happened to your clothes and possessions as..."

WHOOSH!

CRASH!

Terrance swung at Kaiti and his punch passed straight through as he fell on his face once more. He leapt up and swung wildly at the politician. "What the hell is up with you two?! Are you ghosts or something?!"

He chuckled. "Hardly. Today, I am as alive as I have ever been." He nodded at me. "Also, I meant no disrespect, Mr. Touvtpa. I was only stating the obvious and providing some clarity for our newcomer. Let us be on our way." He dismissively walked through Terrance's punches.

We descended the last set of steps and entered the lowest level of the wall.

Kaiti turned to me. "You know Mr. Fos, your words have reminded me of another one of my primary purposes for this visit. Finding and securing a wife for my son. It has unfortunately not been going well. I am quite saddened that Ms. Thracas has turned down my offer."

She shivered vigorously. "No...way..."

Her arms were wrapped around her body like a strait jacket, and she was drenched in sweat.

Terrance glanced at her for the first time since we got here and his eyes were ablaze with hunger. "You know, it's a shame that you're batshit crazy because your body is absolutely banging!"

Epios looked her up and down. "Even though I despise whores, I must admit the brute has a point. You look quite exquisite when you're not being a..."

"Shut up! Can't you see that she's not in the mood?" I roared.

Her shivering intensified. "Let's just...get out...of here..."

How can they not see that she isn't feeling well?

She smiled weakly. "Th...Thanks...James..."

I looked away. "I didn't do it for you."

Tari arrived from around the corner with a fresh set of rags.

"Here you go, beautiful."

"Th...Thanks."

She pulled the clothes over her body and sighed. "Thank you. I'm starting to feel much better now."

Oh, come on! This is ridiculous! Was this all an act or something? I can't stand her!

He winked. "Anything for you, beautiful."

I'm gonna kill him.

We turned a corner, and I noticed the prisoners in these cells didn't look as sickly. They were all men, and they looked confused, as if they had lost something important to them.

Some cat-called from the cells. "Hey sweet thing!". "What is someone like you doing in a place like this?". "You're not like our slave masters are you?" "Come a little bit closer."

Tears ran down her face. "I...I can't..."

"**Sure, you can!**". "**I'm right here!**". "**Come to *this* cell honey!**"

Their voices intensified and before we knew it, the entire cell block was trembling with their desperate cries. She flinched as a dirty hand grabbed her shoulder through the bars. She ducked away as the prisoners pressed and reached through their restraints, desperately grasping for her.

"**I haven't touched a woman in years!**". "**She's mine!**". "**I need her!**"

Kaiti sighed. "This is precisely what I was hoping to avoid."

She whimpered as she crumpled to her knees. "No...please!"

Her eyes looked lifeless.

I picked her up and sprinted toward the exit. "We're getting out of here!"

"**WHAT DO YOU THINK YOU'RE DOING!**". "**WHERE THE HELL ARE YOU GOING WITH MY WOMAN!**". "**GET YOUR ASS BACK HERE!**"

CRASH!

The bars shattered as the ravenous men barreled through. The entire cell block stormed after us as they trampled each other like animals. Men grabbed and clawed at me, ripping off my flesh, but I shrugged them away as I blindly sprinted down the corridors. I ducked around corners and leapt over bodies as naked men filled my vision from all sides. We turned down the last passageway and saw the exit.

CRASH!

The men in the cells near the door burst through the bars and my sight was flooded with flesh.

I charged at the steel gate. "AAAARGGGHHHHAAA!"

WRENCH!

Suddenly, tree roots formed around the door and ripped it off its hinges. I dove into the light and tumbled through the dust. Kayla and I rolled in the dirt until we slid to a halt. I looked up as the rest of our group leapt through the opening and tree roots barricaded the doorway.

SLICE!

GUSH!

SPLAT!

The roots rose and mutilated the men that spilled across the prison's threshold, splattering their blood and guts across the sand. Blood spatter filled the air, and it rained down upon us like a crimson mist. Red ooze splattered across my face, and I shifted my body to shield Kayla from the spray. I squeezed my eyes shut as the horrific sounds of carnage rattled within my skull for an eternity.

It...stopped...

I looked up and saw the politician, soaked in blood, casually wiping his robe with a handkerchief. Tari looked upon the aftermath of the carnage with a wild grin.

Who are these people? What kind of hellhole did we just walk into?

Kaiti yawned. "Well, that was eventful. I wasn't expecting a workout this early in the morning. Apparently not *all* beasts support me..." He spread his arms wide with the city at his back. "But I digress! Welcome to paradise!"

Tari winked. "I'll be seeing you again soon beautiful!"

"That's all you have to say?! What about all those people who just...and you! I...urgh! I don't have time for this! Kayla! Are you ok?"

She shivered and trembled despondently in my arms.

"Now you see the depravity I have come here to fix. I believe the time has come for us to take our leave."

"Wait! Who the hell are you?! Don't lie to me! And what happened to Kayla?"

"I think we all know that Ms. Thracas has her...issues. I believe she will recover in due time." Kaiti said.

He started down a dark alley before turning and offering us a wide smile. "And as for me. I told you; I am nothing but a humble politician seeking to change the world. I offer kindness to all, and I do hope you will return that kindness one day." He faced the darkness. "Stay safe. This city is a dangerous place."

He disappeared into the alley's shadows.

We waited outside the wall until Kayla recovered.

She held her head and spoke groggily. "Wh...What happened?"

"You passed out in there for some reason. Are you alright?"

"Yeah, I'm..."

She looked down and noticed that she was in my arms. She leapt to her feet and dusted herself off. Her cheeks were rosy as she looked away. "I'm fine. Let's find the Archigos and get out of here. Preferably after we buy some clothes first."

I looked down and realized my rags were barely intact. I was virtually naked, and my clothes were in the best shape out of everyone's.

Epios scoffed. "And exactly how are *we* supposed to find the Archigos in this massive city? The authorities have been searching for years."

"Well first let's see if we can gather any information...and buy some clothes. Does anyone know how we can get some money?" I said.

"No clue. I've only been to the palace a few times and everything I had was in my backpack." Kayla said.

"Money is no problem! I'm the prince of the Ocean Tribe! My mere presence will inspire the generous donations of my adoring fans from across the world! I am a He-Man after all!" Terrance shouted as Sesame climbed out of his shorts to flex.

Epios chuckled. "Money is a trivial matter for a prince such as myself! I shall simply write to my father, and he will certainly send a few million for me to toss around." He turned his nose up as he looked us up and down. "I may be willing to spare a few pennies to allow you dregs to cover yourselves less scandalously."

I face palmed. "Those are both terrible suggestions. Epios, how long do you think that's gonna take? I'm trying not to punch you in the face right now. And how are we supposed to defend ourselves if we get attacked again when we don't have any weapons?"

Kayla looked around. "We'll need to avoid conflict as much as possible. Most of the people living here can use Earth Craft at some level, and in a place like this we're at a severe disadvantage. If we get into some kind of confrontation, you'll have to use your fists, or whatever techniques you have that don't rely on your sword or armor."

"That's basically nothing." I said.

Terrance threw his arms wide. "Have no fear servants! I, the great Terrance Touvtpa, personally take it upon myself as your fearless leader to ensure we find the Archigos and lead our outfit to victory! That's rule three of the Ocean King's Ten Rules of Manhood! Follow your fearless leader and everything will work out perfectly! Especially if you're a woman!"

A vein popped out of my forehead. "You'd call what just happened 'going perfectly'?! In fact, it's been nothing but disaster after disaster since we started following you! And you're *not* our leader!"

"I am your prince you arrogant troglodyte!"

"This is why I hate men."

"All I hear is irrelevance! I got us here in one piece and you all should be grateful! And besides! We shouldn't get into any conflict in the first place because all we must do is find my friend Machari. From there he can help us out." Terrance pulled out a letter.

I stared. "Where have you been keeping that? And why didn't they steal…You know what. Never mind. Let's just go."

We walked down an alley and on the other side was a massive, bustling street. Enormous sandstone buildings were packed together as they towered in every direction. Thousands of citizens filled every crevice of my sight as they hustled down the street. Ahead of us was a wide road where hundreds of stone vehicles barreled through at rapid speeds. It was like a sandy, hot, tan, Times Square. We stepped out onto the sandstone sidewalk, but Kayla wasn't with us. I looked back and she was trembling and sweating like before.

"What's wrong?"

"Do we...do we have to go out here? With all of these...people..."

"We can't get to Terrance's friend's house any other way."

"O...Ok..."

I extended my hand and smiled. "Here, stay close to me and hold my hand."

She hesitated as she slowly reached out. "O...Ok...but just this once."

She grabbed my hand, and we started down the street. She pressed her body against mine, and I loved feeling her warmth as our skin touched all over. I felt a rapid heartbeat pulsing through her skin, and her gentle breaths gave me goosebumps as they grazed my neck. Even though she was covered in dirt and sweat, whiffs of her heavenly scent remained. My stomach was flooded with primal emotions, and I struggled to keep myself together as we forced our way through the mass of bodies behind Terrance. I felt cool tears running down my back and they filled me with determination to protect her. *I'll get us there safely!*

"AYY! I'M WALKIN ERE'!" Someone cried out in a New York accent.

James looked down the street and saw Semaj in a New York Knicks Jersey. He was shaking his fist as he walked directly into speeding traffic.

James stared. "What the hell..."

A vehicle swerved to avoid Semaj.

CRASH!

It smashed into another, causing a massive accident.

CRASH! CRASH! CRASH! CRASH! CRASH!

Stone collided and dust clouded the sky as people were thrown from their cars and rubble filled the highway. Blood and gore splattered in the street as the survivors leapt out of their cars enraged.

"WHAT THE HELL IS WRONG WITH YOU?!"

"YOU DIDN'T SEE THAT GUY!?"

"THERE WAS NO GUY!"

"WHAT ARE YOU DRUNK?!"

"HE WAS RIGHT THERE!"

They roared at each other in the street as they came to blows.

Kayla glanced up at James with teary eyes. "W...what happened...What was all of that...that noise..."

James smiled reassuringly. "It's alright. Just keep your head down and stay with me."

Only one person stayed in their car. He was an average looking man in a plain white tee. He had tan skin and his yellow eyes glowed in the reflection of his windshield. He impatiently tapped his sunglasses against the steering wheel with a hand pressed against his temple. He sighed. "Why do these things always happen to me?"

The man looked up and saw Semaj whistling as he crossed the street completely unscathed. He gawked as Semaj disappeared into the shadows of an alley. The people on the sidewalk stopped to spectate, until the mass of bodies continued in their hurry as if nothing happened. The authorities arrived in stone vehicles and quickly attended to the scene.

James shook his head. *That was terrible, but at least the police are here to help. I wish I could do something about this, but we need to keep moving.*

James

I'm going to let Semaj **have it** *once we have some time to ourselves!* My stomach was filled with sorrow after witnessing that accident. The joy from having Kayla on my arm went a long way in tempering my rage.

As we continued, Terrance started flinching and waving his hands around his head. "OUCH! WHAT THE HELL IS GOING ON?!"

I sighed. "What is it now Terrance? Did you finally realize that you don't know where you're going..."

"NO! I keep getting hit by bugs or some shit! I swear I'm going to kill them! EVERY LAST ONE OF THEM!"

I looked closely and saw white spheres bouncing off his head. Semaj was ahead of us rattling ping-pong balls off his skull like a professional tennis player.

He wore a polo and a visor for some reason, "40 Love! WOOOHOOOO!"

I yelled under my breath. "*Semaj!* What are you..."

His eyes widened and he vanished.

What the hell?! Just wait until we get where we're...

Semaj suddenly sprinted from the left and stuck a "KICK ME" sign on Epios' back.

"Who dares touch the future king of this..."

Semaj whistled casually as he walked past Epios from the right.

I glared. "Don't you dare..."

He glanced at Epios and excitement filled his eyes as he saw the sign. He spoke in a British accent. "I might as well then mate!"

POW!

He cocked his foot back and devastated Epios with a kick to the balls.

"GAHAHAHAHAHAHAHA!" Epios cried as he crumpled to the ground. He rolled around the dirt in tears as he cradled his jewels.

Kayla raised her head from my back for the first time. "Wh...who are you talking to James..."

"It's nothing...I..."

"OUCH!" She yelped as she was knocked to the floor.

"Kayla!" I helped her up and looked for what knocked her down.

Her hoodie and sweatpants had socked her in the head. I looked up and saw Semaj in the window of a building above us.

"I'm finished with those!" He shouted as he held up a framed replica of the outfit.

"Oh my God! My clothes!" She looked around. "But how did they get here..."

"Uhh, I'm not sure. But at least you've got them back, right?!"

"Absolutely!"

I averted my eyes out of respect as she sprinted into an alleyway, turned away from me, and ripped off her rags.

She swiftly redressed and sighed in relief. "Phew! I feel so much better now!"

I feigned enthusiasm and gave her a thumbs up. "That's...great..." *I know she was in distress but why did Semaj have to go and do that? She looked so good in those ripped clothes, and I was enjoying having her so close to me.* I balled my fists. *He's gonna pay for this.*

I walked toward the alley. "Excuse me for a moment." I looked back to make sure Kayla wasn't within earshot.

"SEMAJ BRING YOUR ASS HERE THIS INSTANT!"

"Kommichie wa!" He bowed in a samurai outfit.

SLAP!

I slapped the shit out of him, and he fell to the ground.

"Oi mate! The hell was that for?" He said in a British accent. He had somehow switched into a soccer uniform.

"I've had enough! What the hell do you think you're doing here?!"

"I just came to assist you, mate! Those bloody wankers were getting on your nerves, and your girl was cowerin' so I thought I'd..."

"But what about when you caused that car accident and killed all those people?!"

"That was nothin' but an accident, mate. I was late for me tea and crumpets!

"You tried to walk across the highway in rush hour traffic! Are you an idiot?! How are you even out of my body in the first place!"

He switched into a kimono. "Wǒxiǎng zhǒngxià yìxiē zhǒngzi, wándé kāixīn..."

"And why are you talking in all of those accents?!"

"I thought you were mixed mate."

I face palmed. "No! What the hell are you talking about?! I never said...You know what?! I've had enough! Get back inside my body and never come out! I don't want to see you ever again!"

He blushed and became flustered. He spun around and his outfit changed to a colorful button up with a sombrero, "¡Bondad! ¡No sabía que querías llevar nuestra relación al siguiente nivel! Todo esto también se está moviendo un poco..."

"I told you I can't understand you and I'm sick of this! Go away! All you do is cause trouble!"

He switched back to his soccer uniform. "What are you talking about mate? I've done nothing but give my all to help you buggers, and all I see are bloody ingrates! I told you I would give you a great pillow and I did mate! I called those shady looking buggers in the desert to save you lot and if I hadn't you would be vulture slop mate! I scared off that tall bugger, who was hitting on your girl mate! I should have killed that bloody *bastard*...but I even returned your girl's clothes and..."

"Enough! I never asked you to do any of that! Go away and don't come back! We have a mission and you're doing nothing but causing problems!"

He teared up. "Fine then you ungrateful bugger, you! I've provided nothing but good things for you and this is how I'm received?! Outrageous! Cripey! Don't come crying to me when you and your friends get into danger, and I can guarantee it's coming soon! You'll rue the day you rejected a helpful bloke like me! I'd sooner watch you bleed out before I lift a finger to assist you sorry lot! And don't even *ask* me to help find the Archigos, because I do know where he is!"

"We'll find him ourselves! You're nothing but a suspicious troublemaker and I don't want to have anything to do with you! How you're even here still escapes me, but those guys at the round table were right about you and I don't trust you as far as I can throw you!"

He held up a scale without a reading. "Well, I am part-spirit so I'm rather light…"

"GO AWAY!"

He held up his hands. "James…please…I didn't mean to…"

"GO NOW! GET OUT OF HERE!"

He burst into tears as he despondently trudged into the shadows.

I shook my head. "What the hell is wrong with that son of a…"

"James? Are you ok? Epios is better now, and Terrance is ready to go so…"

"Yeah, I'm fine. Let's find Terrance's friend and get the hell out of here."

We pushed through the city's dense crowds. Every block looked the same due to the monotone nature of the sand and the nearly identical sandstone houses that were packed together on every street. As we got further from the city's center, the height and quality of the buildings' construction decreased. Every alleyway we passed was filled with passing civilians or homeless people who had made them their personal residences. People were in such a rush that they constantly shoved past each other with no regard for anybody but themselves. We were getting a bunch of dirty looks for some reason, but I was too tired to care. As we walked, I noticed that Kayla had completely gone back to normal. *What caused her to act crazy like that in the first place?* I thought about asking her, but we were all starving and exhausted from another day of walking in the heat. After several grueling hours we eventually reached a house that matched the address on Terrance's letter.

"Ta-da! The residence of my long-time friend Machari! He's the man here so he should be able to give us a place to stay until we find the Archigos."

CRASH!

We were too tired to speak, and we collapsed in the shade as he approached the steps.

KNOCK! KNOCK! KNOCK!

No response.

"Hey! It's me Terrance!"

Crickets.

I rolled my eyes. "Yay! Our fearless leader is the best..."

Epios moaned. "Once a trog...always a trog..."

Kayla sighed. "Can't trust a man for anything."

He glared at us and placed his hand on the doorknob.

CRASH!

The door fell off the hinges.

"What an auspicious sign." Kayla said.

"SHUT UP!" He roared as we went inside.

The house had been completely ransacked and dilapidated.

"Something must be wrong. I've been writing Machari for years and I always sent the letters to this address!"

For the first time, he had a look of genuine concern for another human being.

I didn't care. He pissed me off.

"Look, you've wasted enough of our time. Let's just head to the palace and try to get a meeting with the Archigos." I said.

He looked away. "Fine. I hope Machari is alright."

As they walked away, a figure appeared in the window of one of the house's upper rooms.

James

Terrance led us toward the palace. The crowds were thickening as we entered the royal district. As we maneuvered, people gave us death glares and others seemingly went out of the way to impede our progress. We pushed forward until we heard shouting and realized that the mob was at a complete standstill. The crowd was over a mile long, and it was full of enraged protesters.

"MY CHILDREN ARE STARVING!", "WHERE IS THE ARCHIGOS?!", "WE CAN'T LIVE LIKE THIS!"

I tapped a man on the shoulder. "Excuse me, but why exactly are the people protesting here? We need to get to the palace."

He spat at my feet. "You filthy foreigners are the reason! We're overpopulated and nobody has enough because you and your kind keep barreling in here like you own the place!"

Their cries were deafening, and the palace security were barely able to keep the people back. I could tell that things were about to get violent.

"I HAVEN'T EATEN IN DAYS!", "MY CHILD STARVED TO DEATH BECAUSE OF YOU!", "MY DAUGHTER WAS KIDNAPPED FROM MY LIVING ROOM!", "HOW ARE WE SUPPOSED TO WORK WITH ALL OF THESE GANGSTERS AROUND?!", "WHAT ARE YOU GOING TO DO ABOUT THIS?!", "YOU'RE IN CHARGE! HOW ARE YOU GOING TO FIX IT?!"

I yelled to my friends and Terrance. "We need to get out of here!"

We started exiting the crowd, but we were slowed by the people's increasing ferocity. The air was hot, thick, and suffocating as we shoved through the mob of flesh. We were gasping for air once we finally slipped through and made it back to the sidewalk of the city's main street. Once we reached a safe distance from the crowd, Epios plopped into the sand and groaned. "This place is truly detestable. I should raze every inch of it once I become king."

"I'm just glad we made it out of there in one piece. Let's try to find a place to stay for the night so we can recover and start our search again in the morning." I said.

Kayla moaned. "But how are we going to stay in a hotel without money?"

"It's probably around 2 o'clock. Maybe we can find somewhere that will let us work for the afternoon in exchange for one night of sleep."

We scoured the city for a place to stay the night.

"NO VACANCIES!", "WE DON'T ACCOMMODATE FILTHY PRISONERS!", "NO SHIRT! NO SHOES! NO SERVICE!", "GET THE FUCK OUT OF HERE YOU FILTHY BASTARDS!", "DO I LOOK LIKE? A CHARITY CASE?!"

Those were the nicest responses we received that afternoon. The police were equally hostile when we asked for help, had no idea who any of us are, and looked like they were in worse shape than we were. We solicited hotels and stores for hours, only to face rejection each time. Not a single hotel had a vacancy, and no store was willing to allow "ex-convicts to work for them". Every inn we visited had long lines of people waiting to get in that spilled out into the streets. As the afternoon wore on, people laid down and slept in those lines. We were starving after not eating for a day and a half and we had no hope of securing a place to stay for the night. We aimlessly wandered the streets as night fell.

"What are we gonna do..." I moaned.

"This is a disaster..." Kayla moaned.

"So...tired..." Epios moaned.

"My plans never...fail..." Terrance moaned.

My mind was weary as we slogged through the streets. It was pitch black and we had only the moon to guide our path.

Suddenly, noises rustled in the shadows around us. *Shit. I must come up with something or we'll all be raped and killed.* A dim light caught the corner of my eye. I looked up to see a small inn with a sign that said. "ROOMS AVAILABLE".

"Look guys!"

"Oh, thank God!" Kayla said.

"Finally! A place for a weary prince to rest his tired soul!"

"It's about damn time!"

We walked inside and saw an obese man sitting behind his desk eating a steak. He shook his head. "MHM-MHM! No way! No convicts!"

I held up my hands. "Please sir! Would you really leave a few kids out to suffer in the streets?! We're not actually convicts. I promise if you let us work, we can pay you back..."

He buttered his bread rolls. "So, you don't have any money either? Denied! Exit the premises before I call the authorities!"

We despondently shuffled out of the inn. I looked around and felt the shadows converging. *There are people out there and we're in no shape to fight.*

"Guys, stay over here by the light."

Kayla looked around weakly. "Why? Is someone..."

"Just trust me."

"NO LOITERING! IF YOU BUMS DON'T GET OFF OF MY PROPERTY BY THE TIME I'M FINISHED EATING, I'M CALLING THE AUTHORITIES!"

"Sorry sir! We'll be on our way shortly!" I said in the kindest tone I could muster to that fat bastard. *How is he eating a steak when everyone else is starving?* My growling stomach made me want to go back and snatch it from him.

"We must find a way to convince that guy to let us in. We can't survive all night out in the streets."

"Maybe we could sell him the mammoth for a night's rest." Epios said.

Sesame's eyes went wide with horror.

"No chance! Sesame is off limits! I'll sell you first!" Terrance said.

We racked our brains for solutions as the shadows crept closer.

"Maybe the princess could try to charm him to let us in?" Epios said.

"Absolutely not! I refuse to..."

"That's the first time you didn't call her a wench or a whore!" I said in shock.

Terrance perked up. "Absolutely! That's a great idea you pompous bastard! She should just let him feel her up a bit and he'll let us in for sure!"

"No way! I refuse to be treated like a sex slave!"

I'm against making her do something she's uncomfortable with, but at this point we're out of options. We are minutes away from one of us getting snatched into the shadows. If we called the police, we might even get thrown back into prison because of our clothes. We must try something.

"Kayla I would never ask this but..."

"No, James! How could you ask me to do that?!"

Terrance stepped forward. "Oh, come on! Settle down kids! This is the perfect time for the Ocean King's fourth rule of manhood! When you don't want to do something, send one of your underlings to do it for you! Especially if it's cooking and cleaning and *especially* if they're a woman!" Terrance boasted as Sesame weakly flexed his muscles in support.

She crossed her arms and looked away. "Now I'm definitely not going to do it."

I face palmed. "Did you really think that would help?"

Epios greedily eyed Sesame. "I saw we eat the mammoth..."

CLINK!

I heard the clink of a chain, and a jagged piece of metal reflected light from the glowing sign a few feet away. I started into the darkness, and the bloodied hook retracted into the shadows.

"Look, we're running out of time! We just need to take a vote at this point. All in favor say..."

"I don't give a damn what you say! I'm not..."

"**I.**" The men declared in unison.

"That doesn't mean anything! I'm still not going to..."

Chains rattled in the darkness.

I grasped her hand. "*Please* Kayla. This is our only chance. I've been wracking my brain for hours and I promise you I wouldn't ask you to do this if I could see *any* other way out of this. You don't have to let him do anything you're uncomfortable with but please just try to convince him." I swallowed as I glanced at a pair of eyes in the shadows. "*Please*. We're almost out of time."

She stared into my eyes and her face softened. "Fine. I guess I can ask him, but I'm not making any guarantees."

She started toward the doorway.

"Psst! Kayla" Terrance said.

She turned around and Terrance squeezed his nipples. Epios pulled his shorts tightly to show off his butt.

I face palmed.

She glared as she entered the inn. "I promise I will kill *every single one of you* before this is all over!"

The boys watched Kayla enter as they hid outside under the windowsill. Kayla approached the desk, and the innkeeper lifted his eyes.

Kayla grimaced. *I can't believe James would ask me to do this. I'm going to murder him in the morning after we find a place to sleep tonight. I suppose this is what I deserve for trying to get back at him for assaulting me in the desert by flirting with that politician's son...*

"You again..."

Despite the dirt and grime, her beauty was undeniable. The innkeeper looked upon her and he instantly was infatuated. He raised an eyebrow. "Why hello there! What can I do for you this evening?!"

It took everything in Kayla's power to keep from rolling her eyes. "Disgusting! Am I a piece of meat to you?! I was just in here and you..."

Oh Shit!

"Oh...uh...hey...?" She muttered nervously.

Crap! I don't know how to be sexy, or feminine, or seductive, or anything like that! How am I supposed to pull this off?!

The innkeeper leaned forward. "I apologize for my rudeness earlier. I didn't get a good look at you before. How can I help you?"

WHAT THE HELL DOES THAT MATTER!? HOW I LOOK HAS NO BEARING ON WHETHER OR NOT YOU SHOULD LISTEN TO WHAT I HAVE TO SAY! I HATE MEN! I HATE MEN! I HATE MEN! I HATE MEN! I HATE MEN! I HATE MEN! I HATE MEN! I HATE MEN! I...

She laughed awkwardly and playfully brushed his shoulder with her hand. "Oh...that's...ok...I guess...te-he...te-he...Do you have any vacant rooms...Ha-ha...ha-ha..." Her fingers were extremely warm to the touch as she fought to restrain herself from burning him alive.

"Ooh, I like that sweet thing! I certainly have a room for you. But first, tell me where you're from?"

"Oh me? Ha-ha-ha I'm from the...Flame Tribe. Ha-ha ha..."

I SHOULD KILL HIM WHERE HE STANDS AND BURN THIS ENTIRE INN TO THE GROUND!

The innkeeper came around the booth and placed his hand on her lower back. He slipped it underneath her hoodie. James crept closer to the doorway as he watched.

"I can't believe I asked her to do this! What was I thinking?! I can't have her talking to other men like that!" James whispered in a panicked tone.

Her body tensed up and flames danced in her eyes. She quickly looked away and took deep breaths to hide her rage. He slid his hand down until it was right above her butt.

"You're kind of tense sweet thing. Tell you what. I'll get you a room and I'll even give you a special offer. How does that sound?"

A guttural, feral sound emanated from her throat as she gritted her teeth. "RRRRRRGGGGGGGHHH!"

"Whoa! Are you alright, Hun?"

Terrance face palmed. "This is terrible! She's so bad! She's gonna get thrown out and we're gonna get raped by savages!"

"For a whore, she is not very seductive." Epios whispered.

She gritted her teeth and clenched her fists. AAAAAAAAAAARRRRRRRRGGGGGGGG!

Kayla's face shifted to a wide grin as she spoke in a high-pitched voice and softly put her hand on his chest. "Absolutely sir!"

"I like it when you call me sir." He lowered his hand and grabbed her butt cheek.

"I'm putting a stop to this." James whispered as he stepped forward.

"Stop! You're the one who said this was our only shot!" Terrance hissed.

Steam rose from her head and poured from her ears as she smiled even wider. Her hand moved from his chest to his shoulder as she felt for his vital nerves.

"I like a man with big shoulders." She said as she moved her hand from his shoulder to his neck.

"Thanks! I've been hitting the gym recently if you can't tell..."

She rubbed her hand on his neck. I'VE FOUND ALL THE NERVES THAT I NEED TO PARALYZE YOU FOR LIFE!

She beamed as she gripped one of the nerves.

"OUCH!"

"I'm so sorry! Te-he! I guess I can be a bit too rough sometimes! Te-he!"

"No! What is she doing?!" Terrance moaned.

"Serves him right!" James said.

"Fiend, are you actually jealous of that bloated buffoon right now?!" Epios whispered aggressively.

The innkeeper rubbed his neck and smiled. "Rough you say? I like an aggressive woman! Tell you what, I'll let you and your three creepy friends who have been watching us spend the night here!"

Terrance, James and Epios ducked under the windowsill.

"Hooray!", "We did it!", "Hi-five!" The boys rejoiced under their breaths.

"Really?! Thank you so..."

"But in exchange you and I are going to spend the night together in my fanciest suite. I've got steaks, condoms, chains and all of the fixings! I promise I'll show you a good time. How does that sound?"

Dread filled the boys' hearts.

"Oh fuck."

"Oh God."

"Oh dear."

Kayla looked up at him silently with a face of unadulterated disgust. Her malicious aura could be felt for miles. Her murderous intent even caused the criminals in the shadows to retreat.

"I've had enough of this."

CRACK!

She ripped the innkeeper's hand from her back and broke his arm.

"GAAAAAAAAAAAH!"

POW!

She chopped him in the neck and his body limply fell to the ground. Kayla's blazing Spirit Energy spiraled around her body and ignited the tavern's wooden floor.

"This is why I HATE men! All of you are nothing but filthy, unkempt swine who can't do anything but get erect and throw shit around at each other! Why on earth you felt you had the right to touch me like that is literally beyond the scope of my comprehension! And let me tell you something else..."

James ran into the inn as the fire spread. "Kayla stop! We have to go!"

The innkeeper writhed in pain on the ground as she spat in his face. The heat from her energy was searing his skin.

"No! I'm not finished with him yet!" She stared daggers into his soul as he burned. "You think you're some big man, but let me tell you what I see. You are nothing but a fat, sexist, horny, pig, bastard who doesn't deserve to have the right to reproduce! And here's another thing..."

James grabbed her hand as his skin was scorched by flames. "Kayla, we have to go now!"

"I'm not done with him! I..."

James pointed and she looked up. A woman was standing in a doorway that led toward the inn's rooms.

"POLICE! HELP! TERRORISTS!"

James and Kayla turned and sprinted out of the inn. As the group sprinted into the shadows, James glanced behind them. "Do you guys think they have police all the way out here in the...GAAH!"

BOOOM!

The ground beneath him exploded into a steam geyser that launched him into the air. They stopped as stone barriers rose high into the sky ahead of them. The group was blinded as massive spotlights illuminated the shadows from behind the walls.

A soldier walked through the barricade. "This is Gi Squad 3! Come quietly and you may be allowed to live!"

"Shit. This is bad. That's the Gi force. They're the palace's elite guard. What are they doing way out here in the slums?" Terrance said as the group put their hands up.

James flipped wildly through the air. He caught a glimpse of a reflection in a building's mirror.

ZIP!

He beamed into it and out onto the street with his friends. His clothes had completely disintegrated.

The lead officer spoke into a walkie talkie. "This is Reggie from Gi Force Squad Three, over! We have four targets in custody. Three escaped prisoners and one pervert!"

"Why does everyone keep calling me a pervert?!"

Kayla rolled her eyes. "Please put that little thing away."

James looked down and was filled with embarrassment. He quickly covered his privates. "You didn't have to say *little*. I'm not even hard right..."

"SILENCE! YOUR DAYS OF TERRORIZING THIS KINGDOM ARE OVER! STAY WHERE YOU ARE! PUT YOUR HANDS ON YOUR HEADS AND GET ON YOUR KNEES! SLOWLY!"

They followed instructions. As James was kneeling, images from the riot at the palace flashed into his mind.

He stopped.

He rose to his full height as his body trembled with rage.

"WHAT THE HELL ARE YOU DOING?! IF YOU DON'T..."

"NO! YOU SHUT THE HELL UP AND LISTEN! THIS CITY IS IN SHAMBLES BECAUSE YOU GUYS DON'T KNOW WHAT THE HELL YOU'RE DOING! WE'RE NOT EVEN TERRORISTS! WE'RE SOLDIERS ON OFFICIAL GOVERNMENT BUSINESS! THERE ARE PLENTY OF BAD GUYS ALL AROUND US IN THESE SHADOWS WAITING TO RIP OUR HEADS OFF BECAUSE YOU GUYS HAVEN'T APPREHENDED THEM! YOU GUYS ARE A JOKE AND I'M NOT GOING TO SIT HERE AND LET YOU WASTE ANY MORE OF OUR TIME! NOW LET US GO SO WE CAN..."

"Gi Force, engage."

Soldiers leapt out of the mud at James's feet and grabbed him.

POW!

They slammed him to the ground and knocked the wind out of him. Dark energy surged within his veins. *I refuse to let these bastards take us in! I won't let tyrants control me* EVER AGAIN!

ZIP!

He beamed into a mirror in a nearby building and exploded out of it.

POW! POW!

He punched the first guard in the face, spun, and roundhouse kicked the other guard in the head. Dark shockwaves erupted from each hit that shattered nearby windows as the guards crumpled to the ground.

Kayla raised her head. "James! What are you..."

"Let's go!" He shouted.

"Gi Force, fire at will!"

Rocks and chunks of metal soared at James from the shadows. As they approached, time seemed to slow. James extended his left hand toward the floodlights and took a deep breath as beams of light materialized on his fingertips. His eyes glowed with a purple aura as he took in his surroundings with Spectrum Vision. In his right hand, a blade formed from pure darkness.

CRASH!

As time resumed, he fired the beams and they shattered the floodlights.

SLICE!

In the same instant he swung the blade at incomprehensible speeds.

BOOM!

The projectiles exploded into a cloud of dust.

"Dammit! Get those lights...ARRRGHAAA!"

Bandits swarmed the guards and brutalized them mercilessly. Epios activated Spectrum Vision while Kayla activated Thermal Sense.

Terrance groped around in the darkness. "Hey! I can't see..."

A hoodlum rushed Terrance with a hook and chain. James raised his right hand.

SWIP!

GUSH!

He brought it down and the hoodlum was slashed to pieces as his blood gushed across the sand.

James grabbed Terrance's wrist. "I got you! Let's go!"

As they sprinted toward an alleyway, criminals descended upon them from every angle, James led the group and he swung his arm in an X motion.

SLICE!

GUSH!

Dozens of criminals were slashed to pieces in an instant as James led the group down an alleyway. They blindly charged through the back streets as they avoided their pursuers in the shadows. The group was weak and low on stamina and their foes steadily gained on them.

James gasped for air as his stomach and sides burned from fatigue. *Dammit! What do we do?!*

SLICE!

A criminal leapt from the shadows with a scimitar and his blade grazed James' neck.

WHOOSH!

Suddenly, a sand cloud washed over the alleyway. James and his friends burst through the cloud unscathed.

The criminals in the cloud were reduced to bone. The sand dissipated, and in its center was a tall man with two curved blades, dripping in blood.

The criminals froze in their tracks.

"Boss, what are you..."

The man with the blades held up a hand. His muscular, scared body was illuminated in the moonlight.

"Let them go for now. I want to see if that bastard has grown soft or not."

James and his friends ran until they stumbled and collapsed in an alleyway. They doubled over on the cool sandstone gasping for air as they clutched their stomachs.

As they recovered Kayla sat up. "James...*huff*...that was crazy!"

James huffed as he laid in the sand. "They would have just...*huff*...*huff*...slowed us down...Then we never would've...found...the Archigos...*huff*...*huff*..."

"You...fiend! You've made your king...*huff*...*huff*...a fugitive...*huff*...*huff*..."

"I...don't know how you...pulled that off...simp...but that was...*huff*...*huff*...pretty damn slick...."

After they recovered, James sat up.

"Well, I think that's enough excitement for one day. I don't think I can walk any further without getting some rest."

"Agreed." Kayla said. She stood and averted her eyes. She pulled the criminal outfit from her hoodie's front pocket. "Here. Put these on so you can cover that thing up."

"Gladly. But what was with that *little* comment earlier? If you claim to be celibate then how can you judge?"

Kayla smiled. "A woman's intuition."

James laughed. "What does that even mean?! That makes no sense!"

They laughed and joked as they rested in the alleyway. They took shifts at the lookout while the rest of the group slept. They enjoyed their first reprieve in days.

A short distance away, a massive factory was in full operation. There was a small boy working on the assembly line inside the building. He was covered in filth, grime, and he had a dirty mop of unkempt hair. His body was gaunt, and his limbs looked as if they would snap if subjected to a miniscule force. He sobbed as his slight frame trembled. His thin fingers were covered in blood and filled with glass fragments as he tried to manipulate the shards with Earth Craft. Everyone around him created glass products efficiently.

SMACK!

The foreman smacked him in the back of the head.

"Goddammit Gialli! If this is the best you can do then pick your wilted ass up and get the hell out of here!"

The boy put a trembling hand on the back of his skull. His head was caked in blood. His sobs intensified. "Sir...*sniff*...*sniff*...please...I'm doing the best...that...that I can!"

"Shut up, boy! If you can't get any work done like everyone else here then you're fired!"

"But please...sir...this is my twelfth job...this month...I have to help support my...support my family...I..."

"I don't give a damn! This isn't a charity shop!"

On a nearby rooftop, Gray stood overlooking the factory.

He had thick bags under his bloodshot eyes. "Finally, our last stop of the night in this miserable den of thieves." He raised a hand. "Shadow Craft Art 7, Seeking Shadows."

Inside the factory, the foreman saw something shift in the corner of his eye.

"What the...GAAAAAAHAAA!"

SLICE!

Shadows rose from around the factory and swiftly sliced through it.

BOOOOOOOOOOOOOOOOOOOOOOOOOOOOOOOOM!

There was a massive explosion as flames burst through the factory windows. Machines exploded and the people screamed as they fled for their lives.

"Gray squad, engage."

Soldiers leapt through portals in the shadows and rushed the factory from all angles. They burst through the doors and slaughtered the workers.

As James slept, he was tormented by thoughts of his experiences in the capital's slums. He reached out as he tried to save the man who writhed on the ground in front of him, only to watch him convulse until he succumbed. His mind drifted back to his time on the football team and the weary faces of his teammates after their multitude of losses.

His wrath grew as he endured a terrible nightmare. He was chained in darkness, as he watched his teammates approach his head coach one by one. Each player had a smile on their face, and they offered the coach words of gratitude.

"Thank you for giving me a chance! I've been dreaming of this since I was little, coach!". "Football is my life, coach! I'd give anything for this team!". "I've always wanted to play for university! My parents are going to be so proud of me!"

As each one approached the coach, his smile grew wider and wider. Until his eyes glowed green and he grabbed a player by the neck.

"NO! Stop it!" James roared.

The coach choked the life out of each player and watched as their dreams and aspirations flew out of their body and disappeared. James saw visions of office buildings being razed, and visions of his teammates on professional teams being shattered. He watched as dreams of affluent, smiling families were erased and thrown down into the fires below.

"NO! GET AWAY FROM HIM!" James cried out.

The players continued shuffling forward smiling, as each one met their fate.

James bawled as he watched each of his friend's deaths. "PLEASE STOP! YOU DON'T HAVE TO DO THIS! OH MY GOD, PLEASE STOP IT! NO! PLEASE!"

Suddenly, hands appeared in the shadows and gripped James by the neck. He gasped for air as he looked up and saw his position coach smiling down at him.

"You were never that good son." The coach said as he strangled James to death.

James struggled against him until his vision went black and he leapt out of the nightmare. He sat up quickly and grasped his neck as he panted for air.

Kayla ran over. "James! Are you ok? What happened?"

"It's nothing...huff...huff...huff...bad dream..."

She sat next to him and put a hand on his shoulder. "Tell me about it. What happened..."

BOOOOOOOOOOOOOM!

A loud explosion reverberated through the area. Terrance and Epios jolted awake.

"What the hell is going on here!" Terrance said as he leapt up and formed icy axes. Sesame jumped out of his pocket and flexed alongside him.

"What in God's name could possibly be happening at this hour?" Epios moaned.

"It's nothing Kayla. Let's go make sure nobody was hurt in that explosion." James said as he rose to his feet and sprinted toward the sound.

The group followed James, and they stopped as they took in the carnage. Soldiers with uniforms from every tribe were slaughtering civilians and destroying the factory.

"NOBODY GETS TO WAKE UP THE OCEAN KING AND GET AWAY WITH IT!" Terrance bellowed.

"These are the bastards that attacked my island!" Kayla roared.

"And I was finally catching up on my beauty sleep! Such a treasonous act against your future ruler shall not go unpunished!" Epios cried as they raced toward the building.

James cracked his knuckles. "These guys again? Well, I've been looking for a chance to blow off some steam."

17 – The Weakling

GRAY OBSERVED THE CARNAGE FROM A ROOFTOP AND TURNED TO TAKE HIS LEAVE. He sighed in relief. "Just one more assignment. Then I can get some rest until those dimwits finally get their act together."

He stepped off the skyscraper and plunged into the shadows as he disappeared.

※

The factory was massive and there was a large conveyor belt that ran through the center of the first floor. The roof was vaulted and the second story expanded outward into separate sections of the factory. There were several areas of the second story that hovered over the first, and if a person looked over the rails they could see the entire factory operation. Smoke filled the air as massive flames roared throughout the building.

James and his friends rushed inside as carnage ensued around them. There were dozens of soldiers in the uniforms of various nations slaughtering civilians and destroying equipment across the building's two stories.

"Let's split up! Epios and I will take the upper floor! Kayla, Terrance, you take the ground level! Protect the civilians and watch each other's backs! Remember we don't have weapons or armor, so be careful and use the environment to our advantage!" James commanded.

The group stared at him in silence.

Epios squinted at James. "There's no need to shout, fiend. We are standing right next to you."

Kayla clapped. "Okay James! When did you get all assertive?"

"HEY! SINCE WHEN DID I DIE AND MAKE YOU LEADER?! LET ME ANSWER THAT! I DIDN'T, SO SHUT YOUR ASS THE HELL UP!"

James face palmed. "It's not about that! We're here to help keep these people safe. And Kayla, just so you know I've always been assertive so..."

"SHUT THE HELL UP! IT'S TIME FOR THE REAL LEADER TO GIVE HIS SPEECH! AHEM! THIS IS THE PERFECT MOMENT FOR THE OCEAN KING'S FIFTH RULE OF MANHOOD! RULE 5: ALWAYS PROTECT PEOPLE IN NEED! ESPECIALLY IF THEY'RE WOMEN AND CHILDREN! NOW LET'S FOLLOW THAT RULE AND KEEP THESE PEOPLE SAFE!" Terrance roared as Sesame jumped out of his pocket and flexed.

Sesame unleashed a war cry. "MMMMHHHHAAAAA!"

"THAT'S HOW YOU DO IT BUDDY! WAY TO GO!" Terrance said as Sesame jumped up and they high fived.

When Terrance looked up, his friends were walking away in disgust.

"I hate praising the fiend, but his speech was better." Epios scoffed.

"That speech sucked ass." Kayla complained.

"That was literally what I said but in a less succinct way." James grumbled.

James beamed up to the second story and stretched. "Ok! It's been a while since I...WHOA!"

SWIP! SWIP!

James leaned away from two sword slashes from a soldier. The soldier swung left and right, but James easily avoided his attacks.

"Hey! It looks like getting my ass kicked for weeks is finally starting to pay off!"

SMACK! SMACK!

POW!

James swiftly struck the soldier in the wrist and chest, finishing him with a hook across the face, knocking his sword free and sending the soldier staggering backward. James reached and grabbed the sword before it hit the ground.

SLICE! SLICE!

He funneled Spirit Energy into the blade and sent two energy slashes at the soldier that mutilated his chest and sent him over the balcony railing.

James looked down at the sword in his hand. "Man! I'm getting pretty nice!"

"Terry! No!" A soldier near James cried.

"NOOOOO!", "Not Terry!", "He was such a great guy!", "He was my roommate!", "He was supposed to be the best man at my wedding!", "He's the godfather of my kids!", "He was supposed to help me with my taxes this weekend!" A cacophony of soldiers shouted.

Malice gleamed in their eyes as they turned their heads to James in unison.

He glanced over the railing at Terry's body. "Damn...Is it too late for me to apologize?"

"KILL HIM!"

Eight soldiers rushed James from all sides.

"Yeah, no. Gotta go!" James said as he leapt over the edge of the balcony.

The soldiers ran to the railing and looked down into the carnage.

"Where is he?"

"I don't see him any...WHERE!" A soldier shouted as he and three others were sent flying.

CRASH!

James burst through the floor below them and landed in a heroic pose. "I've always wanted to do that! This will be fun!"

The soldiers began their assault. James engaged a foe head on, ducking his first slash and deflecting the second. He slipped past a strike from behind and fired a laser from his finger into the first soldier's side. He spun away from a thrust aimed at his side and he beamed into a nearby cracked window.

ZIP!

SLICE!

He burst forth, cut down a soldier and gave a kung-foo scream. "HUOOOAAA!"

He Mirror Dashed in and out of the window twice more and instantaneously cut down two more soldiers. "HUOOOAAA!", "HUOOOOOOOOAAAAAAAAA!"

The four remaining soldiers stared in confusion.

James spoke in a deep voice as he raised his blade high. "Face me! For I am the chosen one!" Visible heat waves emanated from his body.

CRASH!

A soldier tossed a brick into the cracked window and shattered it.

James stared at the shattered glass. "Shit."

"VENGEANCE FOR TERRY!"

"Yeah, let's not do that."

James dashed forward as the soldiers surrounded him. He charged hard at the soldier directly ahead, but suddenly ducked and attacked the soldier to his right with a hard vertical slash, knocking his sword from his grasp. James cut down the soldier with a downward slash as the remaining three closed in on him. He sprinted away from them toward a shelf made from iron beams. He fired a Photon Beam at the shelf and ducked, as the beam reflected over his head and hit the soldier behind him in the face. He front flipped over a swipe at his legs from a soldier to his left, but as he flipped the other soldier's blade was inches away from coming down on his back. In midair, he swiftly reached out and ripped off a piece of the melted iron beam that he hit with the laser and flung it into the face of the soldier whose blade grazed his skin.

CRASH!

He quickly grabbed the shelf and pulled it down onto his last pursuer and himself. James flipped the shelf off his body but couldn't find his sword. He leapt backward as the last soldier slashed at him ferociously. James leaned left and right as he avoided the vicious assault. He consistently lost ground as the soldier swiftly slashed twice more, slicing James on his side and across his cheek.

James glanced behind him and smiled.

The soldier brought down a strike with lethal force, but James beamed into the window behind him, zoomed out, and socked the soldier in the face as he screamed. "HUOOOAAA!"

The soldier staggered backwards, raised his blade and received another light speed punch to the face with a scream. "HUOOOOAAAAA!"

ZIP! ZIP! ZIP! ZIP!

James zipped into the window seven more times and delivered a savage flurry of blows. "HUOOOAAA!", "HUOOOOOAAA!", "HUOOOOOAAA!", "HUOOOOAAA!", "HUOOOOOAAA!", "HUOOOOOAAA!", "HUOOOOOAAA!"

He beamed in and launched himself out one final time as he delivered a spinning roundhouse kick to the soldier's skull.

POW!

"HUUUUUUUUOOOOOOOOOAAAAAAAA!"

He landed in a kung-fu stance and bowed to his opponent. "You fought well. Terry-Squad-Sama's."

Another nearby soldier looked over at James' naked body bowing over his opponent. He roared into his walkie-talkie. "Terry Squad is down! I repeat! Terry squad is down! Send reinforcements to the upper deck!"

CRASH!

Hooded soldiers glided in and crashed through the broken windows as they surrounded James. They had more advanced equipment, donned cowboy hats, and were in high-tech, black combat suits. James glanced at them with one eye from his bowed stance and smiled. He leapt into the air and assumed another kung-fu stance.

"You seek vengeance for Terry-Squad-Sama?! Fine then, face me! It is me! I shall be your opponent!"

I am having way too much fun with this.

Two soldiers looked at each other in confusion.

"Is this perverted kid being serious right now?"

"I don't know. I hate perverts. Let's just kill him."

James' eyes widened as the soldiers aimed pistols at his head.

Epios zipped up to the factory's second deck. He was completely unmoved by the civilians being slaughtered around him as he casually surveyed the carnage below. "Hmm, not having a blade could be quite problematic. And I am still *quite* drowsy. What to do..."

SLICE!

A soldier slashed him in the back. Epios had a large, gaping wound, but he was stiller than a statue. He turned and looked at the man with pure hatred in his eyes. His pupils had a crimson, flaming hue.

Epios stared at the soldier with a face filled with rage and condescension. "*Tell me*...what is the purpose of this attack on the factory?"

The soldier felt his malice and backed away. "T...to cripple the nation's economy s...sir."

"*Tell me*...Why is this operation being conducted at such an hour when royals like myself are likely to be sleeping?"

"Uhh? I think that's the point sir. We gotta make sure nobody sees us and lower our chances of getting caught."

Another soldier ran toward them. "Why are you talking with him?! This guy is our primary target!"

"Oh really? This guy? I thought he would be tougher looking or at least more muscular..."

"It appears that you are aware of my identity. *Now tell me*...what is the penalty for interrupting a king's slumber and then assaulting him as he attempts to assess a critical situation?"

"Uhh, I really don't know...I doubt that it's really ever happened before..."

"Kyle! Stop talking and capture him!"

"*I see*...Allow me to educate you."

GUSH!

Epios swiftly blasted them both in the heart with twin laser beams from his hands. He picked up their swords and tossed them in his palms as a group of soldiers surrounded him.

A soldier shouted into a walkie-talkie. "Gray! We've found the target! He will be captured and processed shortly!"

Gray spoke back through the device. "*They're* here? Perfect! He should be easy to capture. Father will probably give us a bonus for a haul like this."

Epios raised his blades. "Allow me to teach you what happens when you interrupt a prince's beauty sleep."

GUSH!

Epios rushed the nearest guard and viscously cut him down with both blades before he could react. He charged, deflected a soldier's strike with his right and cut him down with his left. He deflected a slash with his off hand and sliced the soldier in the neck. Two soldiers attacked and he leapt over their slashes, slicing off both of their necks at once. He casually pointed a finger and fired a laser beam that ricocheted off several reflective surfaces and pierced through seven soldiers surrounding him.

Several dozen soldiers approached but hesitated when they saw the multitude of bodies on the ground.

"Kenneth! I thought this guy was supposed to be weak!"

A soldier pulled out a manilla folder "It says right here he's an average fighter at best!"

Epios spat at their feet. "If I am as weak as they say then come over here and show me!"

They swarmed him with attacks, but he dodged every blow with ease as he swiftly cut them down. His technique was masterful, as he either ducked or parried every strike and massacred the mob of soldiers in a swift succession.

"This..."

SLICE!

"...is what happens..."

SLICE!

"...when you interrupt..."

SLICE!

"...my..."

SLICE!

"...BEAUTY SLEEP!"

SLICE!

He was drenched in blood as he looked down at the dozens of bodies surrounding him. He shook his head. "It's a shame you were not able to collect your bonuses today. But the penalty for treason is death."

Kayla and Terrance gave each other dirty looks.

WHOOSH!

They sprinted in opposite directions on the ground floor. Kayla stared at the carnage around her. *I don't have the wooden part of my daggers so I can't channel my Spirit Energy into them like normal.* She concentrated her energy and daggers made of pure flame formed in her hands. *This is so hard to control, but it will have to do.*

A soldier saw her sprinting toward him, and he raised his blade.

She calmly inhaled. "Flame Craft, Art 4..."

He pressed a button on his walkie talkie as he prepared for battle. "Gray! Come in, Gray! The Flame Tribe princess and her friends are...GAAAHHHAAA!"

GUSH!

She leapt and drove her daggers into his eyes as she used her momentum to knock him down.

"Who's there? Come in! Where is the princess…"

SMASH!

Kayla stepped on the walkie-talkie, crushing it to pieces. Nearby soldiers heard the scream and stared. She was drenched in sweat and heat waves emanated from her body.

"It's the Flame Tribe princess!". "Is she a target?". "I don't know!". "Isn't Gray in love with her or something?". "I don't know!" "Should we capture her?". "I think so!" The soldiers clamored.

FWOOSH!

She blitzed them faster than the eye could see.

SLICE! SLICE!

She swiftly leapt left and right as she slashed 2 opponents across the face. The soldiers snapped out of their stupor and charged her.

GUSH!

She sprinted forward and tossed her dagger into the face of the soldier leading their charge. She forcefully pulled her hand backward and the dagger in his face dragged him forward. She sprinted, grabbed the lodged dagger, and used her momentum to swing his body upward and smash it into the soldiers behind him.

SLICE!

She leapt up twice more, slitting the throats of two foes. A soldier brought his blade down above her, but she swung upwards with her right dagger and the flames burst forth and tore a deep gash across his torso. She swung downwards with her left dagger and the flames raged out, ripping through his body and mutilating the two soldiers behind him.

She looked around and saw several soldiers attacking civilians across the factory. She raised her palms and fiery, winged serpents rose from the flames across the first floor. They swayed from left to right as they rose out of the smoke. She pressed her hands together and the serpents raged across the factory, devouring every enemy in sight.

More soldiers piled in from an opening about 30 yards in ahead of her. They sprinted at her, and she remained still as they approached.

She calmly took a deep breath and exhaled white-hot steam. "This is for my people. Flame Craft Art 4, Graceful Flame Tempo!"

She sprinted toward the soldiers, and her steps became gallops as she bounded from left to right.

WHOOSH!

She vanished from sight in a burst of flames.

SLICE!

She reappeared to the right of the nearest soldier and viciously tore through him.

SLICE, SLASH, SLICE, SLASH, SLICE, SLASH, SLICE!

She instantaneously vanished and reappeared next to each of the soldiers in the group, swiftly devastating them before they could react. She materialized in a crouch behind the last soldier.

SNAP!

The soldier's bodies exploded.

FWOOOOOOOOOOOOOOOOOSH!

Flames burst forth from every extremity as their limbs were blown off and they crumpled into the sand.

Terrance stomped away from the large door the group entered from.

He grumbled. "How dare they say that simp's speech was better than mine! He didn't say anything that great. I'll show them!" He flexed. "Alright, Sesame! It's time to show our underlings how a real man gets shit done! Are you ready?!"

Sesame leapt out of his pocket and with a determined expression as he assumed a battle stance.

"Excellent! Let's put on a fucking clinic!"

A soldier cornered a woman holding a child in the corner of the factory. He raised his blade over their heads.

"MMMMMMHHHHAAAAAAA!" Sesame roared.

The soldier turned around.

"Hey! What the hell are you picking on them for? Bullying women and children is for simps! Come fight *me* if you're a real man!" Terrance shouted.

The soldier trembled with rage. "I'll show you a real man you little punk!"

The soldier charged and Terrance formed an icy ax in his hand.

CLANG!

He swung the ax, but it shattered in his grasp as it made contact with the soldier's blade.

What the hell? Why is it so weak?

SLICE! SLICE! SLICE!

The soldier sliced him across the neck and chest before following it up with two more slashes that mutilated Terrance.

GUSH!

He thrust the blade into Terrance's gut and his head slumped as he fell to his knees.

"Stupid kid." The soldier said as he went to remove his blade.

The blade refused to budge.

Terrance lifted his head.

The deep gash across his face was replaced by a sadistic grin.

"My turn."

WHOOSH!

POW!

Terrance snapped the blade in his stomach with an open palm, swept the soldier's feet from under him with a sliding kick, leapt up, and pounded the soldier's face with a devastating punch in midair.

Terrance flexed his abs and the blade popped out of his stomach. "At least Depth Command still works."

The soldier on the ground held his face as he writhed in agony. He reached down and pressed a red button attached to his walkie-talkie. Soldiers in the immediate area stopped, rushed over, and surrounded Terrance.

Terrance looked down at the soldier and shook his head. "Such a weak move. Real men handle their issues one on one!"

The soldier cried out as Sesame violently kicked him in the skull. "GAUAHAGHA!"

Terrance cracked his knuckles. "But fine. I'll teach every one of you a lesson about manhood. Anyone can learn from an ass kicking!"

He formed frozen axes in his hands. *My Ocean Craft must be weaker because of the dry air and these flames all over the place...*

A soldier swiftly ran up and slashed him across the chest.

SWIP!

Terrance sliced his head clean off. Another soldier sliced him in the back.

SLICE!

Terrance effortlessly spun and decapitated him in one smooth vertical slice. The heads flew and bounced on the ground at the feet of a soldier in the circle. The soldiers stared at the heads in shock.

Terrance smirked. "No problem! I'll just have to make my strikes one shot, one kill!"

The soldiers rushed him from all angles. Terrance received a multitude of slashes, but he endured their attacks and swiftly responded with lethal blows. He quickly rampaged through the swarm of soldiers until none were left standing.

As Terrance's wounds healed his stomach growled fiercely.

GROOOOOOOOOOOOOAAAAAAAN!

Sesame looked up at him with a concerned expression.

Damn! I'm starving. I forgot that I haven't eaten today. If I don't throw down on something soon, I won't be able to regenerate any...

BANG!

Terrance's head exploded as he was blasted by a gunshot.

He crumpled to his knees and slumped into the dirt.

Soldiers in black hoods zipped down from the upper deck and surrounded him. Lights were attached to their pistols, and they aimed at Terrance's limp body lying in the sand.

"Is he dead?", "I'm not sure.", "Let's make sure the job is finished!"

BANG! BANG! BANG! BANG! BANG! BANG! BANG!

They opened fire and filled his body with holes until only a bloody, gory mess remained.

A soldier nodded at the others. "That's one down. Let's finish off the others and..."

"MMMMMMHHHHAAAAAAA!" Sesame roared as he tried to shake Terrance's body. Tears fell from Sesame's eyes as he desperately pulled on Terrance's shorts.

They swiftly turned and aimed at Sesame.

"Is that a fucking mammoth?". "Where did it come from?". "Should we eliminate it?"

The soldiers trained their guns on Terrance as he stirred. *I have to...protect...him...*

FWOOSH!

Blue energy burst from his wounds as they rapidly healed, and his head regenerated. Mist poured out of small cracks spreading across his body as tendrils of blue energy zipped off his flesh. The soldiers opened fire and Terrance's flesh exploded.

BANG! BANG! BANG! BANG! BANG! BANG! BANG!

As the bullets tore into Terrance, his flesh morphed as each wound instantly regenerated.

BANG! BANG! BANG! BANG! BANG! BANG! BANG!

He slowly rose to his feet amidst the gunfire with a wild smile.

CLICK! CLICK! CLICK! CLICK! CLICK! CLICK! CLICK!

The soldiers pulled their triggers, but no bullets came out.

Terrance picked up Sesame and smiled. "It's alright buddy. You don't have to worry. I'll be just fine." He stared at the soldiers with rage in his eyes. "These guys on the other hand..."

The soldiers reloaded and kept their guns trained on Terrance. "How is this possible?!", "We just killed that son of a bitch!", "Sergeant, how should we proceed?!"

Frozen axes materialized in Terrance's hands. "Man. What a pussy move. Bringing guns to an ax fight."

"Men, if guns alone won't put this bastard down, then he must be a spirit! If that's the case, we'll have to use Shadow Craft to make sure he says down! Engage Split Offensive Position!"

Half the soldiers vanished into the shadows and reappeared on the second level. They equipped heavy rifles strapped across their backs. The soldiers on the ground floor holstered their pistols and demagnetized swords attached to their hips. The blades radiated dark energy as they raised them against Terrance.

"We will not allow a single child to threaten this operation's success. Lawbringer Squad 3, ENGAGE!"

Terrance smiled with a wild glint in his eyes. "I'm a grown ass man. Bitch."

BANG! BANG! BANG! BANG! BANG!

The upper deck soldiers opened fire, but Terrance effortlessly torqued to avoid their shots. His mind was in a daze as he observed the foes around him. *Everything seems to be moving slower now for some reason...*

BANG! BANG!

GUSH!

As shots rang out around him, he contorted to avoid a sword slash and instantaneously removed the head of an attacking soldier, sending a spray of blood everywhere. He instantaneously reacted to avoid gunfire as two more soldiers engaged him.

CLANG!

GUSH!

Terrance met the first soldier's slash with his own, but his ax shattered as the other soldier impaled his back. The blade's dark energy raged and Terrance roared as it seared his flesh.

Time seemed to stop as pain flooded his veins.

His nervous system was in overdrive as his calm mind steadied. Terrance looked down at his broken ax on the ground and saw that it had almost completely evaporated. *Hmm, I wonder if that would work.*

SLICE!

He twisted his torso and instantly decapitated the soldier who sliced him in the back. He swiftly turned and tossed his ax at the soldier ahead of him and impaled his skull.

BANG! BANG!

Two shots rang out and his chest exploded, but his flesh regenerated as more cracks spread across his body. He charged at the remaining soldiers as he ducked and dodged rifle fire. Terrance slashed at a foe, but the his blade shattered as he was sliced across the chest and liquid from the ax soaked the soldier. While impaled, Terrance tossed another ax at a nearby soldier who was keeping his distance, but the soldier sliced it and was soaked in water.

BANG! BANG! BANG!

Three shots destroyed Terrance's back, but he snapped the blade in his chest, spun, and slung seven axes at the soldiers on the upper deck.

BANG!

The axes were inches away from the upper deck soldier's faces as they fired and were soaked with water. They swiftly ceased fire to wipe the blinding water from their face masks. Terrance rushed the remaining soldiers on the ground floor. He swung at an enemy and his ax shattered, soaking the soldier as Terrance was sliced through the gut. Another soldier swung at Terrance and Terrance met his blade, but his ax shattered, soaking the soldier as he sliced off Terrance's right arm. Terrance raised his left arm to deflect another slash, his ax shattered, the soldier was soaked, and Terrance's arm was severed from his body.

GUSH!

Terrance was pierced through the back, and he crumpled to his knees as the soldier with the blade in his gut looked down on him. The soldiers in the upper deck aimed their rifles and there was a moment of silence.

The soldier spoke smugly. "You fought well..." He smirked. "For a *child* that is."

Terrance's voice trembled as cracks fully covered his face. "I told you...I'm a grown ass man. Bitch..."

Suddenly, the water covering the soldiers glowed with a blue aura.

BOOOOOOOOOOOOOOOOOOOOOOOOOOOOOM!

The combined explosion was massive and blue energy burst through the factory's openings and decimated nearby buildings. The eruption of Spirit Energy could be seen for miles as it illuminated the night sky.

A figure with curved blades stood on a nearby building as he observed the lightshow. "Hmph. Not bad. Looks like that bastard has still got it."

Terrance sat on his knees with a blank expression as azure mist settled across the factory floor. His body was entirely covered in cracks as blue steam poured from every crevice. Sesame leapt out of his shorts and stared at him in awe. He raised his hand and Terrance weakly high fived him.

Terrance smiled. "You're right buddy...It looks like we did it."

In an unknown location, Gray's mother observed the world through a wall of shadowy monitors. She watched as James faced off against hooded soldiers on the factory's second story. James was surrounded by armed foes as two looked at each other in confusion.

"Toby, is this perverted kid being serious right now?"

"I don't know Larry. I hate perverts. Let's just kill him."

The soldiers aimed at James' head.

"Light Craft, Art 8, Reflect!"

Transparent walls of light surrounded James.

BANG! BANG! BANG! BANG! BANG! BANG! BANG!

The bullets contacted the barriers, and bounced off, reflecting with greater force and speed back toward the soldiers who shot them.

GUSH!

The soldiers in the circle collapsed simultaneously.

James bowed in the circle's center.

Gray's mother watched with an annoyed expression as the rest of James' group massacred the soldiers. The explosion at the factory appeared on several of her screens.

CRASH!

She shattered a monitor in anger. "That boy can't seem to do anything right! Even Jedediah's troops have failed! It looks like I will have to step in and make sure this *routine* operation is handled."

Back at the factory, after James deflected the bullets and defeated the hooded soldiers, he bowed.

He spoke in a deep voice. "You fought well. It is a shame when a man is defeated by his own hand."

Suddenly, a blue wave of energy exploded through the building, knocking him from his feet. He looked down at his body and saw that he was unscathed. "The hell was that?"

"It appears you have survived fiend." Epios said as he rounded a corner holding two blades in his hands. He was wearing a light craft suit that he pilfered from one of his victims.

James noticed Epios' blood-soaked body. He smiled playfully. "*Shoot*, I should be the one saying that to you! I'm surprised you made it this long Charmin!"

"You will explain this Charmin insult to me at once!"

On the ground floor, Kayla picked herself up after being thrown from her feet by the explosion. Several soldiers and civilians across the factory had been knocked unconscious. She saw Terrance's cracked body as he knelt on the ground and ran over to him.

"What happened to you, *boss man?*" She said sarcastically.

He slowly turned his head as dust fell from the cracks in his body. "I'm...not...in...the mood..."

Sesame growled as she rolled her eyes. "*Please*, what could you possibly do to me you little punk. You're just as bad as he is."

Suddenly, spirits formed in the shadows surrounding the factory.

RMBLRMBLRMBLRMBLR!

The earth trembled as the dark figures covering every grain of sand sprinted inside the factory. In the center of the mob, a tall spirit resembling a woman strutted confidently through the masses. Civilians heard the spirit's detestable cries, and ran for their lives. The soldiers' hearts were filled with fear as they abandoned their mission and sought any means of escape. The spirits violently slaughtered and devoured anyone in their sight. Kayla felt the ground rumble as she saw the spirits approaching.

"Oh shit!" She said as she grabbed Terrance and leapt up to the second floor.

She landed on a platform across from James and Epios. She laid Terrance down against a wall and he passed out

Epios tapped his head. "I see...so Charmin is a waste product that is used to..."

"What the hell are you two talking about?!" Kayla roared. She looked upon James' naked body and averted her eyes. "AND JAMES! WHY ARE YOU NAKED AGAIN?"

James was filled with embarrassment as he covered his privates. "It happened while I was fighting! I don't do this on purpose! And besides, why does it bother you so much if you..."

She pointed to the lower floor. "Never mind that! We have much more important problems right now!"

Wrath spirits swarmed up the stairs. In their center was a Lust spirit. The spirit appeared to the men as a tall naked woman who was the pinnacle of beauty and female form. She was voluptuous, and she stared at the boys with a seductive, hungry gaze. They looked upon her and their stomachs were instantly filled with primal attraction.

"Who in the world is that..." James asked in a daze.

"I have no clue. But she must be mine." Epios said with a mind full of haze.

Kayla watched them and rolled her eyes in disgust. "So disgusting. Stupid apes."

She looked upon the Lust spirit and saw a devilishly handsome, naked young man. Primal attraction instantly flooded her entire body, and she pressed her legs together as she wiggled in joy. She squealed in a feminine, high-pitched voice. "SQUEEEEE! Oh my God! Who is that beautiful man, I need him!"

James and Epios stared at her with disgust.

James glared. "I've never heard her make *that* sound before."

"And I thought we were supposed to be the dumb apes." Epios said.

James shook his head. "Isn't she the same one who said she hated men?"

Epios scoffed. "*Indeed*, and on numerous occasions. She continues to prove herself to be nothing more than a *skanch* and a *whore* in my eyes."

The Lust spirit rose to the second story on a stairwell created by the Wrath spirits. It walked across their piled bodies as it stepped down onto the platform.

It spoke seductively. "Hello there boys."

(Kayla heard. "Hello there beautiful.")

James was starstruck. "Hey there..."

Drool fell from Epios' mouth. "Marry me! Become my glorious queen!"

Kayla stammered in a submissive tone. "H...hi...hi

The Spirit waved playfully. "Would you boys like to do me a favor?"

(Kayla heard. "Can I ask you to help me with something sweetheart?")

"OF COURSE! I'D DO ANYTHING FOR YOU!" James roared.

"I WOULD SELL MY KINGDOM FOR YOU!" Epios shouted.

"YES! JUST TELL ME WHAT YOU NEED HANDSOME!" Kayla said in a high pitched voice.

The Lust spirit gave a seductive wink. "Great! Just sit still for me while these Wrath spirits devour you ok!"

"Sure!"

"Absolutely!"

"Of course, I'll get right on that for you honey!"

"**WAIT WHAT**?!" They declared in unison.

They snapped to their senses and were surrounded by a horde of Wrath spirits. The spirits surrounded them in separate circles, isolating them from each other. Kayla raised her flaming daggers as she backed against a wall to defend Terrance's sleeping body.

"These little ones might not be enough, so I'll let some of my other associates soften you up first." The Lust spirit said.

The crowd of spirits parted and a dark spirit wearing a mask stepped into James' circle. A spirit in a fancy suit strode through the crowd and counted money as it entered Epios' circle. A large, obese spirit rolled on its side through the crowd and entered Kayla's circle.

"The time has come for me to reveal your truth." The masked spirit said.

"Bring it on!" James barked as he raised his blade.

The suited spirit extended its hand. "It's a shame that you are standing between me and what I want, but it cannot be helped. Oh well. What's mine is mine. I'll be taking this kingdom from you now."

Epios raised his blades. "You have no claim to the throne, *spirit*. Allow me to make the difference between us quite apparent."

The obese spirit reclined and closed its eyes. "UGGGHH! Killing people is so much WORK! I'll just let these angry guys kill you and I'll eat whatever's left."

Kayla's daggers blazed. "You remind me of my brother, you fat bastard! And I *hate* my brother!"

The Lust spirit longingly glanced out the window. "Dispose of them so we can be on our way. There is an entire city out there that I am just *yearning* to share my love with."

✦

The battles began simultaneously. Epios faced off against the well-dressed spirit. The spirit's cocky grin filled Epios with rage. His mind flashed back to his encounter with the cowboy. "*Aww, the little prince saw his friends get iced and now he's too much of a spring chicken to step up to the plate. Yer a lily-livered coward, boy.*"

Epios spoke with a determined expression. "Today is the day of redemption."

He charged and the spirit casually side-stepped his first slice. It grabbed the blade in Epios' off hand with its bare palm. "Shabby craftsmanship, but *I'll* be taking this."

BLINK!

Epios' blade vanished.

He leapt back, swung his arm, and fired three Photon Beams at the spirit.

The spirit sighed. "They're garbage, but I guess I can take these as well."

BLINK!

The spirit swiftly grabbed the beams and they disappeared.

I see. Apparently, this spirit can take whatever it touches into its possession. Let's see what his limit is.

Epios slashed a nearby Wrath spirit, grabbed it, and slung it at the spirit.

The spirit pouted. "More junk, but I guess I'll take it." It touched the Wrath spirit and it vanished. The spirit covered its eyes. "Please stop giving me junk and..."

Epios was ducked behind the Wrath spirit.

SLICE!

He ripped his blade across his enemy's torso.

SNATCH!

Before Epios could react the spirit grabbed his chest and lifted him from his feet.

It shook its head. "That's not very businesslike."

The spirit clutched Epios' chest and he roared in pain. "AAAAAAARGHAA!"

Dark energy enveloped the spirit's hand and it tossed Epios to the ground. The spirit's wound regenerated and there was a gaping, bloody hole where it had grabbed Epios.

It dusted off its suit. "*There.* I had to take a bit of your lifeforce to become whole again after you attacked me. Let that be a warning for attempting foul play."

Epios was dazed and his vision was blurry. He struggled to his feet but his legs warbled and he collapsed to the ground. *Dammit, the fatigue from starvation is starting to affect me. On top of that, who knows how much of my life energy he just stole. This may not be a fight that I can win through sheer force.*

Epios slowly staggered to his feet. "Tell me. Who exactly are you, spirit?"

"Finally! It's about time you asked me for my name! I can tell you'd make a lousy business partner! You are terrible at negotiations!" The spirit bowed. "I am an Envy spirit. *The* Envy spirit of the Earth Tribe to be specific. It is a pleasure to make your acquaintance, crown prince of the Union of Tribal Nations."

Epios bowed in response. "Finally, *someone* with manners. Tell me. What exactly is it that you desire, Envy spirit of the Earth Tribe."

"It's simple! I'm here to strike a deal and take you for everything you've got! You've noticed these guys haven't laid a finger on you, haven't you?"

Epios glanced around at the Wrath spirits. The mob of savage brutes were salivating; eyeing him with feral hunger as they maintained a circle around them.

"Alright then. What kind of deal do you propose?"

"First, I think we should both discuss what it is we want. Then we can talk about what we are willing to trade to acquire it." The spirit spread its arms wide. "I want the entire world. Every blade of grass and every speck of sand. I want to collect every last thing that has ever existed for myself, and I will stop at nothing to have it all." It greedily glanced at Epios. "What is it that you desire, *crown prince?*"

What should I tell it? If I give a humble answer, that may anger it, and I'm not in a position to face him currently. If I give a vain response, he is likely to grow even stronger. What should I do? What can I say? Epios glanced at the tear in the spirit's suit. "*It was quick to heal itself after I hurt it earlier. It may not have as much durability as other spirits. I need to catch it in a lull during our negotiations and find a moment to finish it in one decisive blow.* Epios eyed the salivating Wrath spirits. *Though I cannot say I know what will happen after I dispose of this fiendish* **bastard.** *I am entirely out leveraged. What exactly does it think I have to offer it that it cannot acquire on his own?*

"I want this kingdom! I want to sit on the throne and become the most benevolent ruler this nation has ever seen!" Epios boldly declared.

The spirit grew larger, and its biceps stretched its suit at its seams. "Excellent! I love aspirations of grandeur! It's my turn again so let me tell you! I want women! I want money, sex, POWER! I NEED EVERYTHING THAT THIS WORLD HAS TO OFFER!"

Epios shivered.

The spirit eyed him with admiration and hunger. "I can sense that you were raised in affluence, yet that despite that, you have been deprived of the things you truly desired! Ah yes! I can feel it! There's one woman you want in particular! Tell me! What else is it you desire *Epios?*"

Epios grimaced. *Dammit! I may have had a moment to strike while he was going on and on spouting nonsense. Now it has grown even more powerful. Are there any mirrors or reflections I can use to make my advance?* Epios subtly shifted his eyes toward the gleaming moonlight beneath his feet.

He smiled. "I desire nothing more, spirit. The kingdom is all I want."

The spirit's grin faded as it shrunk back to its normal height. "Oh come on! There has to be more! No! No! No! No! No! No! This can't be right! You must want more than that!"

Epios shrugged as he subtly placed his hand on his blade. "It's true! That is all I..."

WHOOSH!

The spirit was directly in Epios' face. "You're a liar. Let's have a looksy!"

The spirit grabbed Epios by the head with both hands and placed two fingers on his temples. Epios' consciousness retracted into his mind as the spirit's voice rattled within his skull. "What do you desire. Who are you envious of...*Crown Prince.*"

In his mind, Epios stood at the front of a classroom in the academy with Milliard.

"Just a 90 Epios? That must suck! I got a 100 on the exam and I didn't even study!" Milliard said as the other students pointed and laughed in Epios' face.

Epios teared up and trembled with rage. "I hate you, you muscle bound..."

The Envy spirit's voice boomed in his mind. "Good! Show me more!"

Epios was whisked away, and he stood in his father's throne room. The king patted Akri on the head and hugged him tightly. "This is an *excellent* invention my son. Without you, our nation would be nothing."

The king glared at Epios as he pulled Akri closer. "Epios! Get out of here! Get back to your studies! I don't want to see you again until you can wield the Kai Fos!"

"Father, I've been giving it my all and..."

"Not, good, enough. Leave my sight."

Tears filled his eyes and Epios crumpled to his knees as the vision vanished.

"That's just more of the same. Show me more." The Envy spirit said.

Epios found himself in the dirt at the academy's training grounds. He was bruised and battered as he looked up at Milliard. The sun shone behind Milliard's face and illuminated his handsome features.

He pointed and laughed in Epios' face. "Oops! Sorry if I went too rough on you little bro! This must suck for you! What's our record now? 21000-0? *Damn* you're weak!"

Epios glanced at the sword on the ground. "I'll kill you! I'll kill you if it's the last thing I ever..."

Laura walked into the fighting circle. "Wow Epios, are you ever going to get it together?"

His heart sank. "Laura! I promise I will get better...I..."

"All I hear is 'I'll do this' or 'I'll get better at that'. Or 'I'm going to be king one day'." She rolled her eyes. "Fat chance. Are you really delusional enough to believe something stupid like that?" She leaned against Milliard.

"Can't you even muster up the strength to beat Milliard, *one* time?"

"Laura...I..."

"No? Didn't think so. That's why I'm with *him* and *not* you."

Laura put her hand on Milliard's chest and kissed him.

Epios' heart shattered.

They kissed passionately as they exchanged tongues and spit dripped from their lips.

She glared at Epios in disgust. "Quit ogling us you freak! And by the way. I *never* loved you." She turned back to Milliard. "I could barely even stand you."

Epios' body grew numb as his soul was plunged into despair

"Yes! Yes! That's the stuff! But show me more! MORE!" The Envy spirit cackled.

Epios bawled his eyes out as he was whisked away to the Ocean Tribe. He watched James and Brooklyn's kiss, and rage filled his heart.

James smiled as Brooklyn stared at him in adoration. "And that's how I became so smart and sociable and popular and handsome! I'm a natural at everything! Just like Milliard! I barely even have to put in effort to be better than Epios! And I just got here!"

Epios trembled as he grasped around and found his sword. "FIEND! I SWEAR TO YOU I..."

"SHHH!"

Epios looked up and saw Brooklyn with a finger to her lips. "Quiet down white-boy. Can't you see we're talking here?"

Brooklyn grabbed James' head and passionately made out with him.

"JAAAAMEEES!" Epios raged.

"YES! I think I get the picture now! But what were you planning on doing about all of this?" The Envy spirit said.

Epios found himself standing outside the Prism Palace within a massive crowd. He looked up and saw Basilas placing a crown on Milliard's head.

"Your next ruler! King Milliard Iliaktida!" Basilas exclaimed.

Epios sprinted toward them with his sword. "NOOOOOO! THE THRONE WAS SUPPOSED TO BE MINE! I REUNITED THIS COUNTRY WHILE HE SAT ON HIS ASS IN THE PALACE! NOT HIM!" He stopped and pointed to the sun. "YOU SEE! THE SUMMER IS NOT OVER YET! THERE IS STILL TIME! AS LONG AS WE MAKE IT BACK BEFORE AUGUST, I CAN CONTEST THIS AND MAKE MY APPEAL TO BECOME KING! I'M THE ONE WHO SAVED THIS COUNTRY! I AM YOUR RULER!"

Milliard walked over and put his hand on Epios' shoulder. He gripped Epios' hair and lifted him from his feet. "Silly brother. Did you really think that was going to work? You rushed your friends all summer, and deprived them of fun and memories because of *this*? I wish I could be as envious as you are...but I just can't." He dropped Epios and patted him on the head. "Sorry little bro it looks like you'll just have to wait your turn..."

"Mirror Dash!"

SLICE!

Outside the dream, Epios beamed into his reflection in the floor, and he rocketed out, piercing the spirit in the heart.

"GAAAAAHAAAA!"

Inside the dream, Epios stabbed Milliard in the heart.

"Sorry brother, but this is one battle you will *not* win."

Epios' mind returned to reality as he stared into the spirit's frenzied eyes. It desperately clawed and scratched his face. A black liquid dripped from its mouth as its eyes darted around, desperately searching for a means of escape.

"NO! I CAN'T LOSE IT ALL! NOT LIKE THIS!"

Epios funneled Spirit Energy into the blade and it burst out, burning the spirit from the inside as it writhed in agony.

"GAAAAAHAAAAAAAAAAA!"

"Do not attempt to negotiate with a king when he's angry, *foolish spirit*..."

Suddenly, the Lust spirit loomed over Epios. "Those were some interesting desires of yours. But I would like to see more."

She kissed Epios and his mind faded away as his consciousness descended into darkness.

"Show me more. Give me *all* of it. Show me who you lust after." She said erotically as Epios passed out.

Epios' mind drifted into his fantasies. He held hands with Laura as they walked through the capital. He brought her to dinner to meet his parents. He kissed her passionately under a fireworks show in the capital. They made love in the dorm room under the cover of night. He proposed to her on the night of his coronation as king. They were married and enjoyed a honeymoon trip to the dragon isles. They raised three strong young boys who were incredibly handsome. They watched their children get married and cried in the audience together. They grew old together in rocking chairs as they sat out on the palace balcony.

The Lust spirit's voice rang out in his mind. "I see! These are wonderful desires. *Lustful* desires. You *crave* her. You *want* her. You desire to make every part of her known to you with every fiber of your *being*." The Lust spirit nodded. "She's a beautiful girl and you two would go well together...wait? What is this?"

Epios's mind flashed back to the day Milliard was crowned Archigos. He sat in the crowd and sneered as the ceremony came to a close.

His father beamed. "And now we have a special announcement."

Epios scoffed. *What more could there **possibly** be. Let me guess. He's impregnated a woman and is to be with child as well?*

Milliard's hands trembled as a bead of sweat rolled down his forehead. "Laura. Would you come to the stage please?"

Epios raised an eyebrow. *That brute is never unsure of himself. What could possibly...no...*

She reached the stage, and she smiled radiantly as her cheeks gushed with color.

NO! NO! NO!

"Laura. The time that I've had the privilege of getting to know you over these past few years have truly been the best moments of my life..."

*HE CAN'T! HE CAN'T DO THIS TO ME! HE KNOWS THAT I LOVE HER! I'VE **ALWAYS** LOVED HER!*

Milliard knelt and opened a small case housing a beautiful diamond ring. "Would you do me the honor of..."

"OH MY GOD YES!"

NOOOOOOOOOOOOOOOOOOOOOOOOOOOOOOOO!

Epios blinked and he was backstage after the ceremony ended. He stomped through the palace, fuming as he searched for Laura. He finally found her showing off the ring to her friends.

His voice trembled. "Laura. Can I speak with you for a moment?"

"Sure, Epios. What's wrong?"

"Come with me." He grabbed her hand and pulled her over to a secluded balcony.

She gave him a concerned look as he stared into her eyes with feral desperation. "You can't possibly be going through with this, right?"

"Epios what do you mean? Of course..."

The damn restraining his emotions shattered.

"YOU CAN'T MARRY HIM BECAUSE I LOVE YOU LAURA! I'VE ALWAYS LOVED YOU SINCE WE WERE LITTLE! I AM OUR NATION'S DESTINED FUTURE RULER! YOUR FATHER IS THE LEADER OF THE NATION'S COUNCIL! WE ARE TO BE TOGETHER BY DESIGN!"

"Epios. Why are you telling me this right now? You saw that I just..."

Tears streamed down his face. "IT'S NOT FAIR! HE'S SO SELFISH! AND YOU! YOU'RE SELFISH! HOW COULD YOU DO THIS TO ME..."

"Epios you're scaring me. I..."

He bawled as he fell to his knees and clutched his chest. "YOU KNEW THAT I LOVED YOU AND YOU STILL CHOSE HIM! YOU'VE RUINED ME! I HATE YOU! I HATE YOU BOTH! YOU'RE SO SELFISH THAT IT HURTS!"

Laura stared at him and a tear rolled down her face.

"Epios...I'm going to give you some time to yourself. I love him and I am going to marry him. You're the one who's selfish for springing this on me like that." She said as she walked past him.

"Laura. Please don't go." He sobbed.

She stopped in the doorway. "I promise I won't tell him you did this, and we will *never* speak of this again. I at least owe you that much for being such a great friend to me all these years."

She left the balcony as Epios bawled his eyes out for the rest of the evening.

The Lust spirit applauded as she held his captive mind. "I commend you! Your desire is pure!" It hesitated. "But what is this sorrow you feel toward her..."

A vision of her tombstone flashed into his mind. He found himself standing on the palace balcony reaching out to her with all his strength as she hovered over the edge.

The distance between them was too great.

She faded away and dissipated into the wind.

FWOOOOOOOOSH!

Outside of Epios' mind, the Lust and Envy spirits stood together a few feet away in shock as Epios broke free from their control. His body was ablaze with a crimson fire that incinerated nearby Wrath spirits.

"What kind of power is this?" The Lust spirit said.

PUFF!

The fire faded as he fell to his hands and knees.

BANG! BANG! BANG! BANG! BANG!

He pounded dents into the iron floor as he bawled his eyes out. "LAURA NO! PLEASE DON'T LEAVE ME! YOU CAN'T DO THIS!"

The spirits stared at him in disgust.

He sobbed. "WE WERE SUPPOSED TO BE TOGETHER! YOU WERE SUPPOSED TO LEAVE HIM AND BE WITH ME LAURA! PLEASE DON'T GO! WE WERE SUPPOSED TO BE TOGETHER FOREVER..."

"How truly lustful!" The Lust spirit shouted.

The Envy spirit mourned. "And how truly *selfish*. His greed rivals even my own..."

"Let's finish up here. This is the one mother wants, so we need to take him back with us after we break him. We still have to make sure the others are handling their food." The Lust spirit said gleefully.

Inside of Epios' mind, the spirit's voices rang out in unison. **"I see what's going on here. The person you lust after most is your brother's fiancé. A dead girl."**

"NO!" Epios screamed.

"And you desire her greatly, even though she *never even loved you*."

"NO! DON'T SAY THAT!"

"And deep down you knew she would never desire you. But you still pursued her anyway! Even though she was engaged! Such lust is incredible!"

"WHY WOULD YOU SAY THAT?!"

"**And we discovered that this entire time you've been planning to use the recognition you gain from reuniting the nation to overthrow your brother's coronation at the end of the summer. I envy such remarkable greed!**"

Epios muttered despondently. "It...It's the only way for me to become worthy. It's the only way for me to show Laura I'm worthy of her love..."

"**You still love her this much even though she never once reciprocated your feelings. Your delusion is astounding! You truly haven't registered the fact that she's dead. And long dead at that. The depths of your devotions are remarkable!**"

He whimpered. "Stop. *Please...*"

"**And to make matters worse she loved both of your best friends instead of you! You're the *only one* who never even got to kiss her! How truly lustful!**"

"NOOOOOOOOOOOOOOOOOOOOOOOOOOOO!"

"**HAHAHAHAHAHAHAHAHAHAAHAHAHAHAHA!**"
The spirit's laughter raged within his skull.

Epios' mind shattered.

He tumbled and slumped over. He foamed at the mouth as he laid on the ground. Tears rolled down his face as despair gripped his being.

The Envy spirit picked him up by the collar.

The Lust spirit shook her head as Epios' empty pupils stared lifelessly into the void. "All the power in the *world.*

All the lust, all the pride, all the greed. But no capacity to use them to take what he wanted in life. Such a waste."

The Envy spirit reached its hand deep into Epios' throat and started pulling his soul out of his body.

"The mistress just needs the body. I'll be taking this soul."

Kayla was surrounded by Wrath spirits, and she raised her daggers as they slowly backed her into a corner. The Gluttony spirit laid on its side as it nonchalantly grabbed unaware Wrath spirits and piled them into his mouth. The Gluttony spirit laid on its side as it nonchalantly grabbed unaware Wrath spirits and piled them into his mouth.

"Flame Craft, Art 2, Ember Dance."

Her body temperature rose, but she did not feel the strength boost she was accustomed to. Her stomach growled in protest and as her vision blurred. *Damn! I must have spent too much energy earlier. And it doesn't help that I'm freaking famished.* She glanced back at Terrance who laid unconscious on the ground. *I hate him, but it would be irresponsible for me to let him die. It's always up to a woman to get a man's job done.*

"What are you guys waiting for? Kill her so I can eat the rest!" The Gluttony spirit complained.

The spirits charged her, and she sprinted toward them.

SLICE! SLICE! SLICE!

She ducked an attack and swiftly sliced three spirits in their sides as she darted into the crowd. She stayed low to the ground as she zipped through the mob. The spirits clawed, scratched and dove at her but she skillfully avoided their attacks. She slid to a halt in the middle of the swarm and began her assault.

SLICE!

GUSH!

SLASH!

GUSH!

SLICE!

She leapt, ripped, slashed, and tore at the spirits; massacring them, as she gracefully dodged every strike. Black liquid splattered across the ground and permeated the air.

GUSH! GUSH! GUSH!

Kayla was soaked in the thick goo, and it dripped from her hair as she violently culled the endless mob.

SLICE! SLICE! SLICE!

The Wrath spirit's aura multiplied her rage grew as she battled. "I'll murder every last one of you worthless spirits! YOU DON'T DESERVE TO EXIST!"

The spirits continuously swarm her, but their fervor waned as some approached more hesitantly.

GUSH!

Two spirits in the mob sprinted toward her and watched as she ripped the heart out of their comrade's chest with her bare hands. They glanced at her violent expression and were filled with fear as they watched the slaughter of their allies

"I'm outraged! But this doesn't look good." The first spirit said.

"I'm enraged! But she can't keep this up forever. Right?" The other spirit said.

They shuddered as she mercilessly brutalized her foes. "EVERY LAST ONE OF YOU WILL KNOW MY WRATH! I'LL SEND YOU RIGHT BACK TO HELLHOLE YOU CAME FROM! YOU'RE WORTH NOTHING MORE THAN MEN TO ME! AND I HATE MEN! DIE AS IF YOU NEVER LIVED!"

The spirits quaked as they glanced at the thinning crowd.

"This is infuriating! But we have to do something brother!" The first spirit said.

"My blood is boiling! But I agree! I still want to live to be angry again tomorrow!" The second spirit said.

The spirits stopped two other Wrath spirits as they charged toward her.

"I'm pissed! But are you two stupid? We can't just swarm her like this! It's not working!" The first spirit said.

"I'm livid! Well, what do you have in mind? These are our orders!" The third spirit said.

"I'm furious! And besides! We must take vengeance for all of our fallen brothers! SHE CAN'T KEEP GETTING AWAY WITH THIS!" The fourth spirit roared.

"I'M FUMING! YEAH! SHE CAN'T KEEP GETTING AWAY WITH IT!" The third spirit raged.

"My rage is eternal! But I have an idea." The first spirit said.

The third spirit nodded. "My rage cannot be quelled. What are you? HEY!"

The first Wrath spirit absorbed the third Wrath spirit and grew slightly bigger.

The fourth wrath spirit stood in shock. "I'm vexed! What did you just do to...AAAGHA!"

It was absorbed by the second Wrath spirit.

The two spirits looked around at their charging comrades. "I'm livid! Hey angry, Wrathy, Ragey, Violenty, Murdury, and Bloodlusty! Come here!"

The spirits gathered within the horde.

"I'm raging! Let's combine powers and take this bitch down!" The first spirit shouted triumphantly.

"I'm irate! Lets do it!". "I'm heated! We'll crush her!". "I'm indignant! Hell yeah!". "I'm seething! Let's maul her!". "I'M SO DAMN ANGRY! SHE CAN'T KEEP GETTING AWAY WITH THIS!". "I'M INCENSED! SHE CAN'T KEEP GETTING AWAY WITH IT!"

The spirits combined and grew into two larger spirits. They continued absorbing spirits until Kayla noticed that there were only a few remaining. She ripped through the last few and gasped for air. Black ooze dripped from every extremity and her long hair was matted to her body, thick from the spirit's blood.

She doubled over and held her sides. "I'm...*huff*...*huff*...so angry...but at least...it's finally..."

POW!

An uppercut devastated her, connecting with her jaw and sending her soaring limply into the air.

BANG!

She landed hard and blood flew from her mouth as she crashed onto the rigid iron floor. Her vision was blurred as she struggled to raise her head. She looked up and saw two massive Wrath spirits before her. They had pitch black skin, bulging muscles, and their claws were razor sharp. The spirits were over seven feet tall and dark energy zipped off their bodies like tendrils of lightning as they approached her with snarling expressions.

"I'm Outraged!" The first spirit said.

"I'm Enraged!" The second spirit said.

Kayla struggled to her feet as dark emotions swelled within her. She stared at the spirits with a feral rage. "What could you two possibly have to be angry about! I've been angry every single day of my life!" She growled. "I'll show you *anger*!"

Rage filled every crevice of her being as she raised her hands. Long daggers formed in her palms and the flames were pitch black. Sweat poured from her skin as her temperature rose to dangerous levels. Visible heat waves emanated from her body as the floor beneath her melted.

WHOOSH!

SMACK!

She vanished, reappearing as the first spirit effortlessly deflected her strike.

CRASH!

The speed from their movements caused wind pressure to shatter the area around them. She rose up and cocked back her daggers.

POW!

The other spirit pounded her spine, and she crashed through the floor into the massive flames below. The spirits hovered to the ground floor. They turned away as the searched for other prey

FWOOOOOOOOOOSH!

Suddenly, the roaring flames turned pitch black, and Kayla walked out of them with eyes of pure malice.

Outraged marveled. "My blood boils, but I like her Enraged!"

"My blood runs hotter, but she intrigues me Outraged."

Enraged turned to Kayla. "I'm pissed, but I sense we share the same rage woman. Tell me, what is it that irks you so..."

WHOOSH!

Before it could react, she soared through the air and plunged her daggers into its face.

SHANK! SHANK! SHANK! SHANK! SHANK! SHANK!

She wrapped her legs around its neck as she ferociously tore and stabbed and ripped at its flesh over and over. Black ooze gushed into the air until it dropped to its knees. She stared up at the other spirit with murderous intent.

It smiled. "I'm livid, but I applaud you! I..."

CRASH!

She leapt and drove her daggers into his chest as she blasted him into the factory wall. Its head went limp as black ooze dripped from its mouth.

SNATCH!

Suddenly, the other spirit grabbed her by the hair.

SLAM!

It violently torqued its body and decimated the concrete with her body. It held her to its face and stared into her dazed eyes.

Enraged's wounds regenerated. "My rage is eternal, but this is an impossible battle for you."

Outraged's wounds regenerated. "My rage cannot be quelled, but this is a fight that you cannot win."

She weakly lifted her arms as she tried to slice at the spirit.

POW! POW! POW! POW! POW! POW!

It jabbed her skull at an incomprehensible speed, and she lost consciousness.

"My wrath is unquenchable, but she interests me."

"My malice is insatiable, but she has my attention as well. Let us see what has caused her to share our same rage."

The spirits delved into her mind as they ripped her memories to the surface.

What...What's going on... Kayla questioned.

She was ripped into a flashback. She found herself back as a child in her mother's room. Her mother was wrapped in a towel in front of the mirror as she curled her hair. She was a tall woman with beautiful golden skin and curly black hair that ran down her back. She was stunningly beautiful, and her crimson eyes gleamed like her daughter's. Kayla sat at her desk as she prepared her mother's makeup.

"Tell me about him again mommy!" Kayla said enthusiastically.

Her mother blushed. "Well, he's tall and very handsome. He looks quite strong and he's a gentleman as well! I think he said he runs a business in the Earth Tribe...but I honestly can't remember..."

"Wooooooow! He sounds amazing! Will I get to go on a date with someone like that when I get older?"

Kayla's mother lifted and held her above her head as she beamed. "Of course sweetheart! You're so much more beautiful than I am. I'm sure you'll meet somebody even more amazing!"

"Really?!"

"Absolutely! But until then focus on your studies so you can become as smart and strong and beautiful as you can be." Kayla's mother said as she sat Kayla on the bed. She put on a bright red dress that accentuated her impeccable form.

Kayla's older sister entered, and her jaw dropped. "Oh...my...God mom! You look gorgeous! Can I wear that dress when I go out with Terrance next week?!"

"Of course, sweetheart! I'm sure you'll look even more beautiful in it! I'm so jealous of you! I still don't know how you got that beautiful golden hair!"

Kayla's sister walked over, and her mother gently stroked her head as she applied her makeup. "You always say that mother, but my hair doesn't get curly the same way that you two's does, and I can really only wear it straight!" She sighed. "I hope Terrance doesn't get tired of seeing me look the same every day."

"I wouldn't worry about that sweet heart. I believe with my entire heart there isn't a man alive that wouldn't be delighted to have you!"

Kayla's sister looked away. "Thanks mom, but you don't have to flatter me so much. I'm not that great. If I was that pretty Terrance would have asked me out instead of me having to ask him."

"Kaia, Terrance is a handsome boy and I'm sure he gets attention from a lot of girls. If he said he wanted to go out with you then that means he likes you! Though I do think there are better choices out there...but I say you should go after that boy Milliard from the capital! Okpa's son is a bit rude and I'm not sure if he's mature enough for someone like you."

Kaia stomped. "Mom, everyone already knows Laura likes Milliard and if I went after him everyone would say I'm a total snake!" She stared into the distance. "He's so *hot* though...But anyway, Terrance and Machari are literally the cutest things in the world! The way they walk around, all brooding and edgy! AGHH! It makes my heart sing! They're like a cute little edgy boy band! I would be lucky to get either of them to marry me..."

"I love Terrance too mama!" Kayla said.

Kayla's mother's smile wilted. "Really...is that so..."

Kaia ran over to Kayla and patted her on the head. "I'll tell you what sis! If things go south or if I find out Terrance cheated on me or something, he's all yours!"

Kayla's mother turned away. "How...generous of you..."

"Thanks, big sis! You're the best!"

Kaia winked. "Of course! If that happens I'll just go after Milliard. Who cares what other girls say anyway right? Besides, I can't wait all year for her to finally make a move on him."

Kayla's mother approached the door and smiled. "Well it seems like you girls have it all figured out. Hopefully my date goes at least half as well as the beautiful futures you two have in front of you!" She waved with a radiant smile. "I'll see you girls when I get back and I promise to tell you all about it!"

"Bye mom!" Kayla yelled.

"Bye mom! If he's a jerk I'm gonna beat the shit out of him for you!" Kaia said.

"Bye now! You two are so sweet!"

The older Kayla watched the scene from inside her mother's mirror and tears ran down her face as she banged against the glass.

"NO MOM! PLEASE! DON'T GO! DON'T GO, HE'S A MURDERER! YOU HAVE TO LISTEN! PLEASE!" Kayla screamed as she smashed her bloody knuckles into the mirror.

Kayla's mother disappeared as the door closed behind her.

BANG! BANG! BANG!

Cracks formed as Kayla smashed the glass even more violently. "NO! MOTHER! PLEASE DON'T LEAVE ME AGAIN! YOU CAN'T LEAVE OR YOU'LL DIE!"

The door shut.

That was the last time Kayla ever saw her mother.

CRASH!

"NOOOOOO!" She roared as she broke through the glass.

Kayla tumbled into the room and the floor disappeared as she dropped into a dark abyss. As she descended into nothingness, she heard voices from her memories.

"THIS IS YOUR FAULT! YOU WERE SUPPOSED TO WATCH OVER HER!" A voice said.

"I AM THE ARCHIGOS! I CANNOT STAY AT MY SISTER'S HOUSE AND DEFEND HER AT ALL HOURS OF THE NIGHT! YOU ARE HER HUSBAND! IF YOU HAD NOT ABANDONED YOUR FAMILY, THIS WOULD NOT HAVE HAPPENED!" Kalarono's voice cried out.

She saw a blurred vision.

"I'm going to find that bastard and kill him." Kaia's voice said.

"Please don't leave me sister. Take me with you! I..."

Kaia leapt as she turned around. "Oh, you heard that little sis? It's alright. I'll be back after I find a way to heal mommy." She smiled as she patted her younger sister's head. "I'm the strongest there is so you don't have to worry! I promise I'll come back, and we can play and talk about boys all day like we always do!" She wiped a tear and smiled even harder. "I'm sure dad will even come back once mom gets better. We'll all be a happy family again!"

Liar.

SLICE!

Outside the dream, Kayla violently sliced off Enraged's head.

POW!

Before she could react, Outraged pounded her spine and she smashed into the iron roof. She landed on her feet in a daze as the spirits levitated to the second floor to meet her.

"I'm enraged, but I sympathize with your anger."

"I'm outraged, but I'm sorry for your loss."

She snapped back to reality and ignited her daggers. "SHUT YOUR MOUTHS! THOSE WERE MY MEMORIES! AND YOU HAD NO RIGHT TO INVADE THEM! THEY'RE MINE!"

Kayla vanished.

SLICE!

She reappeared, spinning and whirling through the air as she sliced Enraged across the chest before it could react. Black liquid gushed from its chest as she was smashed in the side by the other spirit with a devastating blow that shattered her ribs.

SLICE!

She spat blood, but quickly whipped around backwards, her blade extended, and dark energy exploded out as she sliced Outraged's head clean off.

POW!

Enraged rattled her skull with a bone crushing strike to the head. Kayla flipped the blade in her left hand, pierced Enraged's chest and dropped down as she ripped the blade through its torso. Dark energy exploded from its wound and she landed in a crouch.

SNAP!

FWOOOOOOOOOOOOOSH!

Dark flames exploded from Enraged's wounds and erupted from the gaping hole in Outraged's neck as they crumpled to the ground. The spirits writhed in agony as they slowly disintegrated.

She wheezed violently as she crouched down and held her ribs. "They're...*wheeze*...gone...*wheeze*...so why...*wheeze*...do...I still feel...*wheeze*...so..."

The Lust spirit was directly in her face. "My, my. You're quite a tough one. I wonder who it is that you lust after?"

Kayla's eyes widened as the spirit passionately kissed her and delved into her mind. Kayla found herself in a void with two doors before her. One was blue and had a "1" caved into it, and the other was black and had a "2" carved into it.

"I see! You hold affection for two strapping young men! You're quite the promiscuous girly aren't you."

Kayla looked around in a rage. "Shut your mouth bitch! Get out of my head!"

"My! My! You've blocked me from your memories! Your mind is quite a bit stronger than the other one that I'm currently having my way with. He couldn't last very long, and at the moment he's going out quite, *sadly*."

"I swear to God when I get out of here I will..."

"I sense great anger within you, but why? Does it have something to do with what's behind these doors?"

"Shut up! It's none of your business and I'll never..."

"Oh, but *you will*. You will do everything I command because though your mind is strong, your body and soul are too weak to resist me. I figured you would be trouble like that other one, so I had those two big strong boys tire you out first. From this point on you will give in because *lust is your master*."

Kayla's mouth vanished and she clawed at the flesh where it used to be. "MMMMMMMHHHMMM!"

"Now, I'll let you talk again when you learn to be a good girl and answer my questions. Let's see who it is that you truly desire."

Kayla's body went stiff. She mechanically walked over to the blue door and opened it. Inside, she was having passionate sex with Terrance under the covers. Their moans and groans of passion filled her with rage. Dark flames filled Kayla's eyes and she slammed the door shut, only for her body to stiffen once more.

"I see! That boy on the ground over there is the one you *truly* desire. You want *all* of him, and you want him passionately! I can sense that you've desired him since you were a little girl. *How truly lustful.* But who could be behind door number two if you desire him this strongly?"

"MMMMMMHHHHHHHHHHHHMMMMMMMMM!"

"Hush now. Be a good girl and open the other one for me."

Kayla's screams rattled within her skull as she mechanically approached the other door. She opened it, and on the other side she was on a date with James in the capital. They laughed and played together as they enjoyed each other's company.

"MMMMMMHHHHHHHHHHHHMMMMMMMMM!" Kayla roared as her body was racked with sobs.

"I see...this is not very lustful at all. Your feelings for this one are more of the 'platonic' variety." The spirit face palmed. "There is not much lust here, though it does look like there has been some...*sigh, slight* attraction growing as of late. You do desire him though, and you love many qualities about him. So why don't you..."

FWOOSH!

Kayla broke free from her control and fired a beam of concentrated heat into the void.

"Please stop wasting my time and listen." The Lust spirit said as Kayla's body stiffened

"I only have the power to perceive your lusts. Your mind is too strong for me to get any more information. So, I will make you a deal."

Three visions appeared before Kayla. In the first, Epios' soul was slowly being ripped from his body by the Envy spirit. In the second, James was being devoured by a swarm of Wrath spirits. In James' feed, a shrouded figure ate popcorn as it reclined in midair above the swarm. In the third feed, Terrance was being swallowed whole by the Gluttony spirit.

"These visions reflect the inevitable future. I was also sent on a mission to collect information for the mistress. The fact that you were able to kill two Prime Wrath spirits, with Shadow Craft like her son's no less, will certainly pique her interest. If you tell me the source of this immense rage that burns within you, I will take your friends captive and allow them to live."

Kayla watched in horror as her friends neared their ends. Epios' eyes were lifeless, and Terrance's head was almost completely inside of the Gluttony spirit. James' blood gushed into the air as Wrath spirits tore him to shreds.

Kayla violently clawed at her mouth until it reappeared. "FINE! I'M SORRY! I'LL TELL YOU

EVERYTHING! ANYTHING! PLEASE JUST LET THEM LIVE!"

"Good girl! I'll stop my subordinates when I determine that you're telling me the truth. Now answer me. Why are you so..."

Kayla sobbed. "Look...I'm angry and I hate myself because I've never been good enough, ok?! For my entire life I looked to my sister and my mother for everything, THEY MEANT THE WORLD TO ME! Mother was so beautiful, and Kaia was the strongest warrior in the entire world!" Her voice broke. "But I never measured up. I have to struggle and fight every day, WITH EVERYTHING THAT I HAVE...to even take half a step closer to becoming the women they were." She trembled. "But now they're gone and I'm not even close enough to being able to fill their shoes. I'm too weak in battle, too weak to lead my country, and too weak to punish the person that MUTILATED THEM! AND I HATE MY UNCLE FOR REFUSING TO TELL ME WHO THAT BASTARD IS! I hate my brother for being too soft and lazy to rise up and become the leader our people need, BECAUSE I CAN'T DO IT OK?! I hate my dad for abandoning us for some stupid crusade when he knew that we needed him. The men in my life have let me down since the beginning and THAT'S WHY I HATE THEM!"

The spirit clapped. "Excellent! The mistress didn't know that! Mother will be so pleased to have this leverage on those two! But I can tell there's more! Why don't you desire the boy behind door number two? Why does your lust not burn for him as well?"

Kayla fell to her knees as she stared despondently into the void. "I hate myself. I'm selfish and I'm a hypocrite. I make the wrong decision at every turn, and I always have, even though I know I should do what's right! I have an amazing guy right in front of me who loves me and would give his life for me...but I break his heart at every turn because I just don't want him! I'm in love with an idiot man child who hates me and has never liked me! He cheated on my sister, who is the most amazing girl in the entire world! And I hate him with my entire being for that!" Her voice broke. "But my heart still yearns for him and there's nothing I can do to fix it." Kayla looked up in despair. "PLEASE THAT'S EVERYTHING! I'M BEGGING YOU! LET MY FRIENDS GO!" She sobbed. "They're the only ones that I have..."

The Lust spirit nodded. "Yes! How very lustful! One final thing. Tell me..."

POW!

CRASH!

Outside the dream, Kayla was kicked in the skull as she zipped backward and crashed into the wall, denting the steel. Blood dripped from her mouth and her eyes stared off into nothingness as she lost consciousness.

The Lust spirit trembled as it looked up at the regenerating Wrath spirits.

"I'm enraged! She almost killed me with that last one!"

"I'm outraged! I'll cave her skull in for that!"

"YOU FOOLS! I WASN'T DONE WITH HER YET!" The Lust spirit swiftly extended its hand.

FVOOOM!

Invisible waves of energy zipped through them, and they disintegrated.

It shook its head. "*Fools.* I was this close to breaking her mind and discovering the secrets of the vault for the mist..."

SLICE!

"Gotcha bitch!"

Terrance crashed his ax into the Lust spirit's head, and it crumpled to the ground. He took in the Lust spirit's nudity as it writhed in agony. "Goddamn this bitch is bad!"

He glanced at Kayla. "That's not good. But it serves her right for being a..."

The lust spirit was in his face. "You're the one I've been waiting for!"

It kissed him but he swiftly bit her tongue and decapitated it with his ax.

"Hey whore! These lips ain't free! You gotta pay if you want to taste these!"

The spirit's head regenerated.

It shuddered as it moaned sensually. "Oh yes! Oh yes! This is the one I've been waiting for! I've only dreamed of a human with such lust!"

He shouted as he sprinted toward her. "You don't know what the hell you're talking about! And I'm gonna kill you for spreading slander on my fucking name!" His mind raced as he closed the distance. *My body isn't cracked anymore but I doubt I have much left in the tank after that last fight. I probably can't regenerate anymore either. If I get hit too much I'm...*

"Her name was *Luna*, right?"

Terrance froze. "What the hell are you..."

The Lust spirit bit its lips. "And it was *Taylor* before that."

"Listen *thot*, I don't have time for your games, so I'm about to kill you..."

The spirit gleefully spread its arms and spun in circles. "And before that it was Becca and Zina and Rachel and Leah!"

His throat tightened. "Stop it...How do you know those names..."

"And Brea and Tamara and Hannah and Nia and..."

He violently clutched his head. "Make it stop! Make it stop! Make it stop! Make it stop! Make it stop! Make it stop! Make it stop!"

The spirit shuddered as it breathed heavily. "Yes! This is truly lustful. Then it was Hazel and Charlotte and Violet and Nora! Yes! Your lust has no bounds! And Aurora and Iris and Sophia and..."

SLICE

Terrance shuddered as he crashed his ax into the spirit's head.

"Make it stop. Please just...stop..."

A woman's head grew from the spirit's chest. It had curly hair and bright blue eyes. It stared at Terrance as tears ran down her face. "Why did you do this to me?"

FVOOOOOOOM!

Darkness burst from the floor and sent Terrance flying backwards. He landed on his back as the ground morphed into a dark swamp. Hands raised up from the nether and ripped at his flesh.

Voices rang out in his head. "**Why did you leave us**?"

"Get off me!" He cried as he sliced the hands and leapt to his feet.

The hands continued to pull on him as spectral women wrenched themselves out of the darkness. Some had faces Terrance recognized and others didn't.

"Why did you leave me?", "How could you do this to me?", "I loved you."

He frantically sliced off their heads. "No! I don't know any of you! Stay back!" His eyes darted around, searching for any means of escape. He sprinted toward a stairwell behind the Lust spirit.

"You were my everything.", "I would have given my life for you.", "I wanted to have my children with you.", "You used me."

He sliced, murdered, and massacred the women as they rose from the shadows.

"I don't know any of you! Leave me alone, please!"

"I did everything you asked.", "You said you loved me.", "You said you would never leave me.", "You said that you would always be there for me."

A woman grabbed his ankle and stopped his sprint. Another shoved his chest and he fell back into the arms of the mob.

"He's mine!", "He said he loved *me*!", "I'm the one he had sex with!", "He had sex with me first!", "He's coming home to meet *my* parents!"

Tears filled his eyes. "This is all too much! Stop just..."

The Lust spirit leaned into his face. "But you do know them, *ocean prince*. You know each woman intimately and your soul is tied to every single one. You are truly. *Lustful*."

It kissed Terrance sensually and his mind faded as he stopped struggling. The women pulled him into the shadows as his mind drifted away.

Terrance found himself back in his palace bedroom. He was naked, sweaty and he watched as a nude woman got dressed in front of him.

She spoke sweetly. "That was so much fun Terrance! But this can't get out, ok? If my supervisor finds out, I'll be finished! You won't tell anyone, will you?"

He looked her up and down. "Of course not. I would never do anything to lose you. I *have* to hit that again!"

She stuck her tongue out. "Of course! Well alright, I've got to get to my shift, so I'll see you tomorrow night!" She smiled and ran out.

He reached under his bed and pulled out a pill bottle. He took one as he heard a knock on the door. He opened it and a scandalously dressed woman was standing there.

"Hey Terrance! I've been so excited for this! I..."

He grabbed her by the head and passionately made out with her. He tossed her onto the bed and ripped her clothes off.

She stared up at him and blushed. "Terrance you dog! I..."

He put his finger to her lips. "*Shh.* No talking. Let's get to the action. Sorry about the smell by the way."

"It's no problem. I...AHHH!"

They made love until his next suitor arrived.

Adult Terrance watched himself from his closet. "That can't be me! I would never..."

The Lust spirit ran its fingers down his neck. "But you did! And you did it every night for *years*! And that's what makes you truly lustful!"

He swung at it. "Stop it! Get off me! I..."

Terrance blinked and found himself in the palace's training facility. It was a large multi-storied building made from blue ice. It had large, open windows high along the walls, and soldiers stood in the center of the room. Okpa paced near Terrance as he trained with his fellow soldiers.

"Ehh, your form is good enough for now. I need like...hmm...I don't know, a thousand more sword swings from each of you before the day ends." Okpa said casually.

"**Awwwwwwww**!" They groaned.

"Why a thousand dad?! Can't we move on to more advanced stuff like Polar Bear Style or Slush Rush?" Terrance complained.

Okpa held back a yawn. "Most of you will never become strong enough to use Polar Bear Style and only a few of you will ever learn Slush Rush. Even the strongest warriors usually only have enough Spirit Energy to use three abilities in a battle. And that's if it's a long battle and they're not already dead. The fundamentals like Depth Command for survival and basic swordplay are essential to your success as warriors. What is the Ocean Warrior Code?"

"**Control yourself as all you do flows from you**." The students grumbled.

"Excellent. Now I'm gonna go…uh…sign some papers or something. It's a Friday, so get all your training done and you can enjoy the weekend. Otherwise, you'll be training with me all the way through to Tuesday, and I HATE TUESDAYS!" Okpa said as he left.

Terrance started his sword swings when he heard girls giggling outside of the window.

The other soldiers chuckled. "Oh great!", "We all know where he's going.", "Make sure you wrap up this time!", "Save some for the rest of us you bastard!"

He tried to block out their jests as he continued swinging. "Guys come on! You know I'm not the kind of guy to…"

"He-he!", "I think Okpa's gone!", "Terrance, come out here!" The girls called.

He approached the window. "Maybe I'll just take a *quick* look."

He looked down and saw three beautiful women clamoring for him.

"Jump down!", "We're right here!", "Let's go!"

One of the soldiers looked over. "Hey Terrance. Aren't you dating Kaia though? Shouldn't you …"

He winked as he put his foot in the windowsill. "Nah, that's just a rumor. And let's keep that rumor between *us*, ok?"

Suddenly a hand gripped his shoulder.

Machari had two curved blades in his hand as he stared into Terrance's eyes with pure disdain. "You know you need to stay here and train, right? What kind of leader would you be if you ran off and neglected your training every time a pretty girl came around?"

Terrance beamed. "The best leader!"

Machari smiled. "Damn straight!"

They both leapt out of the window.

Terrance and the Lust spirit watched from the second story of the training facility. "That's not me! I would never!"

"But you would! And you did! *Every single time*! You have *no* restraint, and that's what makes you truly *lustful*." The Lust spirit whispered in his ear.

Terrance found himself ducked behind a house with Machari smoking a blunt. Between them was a large dumpster fire.

Terrance giggled wildly. "Isn't Depth Command amazing!"

Machari giggled and snorted excitedly. "I know right! No lung damage!"

Machari chuckled as he stared into the evening sky. "Didn't you have some kind of assignment from your dad or something that you were supposed to do today? Wasn't that family going to get evicted and all that if you didn't sign those papers?"

"I think so! But I don't really give a shit! He left a whole stack of papers on my desk, and I don't know what the fuck any of them are about!"

"That's sick dude!"

"I know right! And to make matters worse. I used some of them...*giggle, giggle*, I used some of them to roll up this blunt that I'm smoking RIGHT NOW!"

"DUDE! YOU'RE A GENIUS!"

"I KNOW RIGHT!"

They laughed and cackled until they heard chatter from around the corner. "Yeah...I still don't really like white boys..."

"SHIT! That's your sister! It's showtime dude!"

"Oh shit! Let me clean up a bit" Terrance said as he brushed the ashes off his pants and tossed his shirt into the fire. He grabbed a bouquet of flowers from on top of a wooden box. He waved a hand over his body and his bloodshot eyes returned to normal. His lungs healed and all evidence of his vice was erased.

He stepped out of the shadows. "Lights, camera, action."

Brooklyn was laughing with two of her friends as they walked down a street. They saw Terrance approach with flowers and rolled their eyes in unison.

"Terrance, what do you want?" Brooklyn said.

He smiled wide. "Hey sis! You look beautiful today."

"Oh so it's 'sis' today? Yesterday you called me a..."

He winked. "I have no idea what you're talking about. But just know that I love you dearly with my whole heart." He held his fingers crossed behind his back.

"I know that you're doing that. You're not..."

He turned to another girl. "Hey there Luna! I got these for you. How's it..."

"This is what we're doing now Terrance? Really?" Luna said.

"What do you mean? I came here to see you and I..."

She brushed past him. "Terrance, you think girls don't talk? I know that you've already run through pretty much every girl in this country *multiple times*, and I am *not* about to be next. I don't know what kind of diseases you've got..."

"Luna please. I'm trying to turn over a new leaf. I think you're smart and pretty and I like that you love God and..."

"Terrance. Save it for the next girl who walks by here. Maybe *she* will want to hear it." Luna said as they kept walking.

Tears ran down his face. He grabbed onto her dress and fell to his knees.

"Please Luna! I need you. You're the only girl that I want in this entire world. I'm really trying to settle down now and walk a new path! I want to be a better man and..."

She slapped his hand off her dress. "I'm sorry Terrance but no! You wouldn't want to be with me if I had slept with a bunch of dudes, right? Who knows how many kids you have out there..."

"I promise I would forgive you if you had slept with a thousand men. I love you and..."

"*Please*, you would *never* take me seriously. And for the record I am a virgin. But the point is that it goes both ways. I don't want to be with a male hoe! How can I trust you to lead a household and guide me in my faith when you can't even lead your own damn self..." Luna said as she left.

He bawled his eyes out in the middle of the road as Machari ran over and consoled him.

Terrance and the Lust spirit watched from a window, and he sobbed.

"I actually loved Luna for real! She was a dope woman, and I ruined it..." He lamented.

"Yes, you did! Now you finally see how lustful you truly are."

A new voice rang out in his head. "He's almost as gluttonous as I am!"

Memories flashed into Terrance's mind. He watched as he chased and pursued Luna for years despite constant rejections. He watched as she burned his love letters and tossed his flowers out of her window. He threw her parties and offered grand gestures, but she always turned him down. He watched the sleepless nights as he cried himself to sleep, and opened his door to other women.

He blinked and found himself back in his bedroom. Luna got out of his bed and bawled as she covered her face.

She sobbed. "Oh my God! I can't believe I just did that!"

He sat up quickly. "Luna, wait! If that wasn't fun, I can do something for you and..."

"No, get back! Get away from me! I was supposed to be saving myself for marriage, but you ruined it!"

"Luna! I'm sorry I..."

"No! I'm leaving! Don't ever talk to me or come near me again!" She said as she quickly dressed herself.

He grabbed and pulled at her clothes as she ran out the door. "Luna stop! I love you! I want to marry you! I'm..."

"Let go of me, are you sick?!"

CRASH!

She pushed him and they spilled out into the hallway. She looked around with panic in her eyes. "If you don't let me go, I'm gonna tell your dad!"

He quickly let go. "Ok! But let's talk this out. I love you! I would die for you! I..."

"If you really love me, you would have waited! I got caught up in a moment where I was lonely and in my feelings…That's my fault, but you're supposed to lead me!"

"I'M SORRY! I.."

She walked down the hall. "Don't tell anyone about this. *Please.* Or my life is over."

She disappeared around the corner as he wept his heart out on the ground and pounded the hallway floor.

"So Lustful!"

"What impresses me the most is that you forgot about her after that day! You couldn't even remember her name! You simply wanted her because she was the one thing that you couldn't have! Your gluttony is unrivaled!" The Gluttony spirit said.

"Please…Stop…" Terrance's soul cried out in despair.

Terrance's mind went blank as he descended into anguish. The spirit's voices rang out in his mind as they tormented endlessly.

"You're an addict.", "A user.", "You broke their hearts.", "They loved you!", "You're a simp.", "An addict.", "A tool.", "A womanizer.", "A glutton."

His mind shattered.

Outside the dream he laid in a ball sobbing on the ground. The Lust and Gluttony spirits stared at him with envy.

"A true *marvel.* His lust rivals even my own. It's a shame that the mistress has no use for him."

The Gluttony spirit jiggled its belly. "Can I eat him now?"

"Absolutely."

The Gluttony spirit grabbed Terrance and started shoving him into its mouth. It lifted its head and Terrance slowly slid down its throat as he sobbed despondently.

＊

James stood face to face with the Deceit Spirit as the hungry Wrath spirits salivated around them.

"I don't know who the hell you are, but let's make this quick!" James snapped.

The Deceit Spirit put a hand to its chest in offense. "How *rude*. I've come all this way to show you the truth and this is the greeting I receive?"

"There's only one truth, and I don't listen to nonsense from random spirits who show up unannounced!" James said as he charged his opponent.

SLICE!

He sliced it across its torso, but it vanished.

It reappeared across the circle and shook its head. "*Sigh*, so violent. No matter. Perhaps some enlightenment will quell your wicked ways."

The factory surrounding James disappeared and became a lush Jungle.

"What the hell?"

Spiders crept toward James from all directions until they completely covered the ground.

"Aw hell naw!"

He fired Photon Beams at the spiders, but they continued their march as they crawled up his legs and started devouring him.

FREEZE!

James froze his lower body in a block of ice, but the spiders crawled through the ice as if it didn't exist. James' legs cried out in agony as the spiders tore into his flesh and he frantically sprinted toward a nearby river.

SLASH!

He was suddenly sliced in the chest by an unseen claw. He fell backward into the spiders and created a wind bubble around his body to blow them away.

CHOMP!

Suddenly, a T-rex charged and scooped him up in his mouth. Teeth pierced his body, and he desperately fired lasers in all directions.

GUSH!

Light beams burst through the T-rex's Jaw in an eruption of blood. James climbed out of its mouth as its body crashed to the ground. He was covered in cuts, gashes, and bites.

"What the hell is..."

"James help me!" Kayla screamed.

James looked up and saw her on the ground being devoured by Wrath spirits.

"Kayla! No!"

SLICE!

SLASH!

James quickly sliced the spirits to pieces and helped her up.

She smiled warmly. "Thanks baby! They caught me off guard!"

Baby?

His heart fluttered and his pain evaporated. "Of course! But how did we get to this jungle? Do you know where Epios and Terrance went? They disappeared along with the rest of the factory."

"I don't know, but we need to go find them." She smiled mischievously. "But first, I have a reward for saving me."

James' mind went to devious places, but he pushed away those thoughts. "A reward? What are you talking about? It should probably wait until after we save everyone here from certain doom. I'm sure there are more civilians that need our help..."

She playfully tugged at her top. "Nope! I'm in the mood, so it's now or never." She pouted. "But it's your choice. I won't *make you* take it. All you have to do is close your eyes."

He raised an eyebrow. "You're usually not like this...But ok, let's make it quick."

His skin tingled with anticipation as he closed his eyes.

"Great! Now just a moment. I'm working up the courage."

"Alright, but we need to hurry."

Is she really this nervous to kiss me or something?

As he heard her footsteps approach, he thought back to the spirits and the battle that was raging around them just a few minutes prior.

"Hey Kayla, how did you beat all those Wrath spirits so quickly. I just saw you get surrounded and..."

James relaxed as he felt her soft hands on his face. He suddenly felt dizzy and lost his balance. He opened his eyes to see the Deceit Spirit before him.

"Easy as pie."

His mind faded away as he sank into the depths of darkness.

The Deceit spirit appeared before James in the void. "Now, let us begin. Show me..."

A voice rang out in the darkness. "I can't allow this mate."

Suddenly, a hand reached out and pulled James from the depths. He found himself back inside his body on the factory's second floor, surrounded by Wrath spirits. Semaj stood between James and the Deceit Spirit.

POW!

Semaj socked the Deceit Spirit in the face, and it hit the ground so hard that it dented the metal floor.

The Deceit spirit shuddered as it stared in horror. "Who...who are you?"

"This town ain't big enough for the both of us mate! Get your bloody own!" Semaj shouted in a British accent.

James' mind was frazzled. "Semaj...what are you..."

SLAP!

Semaj slapped James in the face and knocked him to the floor.

"Bloody hell mate! I suggest you get it together, and *quickly*. This bugger is trying to kill you, and I can't have that happening yet!"

The Deceit Spirit covered its face and trembled in fear as it watched Semaj scold James. It could sense an immeasurable amount of Spirit Energy radiating from Semaj. The spirit peeked through its fingers, but the power swirling around Semaj was so intense that it blinded him.

It stammered. "W...what kind of spirit are you? I've never seen..."

Semaj glared annoyedly. He walked up and pointed his finger in the spirit's face. "First off I'm a human you bloody wanker. Secondly, I'm the kind of passenger that doesn't like to share, *mate*. I'd kill your bloody arse and send you straight to hell this instant for what you've done if I didn't think you had something good to offer me." Semaj lifted the spirit by its collar. "Now, this'll be a proper good learning experience for my best lad James here, so I'll allow you to have your way for now. But if you try something like that again I'll toss you over my knee and paddle your backside!"

"Y...Yes sir..."

James started regaining his faculties.

Semaj dropped him and put a hand on the Deceit spirit's shoulder. "Now listen ere' mate. You're gonna do your best to kill him and make him feel all depressed and alike, as you spirits usually do. But do not dredge up too many of his bloody memories or I'll end you. *Viciously.* Alright mate?"

"S...Sure..."

Popcorn appeared in Semaj's hand. "Also in 3 seconds you're gonna forget this conversation happened but you will do what I instructed you. Give it your best bloody effort and put on a good show for me. Make sure you introduce me as Semaj Fos and..."

"Semaj! What the hell are you doing?!" James shouted as he staggered to his feet.

Semaj held out an empty gift basket. "I was just leaving now mate. I had to discipline this bugger for trying to take over your body and invade your memories. You should be thankin' me instead of blubberin'."

"I don't have anything to give you but if what you're saying is true, thank you. Now get the hell out of here before you make things worse!"

Semaj floated into the air above James and sat with his legs crossed. "It's about bloody time mate! But I'm going to sit right up here and make sure these spirits don't try and get too froggy with your body if that's alright."

"I guess that's fine but stay out of my way! Go help my friends if you want to make yourself useful."

"I would mate. But are they really your friends mate? Do you even know them all that well? I can guarantee they're keeping secrets from you and..."

"Shut it! I don't need that from you!" James said as he faced the Deceit Spirit.

A look of recollection entered the Deceit Spirit's face as Semaj's command took effect. The factory disappeared and morphed into the stage of a packed grand opera house. Each audience member was outfitted in a fancy suit.

"Behold! The time has come for me to put on the performance of a lifetime! Today's show will be titled, 'The Truth about James Fos!' Featuring our special guest, James Fos!"

The audience roared. "**WHOOOOOOOOOOOOOOOO!**"

"What the hell are you...You know what? I'm getting sick of trying to figure these things out. I'm just going to kill you." James said as he raised his blade.

An audience of well-dressed onlookers sat on the edge of their seats in anticipation. Semaj was front and center in a tuxedo as he stuffed popcorn into his mouth.

"WHOOOOOOO! LET'S DO THIS! GIVE HIM HELL JAMES!" Semaj roared.

"In the audience we have another special guest. He's quirky, adorable, clever, and a self-proclaimed love master! Give it up for Semaj Fos!"

The crowd gave him a standing ovation, and he blushed as he looked around in shock. They showered him with cash and expensive gifts. "Oh my goodness. You all are too kind!"

James looked down at Semaj in disgust. "Why do I get the feeling that this is all his fault?"

He rushed at the Deceit Spirit.

"Oh my! It looks like the show is starting! Our first act is titled, 'The Law of Murphy'! Featuring the Middle Texas Central University Football Program!"

POW!

Suddenly, James was tackled by a football player in shoulder pads and they crashed into the stage.

James groaned as his body ached. "What the hell..."

He looked into the player's helmet and saw a zombie of one of his teammates.

"Help...me..." The zombie moaned.

"AAAHA! Get off me!" James screamed.

He blasted the zombie in the face with a Photon Beam and threw its body to the side. More zombies charged him from across the stage. James looked into their eyes and recognized each zombified face.

A tear rolled down his face. "What...What is this..."

"With our first exhibit we have a collection of James' MTCU teammates who had their lives and careers ruined by their terrible coaching staff! Complete with a replica head coach who is prepared to poorly lead them, even in the afterlife!"

The coach pointed its bony finger at James. "Let him live!"

"Look at the authenticity! That is the exact opposite of what they should be doing!"

James raged as dark energy surged within him. "You bastard! I'll kill you for this!" He stared at the ground as his teammates neared him. "I'm sorry guys. I wish I could have done more for you."

CRASH!

James crouched down, shattering the wooded stage.

FVOOOOOOOOOOOOOOOOM!

He leapt high into the air and crashed his blade into the ground, sending dark pillars of energy that disintegrated the players surrounding him. He charged the Deceit spirit as more zombies materialized before him. He darted left and right.

SLICE!

SLICE!

Two players crumpled to dust. Three zombies stood together in his path. James feinted right, and the players crouched as they lunged at him. He spun back left.

SLICE!

James decapitated all three players at once as dark energy exploded from his blade. He continued his advance as wave after wave of players continuously assaulted him.

"WHOOO! YOU GOT THIS JAMES! BULL RUSH THEM! DO THE CROSS-CHOP-RIP!" Semaj shouted.

A screen lowered from the ceiling.

"Accompanying this display of valor, we have a presentation for your viewing pleasure!"

A video played of James working out late at night with his roommate, Micah. They were lifting heavy weights and sweating profusely as the clock read 11pm. The feed cut to James coaching his younger teammates during practice.

"That's how you do it! Now just get your hands inside!" James said excitedly as his teammate won a 1 on 1 rep. James' coach stood off to the side and scoffed.

The scene cut to James dominating his competition in practice. He made tackle after tackle and his teammates celebrated with him. "There you go James!", "J Fos is a Killer!", "Just send that man to the league already!"

James jogged over to the sideline as his backup relieved him. When he smiled and looked at his coach on the sidelines, his coach was silent.

The scene shifted to the first game of the season. James stood on the sidelines as weeks passed in a blur. He smiled as he held onto hope year after year that he would get an opportunity to play, but as time wore on his smile slowly faded away.

As James battled outside the video, he glanced up at the screen. "What is this?! Turn that off!"

The crowd sobbed and wept as they blew snot into their handkerchiefs. Semaj tossed his popcorn at the screen. "BOOOOOOOOOO! I HATE THOSE COACHES! I SAY WE KILL THEM ALL!"

"Shut the hell up Semaj! That won't solve anything!" James roared as he was punched in the face.

The Deceit Spirit sobbed into the microphone. "As you can see this is a true tragedy! Our young hero gave it his all year after year! Only to have his hopes dashed by a wicked coaching staff. He did all that was expected of him and more, and yet he never received the opportunity he deserved. It seems like what can go wrong, in some cases, certainly will go quite terribly wrong."

The Deceit Spirit's words struck a nerve. *That's it.*

SLICE!

He swung his blade violently and a wave of dark energy tore through the remaining zombies in an instant.

"Now. I'm coming for you!" James said menacingly as he pointed at the deceit spirit.

"Sadly not. It's time for our second act! I call this one, 'Snake-bitten'."

Chains burst through the stage and clamped James's wrists. A fancy dinner table and chair appeared before James as the chains forced him into the seat.

"Hey! What the hell is..."

"Allow me a moment to set the stage."

A myriad of beautifully dressed women walked from behind the curtain in a line. They waved and strutted across the stage as the crowd went wild. Semaj ran up to the stage and reached for them as they blew the crowd kisses.

"YEEEAAAAAHHH! I LOVE WOMEN!" He roared as the crowd surged to the stage behind him.

James looked on in awe. "Wait a minute is that..."

"Yes indeed! This long line of women are all individuals who have rejected our eligible young bachelor! Now they're here to tell us their side of the story! Let's hear what they have to say!"

The first woman walked up and sat at the table across from him.

"You're ugly! And your hair is nappy. I never would have dated you!" She said.

James balled his fist. "Oh yeah? Well let me tell you what you did to..."

"Next!"

The woman got up and was quickly replaced by the next. "You were too nice. You just weren't enough of a man for me."

"Well you were a..."

Duct tape appeared over James' mouth.

"MHHHHHMM! MHHHMMM!"

"This is a family friendly show." The spirit said.

The cycle continued as each insult wore on James' spirit.

"We were just friends". "I never saw you as anything more than a little brother.". "I liked your company, but I would never date you". "You're too fat.". "You're just not my type.". "I'm more into bad boys.". "I just didn't like you.". "You're a broke boy". "You're just not that attractive.". "You're so not cute."

The rejections rattled in James' mind as his face fell.

Kayla came and sat in the chair across from him.

His eyes widened. "MHHHHHMM! MHHHMMM! MHHHHHMM!"

She couldn't meet his eye. "James, it's time that I was honest. I've never found you attractive and I never liked you. One nice date doesn't mean that I ever felt anything for you, alright? Like come on! Be real! Did you really think someone like you had a shot with a girl like me? I'm a *princess*, James."

He sobbed as he closed his eyes and shook his head at her words. "MHHHHMM! MHHHMMM! MHHHMM!"

"You're moody, emotional, rude, dumb, immature, a fake Christian, so not a leader, you curse like a sailor, and to make matters worse, I've seen you with your pants down. You're not even *half* the man that Terrance is."

His body shook as he sobbed violently. "**MHHHHHHHHHHMM! MHHHHHHHHHMMMMM!**"

"And one last thing. Don't try to flirt with me *again*. You'd just be wasting both of our time. You *never* had a shot with me."

James sobbed with his head down as the last girl sat before him. She put her hand on his chin and lifted his face. She smiled into his hopeless eyes. A glimmer of hope entered his heart when he saw that it was Brooklyn.

"Hey James!" She said cheerfully.

"MHHHM! MHHM!" He muttered enthusiastically as tears ran down his cheeks.

"I just wanted to let you know that I definitely liked you...and our kiss was *amazing*..."

Hope gleamed in his eyes.

"But I'm gonna be honest. You're crazy. And you ruined everything like you always do. I truly doubt things will ever work out for you. You're basically, like, unlovable at this point. And you'll never get a girlfriend, and if you do it won't be me. Sorry."

James' heart was grieved, and his head slumped. He stared at the table despondently.

Semaj roared as the crowd tossed tomatoes at the women. "BOOOOO! They're all whores anyways James! You don't need em'!"

The women ran off the stage as the table and chairs vanished. James sat on the ground dejectedly. He had no strength or will to fight.

"What a sad sight! Not even *one* of the women was willing to give our eligible bachelor a chance! Did he deserve that folks?"

"**NOOOOOOOOO**!" The crowd roared in unison.

"But sadly, that is the hand he's been dealt in this life. *He's cursed.* For our last act we have our last special guest of the night! James Fos!"

A skinny James who wore a sackcloth shambled onto the stage.

"I call this act, 'Inevitable.'"

Security guards ran onstage and lifted James into a wooden chair. One held his eyes open while the other held his head up.

The shabby James waved weakly. "Hey kid, It's me from the future. I know you're probably excited to see me, but I've got bad news for you."

James didn't respond.

"To keep things brief. You should probably give up now. Nothing that we try ever works. Bad habits, never broke one. Girlfriend, never got one. Success, never seen that. Friends, nowhere to be found. We spent our entire 20's chasing after football. We got depressed and pushed our mental health issues to the side until they overwhelmed us. Our mind became so debilitated that we couldn't even read or do basic math anymore. We had no drive and in our 30's we lost all motivation to live. We tried to end it all a couple times, of course we failed at that too. At a certain point, even our parents gave up on us after they got tired of babysitting a grown man with nothing to show for his life. Now we wander the streets near our old college, begging for pennies and telling all the kids who walk by about what a great player we used to be."

James was motionless.

The crowd sat in silence.

The Deceit Spirit took center stage with its arms wide. "And that concludes the show folks! I hope you enjoyed it and..."

The spirit noticed Semaj was not in his chair.

"**HUUUUUUUUUUUUUUH**?!" The crowd gasped.

The Deceit spirit shuddered.

James stood behind it with a blank expression.

"When did you...GAAAH!"

CRASH!

James grabbed it by the neck and slammed it into the stage, shattering the ground as the opera house faded away. James stared down at the spirit in his grasp with hatred in his heart.

He growled. "I applaud you. Everything you said is true."

"Th...that's right! You think you're a failure and you're right! Your very existence was a mistake! So please let me go and..."

GUSH!

Black ooze gushed across the walls as James drove his fist through its heart.

SPLAT!

He violently ripped it out and the spirit disappeared.

"I didn't need the reminder."

The hungry Wrath spirits surrounding him charged.

He glanced at Semaj in the air. "Are you gonna help me?"

Semaj floated above him and crossed his arms. "Nope. You're the one who said he didn't want my help. Remember?"

"Fine. I'll do it myself."

A dark blade formed in James's hand, and he swung it like a whip.

WHOOSH!

GUSH!

The nearby spirits exploded as black goo gushed into the air. He took on the swarm and brutally slaughtered them.

His mind was calm as he annihilated the mob of spirits. *I know that I've always been a failure.*

WOOSH! WOOSH! WOOSH!

SPLAT!

God has blessed me with so much potential. But I've never been able to do anything with it.

SPLAT! SPLAT! SPLAT! SPLAT! SPLAT!

What can go wrong in my life has gone wrong.

WOOSH! WOOSH! WOOSH!

SPLAT!

I am unlovable.

SPLAT! SPLAT! SPLAT! SPLAT! SPLAT!

My future probably is full of failure.

SPLAT! SPLAT! SPLAT! SPLAT! SPLAT!

He glanced at his friends as they fought their battles.

But deep down something is telling me to give it one last try.

WOOSH! WOOSH! WOOSH!

SPLAT!

He stemmed the tide of Wrath spirits, and overwhelmed them with immeasurable power.

The Lust spirit looked over and her jaw dropped. "Well that is not lustful."

She appeared before James as he slaughtered spirit after spirit.

"Hey there big boy."

He stopped as he turned to face it. When he saw the spirit, it appeared as a beautiful naked woman. The Wrath spirits paused their assault.

"Are you another woman who's come to reject me?"

"Of course not! You're so handsome and I'd love to get to know you. I..."

WHOOOOOOSH!

He stood behind her and wiped her blood from his blade. Its head fell from its shoulders as its body disintegrated.

"You really thought I would fall for that again?"

He turned around and Kayla was directly in his face. "Well, that was rude. You'll *never* woo a woman like that."

He swung his blade, but her lips connected with his just as his sword pierced her flesh. He stopped his blade before it severed her neck. *I could never hurt Kayla.*

Tears ran down his face as he stared into her eyes. His anger dissipated as the dark energy faded. His body grew weak and tired. *This is my dream. I know it's not real. But just this once. I deserve something like this.*

He lost his will to fight, and his blade clattered to the floor. She kissed him with increasing fervor as she pushed him to the ground and fell on top of him. He gave up and let his mind drift off into ecstasy.

Kayla's voice rang out in his mind. "Tell me. Who is it that you...AAAH!"

BANG!

Semaj grabbed her by the hair and slammed her into the ground, denting the iron floor.

"I thought I told you stupid bloody spirits THAT I AIN'T SHARING!"

James laid on the ground as his body was racked with sobs.

Semaj patted him on the back. "James. Take a nap for me would you."

James closed his eyes and sobbed as he fell asleep.

The Lust spirit stared at Semaj in fear.

"Who are you and why could I not sense you..."

"Stop all of that blubbering before I bend you over my knee and paddle your backside! You can do what you want with him, but you spirits need to stop trying to take over his bloody mind! Be like the last guy and shatter his spirit from the outside!"

She stared at him in shock.

Semaj leaned over. "James, wake up. And remember. You were in depression and agonizing torment or something like that."

James woke up and screamed as he cradled his head. "**AAAAAAAAAAAAAAAGGGGGGGGGGGGGGGGHHHH**!"

Semaj put on earmuffs. "That's a bit much. Not agonizing torment. Just depression and minor torment."

"AAAAAAAGGGGGHHH!"

"Much better" Semaj said as he floated into the air and resumed eating his popcorn.

The Lust spirit looked down at James in disdain. "I know the boys want him intact, but I don't care! He almost killed me! He will suffer immeasurably, and I will bring him to meet the family in tatters!"

She waved her hand and the Wrath spirits swarmed James.

GUSH!

SPLAT!

GUSH!

They ripped and tore at his flesh as blood gushed into the air.

She turned and walked away. "I'm sure that strange bastard will stop them before he dies."

✳

On the lower floor, carnage ensued as civilians ran for their lives. Flames raged everywhere as spirits devoured every man, woman, and child. Amid the carnage, a soldier chased an anemic looking boy around the factory.

"Please! Stop! Leave me alone!" The boy cried as he ducked under fallen machinery and stumbled over bodies.

"No can-do son." The soldier said as he steadily walked.

332

The boy leapt onto a conveyor belt and slid through an opening made by two fallen shelves. The soldier smashed through the shelves as he casually paced after him.

As the boy ran for his life his mind raced. *Why do these kinds of things always happen to me?! I just wanted a chance to live a normal life!*

The boy ran into a dead end in the corner of the factory.

"Oh no! I..."

SLICE!

His blood erupted from his back as he fell onto his face. He turned and looked up at the soldier with pleading eyes. The soldier smirked as he looked down on the boy.

"Please! Why won't you just leave me alone!" He frantically looked around and pointed. "Look! There's a window there! We can both escape if we..."

SLICE!

The soldier slashed the boy across the face and he collapsed to the ground. "Sorry son. But none of us are going to be making our way out of here tonight. Those spirits are ravenous, and we've got no shot. I'm the kind of guy who likes to share my misery with little runts like you, so I might as well die doing what I love."

The boy's vision blurred as he groped around in the darkness. He put his hand on the window as he desperately tried to pull himself up.

"P...l...e...a...s...e"

SLICE!

GUSH!

The boy's blood splattered all over the window. His hand was soaked as his palm stuck to the glass.

"Sorry son. But before I go. I'm gonna enjoy carving you up."

SLASH! SPLAT! SLICE! SPLAT!

A crimson pool grew around the soldier's feet as he ruthlessly slaughtered the boy.

SPLAT! SPLAT! SPLAT!

The boy's mind drifted as his life left him. *It looks like this is the end. Every single day, I've prayed for my body to grow. I've begged for God to help me develop some kind of skill. I've pleaded for a chance to actually mean something to someone. I've begged for a chance to be useful. Oh well...*

Life faded from his eyes as he lost consciousness.

GUSH!

The soldier raised his sword and aimed it over the boy's head. "This is it. Thank you for letting me die doing what I love, boy."

He brought down his blade.

SNATCH!

A hand caught the sword.

The soldier looked down and saw that the boy was gripping the blade.

His eyes glowed with a yellow light.

The soldier flinched. "What in the..."

The boy snapped the blade and grabbed the man by the chin. "Don't tread on children of God, yo. This shall be your final lesson, bro."

CRACK!

The boy twisted his neck and the soldier crumpled to his knees. He blinked and stared through the rubble around him. He could see the human souls and the Spirit Energy of the spirits across the factory.

The boy walked forward. "What a desecration of such wonderful blessings, yo."

CREAK! CRASH!

The metal shelves and conveyor belts before him split in two as the metal warped out the boy's way. He raised his right hand and metal pieces formed into a hammer that zipped into it.

He vanished.

BANG!

GUSH!

BANG!

GUSH!

BANG!

GUSH!

The boy blitzed through the factory at an incomprehensible speed. In an instant, he bludgeoned every soldier and spirit on the ground floor. The soldiers crumpled to the ground and the spirits disintegrated simultaneously. The remaining civilians stared up at him in awe.

"Is that Bazek?", "The Archigos is back!", "That kid saved us all!"

The boy flicked his wrist, and the civilians were lifted onto platforms that floated to safety.

The boy glanced up. "Now, for the fans in the rafters, yo."

He walked forward as rubble formed a staircase in his path, and he ascended to the second floor. He saw James being devoured by Wrath spirits, Epios' soul being ripped from his body, Terrance being devoured by the Gluttony spirit, and Kayla being choked to death by the two Prime Wrath spirits. Semaj saw the boy and tossed his popcorn.

He leapt into James' body. "Welp, that's my cue to go!"

The Lust spirit was startled by the boy's overwhelming presence and slowly turned to face him.

"Another interloper..."

GUSH!

The boy ripped the spirit's heart out and it faded away. The boy raised his hand, and a mass of rubble and metal rose from the lower level.

CRASH!

The rubble crushed all the Wrath spirits surrounding James, leaving him unscathed. James' wounds began regenerating as dark energy poured out of them. He walked over to James and put a hand on his shoulder.

"Do not be troubled bro."

James' emotional turmoil was eased, and he opened his eyes. He was too weak to move but he stared as the boy walked away.

James muttered weakly. "Who...are you?"

"To those who love me, I'm one who sticks closer than a brother, yo."

The spirits who were assaulting James' friends turned and faced the boy in shock.

"I'm outraged, who is this?"

"I'm enraged, this is troubling."

Outraged, dropped Kayla to the ground and she gasped for air as she regained consciousness.

WHOOOOSH!

They crouched and launched themselves at the boy, shattering the iron floor as they exploded through the air. The boy leapt, avoided their attack and closed his fist.

CRASH!

GUSH!

Beams of steel soared from across the factory and impaled the spirits until they were completely smothered by the metal. Their hearts were pierced, and they faded away. Kayla stared at the boy in shock as she clutched her neck.

The Envy spirit stopped pulling out Epios' soul and put its hands up. "Look here boss! We can talk about this. Let's make a deal and..."

CLANG!

The boy smacked the Envy spirit through the wall and into the stratosphere. It faded into the distance as it vanished from sight. As Epios' soul reentered his body he regained consciousness and fell flat on his face. He weakly stared at the boy as he approached Terrance.

The boy ripped Terrance out of the Gluttony spirit's mouth.

"Hey! That was my snack!"

The boy set Terrance down as Sesame jumped out of his pocket. Sesame slapped Terrance in the face, and he regained consciousness.

"My...head..." Terrance said.

The Gluttony spirit and the boy stood before each other.

"That's it! I'll just have to eat you instead!" The Gluttony spirit raged.

CRASH!

Its body suddenly expanded and grew exponentially as it burst through the walls of the factory. The boy waved his arm and James' group were raised onto platforms and lifted high into the sky as the factory collapsed around them. The spirit grew over fifty feet tall and the fat from its obese body shattered nearby buildings.

Its roar shook the earth. "**I'LL DEVOUR THE ENTIRE CITY**!"

The boy levitated in front of its face and held his hammer high.

The spirit opened wide. "YOU'RE FIRST!"

CHOMP!

The spirit ate the boy.

"TASTY! NOW I'LL HEAD TOWARDS THE PALACE AND..."

SPLAT!

The boy soared through the spirit's belly and flew high into the sky.

"GAAAAAAAAAAAAHAAAAAAAAAAAAAAAAA!"

The boy raised his hands, and the ground trembled as two skyscrapers were ripped from their foundations. He pointed his hammer at the giant spirit and the skyscrapers crashed into it.

BOOOOOOOOOOOOOOOOOOOOOOOOOOOOOOOM!

"GAAAAAAAAAAAAHAAAAAAAAAAAAAAAAA!"

"What the...hell?" James muttered.

"Who is that scrawny...kid?" Kayla mumbled.

"I've never seen such a strong...fiend." Epios gawked.

"How is that weakling...doing this?" Terrance grumbled.

The boy slowly closed his two hands together as the skyscrapers melded around the spirit's body and pressed it into mush.

"GAAAAAAAHHHHHHHHAAAAAAAAAAAAAAAA!"

The spirit was compressed into nothingness as the skyscrapers crashed into the earth.

The sun started rising, and the boy smiled as the sky was slowly painted a beautiful shade of auburn. He twisted his wrist, and the skyscrapers rose from the rubble and were slowly restored to their original shape. The group looked on in absolute awe. He placed the skyscrapers in their original places and the foundation reattached, just as they were before. He descended and set the group's platforms on the ground. He approached the factory and waved his arms as he slowly restored the building to its original state. The group was stunned as they watched him set every screw back in its original place. When he finished he approached them.

They gushed as they marveled. "WHO ARE YOU SIR?!". "I'M FOREVER GRATEFUL!". "YOU SAVED MY KINGDOM!". "HOW DID YOU DO THAT YOU RUNT?!"

He beamed with joy as the yellow light faded from his eyes. His smile diminished and the boy trembled in fear as he saw their admiring faces.

He cowered. "GAAAAAH! PLEASE DON'T HURT ME!"

They stared at him in confusion and shock. The boy looked down at his body and saw his bloody wounds.

"**GAAAAAAAAAAAAAAAAAAAAAAAHHHHHHHHH**! OH MY GOD! WHO DID THIS TO ME?! I'VE BEEN ASSAULTED BY THESE FOUR WEIRDOS! SOMEBODY PLEASE SAVE ME! I'M BLEEDING OUT! I'M GONNA DIE!"

Their faces of admiration slowly warped into disdain.

Deep in an alley untouched by the sun, Kaiti and his son walked out of a ruined building. They turned into an alleyway and Semaj stood there with a shotgun.

"I've come for revenge mate." He said.

Kaiti stepped in front of Tari and held his hand up. "You'll have quite a hard time with that. Considering the massive debt that you owe me, Fos."

Tari scratched his hair. "Dad? What are you..."

"Hush son. Just stand behind me and be quiet!"

Semaj pumped his shotgun. "He's the one I'm after mate! Stand aside and hand im' over!"

"I truly doubt *that* is the reason that you risked coming this far. I can tell that in your current state, even I could defeat you." Kaiti said.

Semaj smirked.

He tossed his shotgun into a nearby trash can. "Just joshing you mate! I wanted to make sure you weren't a bloody pushover after all these years!"

Kaiti sighed in relief. Tari saw the beads of sweat running down his father's back.

"Dad...tell me what's going on..."

"Not now, son. Your promiscuity has nearly made us a powerful enemy on this day."

Kaiti faced Semaj. "Now tell me. What is the true reason that you have ventured all this way?"

Semaj smiled and held out his hand. "Let's strike a deal mate!"

18 – The Giali Family

JAMES' GROUP STARED AT THE BOY IN CONFUSION AS HE SCREAMED AND ROLLED AROUND IN THE DIRT.

"SOMEBODY! HELP ME PLEASE! I'M BLEEDING OUT AS WE SPEAK! MY ARM IS BROKEN, MY LEG IS BROKEN! I HAVE A CONCUSSION! AAAAAHHHH!"

SLAP!

Terrance violently slapped the child, and he fell to the ground.

"HEY RUNT! SHUT THE HELL UP AND LOOK AT ME WHEN I'M TALKING TO YOU!"

The child held his face and teared up. "Why...would you do that?"

Compassion filled James' heart. "Terrance leave him alone. Clearly..."

SLAP!

Kayla viscously slapped Terrance, and he fell into the dirt.

"OUUUUCH! WHY DID YOU..."

"HOW DARE YOU SLAP THIS LITTLE BOY LIKE THAT! HE JUST SAVED ALL OF OUR LIVES AND THAT'S HOW YOU TREAT HIM? YOU SHOULD BE ON YOUR KNEES THANKING HIM!" She roared.

"I'LL NEVER PRAISE THAT RUNT UNTIL HE LEARNS WHAT PROTEIN IS! AND IF YOU EVER SLAP ME AGAIN, I'LL KICK YOUR ASS! AT THIS POINT YOU'RE SO

ANNOYING THAT I DON'T CARE IF YOU'RE A GIRL! THESE HANDS ARE TURNING BISEXUAL!"

"IF YOU EVER LAY A HAND ON ME, I'LL MURDER YOU AND SEND YOU STRAIGHT TO HELL WHERE YOU BELONG! THIS IS WHY I HATE MEN! WHAT KIND OF MAN OPENLY SAYS THAT HE'S ALRIGHT WITH HITTING WOMEN!"

Sesame shook his fist at Kayla. "MWHHHHAAAAAA!"

James and Epios shook their heads.

"I grow tired of watching whores and brutes bicker." Epios scoffed.

"So immature." James sighed.

As Kayla and Terrance argued in the background, James approached the boy and offered a hand. "I'm sorry about my friends. They can be complete idiots sometimes."

The boy stared at him in shock. His voice trembled at an incredibly low volume. "Y...you're helping me?"

"Of course! Even though you were spouting nonsense, you don't deserve to be slapped! And besides, it's the least I can do. You just saved our lives!" James raised an eyebrow. "By the way, how did you do all that crazy stuff?"

"S...saved your lives? What do you m...mean? I was j...just at work and then I woke up bruised and battered o...out here."

"You don't remember? It was like five minutes ago. You just killed all those spirits, saved our lives and fixed the entire factory! It was the most amazing thing I've seen in my entire life! Here, take my hand already so I can help you up."

The boy was appalled as James helped him up. He trembled as he felt the warmth of James' hand. *I can't remember the last time I touched another human being...*

"W...what are you talking a...about? I c...can't do anything l...like that. D...did the Archigos finally c...come back?"

"Clearly the child's body is not the only thing that is deformed." Epios scoffed.

"Shut the hell up Epios! But I'm being for real. You seriously don't remember any of the crazy things you just did? You literally saved all our lives!"

"No...I can't even use Earth Craft. Let alone..."

"Guys, stop your arguing and come here for a second." James said.

Kayla and Terrance grumbled as they came over.

"Stupid girls. Always getting so emotional."

"I swear. This is why all men deserve to die."

"Enough of that! Anyway, am I tripping, or did this kid just save all our lives?"

"I guess he helped out a little." Terrance spat as he turned away.

"Without a doubt, I owe this fiendish child my life. How should I repay him..."

"Absolutely! It was the most incredible display of Earth Craft I've ever seen! Thank you again by the way." Kayla glowed.

The boy stared at them. These *guys must be* **crazy**. *It's either that or they're trying to butter me so they can kidnap me to sell my organs on the black market or...*

The boy looked upon Kayla for the first time and he froze. Despite her wounds, dirt covered body, and hair matted with dark goo, her beauty overwhelmed him. His mind was bombarded with attraction and lust filled his body. OH MY GOD! IT'S AN ANGEL! AN ETHEREAL BEING HAS DESCENDED FROM HEAVEN TO GREET ME! HOW COULD THIS BE?! GOD HAS ANSWERED MY PRAYERS! LET ME MAKE SURE THIS IS REALLY HAPPENING!

He trembled as he reached out and touched her face. She raised an eyebrow. "Umm...what are you doing?"

"I'm so sorry." He said.

SHE'S REAL! OH MY GOD! SHE'S REAL! I CAN'T BELIEVE THIS IS REALLY REAL! I'VE NEVER SEEN A GIRL THIS BEAUTIFUL IN MY ENTIRE LIFE! ESPECIALLY NOT IN THE SLUMS! THIS IS MY DREAM GIRL! MY SOUL MATE! THIS IS A ONCE IN A LIFETIME OPPORTUNITY! I CAN'T DO ANYTHING TO MESS THIS UP!

James smiled at him. "See! Everyone here saw what you did. Now do you believe me? And by the way, you never told us your name?"

The boy snapped back to reality. "Y...you want to know my n...name?"

"Of course! How could I not want to know the name of the person who just saved my life?"

The boy gawked. *He asked me for my **name**? It's been years since anybody has asked me for my name. And he touched my hand...*

The boy nervously glanced around him. *I don't see anybody else around. And the sun **is** rising. I doubt they would try to kidnap me in broad daylight.*

James raised an eyebrow. "Are you alright? I guess you don't have to tell us if you don't..."

"OUT WITH IT SHRIMP!" Terrance roared.

The boy trembled as he stared at Terrance. He looked him up and down. *I can tell that I don't like this one already. He's so tall and strong and handsome. He's my top competition for...*

Kayla spoke sweetly. "I would like to know your name too!"

GAAAAAAAAAHAAAAAAA! THE ANGEL ASKED ME FOR MY NAME TOO! AND SHE SAID IT SO NICELY! SHE MUST BE IN LOVE WITH ME! WHAT SHOULD I DO? SHOULD I LIE AND COME UP WITH A COOLER NAME? JERRY REALLY ISN'T THAT INTERESTING...MAYBE I

SHOULD SAY I'M POWER GOD! OR I'M THE EARTH KING RULER 3000! NO! I CAN'T START OFF OUR RELATIONSHIP WITH A LIE! WHAT DO I DO! WHAT DO I DO!

Terrance sniffed the ground and looked around. "*Sniff, sniff,* I smell a simp around here. Is that *you* again James?"

"Terrance. If we weren't all injured right now. I would surely beat your ass." James said.

Terrance squared up. "DO IT THEN! LET'S GO! RIGHT NOW!"

James raised his fists. "I just said we're too injured. But since you want that ass whooping I owe you *this* badly, I'll finally have to oblige you."

"Stupid boys. KNOCK IT OFF!" Kayla roared as she stepped between them.

Epios sighed. "Fiends, brutes, whores. What have I gotten myself into..."

The boy stared at them as they quarreled. He noticed that Kayla was holding her side and that the group was covered in a myriad of injuries.

*They're not lying about the fact that something **did** happen to them. They probably just got robbed. But me saving them is just crazy. They do seem like nice people though...* Suddenly he reached a revelation. OH MY GOD! I FINALLY GET IT NOW! THANK YOU, LORD JESUS! THESE GUYS BEAT EACH OTHER SENSELESS AND ARE

MAKING UP THIS STORY BECAUSE THEY WANT TO BE FRIENDS WITH ME! THAT'S THE ONLY THING THAT MAKES SENSE! AND IT LOOKS LIKE THE ANGEL IS THE ONE WHO PUT THEM UP TO IT BECAUSE SHE'S IN LOVE WITH ME! THIS IS AMAZING LORD! YOU FINALLY BROUGHT ME THE FRIENDS I HAVE BEEN ASKING FOR! AND YOU BROUGHT MY FUTURE WIFE WITH THEM! WHAT DID I DO TO DESERVE THIS?! ALL OF MY HARD YEARS OF TOIL ARE FINALLY PAYING OFF! I HAVE FOUND FAVOR IN THE LORD'S SIGHT ON THIS DAY!

"Excuse me!" The boy said excitedly.

The group stared. They were shocked that his voice had risen to a reasonable octave.

He gave a beaming smile. "My name is Jerry Giali, and I would love to be your friend too!"

"Sure! We could use someone with a little more know-how to help us get around the city until we can meet with the Archigos." James said.

"Yeah! We'd love to have you!" Kayla said excitedly.

Jerry gave a sly smile. *She's being modest. She's probably too embarrassed to confess her love in front of the others and admit she set this all up to convince me to be friends with her. I'll take the initiative as a man and confess my love later today.*

Terrance sniffed Jerry. "I FOUND IT! ABSOLUTELY NOT! I CAN SMELL SIMP ALL OVER HIM AND I DON'T LIKE IT! WE CAN'T ADD A THIRD SIMP TO THE GROUP!

THEN WE'LL HAVE TO PAY THE GOVERNMENT SIMP
TAX!"

James face palmed. "Terrance. What the hell are you
talking about? I..."

Jerry glared at Terrance with eyes full of disgust.
Hatred filled his heart. *I see! My rival in love is already
trying to get rid of me, ey? I won't let this stand. I'll have to
kill that bastard off somehow, but first I'll need to rally
allies against him. These other two guys don't seem like
they're that strong, but they're the only potential support
that I have at the moment. I'll have to come up with an
elaborate scheme to gain their support. Once I earn it, how
should we get rid of him? Death by firing squad? The
electric chair? Lethal injection? Being torn asunder?
Sleeping with the fishes? Burned alive? The possibilities
are endless, and we have to make sure it's something he
can't come back from. I wonder...*

Epios came to a revelation. "That's it! I have the
perfect way to reward you, fiendish midget! You will be
promoted and become my royal bodyguard! You're
welcome!"

"Bodyguard? I'm not sure if I can do that, but I accept!
What did you mean by *royal*, exactly?" Jerry said
enthusiastically.

Epios shook his head. "Clearly you are as uneducated
as your other fiendish brethren. I am Prince Epios

Iliaktida, this nation's next king and ruler. You may bow before me."

Jerry's face lit up and he prostrated. "I'm so sorry your majesty! I had no idea! I promise I will defend you with my life as your humble servant!"

"Finally! Someone with manners who respects my station!" Epios shouted.

OH MY GOD! I'VE HIT THE JACKPOT! I'VE MADE AN ALLY OUT OF THE PRINCE OF THE ENTIRE NATION! MY PARENTS WON'T BELIEVE IT!

Jerry stared at Terrance with a sly expression. *There's no way I can defend that prince in an actual fight, but that's one ally secured! He can supply the firing squad for...*

POW!

James shoved Epios to the ground. "Get up Jerry! Don't bow before *this* guy!"

Kayla kicked Epios in the side and Terrance spat in his face.

"Here's what I think of your station!" James laughed.

"I've been waiting to do that you prick *bastard*, excuse of a man!" Kayla said triumphantly.

"I TOLD YOU BEFORE AND I'LL TELL YOU AGAIN THAT I'VE NEVER HEARD OF YOU! YOU'RE NOT EVEN A REAL PRINCE SO QUIT PRETENDING TO BE ONE!" Terrance roared.

"MY ROYAL WOUNDS HAVEN'T HEALED YET! I SWEAR THAT I'LL HAVE EVERY ONE OF YOU ALL EXECUTED!" Epios roared as he rolled around in pain.

James walked over and set Jerry on his feet. "Nah, you love us too much for that."

Jerry stared at them concernedly. *That's weird that they treat their future ruler like that...You'd think he'd have some kind of security or secret service to...*

James stared at Epios in disgust. "Don't be too nice to that guy or it'll all go to his head. Then he'll think you're his slave and start asking you to do weird favors like feeding him grapes or clipping his toenails for him."

"AS YOUR RULER YOU ARE DESIGNED TO SERVE ME! THOSE ARE CUSTOMARY SERVANTLY BEHAVIORS!" Epios roared.

Jerry came to a sudden realization. He glared at Epios. *I just realized...MY WIFE HAS BEEN TRAVELING WITH THE PRINCE OF THIS ENTRE COUNTRY! He's just another rival I'll have to **take down**. It's a good thing I've already made friends with him and he thinks I'm his ally. I'll just have to bide my time and wait for the right moment to **strike**. Keep your friends close and your enemies closer as they say. It will be a tall order to assassinate the crown prince and get away with it, but I'm up to the task. I'll probably need some cyanide and a professional chef and...*

"Nope you're just weird and gross." James said to Epios. He turned to Jerry. "But anyway, do you know a

352

place where we can shower or work so that we can get something to eat? It's been like a whole day..."

Jerry's eyes widened OH MY GOD! *He's asking what we should do for our first ever official friend group hangout! WHAT DO I DO? WHAT SHOULD I TELL HIM! This is our first one, so I have to make sure it goes down in history!*

"I have an idea! Why don't you guys just come over to my crib? It looks like you've been robbed or something...so, you can definitely stay at my place today as you guys regain your bearings and whatnot. We have a shower, food, clothes, and everything!"

James shook his head. "I told you that we weren't robbed. We were attacked by terrorists and spirits...But wow that sounds amazing! I'd love to as long as we won't be a burden or any..."

Kayla, Terrance and Epios trampled over James as they ran up to Jerry.

"OH MY GOSH! A BATH WOULD BE AMAZING!" Kayla screamed.

"YES! LEAD THE WAY! WE SHALL GO TO YOUR HUMBLE ABODE BODYGUARD! YOUR KING REQUIRES HIS BEAUTY SLEEP!"

"FOOOOOOOOOOOOOOD!" Terrance roared.

Jerry stared up at them in ecstasy as they clamored over him. *Wow Lord...I love having friends...*

POW!

James' shoved the group off his back. He rolled his eyes. "I guess that settles it then."

James

The early morning sun lit the sandy streets with an orange hue as we walked with Jerry toward his house. *It doesn't make sense that he claims to have no memory of saving our lives, but that's a discussion for another day. Right now, we need food and a solid place to get some real rest.* He was a strange little kid, and I was interested in getting to know him better. As we walked, Terrance used Depth Command to slowly heal our wounds.

"So, Jerry. Are you enrolled at one of the academies here in the earth nation?" I asked.

Jerry had an incredulous expression. "Academy? Oh, I did go to school for a little while, but I had to drop out. My parents couldn't really afford to keep sending me anyway. Only rich people can afford to go there. It took my family saving up a year's worth of income just to afford to send me for one grading period."

I swallowed. "Really? That's awful. I'm sorry about that."

"Yeah, it's a normal thing around here so there's no reason to apologize. I wasn't very good at all that school stuff anyway so my parents decided to use their funds to send my brother Reggie instead."

"That's awful! They should've given you a chance to finish at least!" Kayla said.

Jerry looked at Kayla with a strange expression before he spoke. "Ah, your voice is a nectar to my ears." He sighed. "But Reggie is much more talented and smarter than I am, so my parents sending him in my place doesn't bother me that much." He stared at the towering academy in the distance. "Still though, I do dream of getting the chance to go back and have a chance to learn to use Earth Craft properly like my uncle can..."

His words made me feel terrible. I'd had the opportunity to go to the world's most prestigious academy for free, just because Milliard asked them to let me in, and I hadn't valued it or tried very hard. Even though I had a great time, I didn't put in much effort on the academic side of things. I was just focused on the fitness aspects so I could stay in shape for when I went home. I never even considered that some people longed to go there.

"School sucks ass anyway." Terrance said.

I wanted to tell Terrance to shut the hell up, but deep down I agreed. My school days back home were not kind to me.

"No, it doesn't! School is the best place in the entire world! You get to learn how to fight and be strong like Bazek! You get to learn important life skills, you get to make friends, you get to stay in air conditioning, you get a chance to make money after you leave, and most importantly there are loads and loads of women there!" Jerry gushed.

Kayla rolled her eyes. I didn't agree with all his points, but he had me on the money and women part. If your school was blessed enough to have beautiful women that is, which my college didn't. He was speaking my language. *This is my kind of guy.*

Epios wrapped his arm around Jerry. "Do not fret my stick-figure bodyguard! Once you have fulfilled your duty in serving your ruler, I will ensure you are admitted into the Earth Tribe's finest academy!"

Jerry leapt with excitement. "Wow! Are you being serious, your majesty?!"

"Absolutely fiendish servant! Once I have accomplished my goal in reuniting my nation, I will ensure you are admitted on full scholarship. It's the least a benevolent ruler, such as myself, can do to repay you for saving my life from those devilish spirits."

Jerry stopped. He covered his face as he teared up. "Wow...I...I...can't believe this! Thank you so much your majesty! This is beyond my wildest dreams!"

When Epios said 'full scholarship' dark emotions swirled within me. My head spun and my skin tingled as a wave of rage washed over me. I couldn't focus, I broke out into a sweat, and my stomach felt nauseous. *The future version of Me's words rang out in my mind.* "We never achieved the success we dreamed about."

The Deceit Spirit's voice whispered in my ear. "You think you're a failure and you're right! Your very existence was a mistake!"

Kayla put her hand on my shoulder. "James, are you alright? You look like you're in pain."

I tried to blink and focus on her words as my mind swirled. *There is no reason for me to be reacting like this. I am genuinely stoked about Jerry getting this opportunity. So why can't I be happy? Why do I feel this way?*

"Yeah. I'm probably just hungry and tired. That's all."

I turned to Jerry and noticed that he was staring at me in disgust. I could have sworn he was glaring at Kayla's hand on my shoulder.

"Are you alright Jerry?" I asked.

His face snapped back to normal, and he smiled. "Yes! Of course! I'm super excited about the king's generous opportunity. I just thought I saw...*a* **snake**! That's all!"

Why did his tone change like that when he said snake? I looked around and we were the only people in the abandoned, run down street.

"Weird. I didn't see one. But that's incredible news Jerry and I'm so excited for you! How old are you and what grade will you be in when you start?

"I'm 25! But I have no education, so I'll likely be starting in kindergarten!" He said proudly.

We stopped and our jaws dropped simultaneously.

"*You're* older than me?" I said in disbelief.

Kayla looked away. "I thought you were in middle school..."

"A dwarf at the least and a midget at best." Epios said.

Terrance sat in a ball and cried. "So this is what happens when children are deprived of creatine at a young age...Deplorable."

I nodded. *That's how he got so jacked. I'll make a mental note for my kids.*

"Why did you guys think I was so young? Don't I look like I'm 23? I've got a little bit of chin hair starting to come in as we speak!" He proudly showed off his one, minuscule chin hair.

"I just...wasn't expecting that..." I stuttered.

"What James said! I didn't mean to insult you!" Kayla stammered.

Epios sighed. "I assumed that your petite demeanor was a result of your age, but now I see it is a result of a deformity in the body and brain."

"You're like 4'9 and you're built like a tree branch. I bet I could snap your arm just by thinking about it." Terrance said.

WHOOOOOOSH!

I felt an overwhelming sense of malice building in the surrounding area. Jerry stared at Terrance and Epios with a look so sinister it could kill. He spoke with such a rage and vitriol that it even made Kayla and I shiver. "I *may be small **now**, but when I grow up, I bet I'll be bigger and taller than both of you **bastards**! And when I do, don't be surprised when I kick both of your asses for calling me short! I let it slide before because we were friends, but next time **I swear to you** there will be serious consequences!*"

They stared in silence.

"BWAAAAHAAAAAAAA! YOU?! KICK MY ASS! THAT'S THE JOKE OF THE YEAR YOU'RE ALREADY GROWN BITCH! FUCK OUT OF HERE!" Terrance shouted as he rolled in the dirt and held his sides.

Epios laughed pretentiously as he slapped his knee. "HA-HA-HA! TRULY COMICAL FIENDISH BODYGUARD! I SHALL RAISE YOUR PAY FOR AMUSING ME SO THOROUGHLY!"

He pointed in both of their faces. "Acknowledge me or not but it's *your* funeral. I'm gonna kick you guys' ass for every single time you've called me skinny or short since the moment we became friends! Prince, you're at 6 and other guy, you're at 4. Mark my words. The day will come where I have *vengeance*."

"BWAAAAAAHAAAAAAAA!". "OH-OHO-HO-HO-OH-OH-OHO!" They roared in laughter.

He was keeping count? I like this guy's attitude.

I shrugged. "I don't know guys...you two do get your asses kicked a lot...I think Jerry might just get you guys one day."

Did they just forget the show he put on when he saved our lives?

"I'm with Jerry. I hope you grow big and tall and kick both of their asses! And if you don't, I'll kick them for you! How does that sound?" Kayla said sweetly.

Jerry's eyes lit up and his face was flushed with color.

He spoke with stars in his eyes. "It sounds...*wonderful...*"

She stared at him in confusion and backed away. "Uhh...great..."

I wasn't sure how I felt about that interaction between them, but Kayla's rejection from the Deceit Spirit still rang in my mind.

"I've never found you attractive and I never liked you. One nice date doesn't mean that I ever felt anything for you, alright? Like come on! Be real! Did you really think that someone like you had a shot with a girl like me? I'm a princess, James."

Is that how she feels? Did she only go on the date because I forced her to? Were the sparks I felt between us all in my head? Is that why she was so willing to flirt with that bitch boy in the prison and make out with Terrance? She never apologized either time and she told me on that rooftop that it was all her fault. Is she just being nice to me and treating me how she would treat any of her...friends? These thoughts weighed on my mind and were crushing me. They filled me with rage, but now wasn't the time to talk about it. I would never treat her differently, but as far as I was concerned, at this point, he could have her. It was better for me to just change the subject.

"So, *Jerry* you were talking about the Archigos like you really liked him or something? Does anyone have any idea where he could possibly be?"

"Nope. He's been gone for years without a trace! I bet he's just on some kind of super cool training mission though, and when he comes back, I'm sure he will wipe out the entire underworld in a single day like he did last time!"

Could he really do something like that?

I tried not to roll my eyes. "It sounds like you're his biggest fan."

"Of course, I am! Everyone is! He's literally the greatest there is! He would wipe the floor with those fake posers like Okpa, Kalarono and Milliard."

"Milliard is *quite* overrated." Epios said.

"Agreed." Kayla said.

"Shut the hell up before I beat your ass Epios! I'll let you slide this time because he's your brother." I roared.

Kayla shrugged. "I hate my uncle, so I'll allow the slander."

Terrance trembled with rage. "*What* did you say about my dad, *pipsqueak?*"

I waved Terrance off. "Pipe down Terrance. He didn't mean anything by it." I grabbed Jerry by the collar and held him to my face. I spoke from a heart filled with malice. "Disrespect Milliard again and you're *finished*. That's my dawg and there will be no slander on his name for as long as I live, *boy*."

"I'm sorry! I'm sorry!" Jerry screamed.

I set him down and smiled. I spoke in my most cheery voice. "It's alright! Well, I'm glad that you like Bazek so much then. I haven't met him, but from my perspective he's a terrible leader for allowing his people to live like this. Once I find him, I'm gonna kick his ass, force him to rejoin the union, and me and my friends are gonna go on our merry way!"

Tears filled his eyes. "DON'T SAY THAT! BAZEK IS AMAZING!"

"Sorry I didn't mean to offend you. I just get worked up about these kinds of things sometimes..."

The rest of the group slowly faced Jerry.

Terrance took a deep breath. "DON'T APOLOGIZE TO THAT RUNT BECAUSE HE'S A SIMP AND A LIAR! BAZEK IS THE WORST!"

I raised an eyebrow. "Have you met him or something? Clearly this kid doesn't think..."

"OF COURSE I HAVE! BAZEK IS A NASTY OLD FART WHO HAS THE WORST ATTITUDE IN THE WORLD! ME AND MY DAD AVOIDED HIM AT EVERY MEETING, BECAUSE HE SUCKS!"

Kayla crossed her arms. "Sorry James, but I have to agree with shit head on this one. Bazek is a very rude and disrespectful old man. He's a really strong fighter, but he's a man whore who neglects his daughters. Just because you're an Archigos, that doesn't give you a license to be a dick."

Epios scoffed. "I am in alignment with the whore and the trog. Bazek is a detestable old prune that I have always despised. He has never respected my father's authority or the throne. He even dared to question my father's lineage! Your future ruler's speculation is that the fiend is missing because he shriveled up and died because his heart is twelve sizes too small. And if so the world would be better off for it."

I stared at them incredulously. "Dang, is he really that..."

"NO, HE'S NOT! I'M SORRY FOR RAISING MY VOICE BUT I CAN'T ACCEPT THIS! HE'S THE GREATEST! BAZEK HAS ALWAYS PROTECTED OUR NATION SINCE HE WAS OUR AGE! I EVEN HAD THE CHANCE TO MEET HIM WHEN I WAS YOUNGER AFTER HE SAVED ME AND MY UNCLE'S LIVES IN A TERRORIST ATTACK! I CAN'T LET YOU GUYS TALK ABOUT HIM LIKE THAT!" Jerry shouted with tear filled eyes.

"I'm sorry Jerry. I didn't know that. We won't talk about this anymore."

We continued chatting about less controversial topics until we reached his house...if you could call it that. It was a very, *very* small one-bedroom apartment. The living room was so little that the long dining table was upon us as soon as we walked in. A tiny kitchen and refrigerator were on our left. There was a children's play area at the back of the main room, a bunk bed, and the living room floor was covered in sleeping bags.

Jerry spread his arms and smiled. "Welcome to mi casa friends! My parent's room and the bathroom are right around the corner. The fridge is over there, and we have plenty of room for you guys to rest up! Make yourself at home!"

"Such a fiendishly small living space. I see now why you fiends turn out so fiendishly. Living in a place like this every day must drive you mad."

I smacked him in the head. "Shut the hell up Epios!"

I turned to Jerry and smiled. "This place is very nice. Thank you so much Jerry!"

Kayla raced around the corner. "You're the best Jerry! I call dibs on the first shower!"

"FOOOOOOOOOOOOOOOOOOOOOOOOOOOOD!" Terrance roared as he ripped open the fridge.

We took turns eating cold noodles and showering. I changed into a suit of Light Craft armor I stole from a dead soldier. It took a long time to find one that fit, and it felt weird stripping a dead man naked and taking his things, but hey, he can't use them anymore! After that we spent most of the rest of the day crashing and catching up on the sleep we missed the night before.

"**HUUUUUUUH**?!"

I awoke in my borrowed sleeping bag to a loud gasp. Six children rushed into the home. Jerry's parents were frozen in the doorway.

Until all hell broke loose.

"Jerry! Who are these people!" His dad shouted.

Jerry waved. "Hey dad! They're my new friends and..."

"Friends?! You have no friends! These people are probably here to rob us all!"

"No dad. I promise I..."

"Jerry. You know you can't just bring company in the house without permission" His mother said concernedly.

"This is unacceptable! Tell them that they need to get out and..."

"But dad!"

I've heard enough.

"Excuse me sir." I said.

"Who the hell are you and what are you doing in my house?! In my son's sleeping bag?!"

I held up my hands. "I'm sorry sir, but we're new friends of Jerry and I promise we mean you no harm. Jerry saved our lives earlier and he offered to let us catch up on our rest from...working the night shift. I'm sorry if we're intruding and if you want us to leave, we will..."

Jerry's mom put her hand on her chin. "Well honey, you know Jerry has been working the late shift recently and it's good that he's finally made some..."

"I don't care! Sir, you and your jabronies need to go! Spouting nonsense about him saving your lives...He can't even save his own life! We don't have time or space for this today! My children have to rest up before work so..."

"Dad, could they *please* stay the night? Just this once? I've never..."

"Absolutely not! How are we supposed to feed them? We can barely feed ourselves..."

Kayla stood. "Like James said, we apologize sir, and we really mean you no harm. We're with the government and we think your son is very talented. We were just enjoying his company, and we appreciate your hospitality..."

Jerry beamed. "You think so?"

Jerry's mom stared at Kayla and smiled. "She seems like a nice girl. She's *very* pretty too..."

Jerry's dad raged. "Talented? Talented at what? Scaring away jobs? Scaring away dollars? Because that's the only thing he has done besides leech away our very limited time, money, space, and resources from contributing family members!"

Jerry's face fell. "Dad...I've been doing my best...I..."

He's really starting to piss me off.

"Sir, with all due respect, you shouldn't be talking about your son like that. He can't help that he's little and he can't help the situation he was born into so..."

He stepped forward. "The situation he was born into?! What are you saying?! Are you saying I don't know how to raise my kids?! Are you saying I don't know how to take care of my family?! If so I'll call the guards *right now* and..."

I held up my hands. "NO! NO! NO! I didn't mean it like that sir! Your words were very condescending and rude. I don't think anyone deserves to be..."

Jerry's mom walked up to me and put a hand on my face. "This boy seems nice as well honey. He's a very handsome young man. Who does he work for again..."

Epios shook his head. "Such fiendish behavior from a father. He reminds me of my own..."

Jerry's dad leaned into Epios' face. "What did you say about me *boy*?! You called me a fiend, I'll show you a fiend!"

Epios gestured toward me. "It is not good for a king to, as the fiend would say, "beat the hell out of his subjects", but it seems that a beating will be in order for today."

Jerry jumped and pulled on his dad. "DAD, STOP! THESE ARE MY ONLY..."

BANG!

He slammed Jerry to the ground and his head hit the table.

"Honey, stop it please! I think we should let them stay the night! They seem like..."

"That's it." I said as I demagnetized a blade from my hip and stepped between Jerry and his dad.

Kayla started toward me. "James! Put that away! We should just leave and..."

Stones ripped out of the wall and swirled around him. "I ain't scared of you, jabronie! I don't give a damn if you're from the government. I'm from the streets! I'll beat the shit out of you and toss your ass the fuck up out of here if you don't turn tail and get your bitch ass gone right the fuck now!"

I raised my blade. "Yeah, people like you are the *worst*."

"JAMES NO!", Kayla yelled.

"GWLAPHAPAHYAPHA!" A voice said sillily.

"MHHHHHHHHHHAAAAAAA!"

We turned toward the source of the sounds. Terrance and Sesame were being swarmed as they played with the kids.

"Who's a good little man! You are! You are!" Terrance said goofily as he tossed a child into the air.

Sesame rubbed against the kids affectionately as they pet his fur. One of the children ran up to their dad and tugged on his leg. He pulled his dad's hand and pointed at Sesame. "Daddy! I want a mammoth just like Sesame!"

Jerry's dad scowled at me, and his face softened as he turned to his child.

"He is a cute little thing. Why don't you go play with him while he's here." His dad said affectionately.

His wife walked over and softly touched her husband's chest. "Pearson, please let them stay for the evening my love. This is Jerry's first-time having friends over and they seem like nice people. The kids are having such a good time, and I can make enough dinner for everyone. Please be considerate of what your eldest son wants for once."

He glared at Jerry as he held his head on the ground, sobbing.

Jerry's dad turned away. "*Fine.* One night and they need to be gone in the morning. I won't have to see much of you jabronies because I'm gonna be leaving for my third shift after dinner."

We settled in as the girls prepared dinner. Terrance and Sesame played with the kids while Kayla helped out in the kitchen.

Terrance sat in front of a white board as Sesame flexed on top of it. His rules of manhood were written on it with phrases like. "Be a man!", "Don't be a simp!", "Get money!", "Get women!"

"Alright kids! These are the Ocean King's rules of manhood! If you master these, your success in life is guaranteed!"

"MHHHHHHHHAAAA!" Sesame roared.

The children clamored. "He's so big and strong!". "I want to be just like him!". "Sesame is so cute!"

"LISTEN UP!" He roared as they sat down and began his lesson. "Now! We'll start with Rule Five! Bullying is the *key* to a better society! Especially for women because they're usually soft! Most people need to go through some kind of hardship in life to reach their full potential, and bullying is the perfect solution! If you see someone weaker than you, BULLY THEM UNTIL THEY BECOME THE STRONGEST THERE IS!"

"Yeah! I love bullying!", "Bullying is the greatest!", "I'm gonna bully everyone I see from here on!", "Let's start with him!" The children shouted as they rioted triumphantly.

As a result of Terrance's teachings, Epios spent his evening avoiding harassment from the kids.

"Stop pulling on my hair this instant! OUCH! Do not throw toys at your future ruler!" He roared.

The kids stared at each other in confusion. "Why is he so mean?", "I don't know. It's probably because he's weak.", "Let's keep bullying him!"

"YOU ARE NOT SUPPOSED TO BULLY YOUR FUTURE RULER!"

One little girl seemed to have sense. She walked up to Terrance and pulled on his shorts. "Excuse me Mr. Ocean king, but why do all of your rules on the white board say, especially for women or especially for women and children?"

He picked her up and sat her on his lap. "Aww, come here little one. I can tell that you're confused."

She looked at him with adorable little eyes.

"Now, you may be wondering, why does the Ocean king do this, or why does the Ocean king do that? But there is always a reason behind it. Take a look at those two simps at the table or that fake ass prince being bullied by toddlers, or that hypocritical woman cooking our food. Our society has grown weak, and I see bullying as the only solution! I know plenty of people who got bullied and later attested that it was the best thing that ever happened to them! I know people who were bullied and later became best friends with their bullies! These are proven results that bullying is our only path forward!" He preached enthusiastically.

"Oh! Ok! That makes sense sir! Bullying for the win!" She said as she ran off and kicked Epios in the shin.

"OUCH! You *fiendish* child!"

I wanted to correct these perverse teachings, but I was tired, and I enjoyed watching Epios suffer, so I let it slide for now. Eventually Epios grew tired of getting bullied, and he stole Terrance's whiteboard while he went to the restroom.

"SETTLE DOWN AND GATHER ROUND CHILDREN! BEFORE IT IS MY TURN TO BULLY YOU!" Epios shouted.

"Make us!", "We're trying to help you not become a simp when you get older!", "We don't listen to simps!", "Bullying is life!" The children rioted.

Epios demagnetized his sword from his hip. "As the future ruler of this nation I am well within my rights to execute anyone I find in violation of our laws!" He glared. "Nobody here would like to be executed, *correct?*"

The children swiftly piled into their seats.

"*Now.* Forget all the false doctrine and troglodytian propaganda you just heard. Your future ruler is here to teach you his ten laws of kinghood that are essential if you hope to rule this nation by my side one day and avoid becoming a *fiend.*"

"Being a fiend sounds bad...", "I don't want to become a fiend...", "Are you even a king mister?", "The Ocean king said you were a faker and..."

"SILENCE! I TOLD YOU TO FORGET THAT TROGLODYTIAN LITERATURE AND LISTEN TO YOUR FUTURE RULER!" He cleared his throat. "*Ahem,* Law One states that a king's subjects must always be loving and gracious toward him. They must serve him with willing and open hearts for the betterment of their own society.

In turn, the king will be loving and gracious toward them. Finally, it also strictly outlaws bullying. Now who here can spell, 'No *bullying*', Anybody?"

"I can do it!", "Pick me!", "Pick me!"

"Ah yes, I pick the especially fiendish looking boy in the brown shirt..."

"HEY! WHAT THE HELL IS GOING ON HERE! GIVE ME THAT WHITE BOARD AND STOP SPOUTING HORSE SHIT TO THESE CHILDREN! IT'S DEPLORABLE!"

"ON THE CONTRARY! THE ONLY ONE SPITTING HORSE SHITE IS YOURSELF TROG! THIS COUNTRY IS AN OPEN LEARNING SOCIETY. WE BOTH HAVE THE RIGHT TO RUN OUR OWN SEPARATE CLASSROOMS!"

"NO! I CAN'T ACCEPT THIS! THERE'S ONLY ONE WAY! THE OCEAN KING'S WAY! AND I'LL KILL YOU TO PROVE IT!"

"IF A DUEL OVER THE TRUE SYLLABAI IS WHAT YOU WANT THEN I SHALL OBLIGE YOU TROG! WE SHALL SEE WHO'S DOCTRINE TRULY RESONATES IN THE HEARTS OF THE PEOPLE!"

"But we all like Terrance!", "Yeah Terrance is the best!", "Bullying is love!", "Bullying is life!", "No! I want to be a king when I grow up!", "Yeah! Epios was spitting facts!", "I don't want to be a fiend, so I'll fight!" The children clamored as an all-out war commenced.

I tried to black out the nonsense ensuing all around me and I sat at the table with Jerry.

He sighed as he stared at her while she cut chicken. "*Man*, I love a woman that can cook..."

I sighed as I stared with equal intent. "I know right! It makes me want to bend my knee as we speak..."

She scowled at us. "You know I can hear you two idiots, *right*?"

I swiftly looked away and whistled inconspicuously. As I casually looked around and pretended to be invisible, I heard a noise. I inconspicuously looked to my left and locked eyes with Jerry. HE'S WHISTLING TOO AND DOING THE SAME EXACT THING!

"GAAAH!" We both yelled as we fell to the floor in shock.

We both got up and I allowed him to grab me and pulled me into the corner.

He whispered aggressively. "I knew it! You're just as bad as the others! All of you are plotting against me!"

"What the hell are you talking about?! I've been admiring Kayla for months! I've loved her since the first time I experienced the sweet nectar that is her voice when she was helping out an old lady! You just got here punk!"

He whispered as he spat in my face. "So! You openly admit it! You admit to being my mortal enemy and rival in love! A foolish error because I will be the victor! I swear it on my name and birthright!"

I wiped my face. "Oh yeah? Well, I already took her on a..."

Her voice rang out in my mind. "Did you really think someone like you had a shot with a girl like me? I'm a **princess***, James..."*

I looked up at her and anger filled my heart. I sighed to calm myself so I wouldn't look like a lunatic. "You know what Jerry? You've got spirit and I like you. From what I can tell, you and I are gonna be great friends. So as a token of our budding friendship, I concede. You can have her."

CRASH!

Everyone stopped and stared as a loud sound filled the apartment. I looked up and saw Jerry's mom running over to Kayla. Apparently, she had dropped a plate on the floor, and it shattered.

"Kayla! Are you alright sweetie!" His mom said concernedly.

Kayla had an expressionless look on her face. She looked up at his mother and gave a half-hearted smile. "It's nothing. I'm so sorry about the plate ma'am! Let me clean it up!"

"It's alright sweetheart don't worry! We have plenty of plates!" She said as they started cleaning up the mess.

Everyone resumed their activities as clamor re-filled the room.

What was that all about?

Jerry suddenly grabbed my collar with a newfound strength and pulled me way too close to his face.

He whispered aggressively. "OH MY GOD JAMES! YOU ARE THE BEST FRIEND EVER!"

I turned my head slightly to the side to keep the ultimate disaster from occurring. "Thanks. But on a serious note, we need to discuss personal boundaries..."

He pulled me even closer, and I aggressively turned my head. *I AM NOT HAVING MY SECOND KISS WITH HIM!*

He teared up. "I WAS SO WORRIED! YOU'RE THE ONLY ONE IN THE FRIEND GROUP WHO ISN'T CRAZY AND YOU'RE ACTUALLY A STAND-UP GUY! I HAD NO CHANCE OF ACTUALLY DEFEATING YOU IN A WAR OVER HER HEART...Of course, I would never admit that...BUT THANK YOU SO MUCH!"

"You kind of just did...but sure! Before you try this though I think there are some things you should know..."

SMACK!

He vanished and I fell on my face. *How did he do that?* I looked up and he was somehow seated at the table patting the seat next to him.

He stared intently into my eyes. "Come friend. I must know everything! EVERYTHING!"

I dusted myself off and slid into my seat. "Well first..."

He put his finger to my lips. "WAIT! I need some background information on you first. That way I'll know how to filter the information you give me so I can proceed efficiently. First, tell me. What kind of woman is your type?"

I moved his finger. "If we're talking physically, I prefer light skins. I like them tall, and athletic, with curly hair. Colored eyes are a bonus..."

CRASH!

We looked over in confusion as we heard another plate shatter.

He looked down and shadows filled his face. "I see...that...you are...a man of culture! We have the exact same type! What a coincidence! We're this great of friends already?!"

"I guess so! But now, about Kayla..."

He put his finger to my lips and my aggravation grew. "SHH! I still need more information. What were the caliber of the girls you went to school with and grew up around? I need to know so I can properly judge your experience level..." He pulled out a pair of expensive looking shades from behind his back and spoke in a smooth tone. "I am a world renown love master, so bagging women is nothing to me." He shuddered as he glanced toward the window. "But here in the slums...they aren't the kind that made you want to bend your knee...let's just say that..."

Kayla rolled her eyes. "Great! Another love master! Maybe this one will actually have some authenticity!"

I gave her a death glare and turned back to Jerry. "Same! I found one good looking girl per year if I was lucky. the kind of guy who always went after the prettiest female. Especially if she was a Christian." I sighed. "Unfortunately, pretty much all my tales ended in disaster..."

He shook his fist at the sky. "Same dude! Life is hard without beautiful women around. But I think I have enough data now. SO, TELL ME EVERYTHING YOU KNOW ABOUT MY DARLING KAYLA SO I CAN CONFESS MY LOVE THIS AFTERNOON!"

"You're gonna confess *today*? Good luck with *that*. But I guess I'll start with the most important thing, she is very religious..."

Epios and Terrance burst into laughter as they slapped their knees and held their sides respectively.

Epios roared as tears filled his eyes. "OH-HO-HO! You call that *wench* religious? What supposed religion could that man hating, hypocrite *bimbo* possibly subscribe to?"

Terrance crushed the children as he rolled around on the ground. "HAHAHAHAHAHAHAHA! I KNOW RIGHT! I'VE NEVER SEEN ANY OF HER DEEDS IN THE BIBLE! THE ONLY RELIGION SHE SUBSCRIBES TO IS HOEISM! AHAHAHAHAHAHAHAHA!"

She turned around with flames in her eyes. "OH YEAH?! WELL, IF I'M SUCH A HEATHEN AND DON'T

KNOW GOD THEN MAYBE IT'S TIME I SENT YOU TO
MEET HIM! AND TERRANCE! I CAN'T BELIEVE YOU OF
ALL PEOPLE WOULD..."

I gripped Terrance's neck as his eyes went wide. I
glanced to my right and Jerry had Epios in an even
deadlier chokehold.

My hand trembled with rage. "If you *ever* say
something like that again about my girl Terrance...You're
done..."

Jerry held Epios' neck in his slender frame with
hatred in his eyes. "She's not his girl, but what he said
holds true. I'll kill you if my woman's name comes out of
your mouth again, *prince*."

SLAM!

We tossed them to the ground in unison.

"I DON'T BELONG TO EITHER OF YOU AND I'M
NOBODY'S GIRL! THIS IS WHY I HATE MEN!"

We ignored her and took our seats. Terrance and
Epios coughed as they picked themselves up off the
ground.

"Body...*cough*...guard this is not how you treat your
future...*cough*...ruler..."

Terrance glared in anger. "A pair of...*cough*...simps.
I...*cough*...*cough*...knew it..."

We glared at them with even greater malice as they
shrunk back in fear. We smiled at each other and
resumed our conversation.

"But anyway, best friend I took her on a date already so I'm your man for all of the insider..."

He pointed and covered his mouth. "Wait a minute...you took her on a date with your hair looking like...like that?"

"KALARONO PAID FOR MY HAIRCUT YOU LITTLE SHRIMP! OF COURSE, I DIDN'T GO ON A DATE WITH THE MOST BEAUTIFUL GIRL IN THE WORLD WITH A NAPPY FRO AND UNKEMPT WAVES!" I shouted as more dishware clattered in the kitchen.

Jerry pointed and laughed. "I was just wondering because Terrance's hair looks like a damn ocean compared to that shallow pond you got up there! And he got robbed just like you did! So what's *your* excuse?"

"His hair does suck." A child whispered.

"This is why we call him *the fiend*..." Epios whispered to the kid.

Kayla chopped vegetables aggressively. "His hair did look nice on the date, but I've been telling him that he needs to get his hair cut for weeks."

Terrance shrugged. "Waves give your anti-simp immune system a one thousand percent boost."

I walked up to each person and pointed in their face. "CHILD, SHUT YOUR DAMN MOUTH BECAUSE YOU'RE TOO YOUNG TO BE IN A GROWN MAN'S BUSINESS! EPIOS, SHUT THE HELL UP BECAUSE YOU'RE THE ONLY PERSON THAT CALLS ME THAT AND YOUR HAIR

LOOKS LIKE SHIT RIGHT NOW TOO! KAYLA, THANK YOU FOR THE COMPLIMENT BUT YOU CAN SHUT THE HELL UP TOO! WE DON'T NEED THOSE DAMN SIDE COMMENTS! HOW ABOUT YOU WORRY ABOUT PAYING THE BILL FOR THOSE CRACKED ASS PLATES AND LEAVE ME THE HELL ALONE! AND TERRANCE, YOU'RE THE ONE WHO'S ALWAYS TALKING ABOUT SIMP, THIS, AND SIMP THAT! BUT YOU STRIKE ME AS THE TYPE WHO WAS A SIMP IN THE PAST AND NOW YOU POINT OUT WHEN OTHER PEOPLE SIMP TO FEEL BETTER ABOUT YOURSELF! I'M JUST SAYING!" I swiftly turned to face Jerry. "AND JERRY! I LIKE THE CAP SON, BUT YOUR HAIR LOOKS LIKE DOG WATER SO YOU HAVE NO ROOM TO TALK! AND I WOULDN'T CAP ON THE PERSON ABOUT TO GIVE YOU VALUABLE INFO, BUT THAT'S JUST ME!"

The room was silent as I stunned them with my words of truth. Everyone went back to what they were doing because there wasn't a *damn* thing they could say to that fire track I just laid down on their asses.

Jerry looked confused. "Sorry, James. I didn't know it was that personal..."

I crossed my arms. "I'm tired of people calling me a pervert and talking about my hair. Let's just talk about something else...like the fact that you keep saying that we got robbed when I told you it was a spirit attack. You really don't remember tossing skyscrapers and saving our lives?"

He patted me on the shoulder, winked and glanced at Kayla. "Ah, James. It's alright. I already know the truth, so you don't have to tell me."

"What the hell are you..."

"Don't be filling his head with stories Jabronie." His father said as he entered the restroom with a cigar and beer bottle in his hand.

I glared at him and decided to stay silent, for now. It was unfortunately his food and his house I was commandeering for the night.

"James don't worry about him...but I can smell the food...is there any advice you can give me before I propose and confess my love to her?"

I put my hand on his shoulder. "I don't think you should do this, but if you do, just speak from the heart and..."

Epios scoffed. "Refrain from this course of action unless you want a thousand years of misery."

Terrance shook his head. "Just don't be a blubbering *simp* and everything will work out."

"I DIDN'T ASK EITHER OF YOU SO PIPE THE HELL DOWN!" Jerry roared.

I smiled at Jerry as I teared up. "Jerry, I love your attitude, and I just wanted to say that I appreciate you. You are the first normal person I have met since I came to this crazy place, and I love that about you. If you just tell her how you feel from the depths of your heart. I'm sure everything will work out swimmingly!"

He teared up as he placed his hand on my shoulder. It didn't reach so he placed it on my forearm. "Thank you James. I love you too bro. Your words have filled my heart with confidence and joy. I'm sure my eloquent declaration will break her out of her shell and cause her to confess her deepest desires and feelings. We'll be on our honeymoon in the dragon isles before you know it. It shall be a sight to behold."

Everyone gathered around the table as the food was served. Jerry's mom excitedly smiled at the group. "So! I've heard a little bit about you guys while we were cooking, but I wanted to get to know Jerry's friends a little bit better! Where do you all work?! And where are you all from?!"

Kayla smiled as James and Jerry ogled over her. "I'm the Flame Archigos' niece and I'm from the Flame Tribe. I don't have a job, but I spend most of my time training. In my spare time I volunteer, I help my sorry uncle run the nation, and I host a Bible study group for young women."

"Wonderful! Who's next!"

"Your fiendish ignorance betrays you as my title should be self-explanatory, but I am *Prince* Epios Iliaktida. The next Light Archigos and future ruler of this nation. Again, you may bow before me."

She bowed. "Oh wow! I didn't know that we were dining with royalty tonight! It's an honor!"

"You most certainly are. I expected your cooking to be fiendish and deplorable. And yet, I regard it as some of the finest in all the land. Your family has found favor in my sight, and I will remember this household for all of the days that I reign."

"Wow! Thank you so much sir!". "Yay! Momma's the best!". "We're gonna be rich! We're moving to the palace!". "We're gonna meet the Archigos!". "I'm gonna buy a castle!". "I'm gonna buy a yacht!" Jerry's mother and the children clamored.

BANG!

Epios pounded the table. "Settle down, *children*! Not all of you have found favor in my sight on this day. I will remember those who betrayed me and allied with the fiendish troglodyte in our prior war. Once I become king, I shall scourge each of you traitors and personally drive you out of this nation for all eternity!"

"Please have mercy on us!", "What's betrayal?", "What's a troglodyte again?", "What's a scourge?", "I'm confused about everything right now...", "I'm bored. When are we buying the castle and the yacht again?"

James glared. "Epios, don't you think those words are a bit too harsh for children?"

"Absolutely not, if they can choose sides in war then they can learn about scourging and..."

"That's enough of that." James said as he turned to Jerry's mother. "Ma'am, I'm sorry about him. You have nothing to worry about and I'm sure he will remember the service you have done us on this day and reward you greatly."

"That's wonderful! You all seem so nice! You two sweet boys haven't introduced yourselves yet!"

James cleared his throat. "I'm..."

Terrance garbled as he shoveled food into his mouth. "Name's Terrance...*scarf*...*scarf*...I'm the Ocean King...*scarf*...*scarf*...and future ruler...*scarf*...*scarf*...of the Ocean Tribe...*scarf*...*scarf*..."

"Wow! You sure can eat! Are all your friends royalty Jerry?" His mother marveled.

"Yep momma! And see dad! Because of your son's charm, you're dining with royals in your very own home!"

His dad scoffed. "Whatever."

His mother turned to James. "That's amazing! And who is the fine young man that we've saved for last?"

"I'm James Fos. I'm just a student...and I work for the government...I guess..."

"Oh, so you're not royalty?", "Boo! You suck!", "You're worthless!", "I see why the prince calls him a fiend now!", "Why are you even here?!", "Let's bully him!"

James gave the children death glares as their mother came to his defense. "Settle down children! Just because he's not royalty doesn't mean that he doesn't have a lot to offer. I can tell that he's a sweet boy. Where are you from? And what do you like to do in your spare time Mr. Fos?"

"Where I'm from...well...that's complicated. Let's just say that I'm from a faraway place. What do I do in my free time...*uh*...I actually host a Bible study like Kayla does but for young men. Most of my days are spent slaving away playing a children's sports game called football. It's very time consuming, but you can get a lot of money and status if you're good at it."

Kayla stared at James in confusion. "Football? James, what are you..."

Jerry clapped James on the back. "There you go James! Always going for the money like your big bro!"

James stared. *How could he possibly insinuate that* **I'm his** *little bro.*

"Wow! That's amazing. Who knew we had so many Bible scholars at dinner with us this evening!", "So you play a games for money?!", "That's so cool!", "I want to play games for money when I grow up!", "Maybe you're not worthless after all!", "He's still not royalty though...", "If I play that game can I still buy a yacht?"

Jerry's mother turned to Kayla. "So, Ms. Kayla. I'm sorry to put you up on the spot like this, but I heard some of my son's ramblings earlier and I had to ask. Are you and my son *involved*?"

"PFFFFFFFFFFFTTT!"

Kayla spat water as she struggled to contain herself. "*Me*? With *Jerry*? Are you..." She froze as she came to her senses. "Well Mrs. Giali, Jerry is a nice young man. But we just met, so I can *definitely* say that we are *not*..."

BANG!

Jerry stood on the table with his shades on. "I see no better time."

"Get off the table boy!" His father said.

Jerry whispered as he jumped off the table. "Dad! I'm trying to propose right now!"

He bent his knee and took Kayla's hand as she stared at him in utter confusion. She trembled as she fought to keep from rolling her eyes. **Please** *tell me this is a joke and he's not seriously trying this right now. I swear this is why I...*

"Kayla. This past day that I've gotten to know you has been the best day of my entire life..."

What the hell is he talking about?! We haven't even had a conversation yet!

"I felt that there was no better time to confess my love and ask if you would allow me to take your hand in marriage."

There's no way he's serious...I can't believe this idiot is really doing this to himself right now...

"Yeah! Jerry's the best", "Go Jerry!", "This is so romantic!", "Just say yes already!", "She's gonna buy us a castle and a yacht!", "I want to marry her next!"

She looked away as she tried to hide her disdain. "Jerry. You're a sweet guy. But don't you think this is all a bit...uh, *sudden?*"

"Yes! I know it's sudden but when two people are in love, why wait? After everything that my main man James told me about you, I knew that were soul mates!"

She glared at James with vitriol. He put his hands up and smiled. She mouthed to him. *I'm going to kill you later.*

She turned back to Jerry. "Look Jerry. I hate to say this but I'm umm...taken?"

He stood. "Who is it that has your heart milady, I promise I will duel them to the death in order to gain your affections!"

"Well, you see...it's not exactly *taken* but..."

Epios scoffed. "Taken? BY WHOM? Please! I doubt I could find a man in the entire kingdom other than the *fiends* at this table who would be willing to have you by their side! Do not lie to my fiendish bodyguard. You're as single as can be *wench*!"

"Who would want to date a crazy whore like her anyways?" Terrance said as he gnawed on a bone.

"Yeah Kayla! Tell us! Who's the lucky guy?!" James said enthusiastically.

She stared at the ground. "Well...uh...let's just discuss this later Jerry."

Silence filled the room.

"I don't think she likes him...". "It looks like we're not getting a yacht or a castle..." The little girls whispered to each other.

"Of course...I know...it's a big decision..." Jerry said as he sat back down despondently.

His dad shook his head. "She doesn't like you boy. And you shouldn't have gotten your hopes up, because I can't think of a single reason why she would."

James clenched his fist.

Jerry stared at the floor as tears welled in his eyes. "Dad...she didn't say no...so maybe..."

"You need to get your head out of the clouds, stop worrying about girls that you don't got no shot with, and worry about making this family some money. These little ones are still out-earning you and you're ok with that?"

"Dad, you know I'm trying my best I..."

BANG!

James pounded the table. "Alright! That's enough! Why can't you treat Jerry with the same decency you treat your other children with sir?"

Jerry's dad stood up. "Because he's a waste of space and a non-contributor! He's the oldest, but his siblings work way more hours than him and bring in much more cash to this family! He's always complaining that he's tired and doesn't have enough energy! Why should he eat if he can't pull his weight?!" He snatched Jerry's plate off the table.

"But if he's doing his best and bringing in what he can right now then why are you so mad at him?! He can't help that he never got an education and that he's small and weak!"

Kayla stared at James intently. *He made me so mad earlier with those stupid comments about letting Jerry have me, but I kind of like it when he gets all angry and righteous like this...*

Jerry's dad pointed at James. "Why are you defending him?! You don't even *know* my son! I've raised him for his entire life, and you just met him! It's not just that he's small and weak, it's the fact that he has no smarts or talent whatsoever! He had the chance to go to school, but he was barely passing because he was always talking about being a fighter or becoming the Archigos, instead of focusing on his books! On top of that, he's always hanging out in the wrong crowds with his good for nothing uncle! When you hang with good for nothings, you become a good for nothing and that's exactly what happened to him! *That's* why we pulled him out and got Reggie in there! We need someone who can get us some results and bring this family some cash. With him we actually have a chance to put the Giali name on the map!"

"Look! Why are children even being allowed to work these long hours in these harsh factory conditions anyway?! They're not even in middle school! You shouldn't be allowing this no matter how broke you are because if they get crushed by a machine *they're dead!* And as a parent you have a responsibility to each of your kids, so if you can't afford to have them wrap up or get from under the covers! It's irresponsible to keep having kids when you can't afford them!"

Oh my gosh! He's so right! Wait, why does he look so attractive right now? Kayla thought.

The dust beneath their feet spiraled. "HOW DARE YOU TELL ME HOW TO RAISE MY KIDS AND TAKE CARE OF MY HOUSEHOLD WHEN YOU WORK FOR THE GOVERNMENT! YOU HAVE A CUSH JOB! YOU'VE NEVER KNOW WHAT IT'S LIKE TO STARVE AND BE HUNGRY AND HAVE A FAMILY DEPENDING ON YOU TO COME HOME AND FEED THEIR HUNGRY BELLIES AT NIGHT! I SHOULD KILL YOU BECAUSE YOU AND YOUR ROYAL PALS ARE THE REASON THAT PEOPLE LIKE US ARE IN THIS MESS! AND..."

James spoke calmly. "What were you sipping on earlier?"

"What are you..."

"What were you smoking on earlier?"

"What I do in my spare time is none of your business! You have no idea what it's like to have to cope and..."

"I DO KNOW WHAT IT'S LIKE TO COPE! AND I'VE HAD TO COPE WITH SOME HARD ASS SHIT SIR! SOME SHIT SO HARD YOU COULDN'T EVEN COMPREHEND IT! IF YOU'RE SO POOR THEN HOW CAN YOU AFFORD THAT?!"

"Look I've been trying to quit and..."

"TRYING ISN'T GOOD ENOUGH! BUT YOU'RE THE SAME MAN WHO HAS THE NERVE TO BELITTLE HIS OLDEST SON WHEN HE'S TRYING HIS BEST AND THEN COMPLAIN ABOUT YOUR CHILDREN BEING HUNGRY! DON'T COMPLAIN ABOUT BELLIES RUMBLING WHEN YOU'RE THE ONE WHO SMOKES AND SIPS AWAY THEIR MEALS AND DOESN'T GIVE THEM THE SUPPORT THAT THEY NEED TO BE SUCCESSFUL, BITCH!"

CRASH!

Jerry's dad roared as he slammed Jerry's plate on the ground. "WHATEVER! THAT BOY IS STILL USELESS AND THAT FACT WILL NEVER CHANGE!"

SLAM!

He stomped into his bedroom and slammed the door behind him.

Jerry stared at the door and burst into tears.

James hugged him and pulled him close. "It's alright Jerry. I can see that you're doing your best and that's all that matters. You don't need validation from a jackass like him. The person that you are is more than good enough and as long as your name is Jerry *fucking* Giali you will always have my support. It's gonna be alright bro."

Jerry grabbed tightly onto James and gripped his clothes as he sobbed violently.

Kayla looked away as she blushed. "HMMMPPPHH!" She screamed to herself quietly as she covered her face.

Jerry's mom put her hand on Kayla's shoulder. "I'm so sorry you had to see that dear. Are you alright?"

"Yes, ma'am. I'm alright. I'm quite alright." Kayla whispered blissfully through her fingers.

The evening ended in a somber mood as everyone finished their meals in silence. The household winded down as the children and their parents rested before the night shifts.

James started putting on his shoes. "Are you going to work tonight, Jerry? If so, I'll work a shift with you and all the money that I earn is yours."

Jerry stared at the ground. "*Sniffle, sniffle.* Thank you, James, but I don't think I can work tonight. It takes all my energy and focus to do the little Earth Craft that I can manage in my factory jobs. There's no way I can get it done when I'm emotionally drained like this" He shuffled despondently across the room.

James' heart broke as he stared at Jerry. He looked like a lifeless zombie, and he was completely enveloped in his sleeping bag.

He zipped it over his head and went still.

James and his friends slept on the ground with the rest of the children.

In the middle of the night, James got up and crept over to Jerry's section of the room. He leapt and tiptoed like a clumsy ballerina as he struggled to avoid the bodies strewn across the ground. He reached into Jerry's small pile of belongings and pulled out his ID and work schedule.

"I'll work for you tonight, Jerry. Just get some rest." James whispered.

James crept through the apartment and tiptoed out the door. As he eased the door shut behind him, he lifted his head and saw a street filled with masked goons.

James put his hand on his blade.

"What are you guys doing HERE..." James yelled as he was dropped into a sinkhole.

Inside the apartment, Kayla, Epios, Jerry, and Terrance slept soundly. Suddenly the ground beneath them shifted into sinkholes and they were swallowed up by the earth without a trace.

Elsewhere, Gray stood on an abandoned skyscraper overlooking the city. The building had an exceptional view of the gorgeous midnight skyline. There were two entrances on opposing corners of the roof. It was a cold, rainy night, and the frigid wind tore through his skintight suit. He had thick bags under his bloodshot eyes. He sighed as he admired the view. "Last job and then I finally get a break. They're working me ragged...but I'm glad that I can give my all for the cause."

He shuddered as he sensed a new presence and swiftly turned around. An ordinary looking man in a plain white tee and expensive looking shades walked out of the rooftop entrance.

The man pulled out an umbrella. "Don't look so scared kiddo. You're the one who called *me*, remember."

Gray forced down his fatigue and sharpened his focus. "You're late, *Slave Master*."

He waved dismissively. "Yeah, yeah. I'm sorry, but not all of us can slink through the shadows alright. And you wouldn't know, but for us normal people, traffic in this city is a bitch ok?." He smiled. "You see something new every day..."

"Father has a request for you, and he is not willing to negotiate."

The Slave Master burst into laughter. "Not willing to negotiate?! What does he take me for? Some kind of B-list crime lord that he can just push around as he pleases? Hilarious." He chuckled as he shook his head. "This had better be *some* request..."

Gray's pitch-black blade gleamed in the moonlight as he pointed it at the Slave Master. "You are *nothing* to the Council of Tromos. Never forget that underworld scum."

The Slave Master yawned. "You're not doing a very good job of making me want to hear you out kiddo. But still, I drove all this way, in this cold ass rain, so hit me with your request. If we're not negotiating, I may or may not have time for it. I've got a busy schedule this week. I've got a show to rehearse for and I need to hire a new drum guy..."

"Father would like you to acquire a boy by the name of James Fos and deliver him to us immediately."

The Slave Master picked his fingernails. "Again, the rudeness and imperatives will get you nowhere son. But this *is* interesting. What kind of kid has the great Dameon Dark so spooked that he would come asking a guy like me for help? *You guys* are the big bad terrorist organization, aren't you? Why do you need an average joe like me to help you guys capture a *kid*?"

Gray's blade was enveloped in milky energy. "That's none of your business! And you shall not insult us again! You will do the job for free or face the consequences!"

The Slave Master face palmed and sighed. "What are you going to do with that son? Honestly you and your father are just alike...How does he expect to get anywhere in life without making compromises? You two just need to relax a little bit and have some fun once..."

"ENOUGH GAMES! YOU WILL DO THIS JOB OR DIE!"

"Oh my gosh, so scary!" The man said as he threw his hands up in jest.

Gray's green eyes flashed with darkness. "This is your last *chance* Giali."

The Slave Master's jaw dropped. "Wooooow! We're throwing government names into this?! Honestly, you kids keep getting bolder and bolder these days." He yawned. "But fine. I'll do it..."

Gray lowered his blade. "I knew you would come to see reason. Now, he was last spotted in a factory attack here in the Earth Tribe. We believe he is hiding somewhere in the..."

The man gave an exacerbated yawn as he held up a finger. "But not for free. Clearly this kid means a lot to you guys, and for some reason Dameon doesn't think you all have what it takes to bring him safely...or *quietly*." He pulled out a small notebook and combed through it. "I'll do it, in exchange for one of Dameon's top guys. Give me

Ji or Kakinos. Or I'll even take that crazy hunter guy that broods in the dark all day. There's gotta be a good story behind him..."

"I told you! No negotiations! ARE YOU GOING TO THROW AWAY YOUR LIFE OR..."

The Slave Master shrugged. "*Actually*, you're his son so why don't I just take you."

Gray flinched. "Absolutely not! Father would never..."

The man took off his shades revealing bright yellow eyes. "Tell me, Gray. Do you have a girl that you fancy? A woman that you love? A female that you would do anything to protect?"

Gray hesitated as Kayla came to mind. "No! Now we're done talking..."

"You're a *terrible* liar. And it sucks for you because I just came back from boning her. Raw. For hours. We had such a great time too! She was just *so cooperative*, and she did some things that I just couldn't..."

Gray trembled as he raised his blade. "YOU'RE A LIAR YOU..."

GOOOOOOOONG!

A gong sounded in Gray's mind and his entire body went stiff. He instantly lost consciousness, and his eyes shifted from green to yellow. He sheathed his sword and stood at attention as the Slave Master approached him.

The Slave Master nodded. "Good. I'm just gonna probe your mind a little bit, wire in a few commands and then we'll go get the kid." He put his hand on Gray's temple and Gray's memories flooded into his mind. "Interesting. You guys have been following this guy and his people for a long time! But there's nothing here that tells me why Dameon wants this boy so badly. Maybe I should just take him for myself now that I know his face."

He stepped back from Gray as he blinked rapidly to clear his thoughts. He stepped forward and delved into Gray's mind. "Alright it's time to add in some commands. When you capture the boy, I want you to bring him to me. *Instead* of your father. And let's see what we've got in these fractured memories as well..."

A few minutes passed and a figure appeared on the rooftop behind the Slave Master. A large samurai in crimson armor cleared his throat. "I'll be taking the boy with me Giali."

The Slave Master beamed. "KAKINOS! We were just talking about you! It's so good to see you! I love the suit by the way. It really accentuates your eyes. I was gonna take you or Ji in the deal for the Fos boy, but this kid was annoying me, so I decided to take him instead. But now that you're here I think I'd rather have you!"

Kakinos unsheathed his blade. "I have no time for games, Giali. You have no hope of breaking my mind. I gave up on earthly attachments decades ago and I refuse to be used by the likes of you." He extended his hand.

"Return the boy to my care immediately or face my wrath."

"That may be true, but don't send someone to me who's rude, not willing to negotiate and then have him try to kill me! That's so not cool! What are you even doing out here this late at night? Still searching for the dude who slept with your wife?"

FWOOOOOOOOOOOOOOOOOOOOOOOOOOOOOSH!

Kakinos' blade ignited. Despite the darkness of night, his crimson red blade burned bright like the sun as it casted the county in a crimson hue. "Yes. And I believe you know exactly where he is. I'll be peeling this information from your corpse after I collect the boy."

The Slave Master shrugged and started toward the exit. "Yeah, I don't think so. You know snitches get stitches as they say!" He turned to Gray. "Gray. Please get rid of this guy for me and let's meet up down the street. I gave you some upgrades so you should be able to handle him."

Gray drew his blade and stepped between the Slave Master and Kakinos.

Kakinos raised his blade. "*Sigh*. Your mind is that weak boy?"

The Slave Master waved goofily. "Well, that's all from me! I'm on my way to pay my nephew a visit in the morning so see ya!" He put his hand on the door handle to the rooftop exit.

BANG!

A bullet decimated his hand, and he fell to the ground. His vision blurred as he stared at his blood pooling on the ground.

"Though I require no aid, did you truly think I was foolish enough to confront one of the Underworld Lords alone, Giali?" Kakinos said.

The Slave Master swiftly turned and peered into the distance. Several rooftops away, Lawbringer laid prone with a rifle. "I've gotta save yer' ass again boy?! You already made me waste good men supplementing yer' sorry ass troops in last night's raid!" He loaded his second rifle shot.

"Shit! GET ME OUT OF HERE!" The Slave Master roared.

BANG!

A man with yellow eyes dove in front of the Slave Master just as the bullet neared his head. The man who took the bullet crumpled to the ground and died as two more men burst through the roof. They shielded the Slave Master on either side as they entered the stairwell.

"Don't let them get away!" Kakinos roared.

BANG!

GUSH!

A bullet hit one of the Slave Master's protectors and his head exploded in blood as they sprinted through a lower floor.

"ROGER!" The Lawbringer shouted.

Suddenly, a man with yellow eyes walked out of the shadows behind Lawbringer.

Lawbringer shuddered. "Shit."

GUSH!

He ripped his hand through Lawbringer's back and out of his chest as his blood gushed into the night sky.

✳

Back on the rooftop with Gray, the two swordsmen paced as they readied their blades.

Kakinos' blade roared with fire. "You have been clamoring for years about joining us in the upper ranks, boy! Now is your chance! Face me!"

Gray spoke as if in a trance. "Art 3, Void Double..."

Seven clones of Gray appeared from the shadows and circled Kakinos.

"This trick again? You really are your father's son!"

"**VOID SLASH**!" The Gray's shouted in unison.

Kakinos remained in place, and he flipped over his blade. It shifted from a bright crimson to pitch black as the Void Slashes careened toward him.

WHOOSH!

As the shadowy blades neared him, they evaporated.

"Nice trick. But you know that Spirit Craft doesn't affect me, boy."

FWOOSH!

Kakinos vanished in a rush of flames as he charged forward.

WHOOSH!

The clones assaulted him from every direction and brought their blades down upon him. He smirked as his blade's darkness deepened, "...Art 9, Burning Heavens."

FWOOOOOOOOOOOOOOOOOOOOOOOOOOOSH!

Before they made contact, he stopped on a dime, pivoted, and sliced through each Gray as a raging tempest of flames filled the night sky. The original Gray leapt back as his entire body was scorched and bubbling.

"Is that all you've got, boy? If so, joining the upper ranks will be nothing more than a dream for you!"

Gray raised his blade, and it was soaked in moonlight. "Orichalcum, Moon's Pale Light."

A dark wing formed on Gray's body, and he rose into the air. "Void Double and Heaven's Wrath, Eightfold!"

Kakinos smiled. "So you've taken the next step."

FVOOOOOOOOOOOOOOOOOOOOM!

Gray pointed his blade and a massive beam of energy erupted from it. The laser split into 8 equal sized beams as they raced toward Kakinos. Hundreds of Orichalcum Gray clones blitzed toward him at immeasurable speeds from every corner of the shadows.

Time seemed to stop as Kakinos gripped his sword. *The boy's potential is quite frightening. I hope he turns out better than his father.*

He flipped his blade and it shifted from pitch black to a bright crimson. "Flame Craft, Progress Art, Raging Flame Tempo!"

FWOOOOOOOOOOOOOOOOOOOOOOOOOOOOOSH!

He vanished in a massive explosion of flames that melted the cement where he stood.

SLICE! SLASH! SLICE! SLASH! SLICE! SLASH! SLICE! SLASH! SLICE! SLASH! SLICE! SLASH! SLICE! SLASH! SLICE! SLASH! SLICE! SLASH! SLICE! SLASH! SLICE!

In the blink of an eye, he elegantly slashed and weaved his way through the beams of energy as he destroyed each of the Grays and propelled himself high into the sky. Gray stared up at him in shock as Kakinos smiled down at him from above.

"Keep training boy."

He rocketed toward the ground and plunged his blade deep into Gray's chest as they crashed into the building.

CRASH!

CRASH!

CRASH!

CRASH!

CRASH!

BOOOOOOOOOOOOOOOOOOOOOOOOOOOOOOOM!

He drove Gray's body through floor after floor until they collided with the surface in an enormous eruption of flames that consumed the entire block.

Back on Lawbringer's rooftop, he fell to his knees as a yellow eyed man pulled his hand out of his flesh.

His gaping wound instantly regenerated.

Lawbringer pointed his finger at the attacker, and he instantly stopped moving. Lawbringer tossed a small round device onto the assailant as he reloaded his rifle.

He leapt from the roof. "Stay right there for me now."

FREEZE!

The ice erupted from the assailant's extremities, and he shattered into frozen pieces. Lawbringer leaned backward and crashed through the window of the building and rolled to a stop. He aimed the rifle and clicked a button on his eye piece. He saw the outline of the Slave Master and his men's Spirit Energy as they raced through the building. He focused his attention on the Slave Master and his target stopped moving.

BANG!

A man leapt in front of the shot as the Slave Master unfroze and continued running.

"Dammit! How many of ye' are there?!" Lawbringer roared.

Suddenly his perception was flooded with hundreds of outlines inside the he aimed at.

He sighed. "Not again."

SWIP!

He pointed his finger at an attacker behind him, freezing him as he ducked under another foe's sword slash.

BANG! BANG!

He quickly drew his pistol and fired two quick shots into both of his attackers as he raced toward the stairwell. He froze opponents, fired his pistol, and avoided a myriad of attacks as he sprinted from floor to floor. Between attacks he drew his rifle and fired shots that picked off the mob of men surrounding the Slave Master, each shot reaching closer and closer to his target.

As the Slave Master reached the bottom floor a shot rang out.

BANG

Blood erupted from his other shoulder.

He sprinted out of the building in pain. "DAMMIT! THERE ARE A THOUSAND OF YOU AND WE CAN'T DEAL WITH A FUCKING COWBOY AND A GODDAMN! SAMURAI!"

He wiped a bead of sweat and glanced back. "Shit."

BOOOOOOOOOOOOOOOOOOOOOOOOOOOOOOOOM!

The building crumbled as the block was engulfed in flames. The Slave Master looked up and the dozens of men who leapt to shield him from the fire had been reduced to ashes. Kakinos stood behind him with Gray slung over his shoulder. A group of the Slave Master's soldiers charged Kakinos.

SLICE!

He sheathed his blade as he effortlessly cut them down. The Slave Master frantically sprinted away until he tripped on a wire and fell on his face on the rainy street.

CLICK.

Lawbringer's pistol rested on the Slave Master's temple.

"Adios, partner."

BANG!

The bullet trembled within the gun nozzle as it was held back by an invisible force.

Lawbringer stared at his gun. "The hell?"

The Slave Master rose to his feet as a yellow eyed woman approached him from the shadows. She had long, golden hair with red accents and sported a black, skintight combat suit with crimson etchings that accentuated her curvaceous body. Her hand glowed with golden fire as she raised it toward the Slave Master and healed his wounds. He waved goofily as she approached. "Ah, Karrina! So good to see you! You're looking as beautiful as ever!"

Lawbringer stared at Karrina. "Ay Kak...that's not her right?"

She put a hand on the hilt of her sheathed Samurai blade as Kakinos approached them.

Kakinos hesitated as he stared into her crimson eyes. *She looks like Kaia...*

FWOOOOOOOOOOOOOOOOOOOOOOOOOOOOOOSH!

He unsheathed his blade as it was set ablaze. "I don't know how you acquired one of my people Giali but know that this offense will not be overlooked."

The Slave Master smiled as he stretched. "I didn't *acquire* her. She's my *daughter* you dingus." He waved. "*Well* it's been fun. I wasn't expecting to get a workout in today, but a little cardio is always good for the lungs."

Lawbringer clicked his pistol. "The hell?! We ain't done here!"

BANG!

SLICE!

Karina sheathed her samurai blade as Lawbringer's hand and gun fell into pieces.

FWOOOOOOOOOOOOOOOOOOOOOOSH!

CLANG!

Kakinos blitzed forward as Karrina met his attack head on. Their blades pressed against each other as Kakinos forced hers toward her neck.

Flames danced in his eyes. "I will free you little one..."

The Slave Master walked away. "Oh! I see! You thought I was using my *good* soldiers to protect me! No, no, no, those guys were just cannon fodder that I picked up off the street a few days ago." He shook his head. "They just looked at me the wrong way, you know?"

CRASH!

BOOOOOOOOOOOOOOOOOOOOOOOOM!

Karrina leapt back as a massive invisible force blasted Kakinos and Lawbringer into the pavement. They tried to fight it, but the force multiplied, and their bones crunched against the cement.

"AAAAAAAAAAAARRRRRGGGGGHH!" Kakinos roared as blood poured from his nose.

FVOOOOOM!

His blade turned pitch black, and an aura surrounded him that evaporated the crushing force on his body. He pulled Lawbringer into the aura just as his skull was about to shatter. Their bodies were caked in blood, and they glared at the Slave Master with unrelenting malice.

The Slave Master smiled at them as Karrina stepped between them. He stared at the blood stains on his shirt. "Dammit! And I was gonna give this shirt to my nephew after this. Oh well."

Lawbringer spat blood and trembled as he spoke. "We...ain't...done...yet..."

"Yeah, you are. Not only are you outnumbered. But you're completely outmatched."

SNAP!

The Slave Master snapped.

Bright yellow eyes illuminated the darkness from every surrounding building. Thousands of men and women rushed from every direction as they surrounded

Kakinos and Lawbringer. The eyes stretched for miles, and they stared at Kakinos and Lawbringer with malice.

The Slave Master started toward an alleyway and waved as he was enveloped in the mass of bodies. "Welp! I'll be seeing you boys! I hope you find that Fos kid before I do, because now I'm REALLY intrigued!" He stopped at the alley's edge. "Oh and you might want to take Gray to see a doctor or something. I kind of shattered his mind a little bit. My fault."

Kakinos stared into the mob. *While I could certainly murder Giali where he stands all, losing all of these lives would be dishonorable...*

Lawbringer's eyes hummed with a blue glow. "I think yer' gonna be pushing up daisies for hurting my boi..."

Kakinos placed a hand on his shoulder. "The mission was a success. The factories are destroyed, and we have gained much knowledge..."

Lawbringer slapped his hand away. "A donkey that's half dead is still kicking Kak! He won't get away with poisoning the kiddo's mind..."

Kakinos sheathed his blade. "This is a battle for another day. We are still waiting for our comrade to develop technology to undo the effects of Giali's ability, and we cannot murder all of these civilians..."

Lawbringer performed a hand sign. "They're in my way..."

Kakinos raised an eyebrow. "This is unlike you Jedediah. I thought you didn't care about the mission..."

WHOOSH!

Lawbringer flipped his pistols into their holsters.

He sighed as he approached Gray with his hands in his pockets. "I don't. I'm just punching the clock until I can get a couple acres and retire."

Kakinos smiled as Lawbringer picked up Gray. *It appears that his heart hasn't frozen over yet.*

SNAP!

The Slave Master descended into the alley's darkness as the eyes that filled the surrounding buildings blinked out of existence.

19 – Banquet

James

I WOKE UP GROGGILY AS SOMETHING WITH A ROUGH TEXTURE SQUEEZED MY ENTIRE BODY. I opened my eyes, and terror gripped my heart as I stared down into a massive spike pit. I was hanging from a rope tied to the ceiling in a dimly lit cavern. The rest of my friends dangled nearby.

"Kayla! Epios! Terrance!" I shouted.

Kayla, Epios, and Jerry stirred.

"What's going...OH MY GOSH!" She shouted.

"Who dares interrupt my beauty...GOODNESS! I'VE BEEN KIDNAPPED!"

"What...AAAAAAH! IT'S A SPIKE PIT! WE ARE HANGING ABOVE A SPIKE PIT! THERE IS AN ACTUAL SPIKE PIT BELOW US RIGHT NOW!" Jerry shouted.

"What the hell happened?!" I yelled.

"I don't know! The last thing that I remember was closing my eyes in Jerry's apartment and now we're here!" Kayla shouted.

"YOU HAVE MADE A GRAVE MISTAKE ON THIS DAY! I AM THE CROWN PRINCE OF THIS NATION AND MY BROTHER MILLIARD WILL SURELY COME AND RESCUE ME! MARK MY WORDS EVILDOER!" Epios shouted into the darkness.

"We're gonna die! We're gonna die! We're gonna die! We're gonna die! We're gonna die! We're gonna die! We're gonna die! We're gonna die! We're gonna die! WE'RE GONNA DIE!" Jerry screamed as he cried.

"Everyone! Get it together! We're not going to die! We've been in worse situations than this before!" I commanded.

"I HAVEN'T! THIS IS A DISASTER!" Jerry sobbed.

"Oh, that's true...Well, there's a first time for everything! Right now, we need to gain our bearings and see if we can find a way out of here. After that we need to get on the same page for when our captors eventually come and interrogate us!"

"Wait just one moment...Where is the Troglodyte?" Epios asked.

We looked around and noticed he wasn't dangling with us.

"OH NO! HE ALREADY GOT KILLED AND EATEN BY SAVAGES!" Jerry mourned.

"Terrance did not get killed and eaten! He's the least of our worries because he can actually regenerate! I'm sure..."

CRACK!

My rope was fraying. I glanced around and their ropes were also giving way.

Kayla's voice shook with desperation. "James?! What's the plan?!"

I quickly glanced around the cavern searching for any means of escape. There were no mirrors or reflections of any kind, and there was a stone platform with a doorway about forty yards ahead of us. I didn't have enough training in any of the elements to come up with a plan that I knew I could execute. *I could try to blunt the edge of the spikes with Earth Craft, but could I do it fast enough to save everyone? Can I Mirror Dash into a Re...*

CRACK!

Our bodies jolted as the ropes weakened.

Jerry wept. "OH NO! THIS IS THE END!"

I heard footsteps and voices outside of the doorway across from us, "...and then I said no because we would have to pay the government..."

"HELP! SOMEBODY COME QUICK BEFORE..."

SNAP!

Our ropes snapped and we fell to our doom. The world blurred and terror filled my heart as I plunged toward the spikes.

"SEMAJ! HELP! DO SOMETHING I...!"

"Did you call me mate..."

SPLAT!

I splashed into a thick, muddy swamp. I trembled uncontrollably as my mind raced. *Oh my God...I almost died.* My stomach turned and my body went limp as I sank deeper and deeper into the murky depths. *What would my parents think if they found out I died in a spike pit in another world? How would they feel if they never got to see me come home?* My eyes widened as I realized that I didn't even know if my parents were still alive. *The last time I saw them, rubble was flying everywhere as my football stadium was being destroyed.* I was numb. *Oh my God... I* wanted to let myself drift in the darkness forever.

I balled my fists. *But I have to keep going. I have to find out if my family is alive. I have to find a way to make it home!* My mind sharpened as my body was flooded with rage. *Whoever did this to us is going to pay.*

I swam back to the surface. I heard laughter as I saw Kayla and Jerry frantically floundering around.

"HELP! I CAN'T SWIM! I'M GONNA DROWN! THERE'S MUD IN MY NOSE AND IT'S UP MY BUTT!" Jerry screamed.

"JAMES! HELP ME! I CAN'T SWIM!" Kayla said desperately.

"Kayla! I've got you!" I said as I swam over and grabbed her.

Epios rose from the mud beneath Jerry and rescued him. "Hang on tight my fiendish bodyguard! Though...this will surely result in a reduction of your paycheck."

As I carefully guided Kayla to the shore, the sound of roaring laughter increased. "AHAHAHAHAHAHAAHAH!". "HAHAHAHAHAHAHAHAH!"

Kayla coughed up mud as we made it to dry land.

She stared endearingly into my eyes. "That was terrible. But thank you for saving me, James."

My heart fluttered. "Of course. Now it's time to pay these bitches back."

I looked up at the source of the raucous laughter. Terrance was with another tall shirtless guy pointing and laughing at us.

"WHOOOOOH! WHOOOOOH! THAT'S HILARIOUS! I BET YOU GUYS REALLY...COUGH...I BET YOU GUYS REALLY THOUGHT YOU WERE GOING TO DIE RIGHT THERE!" The shirtless man laughed.

"I TOLD YOU THAT THESE GUYS ARE IDIOTS! AHAHAHAHAHAH!" Terrance roared.

I set Kayla down as she recovered and stomped over to them. "Terrance! What in the actual fuck is going on here?! Why the hell are you two jackasses pointing AND LAUGHING at us WHEN WE ALMOST DIED?!"

"Calm down simp! It was just a prank..."

Darkness swirled around my body and malice filled my eyes. "Is this some kind of sick fucking game to you? IT'S NOT COOL TO PLAY WITH PEOPLE'S LIVES! I SWEAR TO GOD I WILL..."

A curved blade was raised between us.

The other man spoke with a serious tone. "Pipe down big guy. It was only a joke."

"Who the fuck are you? And honestly, you have five seconds to tell me why I shouldn't beat the shit out of you both *right now*?"

"I'm Machari, an old friend of Terrance's..." He gave a wide sweeping gesture to the massive blackness of the cavern surrounding us. "And I'm the king of the underworld as a hobby." He leaned close to my face and spoke in a condescending tone. "To answer your second question, you shouldn't *try* to beat the shit out of me because I mess with people's lives whenever I damn well please. I thought it would be funny to dangle you and your friends over a spike pit. So, I *did it*. Do you have a problem with that?"

"Hell, yeah, I have a fucking problem with that, bitch! Playing with my life is one thing. BUT DON'T MESS WITH MY FRIENDS! LOOK AT HIM!" I pointed at Jerry.

Epios helped Jerry as he was doubled over, vomiting mud.

"LOOK AT HIM! ME AND MY FRIENDS ARE TRAINED SOLDIERS! BUT HE'S JUST A FUCKING CIVILIAN! HE DIDN'T SIGN UP FOR ANY OF THIS!"

"Alright! Alright!" Machari said dismissively as he approached Jerry. He waved his hand and mud rushed out of his mouth. Jerry coughed and convulsed violently on the ground.

Machari casually raised his hands. "There! I helped the shrimp out! Are you happy now..."

I drew my blade and aggressively marched toward him. "NO! I'M NOT FUCKING HAPPY YOU SELFISH..."

Masked men burst through the dirt between us. They rose out of the muddy swamp and surrounded us with all assortments of weapons.

Machari shrugged. "You should be careful who you threaten down here. Not everyone is as nice as I am..."

"I DON'T GIVE A DAMN HOW MANY SOLDIERS YOU'VE GOT! I'LL PUT EVERY LAST ONE OF YOU CRIMINALS IN THE FUCKING DIRT! SEMAJ..."

Terrance put a hand on my shoulder. "Calm down simp. He obviously had people stationed in the mud. He wouldn't have let any of you guys..."

I shrugged his hand off. "Don't touch me, *Terrance*. That doesn't make it ok. You should be ashamed to associate with someone like him! THIS IS WHO YOU BROUGHT US TO SEE?!"

Machari said as he applauded as his goons disengaged. "Man! Terrance said you were fiery but seeing you in person is a whole different animal!"

"*Shut the hell up.* You're lucky I don't kill you where you stand, *bastard*." I spat.

Machari made a fake ass pouty face as he walked toward Kayla. "Aww? Are you going to be mad at me *forever*? Hopefully you'll calm down some by dinner." She was still recovering on the ground, and he gently grabbed her face as he examined her. "Now this I like! Terrance, did you say this was Kaia's sister or…"

FWOOSH!

A fiery dagger was inches away from searing through his neck as she glared at him. "Say her name again and *you die.*"

He smiled. "Feisty! I like it!"

The ground swallowed her up and spit her back out. She was on her hands and knees gasping for air.

"I like that one Terrance. I'll take her if you don't mind…"

"KAYLA!" I roared as I charged at him.

I brought my blade down on his neck.

CLANG!

I was knocked to the floor. In my hand was the hilt of my shattered blade. I looked up and Machari stood over me with two curved longswords. He crouched down as he stared into my eyes with disgust. "*Man.* You really are a *simp.*"

I swiftly demagnetized my second blade, but the ground reached up and swallowed my arm.

CLANG!

POW!

Iron chains burst from the earth and clamped onto my wrists, ankles, and neck as they slammed me into the dirt.

Machari spoke smoothly. "Stay right there for me."

I struggled violently against the chains as I shouted at Terrance. "TERRANCE! WHAT THE HELL ARE YOU DOING?! YOU'RE JUST GOING TO LET HIM DO THIS TO US?"

He frantically looked back and forth between me and Machari. "Q...quiet simp! I told you to just calm down and everything would be..."

Epios crossed his arms. "I hope you understand the ramifications of your actions, underworld *scum*. Kidnapping the crown prince is no small offense and..."

Machari stared at him in confusion. "Who the hell is this guy?"

"I AM THE CROWN PRINCE AND FUTURE RULER..."

"Yeah, I don't really care. And you're too noisy." He flicked his wrist.

Mud splattered over Epios' mouth and hardened.

"MHHMMPPH!" Epios said as he clawed at his mouth.

"That will teach you about interrupting when grown men are talking." He said as he approached Terrance.

"Now as I was..."

I took a deep breath. "TERRANCE! HELP SO WE CAN..."

"What did I just say about NOISE!"

SLAM!

Metal burst through the earth and clamped around my mouth as the chains pulled harder and harder on my extremities, contorting them at odd angles.

"**MMMMMMMMPHHHHHH**!" I cried out in agony.

Machari shook his head as he continued toward Terrance. "Goodness Terrance! You have some unruly slaves! It's clear that you've been slacking on the discipline my friend!"

Terrance stared at us with concerned expressions. "Machari they're my..."

"But as I was saying before I was so rudely interrupted, *multiple times*. I like that girl you brought so I'm gonna take her as my wife if that's alright with you. I think she'll be *amazing* in the bedroom and..."

FWOOSH!

There was a rush of flames. I strained my neck to look up and Kayla was struggling in a sandy restraining suit that hovered in the air next to Machari. Flames raged in her eyes.

Machari wiped at a bloody scratch on his face. "S*igh*, you folks are just so damn violent."

"I'm nobody's property you bastard!" She roared.

Terrance stepped forward. "Actually, you are. Remember when we dueled back in the town square..."

The color drained from her face.

"...Well that was a covenant, and I won. I have every right to do with you as I please." He shook hands with Machari. "She's all yours Big Mach."

Machari smiled wide. "Excellent! I'll look forward to getting to know her more *intimately* after dinner time! I've prepared a feast for your arrival!"

He raised his hands, and our restraints were removed. My senses were on fire as I writhed on the ground in agony.

Kayla ran over to me. "James! Are you alright?!"

Terrance stared at us with sadness in his eyes.

Machari turned and started toward the chamber's exit. "I'll be expecting you all for dinner in the grand hall within the hour. There are chambers down the hall with your belongings where you can change and wash up." He glanced back at me. "Oh, and don't start brooding and talking about revenge or anything like that. I was just having my fun." He pointed toward the ceiling. "Plus, you're over a thousand feet below the earth's surface surrounded by the baddest criminals the world has ever seen." He smirked. "Don't get any bright ideas."

I glared at them with a heart full of hatred as Terrance and Machari disappeared into the darkness

✦

After we collected ourselves, we moved down the hall. *I'm so fucking pissed right now, but that guy is out of our league. It would be foolish to try and take him on in the shape we're in, especially when he's in his element underground.* Even though I hated it, the best approach was to stay calm and wait for the right moment to strike.

As my joints ached, I assessed our group's state. I couldn't believe Terrance let his friend treat us like that, and I was especially appalled at how he sold out Kayla. *Is he scared of his friend, or is he finally showing his true colors?* Either way I had lost all faith in him, and I didn't know who's side he was on at this point. Epios was a decent fighter, and he was the least damaged out of our group. Jerry was an absolute wreck, and he sobbed more and more with every step. *I wish he could bust out some of that crazy Earth Craft he used at the factory and break us out of here, but I doubt that's a reliable option right now.* Kayla looked despondent, and I imagined she was envisioning what she might be forced to partake in after dinner. I had no clue how far ahead of us the two jackasses were, and there was no telling how many people lurked beneath our feet or in the shadows of the dark corridors. I walked over to her and spoke softly. I felt her tremble as my breath warmed her ear.

"Are you doing, ok?" I whispered as she snapped back to reality.

I shuddered as her breath warmed my ear. "Yeah, I'm fine. I'm just a little shaken up. All of this is happening so suddenly."

I gave her a thumbs up. "It definitely has, but everything is going to be ok and we're gonna make it out of this just like we always do." I glanced ahead of us. "He's not serious about that covenant thing, right? There must be some way out of it."

She looked away. "Unfortunately, there isn't. Covenants are binding and if you break one, tragic, almost supernaturally bad things happen to the violator. To make things worse, under the government's laws, the other person has the right to put you to death if you break a covenant. Machari could drag me up to the capital and have me executed if I don't comply with his commands and Milliard would probably be the one there waiting to chop off my head. If I'm in violation, Machari has the right to kill me at any time, and that would be easy for him in a place like this. He probably tricked Terrance into giving him the covenant rights so he could keep you in check." She sighed. "What I'm wondering is if Terrance is actually going to go through with this, or if he's going to grow some balls and stand up to him."

"Exactly. I don't know what the hell he's doing right now. But regardless, when we get out of here, I'm gonna kick his ass and stomp him out afterwards."

"And I'll be right there with you! I can't believe he thought that bringing us to the king of the underworld would be a good idea!" She hissed.

"I know right! Well, I'm gonna go check on Jerry. Just stay calm and be ready when the time comes for us to get the hell out of here." I said as she nodded.

Jerry's body was shaking, and I felt terrible for him. *How could Terrance let a civilian get mixed up in all of this? Jerry had a regular life just like everybody else and he shouldn't **be here**.* Staring at him reminded me of when I first came to this world. *Is that how I looked when I was bawling my eyes out in the Forsaken Realm?* Regardless, I had to cheer him up and get him through this, just like Milliard did for me.

I gently put my arm around him and pulled him close. "Hey buddy, I just wanted to check on you and let you know that everything is going to be alright."

"How...*sniffle*...how are things going to be alright? We're in the den...*sniffle*...*sniffle*...we're in the den of the underworld!" He sobbed as he desperately stared into my eyes.

I gave him a thumbs up. "It's gonna be alright bro! It may not seem like it, but my friends and I are government professionals! We kind of get ourselves into situations like this for a living and we've always made it out ok. I promise you everything is going to be alright, and I will personally guarantee your safety!"

A spark of hope gleamed in his eye. "You promise?"

"Yes! I promise you I will keep you safe and get you back to your..."

"Ok! Hands off the midget." Machari said up ahead.

I looked up and we were approaching a well-lit set of corridors littered with identical steel doors. There was a grand hall straight ahead and the corridors ran to our left and right as far as the eye could see. Machari and Terrance stood at the center of the crossroads with two masked men.

I glared at Machari and pulled Jerry closer. "Why?"

He peered at me with an annoyed expression, but his face softened into a childish grin. "Jerry-boy here is our guest of honor. We have to make sure he *stays safe*. He's gonna go to his room and my two homies are going to accompany him to ensure his continued good health. The rest of you can use these rooms to freshen up. Be in the dining hall promptly."

He turned and disappeared into the dining hall. I winced as Jerry's fingernails dug into my flesh.

"I don't want to go! I want to stay with James!" He sobbed.

A masked man stepped forward and bowed. "I apologize but that won't be possible."

"Why does Jerry need all the extra fanfare? He's just a civilian who got caught up in this mess. Let him stay with me."

"Despite the king's chokehold on the underworld, there are many who would like to wrest control from his grasp. I sincerely doubt anyone would attempt to attack us during the banquet tonight, as the majority of the king's forces will be in attendance. But still, the king is cautious, and he simply wants to ensure Mr. Giali's safety."

I probably can't convince them without a fight.

I smiled as I playfully punched Jerry on the shoulder. "It sounds like you're the man of the hour Jerry! I'm sure you can go ahead and trust these guys. Just shower and change real quick. Then we will be back together in the dining hall before you know it!"

He shuddered as he slowly let go of my arm. "O...Ok...then..."

He shivered as he walked over to the guards, and they led him down the corridor. As I approached a room with my name on it, I felt someone staring. I caught Kayla smiling at me as she disappeared into her room. Seeing that encouraged me as I showered and changed into the fancy outfit that was prepared for me inside. The black and white suit was perfectly tailored for my very unique body composition, and I was flabbergasted. How they acquired my measurements was beyond me, and I had never seen a suit this well made in my entire life. My backpack and belongings that I lost in the desert were in the room as well. I re-equipped the bracelet I got from the Flame Tribe, and it filled me with good memories. I smiled as I picked up Brooklyn's pin from the Ocean Tribe. I fastened it to my suit proudly as my confidence surged. *We are going to make it through this.*

I left the changing room and walked out into the massive dining hall. Long banquet tables with fancy tablecloths lined the center of the room. Diamond chandeliers gleamed from the ceiling. The tables were decorated with the finest silverware and high-class decorations I had ever seen. In between the two center tables, at the far end of the room, there was a regal throne with a gold encrusted crown sitting on its cushion. The room could easily seat hundreds, and Machari stood at the center of it all directing workers in suits. People were filing into the hall by the dozen from multiple entrances and an usher walked me to my seat at the front of the room. Epios was already seated three spots away from the throne and he looked heated. I was seated two spots away from the throne across from him ,and the rest of the seats separating me from Machari's seat at the head of the table were reserved for the rest of our group. I looked around as more and more people filed into the room. *Where are the rest of us?*

"How are you feeling Epios?"

He scowled as he crossed his arms. "Enraged does not even begin to describe the animosity that I hold for Terrance and the king of fiends. Why he thinks he can interrupt my beauty sleep and get away with it is absolutely beyond me. AND THROWING ME A BANQUET DOES NOT MAKE UP FOR IT! He's lucky I even came out of my room to receive my honor. I should have remained there just to spite him and catch up on the sleep THAT I SO JUSTLY DESERVE!"

I couldn't help but burst into laughter at his attitude. It was amazing to me that he could remain in his warped perspective at a time like this as he seemed to be completely oblivious despite the perilous circumstances. *Does he not understand that we have been kidnapped by an underworld crime boss?*

"Well, I'm glad to see that you're in good spirits, Epios. Hopefully we can go ahead and get this thing started so he can tell us why he kidnapped us in the first place."

The banquet hall was packed to the brim with well-dressed guests, but the rest of my friends were nowhere to be found. The lights in the hall dimmed as Machari reached the head of the room. A spotlight shone upon him, and he smiled as he tapped his microphone.

BOP! BOP! BOP!

"Test, test, test. Alright it looks like we're good to go! Welcome to the First Annual Underworld Banquet of Vengeance! We are gathered here to break bread and celebrate before we go to war AND TAKE THIS NATION FOR OURSELVES!"

BOOM! BOOM! BOOM!

Cannons fired and neon lights zoomed across the room.

"YEAH!", "WHOOOOOO!", "LET'S DO IT!" The crowd roared.

I stared at Epios. "He can't be serious right?"

Machari's energy was infectious, and you could see his ecstasy all over his face. He was a born leader, and he reveled in this moment.

"WHAT BETTER TIME IS THERE TO CELEBRATE THAN ON THE EVE OF THE ARCHIGOS' DEATH!"

"YEEEEEEEEEEEAAAAAHHHHH!", "WHOOOOOO!", "LET'S KILL HIM! LET'S DO IT RIGHT NOOOOOWWW!"

My heart sank as I realized what we had gotten ourselves into.

He waved his arms to settle the crowd. "I would love to, but first we have some business to handle. First off! Let's welcome the man of the hour. He may be small, but he's a powerhouse with a fiery attitude and a killer personality. Make some noise for, JERRY MOTHERFUCKIN GIALIIIIIII!" He shouted as the crowd roared.

Jerry trembled as he walked out of the corridor in a bright yellow, tailor-made suit. He had four bodyguards surrounding him and he shifted his eyes from side to side as he moved down the center aisle toward his seat. I noticed Epios' rage had grown even further, but I didn't have time to worry about that right now. Jerry shivered as he slid into the seat next to me, directly adjacent to Machari's at the head of the table.

"You made it!" I said enthusiastically.

He trembled. "Yeah...it's...just...a lot of people..."

Machari started his next introduction with a humble tone. "Next. Let's welcome someone I've known for a *very* long time. He's been my best friend since the fateful day his father saved my life, as I was this close to making a tragic, *tragic* mistake. He's been by my side on my quest for vengeance since day one, and I wouldn't be standing before you as the leader, or the *man*, that I am today if it wasn't for him. He's big, he's bad, and he's as sexy as can be! Make some noise for my best friend, the Ocean King himself, TERRANCE MOTHERFUCKIN TOOUUVTPAAA!"

"WHOOOOOOOOOOOOOOOOOOOOOOOOOOO!"

The crowd went ballistic as Terrance walked out of the corridor in a sharp, navy-blue suit. As he came down the carpet, he smiled and waved but he wasn't his usual energetic self. *Normally I would have expected him to be yelling and screaming at a moment like this.* I could tell something was bothering him. *I hope it eats him alive.* He sat in the other seat directly next to Machari as he offered him a falsetto smile. As the crowd roared, I could tell that Machari sensed something was off too.

He leaned over to Terrance. "What's wrong? Was my introduction not hype enough?"

Terrance looked away. "It's nothing. Just continue the show."

Machari gave him a confused stare but quickly shrugged it off. "And last, but certainly not least! You guys know I would be wrong as hell if I didn't introduce you to my newest wife, right? GIVE IT UP FOR THE FLAME TRIBE KNOCKOUT! A SCORCHING HOT DIME! THE LOVE OF MY MOTHERFUCKING LIFE! KAYLA THRAAAAACAAAAAASSSSSS!"

"WHOOOOOOOOOOOOOOOOOOOOOOOOOOOOOO!"

The crowd lost their minds and gave her a standing ovation as she exited the corridor.

"WHOOOOOOOOO!", "GOD DAMN SHE'S BAD!", "WHOOOOOOOOOOOOOOOOOOOOOOOOOOOOOOOOOO!"

Kayla gracefully moved down the aisle in a beautiful crimson dress that looked criminal on her. Her makeup and hair were perfectly done, and she was a total knockout. She smiled as she walked down the aisle, and my mind instantly started envisioning what she would look like in a white dress.

Even Jerry stopped his crying and joined the crowd's raucous cheers. "THAT'S MY KAYLA! WHOOOOOOO! YOU LOOK BEAUTIFUL BABY GIRL! BEAUTIFUL!"

As she approached her seat, she smiled at me and filled my heart with ecstasy. She glanced up and scowled at Machari. He replied with a wink and a wide grin as he egged on the crowd's cheers.

My palms were sweating as she sat down in front of me. "Wow...Kayla. You look amazing!"

She blushed. "Thank you so much James! I can't believe he had an entire team of makeup artists waiting for me in there. I'm just glad they were able to make me look *decent* in such a short amount of time."

Jerry leaned forward onto the table and waved his arms as he shouted. "DECENT? YOU LOOK AMAZING! BENEVOLENT! OTHERWORLDLY! I'VE NEVER SEEN A HUMAN BEING LOOK AS BEAUTIFUL AS YOU DO RIGHT NOW! YOU ARE TRULY GOD'S GIFT TO ALL MANKIND AND I AM HONORED TO BE IN YOUR PRESENCE!"

She laughed sweetly. "Thank you Jerry. You're such a sweetheart."

Machari gripped the mic like a rockstar as he screamed. "LET THE BANQUET, BEGIN!"

The banquet commenced and we dug into the food. It was absolutely delectable and even though I enjoyed Jerry's mother's cooking, it couldn't touch the quality of the gourmet masterpiece set before me. The flavors were heavenly, and I was able to truly eat my fill for the first time since we came to this terrible nation. While the rest of the people around us were making small talk, we were throwing down on the feast. As we ate, Machari took his seat at the head of the table and started chatting with Terrance. We had nothing to say to them because of how they treated us earlier and we kept our conversations to ourselves. I noticed Epios was only picking at his food.

"What's wrong, Epios? You don't like it?" I asked.

"I suppose the food is of an *acceptable* quality, but my appetite has waned after being blatantly disrespected in this way."

"Who disrespected you? Nothing happened. We've literally just been sitting here..."

"Clearly, I shouldn't expect someone as fiendish as yourself to understand such royal nuances, but I suppose I can spell it out for you. The king of fiends gave each of us a royal introduction except for the only person who truly deserves one, *me*. I swear that once I get out of here, I will contact every single one of the Archigos and I will have his *head!*"

"I didn't get an introduction either and you don't see me complaining."

He banged the table. "But that's because you are a fiend and never should have expected one! I am the crown prince of this nation!"

A few people around us turned their heads.

I pulled him close and hissed into his ear. "I'd be careful how loudly I said that in a place like this! It's probably better that he *didn't* introduce you. I'm sure that someone else would certainly try to kidnap you for themselves if they knew you were here, and I *just* ate. I'm not in the mood to fight and have to save your ass right now!"

Epios scoffed. "*Hmph*, I'll still have his head and at his funeral I shall introduce him to the mourners as the fiend who failed to show his ruler the proper respect that he deserves!"

"Alright Epios, you do that." I said as I turned to Jerry.

He was still trembling, and he'd barely touched his food.

"Have you ever been this far from home before?" I asked.

"No. I've never left the neighborhood unless my uncle took me somewhere nice. He would always take me to tournaments and fancy restaurants every once in awhile."

"He sounds like a great guy. Does he work with the government?"

"Yeah, I think he works with the military or something like that. He says they always give him a bunch of benefits that he uses to take me out and treat me."

"That's awesome! My trainer was in the military too! Has he ever taken you on vacation before?"

"Vacation? What's that?"

"You've never been on vacation? Vacation is..."

Kayla glowed as she jumped into the conversation. "Vacation is *wonderful*! *Heavenly*! It's one of the most amazing things in the entire world. You get to travel, go to exotic locations, relax, and eat whatever you want without a care in the world! My uncle has taken me to the deep jungles and the desert hot springs and the ruined mountains and..."

"But how can people afford something like that? I think my uncle travels for his job sometimes, but that's rare. And wouldn't you still have to work while you're out on the trip?"

"Nope! The point of vacation is to get away from work and everyday life! That settles it. Once we get out of here and reunite the nation, I'm taking you on a vacation!" I shouted.

"That sounds nice, but how could we afford that? I don't have any money and..."

I pulled Epios into a hug. "Money is no problem! We've got the prickish prince with us right here! I'm sure he can afford to take us on vacations until we get sick of them!"

"I am not in the mood *fiend*, and if you insult me again, I shall have *your* head first!" He pridefully looked away. "But I do *suppose* I could throw in some paid time off or a vacation benefit on the fiendish bodyguard's salary if he serves me well."

Jerry's eyes watered. "Wow, James. This all just sounds like a dream..."

"And that settles it! We're going on vacation! I've heard a lot of people talking about the Dragon Isles recently! Maybe we could go there! Have you been before Kayla?"

Her smile drooped. "That's unfortunately the one place my uncle won't let me go. The Dragon Isles are an independent nation and the world's premiere destination spot. My uncle refuses to let me visit for some reason. Probably because my cousin Kalios lives there..."

"Kalios? That's Milliard's best friend! I'm sure we can get Milliard to help us sneak you in, and if Kalios lives there, I'm sure he will be willing to help too! I'd love it if we could all go somewhere that we've never been before together." I glowed.

Kayla gave me a half-hearted smile. "That sounds amazing, but my uncle will probably never go for it. He's not serious often, but he's adamant about me never going there and I've just grown to accept it. He can be obsessive about that kind of stuff and when he sets his mind to it there's nobody in the world that can stop him. I'm sure that there are plenty of other places we can visit though..."

"Nah! I'll convince him! He loves me, remember. He was ready to give you over to me in marriage and everything!"

"I still need to kill him for that..."

BANG!

"WHO IS THIS UNCLE AND HOW DARE HE TRY AND BARGAIN OFF MY KAYLA TO ANYONE BUT ME! I'LL BEAT HIS ASS!" Jerry shouted as he banged the table.

We all burst into laughter.

"Good luck with that! He's the Flame Archigos!" I laughed.

Jerry shouted as he beat his chest. "I don't give a damn who he is! I promise you that he's gonna hear from me! Jerry Giali! AND HE AINT GONNA LIKE IT!"

Terrance smiled as he looked over at us. "Hey! What are you guys..."

We gave him death glares.

"Alright then..." He said.

I expected him to get mad at us for treating him like that. Something was *definitely* bothering him.

But I didn't care.

He had pissed me off.

I playfully glanced at Kayla and turned back to Jerry. "So Jerry. You know that if you want to date Kayla you have to be a man of God, right?"

She rolled her eyes at me as he spoke. "Of course! I've always been a Christian and a man of God! I do Bible studies with my siblings every morning before we go to work! My relationship with God is really the only way I've been able to survive and make it through each day of my shithole life!"

"Wow! That's amazing! I'm starting to like you more and more! I was raised as a Christian too! I've always been the kid that got picked on and seen as weird for doing the right thing. I've never really been able to fit in or make a lot of close friends because I'm not into worldly stuff like everyone else is. Back home I ran a Bible study group on my team, and before I started playing football in college, I spent a lot of my time volunteering to help the needy."

"Same here! I always got picked on in the streets for being a Christian too! My uncle is also religious, and every week he takes me to church with him. When the country was safer, we always helped volunteer at homeless shelters and things like that. I always loved serving and getting to know all the people we helped."

"That's awesome. Your uncle sounds like a great man! Does he spoil your other siblings too?"

"No, he doesn't really. If I'm honest, he's always treated me a bit better than my siblings. I think it's because he sees that my father doesn't always treat me the best sometimes...But we've been really close since I was little, and he always goes out of his way to do nice things for me. He buys me expensive clothes that I get to wear when we go to certain events, and he doesn't even mind me selling them afterward so I can bring in a little extra cash! I still remember the day he bought me these custom sunglasses, and we always wear them out when we spend time together!" He sighed. "I haven't seen him much recently though and I really miss him..."

"I'm sorry about that, and I give my condolences for your family situation too. Nobody deserves to be treated like that."

He shrugged. "Ideally no, but I'm not so sure about that James. I mean if you're a worthless noncontributor, do you really deserve to eat? Do you really deserve the same consideration as the people who are making sure the family survives? I'm sure my dad is just doing what's best for the others in the way he treats me. Once my dad saw I didn't have much potential, he focused his attention and resources on the other kids." He sighed. "He thought I didn't notice, but he even started siphoning food off my plate to help feed my younger siblings...But I'm ok with it because it's important for everyone to grow big and strong! I understand how he treats me because everyone else in the house is a strong EarthCraft user, and I'm the only one who can't..."

"That's ridiculous! Them taking food from your plate is probably how you've ended up so small in the first place! That's deplorable and I won't allow you to talk about yourself like this Jerry!"

"That may be true, but you don't understand James. The people of this nation pride themselves on having the strongest resolve and owning a will that can even buck the harsh conditions of the desert. Toughness is the standard, and nobody has sympathy for somebody who can't get the job done. On top of that, once you drop out of the Earth Academies you are forever stained as a weakling, and it's almost impossible to find any work. That just made things harder for my family because of the shame I brought on us. People lost respect for us, and they refused to trade at fair prices anymore. My dad even lost his government job for raising such a pathetic son...After that, we were all relegated to working in low paying factory jobs, and I couldn't find any work at all." He teared up. "I'm telling you James; I deserve every bad thing that has come to me, and I've accepted it so..."

"NO! JERRY THAT'S WRONG! Just because you aren't the biggest and the strongest, or even the most competent, doesn't mean it's ok for people to treat you like that and I won't allow it! This society is warped, and I blame it on the Archigos for letting it get this bad! You are not *worthless* Jerry, and you deserve the right to be treated decently just like everyone else on this planet."

"That would be nice James but it's unfortunately not the way things work here."

Darkness flashed in my eyes. *This is just like my fucking team and those fucking coaches...*

I put a hand on his shoulder. "I know and I'm gonna fix it. Trust me. You are incredible Jerry, and I've truly enjoyed the time I've gotten to spend getting to know you so far. Once we get out of here, we'll have to stop by and pay your uncle a visit so I can thank him for raising up one of my best friends as such an incredible young man."

"Thank you James. I appreciate that, and I think you're amazing as well. I hope we really can do that like you said. My uncle is the best guy I know, and he's the person who inspires me to work so hard. Even though I'm feeble, and I can't get much done on my own, I still give it my all every day so I can be like him and make more money for the family. They've sacrificed so much for me throughout the years, and I want to repay them for all they've done for me. I want to get so big, strong, and make so much money that they never have to work again, or even stop to think about finances!" Jerry said passionately.

"You give your family too much credit, but I feel the exact same way! For me it's my dad. He's my ultimate inspiration. He grew up in the slums, kind of like you now that I think about it. But with only God by his side, he earned a college degree and worked his way up to becoming the CEO of a major business. He didn't have a father figure, or any help or worldly guidance, but he reached the highest level of success and set the ultimate example for me in the way he raised up a Godly family. What he did with such little support is amazing and I strive to build upon his legacy and turn it into something the world can marvel at!" I said passionately.

"That's amazing James! He sounds just like my uncle! I bet they would be best friends! And you're so amazing that I'm sure you'll do even greater things than both of them!"

I sighed. "Thanks Jerry, but unfortunately all my efforts have been pretty much worthless to this point. He had so little...and I've started off in *such* an advantaged position...yet nothing I try ever amounts to anything. Even though I always try to do things the right way, no matter how much effort I put in, it just seems like things always find a way to go to shit."

"That's not true James. I..."

BANG!

I pounded the table as a tear rolled down my face. "I don't even know if my family is *dead or alive Jerry*, but I swear to you I will make it back to them! And I will work myself to the bone, every single day to make sure I give them the life they've always dreamed of. I won't let anything stand in my way."

Jerry reached out his bony hand. "Let's do it together then! Let's become partners and work hard to grow big and strong, so that we can give our families the lives they've always dreamed about!"

Memories of Milliard came to mind as I stared into his bright yellow eyes.

I smiled as I took his hand. "Let's do it then, partner."

SNIFFLE, SNIFFLE!

We looked across the table and Kayla was wiping her face with her dress, as her makeup ran.

"What's gotten into you?" I asked.

Jerry stood up. "DID SOMEBODY HURT YOU? WHERE ARE THEY? I SWEAR TO GOD I'LL..."

She laughed as she wiped at her teary eyes. "No! No. It's nothing. Don't mind me. Just pretend I'm not here."

"Alright...then..." I said as I stared at her in confusion.

Girls are so weird.

As the rest of the group chatted, Terrance and Machari had their own discussion.

"And then I was like, 'I wonder if I could make water explode'. So I splashed it on them and then it went BOOM and the entire factory blew up!" Terrance shouted.

"I saw that explosion from a few blocks away and it was incredible! I was like, 'That old bastard has still got it!'" Machari said as he burst into laughter.

"You know it! I ain't never going out like no hoe!" Terrance roared as they pounded the table in laughter.

James and Kayla gave them dirty looks, but the duo ignored them and had the time of their lives.

Machari glanced around with a smile. "*Man,* I remember when we were just two little Ocean Tribe punks skipping school and chasing ass. Now look at us. I'm the king of the fucking underworld and you're going to be crowned Archigos in a few years when your father retires. Who would have thought."

They clinked glasses. "Who would have thought! And this serves every single one of those whores right for not sticking with us after the Luna incident! I bet they want some now! *Don't they Machari!*"

"You're damn straight!" Machari said as they toasted to themselves.

Machari looked out on the crowd with a heart full of satisfaction. *Man. It's unbelievable to think that I am just a few hours away from attaining what I've worked my entire life for. Nothing could ruin this moment...*

He turned his attention back to Terrance and caught him staring at Jerry. "What's got you so upset bro? Was it what I did to your girl or...?"

Terrance sighed and looked away. "No. It's not that. And she will *never* be my girl. It's just...why did you even bring that shrimp here with us. Couldn't you have done your plan without..."

"I told you that he's insurance if *our* plan goes south. You saw what he did at that factory just like I did. Only an Archigos has that level of..."

"But how could he have possibly done that?! It must have been a fluke or some kind of smoke and mirrors! Are you really trying to tell me that pipsqueak is stronger than we are?"

"Terrance this is *reality*, and in this reality that little chicken head threw two fucking skyscrapers just to kill a Gluttony spirit. I'd never say that anyone could beat us in a fight but..."

"Then don't! And why did you introduce him before me at the start of the banquet?"

"Are you seriously mad about that right now? Have you not been getting enough sex in or something? Look, I just did it to hype the kid up a little bit and make him feel better, ok? It's clear that he's completely spooked to even breathe the air here and I need him ready and on board with the plan, that's all. I wasn't even thinking about the order when I..."

"Whatever. I still think this whole plan is stupid anyway. There has got to be a better way of going about this. You can't just kill the Archigos and expect..."

"I'm going to kill the Archigos and turn this nation into the paradise it would have been if that *scum* was never born. Then the two of us are going to use our newly acquired resources to find that fucking cowboy and *kill him* like we always said we would. Then you'll get to talk to your mom and we can find Luna, just like we always planned! If the other Archigos show up...that's a problem for another day...but this has been my life's ambition since we were kids, and you know that, Terrance!" He stared. "You've never had a problem with this before today. How are you gonna chicken out on me now that the lights are about to come on and it's game time? I'm gonna fulfill my end of the deal, so you had better..."

A butler tapped Machari on the shoulder.

He sighed. "Just a moment please."

Machari stood and walked to the side of the room with the butler. "You had better have a good reason for interrupting me during the only time I get to see my..."

"Sir, despite your warnings, the Slave Master has arrived, and he has brought an army."

Machari gripped his temple. "Fuck! What the hell does that creepy bastard want?"

"He has requested you turn the Fos boy into his care immediately before he 'causes a scene up in this bitch.'" The butler said with air quotes.

"Dammit! I can't give him up because I still need to know about that dark power he's been using. I'm almost positive we'll need it against The Sword. Tell him that he can have him in the morning once we finish the mission and that he had better not bother me AGAIN!"

While Machari was gone, Terrance turned his attention back to his friends. Jerry had his shades on and was gesturing flamboyantly as the rest of the group laughed.

"They call me Swag Jerry when I put these shades on, yo! This is what I do whenever it's time to hit the town and check on the ladies, bro!"

"Ha! Ha! That's amazing Jerry!" James laughed.

"I thought you had to have swag to get 'swag' added to your title!" Kayla laughed.

"Even I find this mildly amusing." Epios chuckled.

"I'm the swaggiest there is, yo! You'd better hide your wives and hide your daughters around me yo, because I'm..."

Terrance stood. "Hey runt! How did you do all that shit at that factory? Tell me now and be honest!"

James sighed. "Terrance. What has gotten into you..."

Jerry stared at him in surprise. "Factory? What are you talking about? I..."

Terance snatched Jerry's shades off his face. "I'm sick of your lying and I'm sick of your damn excuses!"

"Hey! Give those back! Those are from my..."

SMASH!

Terrance threw them to the ground and crushed them under his foot.

"You wanna act all big and bad, but I see right through you! You're nothing! You're just a scared little punk who's trying to trick everyone! You shouldn't even be here! You weren't the one who saved us at that factory, so tell me who did it right now before I beat it out of you!"

James stood. "Terrance, what the hell is wrong with you?! Those shades were a gift from his uncle!"

Kayla banged the table. "You're acting crazy right now! Are you that insecure that someone like Jerry can..."

Terrance turned to James. "You know what James? You and that simp sure have been getting close lately. You're always coming to his defense and whispering in each other's ears late at night and shit. That's not your *boyfriend*, is it? You're not turning into a gay simp bastard now, are you?"

Darkness flashed in James' eyes. "That's its Terrance! I've owed you an ass whooping for a long time now and it's about time I cashed it the fuck in!"

James reached out his hand and a saber made from pure darkness materialized in it. "If you're going to spend all your time bullying others. Then I'm going to bully you!"

Machari's blade flashed between James and Terrance. "Settle down and take a look around you."

James and Terrance glanced around the room and saw that the crowd had gone completely silent. They stared at the conflict in anticipation. Men had their hands on concealed weapons, and they stared at each other with violent greed.

Machari pulled them close and hissed into their ears. "If you two idiots start fighting then this entire banquet will become a bloodbath! This is my special night and you two *will not* ruin it! Sit your asses down and act like you have some *fucking manners*."

James glanced around. *I could probably take both Machari and Terrance, but there's no guarantee I could escape the rest of the carnage and get my friends out of here safely.* He dematerialized his blade and they slid into their seats as the crowd continued chattering.

Machari mumbled to himself in frustration. "I swear, I leave you two alone for ten seconds..."

"If you're gonna get mad, then be mad at Terrance for picking on somebody weaker than him." James scoffed.

Machari smiled. "Why would I be mad at that? That's the Ocean King's 6th rule of manhood. Bullying is the key to a better society, especially for women and children. He was probably just trying to make him tougher and..."

"You subscribe to that nonsense too? I thought he was just making that stuff up. Both of you are bitches in my eyes." James spat.

Machari grinned. "Of course not! We co-authored the rules as kids in the Ocean Tribe! He wrote five and I wrote five!"

Jerry sobbed as he stared at his broken shades. He looked up at Machari with pleading eyes. "*Please sir,* why did you even bring me here? I don't have anything to do with this! Can't you just drop me off back on the surface! I promise I won't tell anyone about what I saw here or..."

Machari pulled Jerry close and smiled. "Absolutely not! Jerry, you are *my guy!* You're the man of the hour, remember?! I can't accomplish any of my goals without you!"

"Wha...what do you..."

James banged the table. "Why? What does Jerry have to do with any of this? Why did you even kidnap us and bring us here in the first place?!"

"Uhh? Were you not listening? I told you, after the banquet we're gonna go kill the Archigos. I thought I made it pretty clear in my speech..."

"What the hell are you talking about? The Archigos hasn't been seen in years! And even if we did know where he is. Why would we help you..."

"Uhh, you're gonna help me because I've got your lady friend in a covenant and if you don't cooperate, I'm gonna slice her fucking head off. Now, I know *exactly* where the Archigos is. He's sitting in his room, sulking and crying like the little bitch he's been since birth."

The group stared at him in shock.

James stood. "How do you know that? Why would the Archigos stand by and let..."

Machari looked away. "Because he's a terrible person and he's selfish, ok! I can't tell you why he does half of the shit he does, but he's always been a dirtbag and that's never gonna change."

James stared at him. "This sounds like more than just a grudge...You're talking like this is personal, or like you know him or some..."

Terrance stood. "James, don't get into this. Let's leave now before..."

Machari sighed. "This *is* personal to me. Because...he's my dad..."

Terrance face palmed as the group gasped.

"Why would you want to kill your own father?" James asked.

"Because I hate him? Because he's a terrible person and an even shittier father? Because he abandoned me to die in the streets? How much more motivation do I need?"

James shook his head. "Look, we all have daddy issues, but we actually came here to speak with him about a matter of national security..."

"You're talking about the terrorists? The Council of Tromos? Dameon's bunch of bitches right?"

"I don't know who that is but..."

"Yeah, I already know all about them and the people I have at my disposal could easily wipe them off the face of the earth. I don't know if you've heard, but the seven Underworld Lords who serve me are pretty fucking strong. If you help me, once I become Archigos, I'll lead the entire Earth Tribe army *and* underworld against them. Then we can wipe them out for good."

"That sounds nice, but there's no guarantee once you get what you want that you are actually going to follow through and do what you said. I'm more interested in *re-*

uniting the nation than I am in fighting a war against terrorists anyway. Now look, I'm sorry you had a terrible childhood, and I hate poor leadership more than anybody but..."

Machari slammed the table. "THIS IS NOT ABOUT DADDY ISSUES! THAT ARROGANT BASTARD LEFT THE UNION OUT OF HIS PRIDE, WHEN HE KNEW HIS PEOPLE WERE STARVING!" He gestured to the ceiling. "And now, look at what has become of them up there! Violence runs rampant in the streets! Women and children are starving and being sold into slavery and prostitution! Corrupt politicians have taken over the country and do nothing but pass laws that line their own pockets! Immigrants are being packed into the nation's walls like slaves, with no hope of ever going free!" Darkness flashed in Machari's eyes. "And what does Bazek do? He sits in his room all day, crying over spilled milk, while his people are in the streets *dying*." He stabbed his blade into the table in the center of his crown. "I didn't become the king of the fucking underworld because I wanted bitches and a nice banquet hall. I left my true home in the Ocean Tribe and became the king of the fucking underworld, so I could save this nation."

Memories of the depravity and corruption James witnessed in the Earth Tribe flooded his mind. He remembered that sickly baby and her ghastly mother. He remembered fearing for his life as they roamed the streets, with the threat of death around every corner. He remembered Jerry, who had been subjected to such a horrible life because of this society's cultures and values.

His blood boiled.

Darkness flashed in James' eyes. "Look, you're right Machari. He does deserve to die. And I want to strangle him with my bare hands right now. But we should try something else first! Everyone deserves a chance to make things right. Maybe we could try to talk to him and..."

"James, I actually kind of like you. I can tell that we're kindred spirits. But you're childish and *naïve*. Bazek is an old man who's set in his ways that abuses women and abandons his children. Let me tell you a story about the man that you want to try and sit down and have a chat with. Let me tell you the truth about *my* father."

Many years ago, Bazek was one of the top scholars at the Earth Tribe's Forge Academy, and he was a finalist in the Tournament of Champions. To celebrate his semi-final round victory, he went out with his friends to celebrate at a strip club. They were rich, tall, handsome, and powerful young men. Their presence was felt by the entire club as soon as they walked through the door. Some of the strippers eyed them as they entered.

"Who do you think *they* are?" A stripper said.

A tall woman pointed. "I don't know, but *that one* looks like eighteen years of tax-free *paradise*."

She walked over and wrapped her arms around Bazek's neck from behind. "Hey there big boy. Why don't you come and spend some time with me tonight."

Bazek stretched his aching back. "I'd love to. I was actually hoping I could get a massage today. I *did* just win my semi-final match in the Tournament of Champions."

"That's amazing. You're so strong and handsome! I could tell you were someone special as soon as you walked in the door."

Bazek blushed. "You think so? Well, if that's the case..."

She kissed him erotically and pushed him against the wall. "No more talking. Let me reward you for your efforts, my king."

"Oh shit!". "Is that Bazek!". "Oh damn! She's going in!" Bazek's friends cheered.

"Shh!" He said as he playfully put a finger over his lips. She led him by the hand deep into the darkness of the club.

Nine months later, she had a baby. She secretly raised the boy in poverty for several years.

"You need to grow big and strong, so you can impress your father when I take you to see him in a few months."

She told the boy as she disappeared in the darkness of the club with another man.

The boy spent his early years bored out of his mind, alone in the back rooms of strip clubs across the Earth Tribe. He dreamed of one day being able to meet his father so they could become a normal family like he read about in magazines he pulled from the trash. From a young age, he quickly learned to cover his ears, so he could block out the sounds of his mother's pleasure.

Years later, after Bazek had been crowned Archigos, the woman showed up at the palace with Machari.

Bazek descended the palace steps in a rage. "What fool thinks they can just show up and request an audience unannounced..."

He saw the woman holding the boy's hand and his heart was filled with terror. "Quickly, come inside!"

She sat down in his private chamber at the top of the palace. The boy ran around and played with Bazek's things, and his heart was filled with joy.

His dream had finally come true.

Bazek paced around the room and ripped at his hair.

The stripper smoked and brushed ashes on his bed. "Now, look. I'm not trying to be here long. I've been raising him by myself for years now and you need to pay me some child support. I reached out to you..."

"You never reached out to me, you lying woman! I was too foolish to see it when I was young, but you tricked me! You seduced me and caused all of this to happen so that you could entangle me in a situation just like this!

"I don't know what you're talking about, but you need to pay up mister. This baby is starving and..."

"He is starving because of your deception! He is only alive because of your deceit!" He broke into a sweat. "What should I do? What do I do?!"

"I don't know why you're yelling, but what you need to do is pay me my child support before I...*gasp*."

The boy's eyes went wide with horror as he watched Bazek grip his mother's neck.

He lifted her above his head. "This information cannot get out or I will surely lose my position as Archigos in this volatile climate. I will not lose what I have worked my entire life for because of one mistake. My enemies would use this against me, and there is too much risk involved in trying to keep this a secret or setting up covert payments." He stared into her eyes. "I'm sorry but this is the way it must be..."

"Daddy! Stop!" The boy shouted as life drained from his mother's eyes.

POW!

He kicked the boy across the face and blood gushed onto the floor. "Shut your mouth child! I am not your father!"

Bazek turned his attention back to the woman as he heard her bones snapping.

She stopped struggling

He sighed in relief.

Bazek looked down and the boy pulled on his leg as he sobbed. "Please don't hurt mommy! Please! I know she's a bad woman, but she's doing the best she can! She really loves me, and she says I need to grow big and strong so that one day you'll love me too and we can be a family together! Please! I promise I can grow faster, just don't hurt mommy!"

Tears ran down Bazek's face as he stared at his child.

Minutes later, the woman desperately ran for her life as she raced out of the castle with her son.

"Mommy! My legs are tired and..."

"Just...*wheeze*...keep running...*wheeze*...if you want to live!"

They ran until they found an abandoned house, and Machari's mother collapsed inside.

He shook her. "Mommy! Mommy! Wake up please! I..."

SLAP!

The boy crumpled to the ground, sobbing as he held his face. His mother's enraged eyes bore into his soul.

"YOU...WHEEZE...WHEEZE...ARE A BAD BOY! YOU'RE WORTHLESS... WHEEZE...WHEEZE... AND I...WHEEZE...WHEEZE...NEVER CARED ABOUT YOU! I

TOLD YOU... WHEEZE...WHEEZE...TO GET BIG AND
STRONG.... WHEEZE...WHEEZE...SO YOUR
DADDY...WHEEZE...WHEEZE...WOULD BE IMPRESSED
WITH YOU...WHEEZE...WHEEZE...AND YOU DIDN'T DO
IT!

"Mommy...I'm sorry. I..."

"SORRY...WHEEZE...DOESN'T CUT IT!

She got up and staggered toward the doorway.

"Mommy! Wait for me..."

She stared out the doorway. "Stay right...there."

"But...why mommy? I want to go with you and daddy
and..."

He shrank back as she faced him with malice in her
eyes. "I never...even named...you...That shows...how
worthless...you are..."

"Mommy! I'm trying to grow! I..."

"You...know what? I'm naming you Machari...because
you're...the dagger...that pierced...my heart."

His lip quivered. "M...mmmachari?"

"If you...ever want to see...me again...you need
to...become the Archigos...then I'll...truly...love you." She
wheezed as she disappeared into the streets.

James

Machari wiped a tear. "Now do you see what kind of
monster we're dealing with? The kind of person who
sleeps with a prostitute but isn't man enough to take care

of his responsibilities afterward! The kind of person who left his only son to fend for himself in the gutters! The kind of person whose son had to become a ruthless killer just to survive!" He beat his chest. "She said I was the dagger that pierced her heart. Well tonight, I'll become the dagger that pierces *his*!"

There was nothing I could say to something like that. *What kind of person are we dealing with? How did someone like that become Archigos?*

A butler tapped Machari on the shoulder and he lifted a blade to his neck. "Can't you see that we're in the middle of something? This had better be important..."

"Sir, the Slave Master is here and..."

"Fuck!" Machari said as he unsheathed his other his blade.

He aggressively stomped away from the table. "I'll be right back. Let that story sink in, as you prepare your minds and hearts for battle."

In a cavern outside Machari's underground stronghold, the Slave Master stood before a massive iron door.

DING-DONG!

The Slave Master stared at the button in confusion.

DING-DONG! DING-DONG! DING-DONG! DING-DONG! DING-DONG! DING-DONG! DING-DONG! DING-DONG! DING-DONG! DING-DONG! DING-DONG!

"Well, that's rude. I told him I was coming."

CRASH!

The iron door folded and crumpled like a tin can as the Slave Master and his yellow-eyed army rushed into the premises. Machari's soldiers attacked the Slave Master's men but were quickly slaughtered by a myriad of unorthodox abilities.

SPLAT!

CRASH!

GUSH!

The Slave Master whistled blissfully with his hands in his pockets as carnage ensued all around him. He casually walked through the bloody corridors as he made his way through the fortress. He turned a corner and entered the corridor that led to the dining hall. A massive iron shutter had dropped down, blocking the entrance to the hall.

He tapped his earpiece. "Holly, I need someone to get this wall down for me so I can pay Machari a visit. Can we get somebody on that?"

A woman's voice spoke into his earpiece as if in a trance. "Right...away...sir..."

He tapped his earpiece to close the line. "*Ahh*, I love hearing her sweet voice in the morning!"

He sat on the ground, whistling as he waited for one of his men to come and break through the shutter. A few minutes passed and he sighed. "We were killing them. What could have possibly slowed us down that..."

"AAAARGAAA!", "WHOOOLAPAA!", "HELP ME!", "ARRRGAHAHAAHAH!" Men screamed from around the corner.

The Slave Master's raised an eyebrow. *Those sounded like some of my elite guards...*

"NO! PLEASE! ARRRGAHAHA!", "DON'T DO THIS! AAAAAAGHAAA!", "HE'S A MONSTER! A MONSAAGHA..."

A bead of sweat ran down the Slave Master's forehead. He got up and dusted himself off. He cracked his knuckles as he prepared to turn the corner.

"Alright buddy. Who do you think you..."

He turned the corner to find Semaj sitting at a tea-table surrounded by the corpses of his best men.

Semaj raised his teacup. "Care to have a chat mate?"

The Slave Master squinted his eyes in confusion. "Aww, sure. What the heck." He slid into the other chair.

CLINK!

He raised his cup, and they clinked them together as they took a sip.

"By George! It's nice to finally meet someone with manners." Semaj said as he sipped his tea.

The Slave Master gestured to the dining hall. "I've been in my fair share of high-status circles. But I've never seen *you* in any of them. You must be pretty in-the-know to be invited to a place like this."

"Unfortunately, I wasn't invited mate. I was kidnapped! And I don't bloody like it one bit!"

"Kidnapped?" He shook his head. "I bet that was Machari's doing. He's never been one for manners or simply asking people to help him with his plans." He raised an eyebrow. "You seem a bit too powerful to get captured by him though."

"I'd say I do well for myself mate. Though, I really came here to help *you* out."

"Help *me*? What kind of deal did you have in mind?"

"It's simple really, mate. I want you to take your bloody goons and get the hell out of ere'!"

"Ha! And why would I do that? I told Machari I wanted that Fos kid and he wouldn't oblige. I can't wait until morning because Dameon knows I'm after him. Besides, he could get killed in that suicide operation Machari is trying to pull. There's no way they can kill Bazek, and I know that from personal experience."

"You'll do it because I asked you to mate, and even though I'm helping you, I'll toss in a favor for you in the future as well."

The Slave Master chuckled. "You must be one bold son of a bitch to have the nerves to come in here and talk to me like this. I don't know who the hell you are, but I'm sure you know who *I am*. *Tell me.* Why shouldn't I just take over your mind right now and make you drag the Fos boy out here."

"For two reasons really! One, because you can't..."

"I had sex with your wife last night."

"Well, that's peculiar because I don't have one!"

"If that's the case, then I murdered your family! In cold blood! I laughed as I split their skulls open with my blade and..."

"My kin are alive and well mate. I'm actually trying to get them passports as we speak, so if you could hurry it up and..."

"Dammit! Who the hell are you?!"

Semaj bowed. "The name's Semaj. I like long walks on the beach and..."

"No! Not that! Why can't I break your mind? I've never been resisted before! Not even an Archigos can resist me!"

"It's simple mate, because I don't have a *mind* for you to break. I can let you in if you want to see what's swirling around up here."

WHOOSH!

Before the Slave Master could react, Semaj grabbed his head as they delved into Semaj's soul. The Slave Master entered a void of nothingness.

He cracked his knuckles. "Finally! Time to get to..."

"I'm afraid you've made a very dire mistake mate."

WHOOOOOOOOOOOOOOOOOOOOOOOOOOOOOOSH!

The Slave Master's mind was overrun with foul memories.

"WHISTLE! IT WAS FOS!", "You're fucking lazy, and your discipline is shit! You have a long way to go if you ever expect to accomplish a fucking thing in this fucking program!", "Did you really think someone like you had a shot with a girl like me? I'm a *princess...*"

An uncountable multitude of dark emotions rushed into the Slave Master. They started to tear him apart from the inside out.

"MAKE IT STOP! PLEASE! MAKE IT STOP!"

The Slave Master fell to the ground as Semaj released him. He gasped for air as he held his stomach and vomited up blood.

"I told you there was nothing in there for you to see mate. I..."

The Slave Master held up a finger as he pulled himself back into his seat.

He smiled sinisterly as blood dripped from the corners of his mouth. "*Cough, Cough.* I like you, Semaj. Please continue...*cough*...telling me what you were about to say."

"Sure mate! My second point is the fact your nephew is sitting right behind that bloody door!"

The color drained from the Slave Master's face. "What? What do you mean? *Jerry?* How could Jerry be..."

Semaj pulled Jerry's broken shades from behind his back and set them on the table.

"I put it on my life. It's the truth and here's your proof! How do you think he'd feel if he knew his bloody uncle was here to kidnap his..."

He quickly rose from his seat. "Ok! Ok! Ok! Ok! Thank you, Semaj. Thank you!" He tapped his earpiece. "Everyone! We're pulling out! I need two on my location immediately!"

He closed the channel and tossed a business card onto Semaj's tea table.

"I appreciate the help, and I look forward to doing business with you." The Slave Master said as he turned down the corridor.

Semaj cheerfully waved goodbye. "Always happy to be of service, mate! Just holler if you need a favor!"

The Slave Master chuckled as he whistled and disappeared down the dark corridor. *Things just got **much** more interesting.*

Machari swiftly changed into a suit of armor in front of a mirror in his room. A butler entered. "Sir, the Slave Master has departed. It is unknown whether he is retreating or..."

CRASH!

"FUCK!" Machari shouted as he shattered his desk.

He stormed back into the banquet hall and snatched the microphone off the stand. "Party's over! We're moving out! We'll have another one tomorrow after we kill the Archigos. Thanks again for coming."

James and his friends sat in silence as he stomped over to their table. "This is it! Ask me whatever questions you want, now!"

Terrance stood. "It's over Machari. We've discussed it and we're not helping you!"

Machari gripped his temple. "*Terrance.* Betraying your friends is totally not cool. It's a good thing I have that pact on your..."

"You don't have anything. I had my fingers crossed when I transferred it to you."

"*Sigh.* I figured you would try and pull that type of thing." He stared at James. "Before I pull out my trump card, is that how *everybody* here feels? I thought I was really getting through to..."

James stared at him. "I'm sorry Machari, but my friends are right. I hate him too, but murder isn't the solution. I just don't think I can bring myself to..."

"*Jerry.* Don't you have anything to say about this?" Machari said smugly.

The group stared at Jerry.

He hung his head in silence.

James was shocked. "Jerry? Why would Jerry have anything..."

"Jerry-boy here should want to kill the Archigos more than anybody. Maybe even more than me. Care to tell them why Jerry?"

Jerry looked around in distress. "No! I..."

"Tell them Jerry! Paint them the full picture of the man it is that we're dealing with here! Tell them what he did to you!"

Terrance pounded the table. "That's enough Machari! You're acting like a psychopath! You can't make him..."

Jerry stared at the floor despondently. "It happened in the evening after one of Reggie's school fighting matches..."

*

Jerry and his uncle walked out of the Earth Academy's fighting gym.

As they left, Jerry shadowboxed and bounced on his toes. "Man! That was so good! Reggie almost had him! If he would have just hit him with a WHOOSH, and a POW and a few more mink-mink-mink-mink's, he definitely would have gotten him!"

His uncle shrugged. "He was *alright*. I don't think he had much hope of winning that match anyways. He's not all that talented."

Jerry stared up at him incredulously. "What do you mean Uncle Ben? Reggie is the greatest and..."

"Don't believe everything your father tells you. I think you would have done much better if *you'd* been the one fighting in that ring instead of him."

Jerry blushed as he looked away. "You think so? I mean no, I could never I..."

"Yes, you could, Jerry. And as the first born, you deserve the right to at least try. It tears me up every single day the way your father wastes your potential..."

"What do you mean Unc? I'm small and weak and..."

"Jerry, never doubt who God made you to be and the impact you could have in this world. I'm expecting *big* things from you." He smiled. "Besides, you won't get any women talking that way!"

Jerry stared at the pavement. "You're *crazy* unc. I love women, but what kind of girl would want someone like me?"

"Lots of them will, Jerry! You're a catch! And until you develop the confidence you need to get girls, I've got something special to help you out" He reached into his back pocket and pulled out a pair of custom sunglasses.

Jerry marveled as the cool plastic touched his fingertips. "Wow! Wow! Wow! These are custom made! Top of the line! I can't afford these Unc. I..."

Ben pulled out a matching pair. "Of course you can, nephew! They're a work gift from a friend, so you don't have to worry about paying for a thing. Don't let your daddy see them though. Now let me teach you how to use them." He crouched down and slid them onto Jerry's face. "Now, when you wear these shades, you're not Jerry Giali anymore. You're *Swag Jerry* and when you're Swag Jerry, you are the biggest and baddest thing on the planet! You're untouchable and nobody could hope to stop you! You see a woman that you like, and she'll be so attracted to you that she won't have a choice but to like you back because you're too damn swaggy yo! If somebody disrespects you as Swag Jerry, you check them and you teach them that they should never even *think* about trying you again if they value their *fucking life*." Ben squeezed Jerry's shoulder. "I want you to use these until you get the confidence from within to be the great man that God created you to be."

Jerry's eyes flashed with a yellow hue, and he beamed as he internalized every one of his uncle's words. "Thank you so much Uncle Ben! I promise I'll take care of them and use Swag Jerry all the time to get tons of money and women!"

"That's the spirit! I'd better watch out before Swag Jerry comes and steals all my girls!"

Jerry slid on his shades and threw up fake gang signs. "Yo, yo, yo! You said yourself bro!"

Jerry's uncle collapsed. "Oh my God! The swag is too much! It might...It might kill me!"

Jerry leapt on top of his uncle and their laughter filled the streets.

Jerry couldn't stop smiling. *I wish this moment could last fore...*

WHOOSH!

Suddenly, Jerry fell on his face. He looked up and his uncle was on his feet.

Ben's hands were shaking. "Jerry. I'm about to go handle some business real quick, ok? No matter what happens. NO MATTER WHAT YOU HEAR, YOU STAY RIGHT HERE, OK?!"

Jerry trembled in fear. "O...ok...I..."

The ground trembled.

BOOOOOOOOOOOOOOOOOOOOOOOOOOOOOM!

A man crashed down into the street, causing a massive explosion of dust and debris. Bazek walked out of the crater in a golden suit of armor with a handcrafted hammer in his right hand.

He looked around for the Slave Master. "After five years I've finally found you Giali! Evil cannot hide from me! You will pay for your crimes against the Earth Tribe!"

Jerry trembled in fear as he stared up at the Archigos. Bazek saw him and glared. "Small child, where did the man who was with you go?"

Jerry frantically looked around. "I...I...don't know...I..."

"Then you're worthless to me." Bazek spat.

He crouched and placed his fingers on the concrete. "Earth Craft, First Art, Tectonic Sense."

His senses were heightened as he felt the vibrations given off by every human being in the entire city. He peered through buildings and saw Jerry's uncle sprinting through alleys a few blocks away.

"Found you!"

Bazek vanished.

POW!

He instantly reappeared, smashing Jerry's uncle with his hammer as they soared at high speeds through the city.

"I've got you now Giali! There's no hope of escaping from..."

Ben snarled. "You're gonna pay for interrupting an evening with my nephew."

Jerry watched in awe as Bazek battled a swarm of unknown figures above the city. Ecstasy flooded his veins as he watched his idol battle before his very eyes. It was more than his frail body could handle. He was so overwhelmed by the moment that he collapsed in the street and passed out.

Jerry woke up in a hospital. *My head is foggy...how did I get here?* He looked around and saw that the room was completely empty except for the bed he laid in. *I'm not hurt so why am I in a hospital? I wonder if uncle is around here somewhere...* Before he left, he patted himself down and sighed in frustration. *Dang it! I lost my shades! I hope uncle won't be too mad at me.* When he opened the door, his uncle was lurking in the shadows.

"Let's...*cough*...go Jerry." Ben said as he coughed blood onto the hospital floor.

"Oh, there you are uncle Ben!" Jerry said enthusiastically as he approached him.

"Here put your shades on." Jerry's uncle said as he handed him sunglasses from the shadows.

"Sure! I was looking for these! I'm so sorry for losing them!"

Ben walked behind Jerry with a hand on his back. "It's ok. Let's just get out of here. We can talk more outside." Jerry didn't notice that his uncle smelled like iron and had bandages wrapped around his entire body.

As they walked through the halls, Jerry's uncle glanced around to make sure he was not seen. If people came too close, he disappeared behind a corner and reappeared behind Jerry before he noticed.

Suddenly, Jerry sprinted away from him toward a hospital room.

He hissed. "Jerry no! What are you..."

"Look! It's the Archigos! And there's nobody else inside! Can I please go in there and talk for a few minutes? Please?"

"No! We have to get out of..."

Suddenly, military officers turned the corner at the end of the hall.

"You have five minutes! Meet me outside when you finish!" Ben whispered as he disappeared into the shadows.

Jerry stared into the shadows "That was weird...but man! It's my lucky day!"

Bazek's leg was in a sling that hung from the ceiling and his bloodied body was wrapped in bandages. As Jerry entered the room, Bazek stared at him in terror. "You! You were with...What did he send you here to do?!"

Jerry ran over to the bed excitedly. "My uncle said I could have five minutes to talk to you before we had to leave Mr. Bazek sir! I'm your biggest fan and..."

Bazek eyed him warily. "That is nice boy, but as you can see, I am currently incapable of writing autographs so you will have to return another time..."

"I don't need an autograph! Just being in your presence is more than enough for me sir! I want to be just like you when I grow up!" Jerry beamed.

"*Sigh*, I doubt I am anything close to the man you regard me as, but I appreciate the sentiment. What exactly is it that you want from me boy?"

"Oh? It's Q&A time! Shoot! I have one million questions! Argh! Which one do I pick? Uncle said I only had five minutes...OOH! I know! I'll ask the most important one of all! Mr. Bazek, sir, do you think I can grow up to be big and strong like you and accomplish my dream of becoming Archigos one day?"

Bazek looked him up and down as he regarded his feeble frame. *Maybe the boy has a specialist ability, or a great potential for Spirit Craft.*

Jerry trembled as Bazek reached out and touched his face. Bazek closed his eyes as he felt for the flow of his Spirit Energy.

He could hardly sense an ounce.

He stared into Jerry's eyes with a solemn expression. "My son, I shall be frank and honest with you on this day. You will not grow up to be big and strong like me and you will never become an Archigos. You are minute, feeble in stature, and you hardly have the potential to master even the most basic tenants of Earth Craft. It is evident that you do not come from a family of affluence, so there is little hope of you securing an education or a proper job. I foresee a harsh life ahead of you filled with many sorrows. I tell you this as a mercy, so that you can focus on living the best life possible and keep your head below the clouds. Otherwise, your dreams will be shattered by the iron wings of reality."

Jerry sulked as he internalized every one of Bazek's words. Life and vibrance drained from his body as his eyes sunk back into his skull. His heart was too empty for tears as he despondently stared into Bazek's eyes. "Oh, ok..."

He turned and exited the room, as the sound of the creaking door echoed through the halls of the hospital.

Jerry slumped into his seat as he finished the story.

Machari pounded the table. "You see! That's the kind of man that you want to have a *pep talk* with! That's the kind of man..."

Kayla glanced at James and Jerry as they sat dejectedly across from her. Her hands trembled. "Machari...I hate you. I hate you *so much right now*. How could you put Jerry through that! How could you make him relive that when you knew what it would do to him! Now look at him! He's..."

James stared at the floor. "We'll do it."

Kayla's head snapped toward him. "James...what..."

"I said we'll do it. I'm gonna make sure that bastard gets put down and I'm gonna do it with my own hands."

Machari clapped triumphantly. "Yes! Finally, someone with sense..."

WHOOSH!

James pressed a dark saber against Machari's neck. "And after we're done. You're gonna rejoin the union as Archigos and me and my friends are gonna go on our merry way." Blood dripped from his neck. "If you try to go back on this deal. I will end you. I will snuff out your life before you can even *blink*."

James walked out of the dining hall.

Kayla leapt out of her seat. "James, wait! We can't do this!"

"Fiend! This is exceptionally unwise!"

Terrance ran after him. "James are you being serious right now? Machari is crazy! We can't..."

Machari raised an eyebrow. "Uh, Fos? Don't you need to hear what the actual *plan* is before you go all killy-killy revenge mode?"

James turned around. "How are we doing this? Just point me to the Archigos and I'll make sure the job gets done..."

Kayla ran up to him and took his hands in hers. She pleaded as she stared into his eyes. "James. I *know* you're angry, but you have to listen to me right now..."

Machari talked over Kayla as she continued. "Excellent! Here's the plan. The bulk of my army is going to attack the palace exterior directly and draw the majority of their defenses. You five are coming with me. We're gonna attack the palace through a hidden passage deep underground. We'll come through the library and avoid as much conflict as possible until we reach the grand hall outside the Archigos' private chambers..."

"...I need you to calm down and..."

James looked past Kayla. "And then what? Why do you need us with you?"

"James!" Kayla shouted in frustration.

"Wow James! You are just my favorite person of all time today! Your group's role will be to distract the Archigos' top soldier long enough for me to slip through and get into the Archigos' chambers. They call her. "The Blade". She would cut through any of my men in an instant. I need you guys to slow her down for just a moment so I can get through. I don't really expect you to win or anything so after I get in you should definitely run..."

"We'll get it done. And then I'll personally come to the Archigos' chambers to make sure the job is finished."

"JAMES, NO!" Kayla shouted as tears ran down her face.

James pointed at Jerry. "But what about Jerry? How does he factor into all of this? He's just a civilian and..."

"Oh, Jerry boy? He gets the safest and easiest job out of anybody on the trip! All he has to do is sit back and watch! He's gonna accompany me to the Archigos chamber as the ultimate backup. If I were to somehow lose, which I can guarantee won't happen, then it will be on Jerry to defeat the Archigos and finish off whatever is left of him! We all saw what he did to those skyscrapers right?!"

Kayla pressed herself closer to James. "See James! It's clear that he is not right in the head! Jerry saved us once, but we don't know how he did that and there's no guarantee he can do it again! He's gonna get Jerry caught up in the crossfire and killed! I know you're not ok with that, are you?! You have to help us stop this right now and..."

"What makes you so confident you can even kill the Archigos? Last time I checked those guys were pretty tough. I know with my power I could probably get the job done." James looked him up and down. "But *you*, you don't look that tough all." James said.

Machari slapped his knee as he burst into laughter. "Ha-Ha! You're a comedian James! I can't deny that the dark energy you wield is something special, but you couldn't take me on your best day. Once this is all over, you'll have to tell me your secret though." Machari slipped a dagger from his coat sleeve. "But to answer your question, this dagger is special. One prick from this will do the trick. Even a small cut has enough venom to kill ten-thousand elephants. I think it should be more than enough to bring down a feeble old man who's past his prime."

"Got it. I'll leave it to you then. But I want to be there before he dies and make him apologize to Jerry for what he said."

Machari shrugged. "Sounds good to me."

"James, *please* listen..."

James dropped his hands from her grasp and left the dining hall.

Kayla stood in silence as she watched James disappear. She swallowed and wiped tears from her face.

FWOOOSH!

She faced Machari as flaming daggers formed in her hands. "I'll kill you for making James feel like this!"

Terrance formed icy axes. "Machari, I love you man, I really do. If you had come to me and asked me to rob the federal reserve, or start a nuclear war, I would have done it without hesitation bro. But killing an Archigos will destabilize this country, lead to an all-out civil war and even more people are gonna get hurt! We're gonna stop you, right here, right now."

Epios demagnetized a blade from armor beneath his suit. "It's time that you paid for ruining my beauty sleep and publicly disrespecting me, king of fiends. I shall have your head this day myself."

Machari chuckled as they surrounded him. "*Hmph,* you guys sure are rude. Trying to stop me right before my big day begins." He pointed at Terrance. "I'm especially disappointed in you Terrance but it doesn't surprise me based on the way your mother is. Rotten apples don't fall too far from the tree."

A tear rolled down Terrance's face. "Machari, don't say that. You're not in your right mind! You've never acted like this be..."

"Terrance. You weren't with me all those years I was alone in the streets. You didn't have to kill to survive or eat shit and drink your own piss just to make it to the next sunrise. I appreciate you and your pops taking me in and saving me from that life...but you just *can't* relate." Machari spread his arms. "This is who I am and it's who I've always been. This is all I've dreamed about since the day we met." He chuckled. "Maybe I'm more like my pops than I thought. I guess you can't teach an old dog new tricks."

"Machari, I'm sorry! I'm sorry for being a terrible brother and for not helping you get through this the right way! You turning out like this is my fault. I knew what we were doing and saying was wrong but I..."

"Who ate the chef's specialty chicken?"

Terror gripped their hearts.

"It was so good right! Perfectly seasoned, crispy texture, and the flavors just bounced off your tongue like..."

Terrance shuddered. "Machari...what have you done?"

"Within that chicken was a carefully measured dose of that metallic elephant poison that we were talking about earlier. At this point, I'd say you have about five hours to live before it binds to your nervous system and you, *well*, die an unspeakably gruesome death."

"THAT'S BULLSHIT MACHARI! YOU WOULD DO THAT TO YOUR ONLY SIBLING? YOUR OWN BROTHER? GIVE ME THE ANTIDOTE RIGHT..."

"We were never brothers!" Machari hissed. "And there is no antidote! Only I can remove the poison by magnetizing it through your skin, back to the source. Which I will only do once I've confirmed the Archigos' body is in a casket!"

He reclined on his throne and crossed his leg. "You'd better get to it."

James

In a room, I quickly gathered my things and shoveled them into a backpack. I was seeing red, and vengeance was all I could think about. I wanted to kill him. I wanted to kill him so bad. I wanted to wrap my hands around his neck and watch the life drain out of his body, bit by bit until there was nothing left. There was only one other time I could remember being mad enough to actually kill someone. And even then, I only would have done it if they had attacked me or escalated things a certain way. When I heard the way that bastard told Jerry he wouldn't amount to anything in life, and that his excuse was that he was telling him as a courtesy, all I heard were my coach's excuses as I sat in front of him and cried my eyes out in his office.

And he would die for that.

As I shoveled the last of my things into my backpack, I heard the door creep open. I glanced over and saw Kayla, gently closing the door behind her like she always did. She leaned against the dresser as she waited for me to speak.

"Look Kayla! I'm sorry ok! But this is just something I have to do and..."

"I know. This really isn't the time, but I honestly think it's cute when you get like this."

My world stopped.

"Kayla...what are you..."

I turned around and she was in my face. She grabbed my hands and pulled them toward her. She rested them in the center of her chest, just above her breasts. "Look James. Is what you're about to do incredibly risky, stupid, and endangering every single one of our lives? Absolutely. Am I mad at you? No. Am I incredibly disappointed in you? Yes, James, I really, really am." She pulled me closer as her breath warmed my face. "Is there a whole lot that I don't know about you? Sure, there is, and that's why I really can't judge you for making this decision. Just know that no matter what happens. I'll be by your side to help you scoop up the ashes."

"Kayla...I..."

She put her finger over my lips. "Don't say anything right now. SHH! Just promise me that everything is going to be ok like you always do. Make me a promise right now, that when this is finally all over, we are going to sit down, talk, and really get to know each other. For real this time. Alright?"

Her bashful smile was absolutely captivating. I wanted to lean down and kiss her, hug her, cherish her, with every fiber of my existence! But instead, I grabbed her pointer finger from my lips and wrapped my own around it.

"I promise."

She smiled as she turned and walked confidently out of the room. She paused in the doorway and rolled her eyes at me. "And by the way, it made me really freaking mad when you just let Jerry propose to me like that. Not very manly of you at all. What would you have done if I had said yes?"

"I mean, what could I have done? He's my friend and I wanted to be supportive and..."

CLANG!

She slammed the iron door.

Girls are so confusing.

James and his friends walked with Machari through the dark tunnels beneath the palace. Jerry had passed out and was strapped to Machari's back. James walked up to Machari and tapped him on the shoulder. "Let's take a restroom break. There's something I need to take care of really quickly."

"Fine. But make it quick."

James walked down a tunnel alone. He looked around to make sure he hadn't been followed.

"Semaj. Come out."

Semaj turned the corner as he was reading a book called, 'Making Friends for Dummies'.

"What is it mate? Can't you see that I'm trying to educate myself ere' and..."

"Stop with the accents. I told you that I'm not mixed."

"*Aww*, you're no fun mate. I was starting to like this British one quite a bit actually..."

"I don't care. Now look, if things go south in there, I may need your help again like I did in the Ocean Tribe. Can I count on you?"

Semaj turned around and walked away. "Absolutely not, mate! With the way you've been treating me you're lucky I even showed up at all! Now, I have my own business to attend to so..."

"Please Semaj. You know how important my friends are to me, and I can't risk anything happening to them. I need your help to ensure they stay safe."

He pulled out a massive spreadsheet. "That's ironic, considering the fact you've been mooching off my power for ages now! I should charge you tax and interest for all the strength you've sapped from me you bloody wanker!"

"What are you talking about?! Are you saying these dark powers are coming from you?"

"Absolutely mate! And they're not dark powers or whatever nonsense that uneducated bloke Machari was spouting! Just because my Spirit Energy is *black* in the same way that Terrence's Spirit Energy is *blue* does not make mine inherently evil! And as a matter of fact, from here on I'm cutting you off! You're always so bloody rude. Always telling me to leave when you know I can only go where you go! Replacing me with all your new friends like that bloody Jerry when I'm the one that's always been good to you since we were little! I'm the one who has always stuck closer than a brother mate, but I get nothing but flak for it!"

"Semaj, I don't even know what you're talking about..."

"Let me make this bloody clear for you mate, the fact of the matter is that if you were smarter, you wouldn't even be getting in situations like this that require asking for my bloody help *in the first place*! What does any of this have to do with getting home, finding a wife, and leaving a legacy? Why do you constantly throw us into life-threatening situations, like sprinting into that factory or running from the police! I swear your bloody mind is warped! How does going out of our way to help even one bloody person who lives here help us get any closer to reaching our goal of getting home you stupid sap?!"

*He's right. Why **am** I here doing this right now? Why did I run into that blazing factory and why do I keep getting myself into situations like this? For my entire life I avoided risks and would have sprinted away from any situation that even remotely resembled something like this...* I stared into the tunnel's darkness. *Even though I've come so far, I'm still such a long way from getting home. I haven't even told my friends about the fact that I need them to help me sneak into the Wind Nation to get that map. And who knows if the sage even exists? At this rate I'm going to get myself killed without even getting close to seeing my family again.*

"Look Semaj. I don't have time to think about this right now. I just need your help so that me and my friends can get through the morning. Whatever happens after that, happens. I'm sorry for being rude and dismissive of you, but if you claim to know me so well, then I think you can understand why I don't trust you. I don't understand any of the crazy things that you do and as far as I'm concerned, all you do is cause problems." James got on his knees. "But I still need you right now and all I can do is ask that you accept my forgiveness."

He crossed his arms. "Well, you don't understand me because you don't make the effort to mate. I told you I only have your best interests at heart and want to do everything I can to make your dreams come true, but *you* still treat *me* like I shot your bloody mum!"

"Look, if we make it out of this, I promise I'll take the time to get to know you, ok? If what you say is true, then help me keep my friends safe. That is the only thing I want right now and I'm willing to do anything to make it happen."

"That sounds good to me mate. All I desire is to be heard, esteemed, respected, accepted, and loved, like anybody else. I'll help you keep your friends safe, but in exchange I require another covenant with you."

"Fine. What is it that you want this time? I won't hurt anybody, and I refuse to do anything weird or immoral like sex or..."

"Pipe down mate! Why would I want you to do anything like that?! I told you that our desires are bloody the same! Though some sexy time with Kayla does sound quite heavenly..."

"Get your head out of the gutter and tell me what you want!"

"Let me think...OOOH! I know! I'm quite intrigued with what Kayla said before we left, and this will go perfectly with another deal I struck recently! If I say 'Tea and Crumpets', then I want you to lend me control of your body for ten minutes. In exchange, I'll grant you unlimited access to some of my power until the morning."

"What about the other deal that we have in place? Isn't taking over my body if I die enough? And how do I know you're not going to hurt or kill anybody and then try to place the blame on me. If we make this deal, I want it to be on the same terms as last time where you can't do anything with my body I wouldn't like."

"I'm afraid I can't do that this time mate. The purpose of this deal will likely be for me to put a few people to the test so I can't promise that things won't get a bit messy. *But* what I can promise is I'll make sure everything works out in your favor. Trust is the first part of any budding new romance or relationship mate."

James face palmed. "This is not a romance, but fine. I agree to your terms of service. If you cross me, I swear to you I'll..."

"James! Hurry your ass up and let's go!" Machari shouted.

"Coming." James said as Semaj waved and disappeared into the shadows.

He rejoined the group, and they continued down the tunnels.

Kayla whispered in his ear. "I thought I heard your voice when I was using the restroom. Who were you talking to?"

"It was nothing. Don't worry about it." James said as they delved deeper into the darkness.

Thick raindrops drenched the Earth Tribe as the moon rose high into the sky. An ominous fog settled over the city, and it was especially thick near the palace. The palace guards dozed off, exhausted from another full day of holding back rioters. A sentry snapped awake as a strange drumming sound was heard coming from the fog.

BANG! Ra-ta-ta-ta-ta-ta-ta-ta! BANG! BANG! BANG! BANG! Ra-ta-ta-ta-ta-ta-ta-ta! BANG! BANG! BANG!

The rhythmic drumming grew in intensity as the fog crept closer and closer to the palace. The guards left the building and stared at the cloud in shock, as the sound of rattling chains mixed into the clamor of the drumbeat. The cloud stopped as it reached the palace's outer gate. Hundreds of soldiers rushed from the palace and stood in formation, with golden spears drawn against the cloud.

For a moment, the world was completely still.

"DENIZENS OF THE UNDERWORLD, ATTACK!"

BOOOOOM!

A mob of unruly criminals burst through the fog and barreled through the palace gates.

"HUUUUUUUUUAAAAAAAAAAAAAAAAAAAA!" The soldiers roared at the top of their lungs as they engaged the underworld mob.

Iron clashed against iron and blood filled the air, as total carnage ensued.

CRASH!

Inside the palace, Machari's group burst through a bookcase in the library, and sprinted into the palace's lower hall. They raced up the spiral stairwell as soldiers stared in shock.

"Intruders! Stop them!" The guards shouted as the group disappeared down a hallway.

The soldiers rode platforms of metal and hotly pursued them through the corridors. Metal barriers formed in the group's path, but they leapt, maneuvered and smashed through them as they darted through the palace.

CREAK!

A massive metal wall rose ahead of the group. They stopped and the soldiers lowered their spears as they rapidly closed the distance.

WHOOSH!

Suddenly, a sandstorm covered the entire hallway and obscured the soldier's vision. They stopped and the storm slowly dissipated. When the dust settled, the group had disappeared.

"Find them! They're somewhere in this palace! We can't let them reach the Archigos!"

Machari led the group as they sliced through soldiers and sprinted down the palace's wide, golden hallways until they reached the top floor. Suddenly, soldiers appeared and blocked the corridor ahead of the group. They stopped and turned, only to find soldiers closing in on their rear.

"We've got you! Stay where you are!" A soldier shouted as they closed in.

Machari panicked and frantically looked around as the group prepared for battle. Machari's head snapped toward a nearby doorway.

"I have no idea where this goes, but we're making a break for it!" He shouted as he barreled through the door.

CRASH!

They burst through the door behind him and on the other side there was a massive locker room where a multitude of women were showering or changing. Machari froze as he took in the scene. The women stared at them in shock.

"AAAAAAAH! PERVERTS!", "THEY'VE COME TO KIDNAP AND RAPE US!", "RUN FOR YOUR LIVES!" The women shouted as they sprinted away.

"This wasn't what I had in mind, but it's not a bad deal." Machari said as they sprinted through the locker room with the guards on their heels.

Jerry woke up from all the screaming and his body was flooded with ecstasy as he stared at the naked women. "I've never seen one of those before...OH MY GOD! HAVE I DIED AND GONE TO HEAVEN?!"

James caught up to Machari and yelled to Jerry. "Nope! But it's pretty darn close!"

"HELL YEAH!" Terrance shouted.

"None of them compare to Laura unfortunately..." Epios sighed.

"This is awful, and you disgusting men are worse!" Kayla spat as they sprinted through the showers.

CRASH!

They burst through a door and found themselves in a massive ballroom. The floors were made of pure gold and there was a beautiful diamond chandelier hanging from the high ceiling. The ballroom was completely empty, and the rightmost wall consisted of arched openings that led out to a magnificent stone balcony. Across the room, there was a massive golden door with ornate silver designs carved into it. Machari pointed at the doorways behind them, and raging sandstorms blocked their openings. The group sat down and heaved as they caught their breath.

Machari stood proudly as he took in the scenery. "This is it! We made it to the grand hall! The Archigos' chambers are just beyond that doorway!"

James stared in the direction of the massive door. "That's great, but who the hell is that standing down there?"

Machari glanced toward the door and his heart sank. "Fuck."

A tall woman in a full suit of ornate silver armor stood proudly before the massive golden door. Her suit was skin-tight, and it perfectly accentuated her incredible form and toned muscles. She had a gorgeous face, long black hair, and striking hazel eyes. She looked upon them with disdain as she stood with her sword before her.

"She's beautiful! A MONA LISA! A MASTERPIECE!" Epios roared as stars filled his eyes.

"I HAVE TO MARRY HER!" Jerry shouted.

Terrance pointed his thumb at her in confusion. "Machari, are you wasting our time? That sexy chick is the one who's supposed to be all big and bad? This will be a piece of cake."

James joyfully clapped Epios on the back. "I've never heard that from you Epios! It looks like you're finally moving on!"

Kayla raised her daggers. "Can you idiots focus and control your erections for once in your freaking lives! SHE'S HERE TO KILL US!"

Machari drew his blades. "I didn't think she would be this hot either. But don't underestimate her because..."

BAAAAAAAAAAAAAAAANNNNNNNNNNGGGGGG!

The woman slammed the tip of her blade into the ground and the harsh reverberations echoed throughout the hall. The group covered their ears as the sound threatened to split their skulls. When the ringing stopped, the woman stepped forward.

"I am Krystal Khalyvas, and I am this nation's top warrior. I am known throughout the land as, 'The Blade of the Archigos'. You have been found guilty in my sight for trespassing on palace grounds and spilling the blood of this nation's loyal soldiers." She raised her blade. "Today, I shall be your judge, jury, and executioner."

20 - The Blade

KRYSTAL SIGHED. "I suppose I shall cut down the weakest first to limit your numbers advantage..."

James braced himself. "Guys! Get ready she's..."

"Polarity."

SLICE!

Krystal viciously sliced Epios across his torso, sending him crashing into the wall as his blood sprayed into the air. James only saw a blur in the corner of his eye. He started turning his head.

"BAAAAAAAAAAAAANNNNNNNNNGGGGGGGG!"

SLICE!

A sonic attack rattled James' skull. He looked to his left and Terrance's torso exploded with blood as he was launched backwards.

CRASH!

James looked down as his sword crashed into the golden floor against his will.

SLICE!

GUSH!

James was sent soaring through the air, and he crashed down onto his back as a pool of blood spread beneath him. A massive, gaping wound covered his chest.

"Ember Dance!"

SLICE!

Kayla leapt backward as she narrowly avoided a sweeping strike. She landed on her feet and the bottom portion of her hoodie was ripped in the chest area. Krystal hesitated as she saw Kayla's flaming daggers.

Kayla ripped off the damaged portion of her hoodie. "What? You don't like these?"

Krystal pointed her blade. "I've never been fond of flames. They're only purpose is to destroy."

Kayla raised her daggers. "I like the way they dance in the wind. Let me show you."

Kayla ducked a swing aimed at her head, spun and tore her daggers into Krystal's side. They did nothing more than leave a black scorch mark in her armor.

Damn, too shallow. Kayla rolled away from another attack.

They engaged in a furious melee as James and Terrance recovered. Terrance stumbled to his feet as he regenerated and charged in to help Kayla. James laid in a pool of his own blood as he writhed in agony. He looked down at his chest wound and it slowly started regenerating. *Thanks Semaj.*

James rose, picked up his sword and joined in the brawl. Kayla leapt backward on the defensive as Krystal assaulted her with a swift sequence of attacks. Kayla ducked right, left and contorted her body to avoid being torn to shreds by Krystal's blade.

SLICE!

Terrance rushed in and swung his ax as Krystal leaned back, narrowly avoiding decapitation.

SWIP, SWIP SLASH!

She gave Terrance three quick slices, and his body exploded in blood.

POW!

Krystal's eyes widened as James sliced through Terrance's torso with violent force and his blade crashed into her stomach. She was knocked through the air, but she gracefully flipped, spun and landed on her feet. James removed his blade from Terrance's body and they stood together, facing The Blade.

SMACK!

Terrence smacked James across the head. "Who gave you permission to do that simp! That hurt! You could have killed..."

"We don't have time for this! We need to make a plan!" James said as he glanced at Epios. He was in a bloody heap on the ground and his body made an indention in the wall. *Dammit! Epios is down for the count. Ok, what should we do? She's unnaturally quick and fast for some...*

"JAMES, LOOK OUT!"

SLICE!

James leapt backwards and bent his spine as he narrowly avoided a lethal decapitation. She turned and swiftly swung at Terrance.

CRASH!

He raised his axes to defend his face, and her blade shattered the axes, sliced through his forearms, into his neck, and sent him flying into a wall across the hall. She wiped the blood from her blade as she stared at her remaining foes. "I see you two can regenerate. It looks like I'll just have to put a stop to that by *beheading* you."

She launched a brutal assault on James and he narrowly dodged and deflected strike after strike. As he leapt backward, his fatigue grew and his defenses waned. *Damn it. I can't keep up like this! I have to think! We have to come up with something. What are the properties of metal...GAAAH!*

GUSH!

Her blade tore into his side. His eyes widened as she swiftly spun her blade and sent it slicing through the air toward his neck.

FWOOSH!

There was a rush of flames and Krystal leapt backward. Kayla engaged her in a furious duel as James held his side in shock. He snapped out of it and fired three Photon Beams at Krystal. They bounced off her armor and careened around the room as they reflected off the walls. A beam nearly hit Kayla, and she swiftly rolled away, narrowly avoiding a lethal blow from Krystal.

"James! Watch what you're doing!"

Dammit! My beams just bounce off her and now they're getting in the way! I have to come up with something! What happens when you heat up metal... He smirked. *I've got it!*

CRASH!

Krystal narrowly avoided a strike from a massive ice hammer.

"Dammit. I missed!" Terrance said as he raised his axes against Krystal.

Krystal stood between Terrance and Kayla and the room was silent.

She patiently waited to see who would make the first move.

WHOOSH!

They rushed her simultaneously and she raised her blade against Kayla. Kayla charged forward, leapt, and brought her dagger down with violent force. Krystal met the high attack with her blade, ducked an attack from Terrance and spun around, slicing him in the torso. She pivoted and shallowly sliced Kayla in the stomach.

BANG!

James beamed out of the wall and crashed his blade into her side, sending her skidding across the golden floor as she came to a stop. James' friends stood side by side and raised their weapons against her.

"Terrance. I want you to bombard her with long range attacks while Kayla and I handle the hand-to-hand combat."

"Why do you get to..."

"Just shut the hell up and be ready when I signal you!" James said as he Mirror Dashed into the wall.

BANG!

James zipped out and Krystal was barely able to absorb the massive impact from his strike with her blade. She ducked an ice lance aimed at her head, and Kayla caught her, swiftly slicing her seven times with her daggers. They left black searing scratches but otherwise had no effect.

"Dammit! James, I can't get through her armor!" Kayla shouted as she backflipped away from a sword slash.

"That's fine! Just keep doing it!" He shouted enthusiastically.

Krystal sliced through an ice lance and absorbed the blow from another Mirror Dash which sent her flying across the hall. *Dammit! What are they planning? The cute one's Light Craft attacks are too fast for me to...SHIT!*

Kayla charged in from behind, but Krystal spun around in midair and raised her blade.

CRASH!

BANG!

An ice lance crashed into her right side as James zipped in and blasted her left side.

POW!

Krystal zoomed through the air toward Terrance, and he smashed his ice ax into her, sending her zooming toward Kayla.

"Flame Craft, Art 4, Graceful Flame Tempo!"

Kayla bounded toward Krystal as she blitzed toward her. She vanished.

SLICE! SLICE! SLICE! SLICE! SLICE! SLICE! SLICE!

Krystal flipped through the air and landed on her feet. She looked down and her armor was blackened with seared slashes. "Ha! A meaningless effort..."

Kayla landed in a crouch across the hall.

She smiled.

SNAP!

FWOOOOOOOOOOOOOOOOOOOOSH!

Krystal's armor erupted in flames, and she was cooked alive in her suit.

"AHHHHHHHHHHHHHHHHHHH!" She screamed in agony as her flesh was seared.

Her body disappeared as she expanded her suit into a large, searing hot dome.

"TERRANCE! FREEZE IT NOW!" James roared.

Terrance raced over to the dome and grabbed it with his bare hands. He funneled Spirit Energy into the bubble as his flesh bubbled from the heat.

"AAAAAAAAAAARRRRRRRGAAAAAAAAAAAAAAAH!" He roared

Frost crept across the dome as it was completely frozen solid.

James took a deep breath.

He funneled Spirit Energy into his blade and its length doubled as a second blade made from pure energy enveloped it. His sword was blinding, and it glowed with a multicolored radiance.

"Light Craft! Art 3! Mirror Dash!"

ZIP! ZIP!

SLASH!

James zipped into a reflection, exploded out, and sliced through the dome.

BOOOOOOOOOOOOOOOOOOOOOOOOOOOOOM!

The dome exploded in a radiant lightshow of multicolored energy.

James huffed and puffed as he looked back at the dome. Its upper half slid down at a diagonal angle as its top half crashed into the golden floor.

James beamed at his friends. "I figured if we could heat her armor enough, and then cool it down rapidly, it would soften enough for me to be able to slice through!"

Kayla and Terrance collapsed in exhaustion.

"Man...*huff*...*huff*...she was tough!" Terrance huffed.

"I'm just glad...*huff*...*huff*...that this is finally...*huff*...*huff*...almost over." Kayla huffed.

Machari waved at them as he casually jogged toward the door across the hall with Jerry strapped to his back.

"Great work team! Now I'll do my part and...OH MY GOD!"

Krystal was completely naked and racing toward him at high speeds. She had a dark scar across her torso where James' blade contacted her. She was swiftly closing the gap on Machari, and he took off in a desperate sprint.

"Oh no!" Kayla said.

"Dammit! There's no way I can close that distance!" Terrance said.

Gold from the floor flew out of the walls and ceiling as it formed a new set of armor around Krystal.

WHOOOOOOOOOOOOOSH!

She suddenly exploded forward with a rapid burst of speed, sending shockwaves that knocked James and his friends off their feet as a golden blade zipped into her hand. Jerry trembled in fear as James' eyes widened with horror. *If she slices through them, Jerry would be the one to die first!*

James' mind raced as time seemed to slow. *No! I can't lose Jerry! I have to think! How did I tap into Semaj's power before?! How was I feeling?! What was I thinking?*

Krystal approached faster and faster and she started raising her blade.

James's mind raged as a tear rolled down his face. *Fuck! Is that the only way? Dammit! I'm out of time!*

James pictured his worst experiences. He sat in a team meeting at his football facility and bawled his eyes out after getting passed over for a scholarship for the fourth year in a row. He remembered a particular day when he sat alone in his dorm room after another day of abuse. He stared out the window in agony as he wondered if four stories was high enough. He thought back to the day he saw Kayla making out with Terrance.

FVOOM!

James' body was overwhelmed with dark emotions, and they overtook him. His mind faded into a sea of blackness, and he fell backward as he collapsed.

Kayla stared at him in shock as he fell. "James! What hap..."

FWOOOOOOOOOOOOOOOOOOSSSSSSHHHH!

James rocketed across the hall as dark energy erupted from his body, sending a dark shockwave that shattered the glass balcony doors.

RMBLRMBLRMBLRMBLR!

The entire palace quaked as the dark wave crashed into the walls. Tendrils of black lightning zipped off his body as he zoomed through the air.

POW!

CRASH!

James instantly caught Krystal and crashed his blade into her as she violently barreled into the wall.

She walked out a crater and stared at him in shock.

His eyes had a red hue and he beat his chest as he shouted in a distorted voice. **"I'LL DO ANYTHING TO PROTECT MY..."**

"A meaningless effort..."

SLAM!

James' blade crashed into the ground.

SLICE!

She ripped her blade from his flesh and propelled herself into the air using his body as she resumed her pursuit. She blitzed toward Machari as he neared the Archigos' doors. She sighed as she raised her blade.

SLICE! SLICE! SLICE! CRASH!

She skidded to a halt as she sliced three ice lances from Terrance. Machari desperately reached out and grabbed the door handle.

CREAK!

It wouldn't budge and he looked back as Krystal raised her blade like a javelin to impale him. Machari shifted Jerry from his back to his front. He squeezed his eyes shut as fear gripped his heart.

CLAP!

BOOOOOOOOOOOM!

FREEZE!

Terrance's broken ice lances exploded, and Krystal was completely frozen solid.

Machari slowly opened his eyes, and the room was covered in blue mist.

"GO NOW! GET OUT OF HERE BEFORE SHE GETS FREE!" Terrance shouted from across the hall.

Machari stared at him in shock. "I...I thought you were going to betray me!"

"I WOULD NEVER BETRAY YOU! I LOVE YOU LIKE MY OWN FLESH AND BLOOD! I'LL NEVER SUPPORT YOU WHEN YOU MAKE THESE KINDS OF CHOICES, BUT I COULD NEVER LET HER TO SKEWER YOU LIKE THAT!"

Machari looked away. "I'm just surprised after everything I've put you through. That's all..."

"Machari, I don't think I could ever forgive you for what you did to my friends, and there's still time to escape..." Terrance pointed past Machari. "If you go through that door, we are *not* brothers anymore."

Machari shed a tear and faced the door. "I'm sorry then. Brother..."

He ripped the massive door open with all his strength and sprinted down the corridor. A raging sandstorm formed behind him blocking the entrance.

CRASH!

Suddenly, Krystal shuddered and broke free from her icy entrapment. She looked into the sandstorm and rage filled her heart.

"NOOOOOOO! I HAVE FAILED!" She roared as she fell to her knees and sobbed.

Sympathy filled James' heart and the darkness faded. He walked toward her. "It's over now. Please, come with us, and we can help stop the carnage going on outside and..."

CLANG!

James narrowly deflected her attack and leapt back.

She stood before them brimming with rage. "Each and every single one of you underworld scum shall die on this day. I SWEAR IT ON MY OWN LIFE!"

She raised her blade as James' friends prepared for battle.

Krystal took a deep breath. Her metal boots shifted and exposed her bare feet to the golden surface. "Earth Craft, Art 1! Tectonic Sense!"

She felt the vibrations given off by each shift of their weight. She vanished.

SLICE!

She tore through Terrance's body and reappeared behind him as his axes clattered to the ground. Kayla and James stood in shock as Terrance crumpled to his knees. She rose and turned her attention to them. Fear gripped their hearts.

James swallowed. *Damn! It's like she's even faster now! How is she doing...*

WHOOSH!

She was upon Kayla in an instant and her eyes were brimming with malice. James' eyes went wide.

"KAYLA NO..."

BOOOOM!

Terrance's ice axes exploded and knocked everyone from their feet.

CLANG!

Krystal leapt up and deflected a slash from Terrance. She struggled as he pressed his ax against her blade and forced it down toward her neck.

"You can't get rid of me that easily you sexy bastard! It was disrespectful to attack me first!"

"You can take your compliments to the grave Terrance Touvtpa!" Krystal spat as her arms trembled.

FVOOOM!

Suddenly, silver energy surrounded her, and her muscles surged. Her strength gradually increased, as she forced Terrance's blade back.

"What the...HELL!" He shouted.

She relaxed, crouched, and used his momentum to send him flying over her head. James rushed her, but she stretched out her hand and his sword zipped away, crashing into the far wall.

"Dammit!" He said as he chased after it.

Kayla charged at Krystal, and she narrowly avoided two swift slashes.

CRASH!

Krystal lifted her hand and Kayla was enveloped in a massive golden sphere.

BANG! BANG! BANG!

Kayla pounded the walls as she attempted to escape. Terrance leapt to his feet and raised his axes against her.

Krystal sighed aggressively. "No more strategies. This time, I'll deal with you *one by one*."

"Bring it on bitch." Terrance said as he prepared for battle.

SLICE!

He rushed her, and she swiftly pirouetted and sliced through him.

"GAAAH!" He shouted.

She calmly stood behind him with her blade extended. He turned and brought down his axes.

SLICE!

She stood in a power position with her blade extended out near the right side of his head.

WHOOOOSH!

A massive gust of wind erupted like a shockwave after her sword swing. It blew golden particles into the wind that glimmered in the light.

James felt the wind from across the hall and swiftly turned around. He looked on at the scene in horror.

Terrance was still.

Krystal sliced through his axes, forearms and head. Blood dripped from the horizontal wound created by her slash.

The room was silent.

His forearms and axes clattered to the ground and shattered.

"Terrance! Get out of there!" James shouted.

Krystal sighed. "A shame. I thought Brooklyn's brother would have been a more skilled fighter. Oh well."

His forearms and head wound swiftly regenerated. He formed a new ax and stared at her, enraged.

"AAAAAAAAAAARGH!" He roared as he swung his ax.

"TERRANCE, NO!"

"A shame."

SLICE!

She sliced his body in half. A gaping vertical line spread through his torso, just next to his neck.

SLICE!

A gaping horizontal line spread through his torso as she sliced him into quarters.

CRASH! CRASH! CRASH! CRASH!

His body's divided sections plopped to the floor and golden beams crashed down from the ceiling and impaled each piece. Terrance's head stared at her in shock as his body writhed in agony.

She walked away. "That should keep you from regenerating. I have only spared you at the moment for

Brooklyn's sake. Think about your final message to her and your father. I shall return to finish you after I deal with these other two insurgents."

James trembled as he watched Terrance's defeat. He grabbed his sword as his mind raced. *Damn! What are we gonna do?! She's way faster than before, and on top of that she's moving before we can even react! It's like she knows what we're gonna do before we do it! I have to think! How is she doing this?*

Krystal heard scratching sounds inside the golden sphere as Kayla steadily chipped away at the bubble's interior.

Krystal sighed as she extended her hand toward the sphere. "I guess she will eventually break free. I suppose I should dispose of it."

CREAK!

The sphere ripped out of the floor, lifted into the air, and rocketed down into the palace courtyard.

GUSH! GUSH! GUSH!

CRASH!

The sphere splattered bodies as it rolled and smashed into the palace's outer gates.

James shuddered as Krystal's gaze fell upon him. *No! I'm all alone! I have to think! I have to think!*

"I don't know who you are, but I assume you're friends with Terrance and Kayla." She glanced at Epios. "And that other guy I guess..." She spat in Terrance's direction. "I hate Terrance, but Kayla and I were friends for a time when we were younger." Krystal tilted her head. "Though I doubt she remembers me. Her and her sister were too boy crazy to notice anyone else. In fact, she was always so obsessed with Terrance that everyone called her a lunatic..." Krystal put her hand to her chin. "Wait a second...You're not dating her now, are you?"

James' voice was laced with rage and fear as he raised his blade. "Why are you asking me this?!"

Krystal sighed. "I shall send her back to her tribe and have her tried there. Kalarono would likely burn down our nation if I didn't grant him this courtesy...I tell you this in honor of the relationship I've observed between the three of you." She glanced at him longingly. "I envy your closeness and would like to at least grant you the mercy of knowing your friends will be alright before I end your life."

James broke into a cold sweat. *Dammit! Think James, think! We can't die here! How is she doing all of this crazy stuff?!* He thought back to his blade crashing into the ground and seeing Krystal lift Kayla's sphere with an unseen force. He drifted back to the moment before Epios was slashed. Krystal's voice saying. "Polarity" rang out in his mind. *That's it! She's using magnetism to do all these crazy feats! She's pushing and pulling the gold in her armor against the rest of the room to allow her to move at high speeds! But what can I do to stop it?*

Krystal spoke compassionately. "Do you have any final words you would like me to give to your friends?"

James analyzed her armor and noticed that it was dented and scratched in several areas. Her blade was chipped and jagged in many spots along its edge. *Her golden armor must not be as durable as the silver one from before. I bet I could slash through it without a problem. It should be less resistant to the heat and cold as well. But that's* **if** *I can free Kayla or Terrance. Who should I free first? I wonder if my Photon Beams will work now...*

Krystal stomped. "You don't have anything to say to your girlfriend or your friends?! That is so not romantic! Have you done this before? What kind of boyfriend are you?!"

James' face was blank as his mind raced.

Krystal sighed. "Oh well...you can't say I didn't try to give *some* grace. Now, are you going to make me come over there and kill you or will you turn from your wicked ways and accept your punishment honorably?"

Ok, I can definitely damage her now and if I can do something to offset her speed or negate her polarity, I'll have a chance to win this. I'll definitely need Semaj's power. I should have asked him exactly what kinds of powers I have access to because it sounded like he has more than one. Maybe I should ask him now...

"Sema..."

SLICE!

Krystal was upon him, and she smashed her blade into his gut. "Why won't you answer me?!"

CRASH!

She sent him flying across the room and he crashed into the wall. His body was a bloody heap, and he laid completely still in a crater.

She groaned as she approached. "*Ugh*, why couldn't you have died on impact. Now I have to come over there and finish you..."

James' mind drifted as he lost his grip on consciousness. *T...hi...ink Jam...es. T...h...i...n...k. I...f y...ou do...n't th...in...k, yo...u're gon...na d...i...e...*

James let his mind drift into despair. He thought back to the day that his coach cursed him out after giving his spot to his teammate. He thought back to the day he found out Mikayla had chosen another man over him. He thought about the day that he woke up in the black dust of this God-forsaken world.

BOOOOOOOOM!

Dark energy exploded out of him, and he snapped awake. Krystal was shocked as a flurry of Photon Beams blinded her vision as they cascaded toward her. She deflected some, but several seared into her armor, leaving black dents.

James rose to his feet as his wounds regenerated. *DAMMIT! They should have pierced through! Why do they seem weaker all the sudden?*

Krystal stared at the black dents in her armor. *Crap, if those spots get hit again, I'll be toast.*

WHOOSH!

She sprinted at James and rocketed toward him at incalculable speeds, sending a shockwave through the hall. James braced against the shockwave and fired another barrage of Photon Beams. She skillfully weaved through them and slashed the ones she couldn't avoid. Krystal neared James and raised her blade to finish him. He continued firing as he formed a dark saber in his right hand.

CREAK!

Suddenly, her armor jolted awkwardly as she sped up faster than she anticipated.

SLICE!

She misjudged her strike, and James crashed his blade into her stomach.

FVOOOOOOOM!

A dark shockwave erupted on impact as she was sent barreling across the hall. She landed on her face and her armor screeched as she skidded to a halt.

"Ha! Maybe school is good for something after all! I added photons to your suit's metal and the electrons inside it gained too much energy and went out of control!" James shouted as lasers cascaded around the hall around them.

Krystal stared at him in a rage as she picked herself up. Her lower torso was exposed through a jagged hole in her armor, but there was only a dark scar on the surface of her skin.

"Oh yeah?! Well, if you're so smart, then why are you still wearing a suit with metal plates in it, DUMBASS!" She shouted as she extended her hand toward him.

James' armor shuddered as the plates dug into his skin and lifted him off the ground.

"Shit, Shit, Shit, Shit, Shit! How do I get out of this..."

SLICE!

WHOOOOSH!

She landed in a crouch as a shockwave of wind exploded behind her.

GUSH!

James' body erupted in blood, and his armor clattered as he hit the ground. He became dizzy as he laid in an expanding pool of his own blood. Krystal turned and paced toward him. He trembled as he struggled to lift his head.

Krystal nodded. "But, you are clever. I'll give you that. At least Kayla didn't pick a complete *dumbass* this time."

James' body shuddered as he feebly lifted his right hand. He desperately fired a proton beam at Krystal, and she easily deflected it.

GUSH!

The beam cascaded off the walls, bounced off the ceiling, and crashed into James' right hand as it exploded in blood.

"AAAAAAAAAAGAAAAAAAAAH!" He roared in agony.

He shuddered as he looked up and saw his hand had been severed from his body. He let his head plop down into the pool of blood.

It's over. I'm...I'm going to die...

His ring glowed with multi-colored energy.

Krystal loomed over him. "Now I shall slice off your head to stop your annoying regeneration..."

"NO! STOP PLEASE! JAMES IS A GOOD MAN! I'M NOT! KILL ME INSTEAD AND LET THE REST OF MY FRIENDS GO!" Terrance screamed.

Krystal snapped toward him. "Shut your mouth promiscuous *filth*! I will *never* forgive you for what you did to Luna! You shall have your turn next *so be patient!*" She noticed the shining ring as she raised her blade over James' neck. "That is a nice family ring, sir. I promise I will make sure it is sent back to them."

"JAMES! YOU HAVE TO GET UP! YOU'RE A MAN OF GOD AREN'T YOU?! YOU HAVE TO GET UP AND DO SOMETHING!" Terrance cried.

James closed his eyes.

Her blade plunged down toward his neck.

FWOOOOOOOSH!

Krystal leapt back as a burst of flames barreled toward her. She looked up and Kayla stood in front of James with flames in her eyes. She was drenched in sweat and visible heat waves clung to her body.

Kayla raised her daggers. "Thanks' for holding out James. Now it's my turn to make sure everything is going to be ok."

Krystal beamed. "Kayla! We were just talking about you! You probably don't remember me, but we were friends when we were little! I told your boyfriend I would spare you so you could be tried in your home country. That offer still stands if you stop resisting and..."

"Flame Craft, Art 4, Graceful Flame Tempo!"

FWOOOSH!

Kayla vanished and was instantly upon Krystal. She stared into Krystal's eyes with overwhelming malice. "He's not my boyfriend. I. HATE. MEN!"

SLICE!

She crashed her blades into Krystal's side, ripped them out, and Krystal narrowly deflected Kayla's next strike as she leapt away in retreat. Kayla rushed after her with a flurry of vicious slashes. Krystal's mind raced as she narrowly deflected the attacks, and her blade grew hot in her hands. The edge of the sword bubbled as it lost its edge by the second.

As Krystal fought for her life, she winced in pain as she glanced down at the searing wound in her side.

Damn, I forgot Flame Craft leaves Critical Burns. I'm so used to being protected by my silver. Her flesh sizzled. *But this is bad. My armor is too thin, my sword is almost finished, and anymore that I make are just going to get worn down the same way. To make matters worse, physically reinforcing my body with Earth Craft doesn't protect me from fire. I'll have to throw her off her game somehow...*

WHOOOOSH!

Krystal used magnetism to zip across the hall away from Kayla.

Kayla raged as she shouted. "Where are you going bitch! Get back here and fight me like a woman!"

Krystal smiled playfully. "Are you really still on that hating men stuff? I thought that you would have grown out of that by now. Not even your *fast* older sister was stupid enough to..."

SLICE!

Kayla sliced Krystal's across the chest, and she staggered backward. Krystal's armor below her neck was gone and her entire torso was pitch black.

"Don't ever mention my sister again you..."

SHINK!

Krystal crashed her blade into Kayla's stomach and sent her cascading off the ground across the hall's floor. She trembled violently as she rose to her hands and knees. She put a hand on her stomach and felt a deep, jagged gash. Blood quickly soaked her clothes and poured onto the ground.

Krystal shook her head as she approached James. "You're still just so *emotional*."

GUSH!

Kayla formed a fiery dagger and stabbed herself in the gut. "**AAAAAAAAAAAAAAAAAAAAAAAAAAAHHHHH**!" She raised a blood curdling cry as she cauterized her wound.

Tears ran down James' face and he trembled as he watched Kayla sear her flesh. "Kayla...stop...please. Just...go...home..."

Krystal looked from James to Kayla and her heart thumped with affection. She spoke in a high-pitched voice as her heart fluttered. "Oh my God! Are you really doing all of this just to save his life even though I offered you a chance to go home and potentially get out of this?! That's so romantic that I could *die*!"

Kayla gasped for air as she panted on her hands and knees. Her body quivered violently as she slowly rose to her feet. Her hands trembled as she weakly raised her daggers against Krystal. Her voice shuttered as she gasped for air. "James...everything...will be...ok."

Kayla weakly raised a thumbs-up.

Hearts entered Krystal's eyes, and she wiggled as she pressed her legs together in elation. "AAAAHAAA! I can't believe Kayla of all people has finally found true love! I'll have to tell everyone about this after I finish here!" Her face dropped as she raised her blade against Kayla. "Still though...It makes me *so sad* that I have to be the one to end it..." She sighed. "Why did you *idiots* have to *come here*? Kalarono is going to kill me for murdering your first boyfriend."

Kayla blitzed Krystal and their blades clashed. They engaged in high level combat as both sides displayed flawless technique. Kayla gracefully danced around Krystal's strikes as she followed up with swift counterattacks. Krystal struck with precision and accuracy as she deflected Kayla's strikes with refined skill. Sparks flew across the battlefield as Kayla's daggers met Krystal's blade.

James couldn't move due to blood loss, and he watched the masterful battle as sparks landed in his pool of blood. *Semaj! I need your help! Please! Heal me again so I can save Kayla!*

Semaj trotted out of the Archigos' chambers with popcorn and a slushie. "By george mate! There's a bloody battle going on out here too?! And I reckoned the one out there was freaking intense! I knew all of my bloody power was being drained, but I never supposed all this was happenin'!"

Krystal unleashed a furious barrage of attacks and Kayla steadily lost ground as she narrowly parried the strikes. Kayla's body grew cold, and it took everything she had to leap, roll, twist, jump, and contort her body to avoid being skewered.

"You can't run from me forever!" Krystal shouted.

James muttered. "Semaj...I'm over here...Please...Give me more of your strength before...Kayla...dies..."

Semaj wore a headset and held an attached microphone out into the room. "I thought I heard something!" He squinted and put a hand above his eyes. "Fos?! Is that bloody you?! What the hell happened mate?!" Semaj tossed his equipment and ran over.

He stopped dead in his tracks when he saw the glowing ring.

"Please...hurry..." James stuttered.

"Sorry mate! But this is the closest I can get to that thing without risking losing me bloody *neck*. With our current relationship level, I'm not sure how much more I can give you mate, especially with that thing in the way. And besides! I've already leant you an immense amount of my power as it is! I could fade out of existence if I give you anymore!"

"Please...there...must...be...some...other...powers..."

Semaj sat down and put a hand on his chin. "*Hmmm*...let me think... "

Krystal's blows grew even more ferocious.

CLANG! CLANG!

Kayla deflected two slashes, and her daggers were knocked from her grasp.

SLICE!

Krystal caught Kayla in the side, and she fell to her knees.

Krystal sighed as Kayla struggled to her feet. "Why won't you just *give up*? Do you really love him that much?"

"Let's...see if this...works..."

A wide red square illuminated beneath Krystal's feet.

Her eyes went wide with fear.

SNAP!

FWOOOOOOOOSH!

A chamber of flames rose and roasted everything inside of the box.

"**AAAAAAAAAAAAAAAAAAAAAAAAAAAHHHHHHH!**" Krystal roared as her flesh was seared.

Kayla held her side as Krystal was burned alive. "I've been...working on that one...for...a long time...I call it...the sausage cooker."

The flaming chamber disappeared, and Krystal's armor had completely disintegrated. She laid face down and her bare body was blackened with burns. Kayla staggered toward James.

A light bulb appeared over Semaj's head. "I've got it! You like women quite a bit from what I've observed mate! You go stiff anytime that Flame Tribe girl gets near you! I bet I could lend you my brother's power! He's a real player! Or no! My other brother's power will really put her in her place!" He folded his arms. "Though, because of our relationship status, I doubt *either* would work very effectively..."

"Kayla! You did it!" James shouted weakly.

Semaj was appalled. "Are you *ignoring* me?"

Kayla smiled as she limped over.

Krystal laid face down on the floor. "I'm...not a whore or anything...but he is definitely...a cutie by the way. I might just have...to take him for myself..."

Kayla's vision went red. "YOU BITCH! I'LL KILL YOU!"

FWOOSH!

She leapt as she raised flaming black daggers over Krystal's head.

SHINK!

Krystal raised a jagged, golden blade and skewered Kayla through.

"**NOOOOOOOOOOOOOO**!" James screamed.

Krystal lifted Kayla up and she slid further down the blade that impaled her.

She passed out from the pain.

Krystal winced with every step as she gently sat Kayla down against the wall, and a new set of golden armor formed to cover her body.

Krystal raised a second blade above Kayla's head. "I'm sorry sweetheart. At least you can be with your sister and mother now..."

"Hey mate? What are you?! HEY!" Semaj shouted as he was suddenly absorbed into James.

James' wounds regenerated and his severed hand with the ring reattached to his body. His hand pulsed with pain, but he blocked it out as blood soaked back into his flesh and he leapt to his feet. His vision was clouded with rage as he charged at Krystal with a dark saber.

FVOOOOOOOOOOOOM!

James rocketed toward her in a dark blur. "AAAAAAAAAAAAAAAAAAH!"

SLICE!

Blood exploded from James' body.

He froze.

Krystal turned back to Kayla. "Sorry, but I really do have to kill her now..."

CRASH!

Krystal gasped as James crashed his saber into her neck.

SIZZLE!

Sparks flew as his blade collided with her unnaturally tough skin. James roared as his power multiplied and he pressed into her neck with every fiber of his being. **"AAAAAAAAAAAAAAAAAAAAHHHHHHHAAAAAAAAAA!"**

Krystal's eyes widened with terror. She fought to pull her neck away as a dark scar formed on her skin and blood dripped from her neck.

This is my chance! I can win this and save everyone! AAAAAAAAAAAAAAAAAAAAAAAAAAAAAAAAAAAAHHHHAAA!

SLICE!

James crumpled to his knees and fell face first onto the golden floor. Krystal dabbed at her neck and felt blood. She scowled at James as he laid motionless on the ground. *Damn he's tough. And this scar is going to be hell to get treated later.* She raised her blade over Kayla's head. *At least this is finally over...*

"AAAAAAAAAAAAAAAAAAAH!"

SLICE!

Krystal sent James flying across the hall and he crashed into the ground, skidding to a halt in defeat.

James laid still.

A tear ran down Krystal's face.

Her hand trembled as she raised her blade over Kayla's head. *He will probably still survive that somehow. But should I do this? Should I give them the chance to live and be happy?* Krystal hesitated as the grip on her blade wavered.

James struggled to lift his head as he stared at Krystal despondently. He reached his right hand out as he desperately grasped at the air.

Suddenly, Krystal's mind was flooded with memories. Hatred filled her heart as she remembered the day terrorists broke into the palace and murdered her brother. She sobbed as she remembered the overwhelming guilt she felt as she watched the falling rubble flatten him. She steeled her resolve and fastened her grip on the blade.

WHOOSH!

The wind whisked as she brought down her sword.

FVOOOOOOOOOOOOOOOOOOOOOOOOOOOOOM!

Suddenly, James's ring exploded with multicolored energy.

GUSH!

Krystal brought her blade down on Kayla's skull and blood gushed into the air.

Confusion struck Krystal as she realized that Kayla had disappeared. She looked across the room and James held Kayla as they laid together in a pool of blood. James' ring returned to normal. Krystal scratched her hair. *What in the...how could he have possibly crossed the room that quickly? I truly do not understand this boy Kayla picked.*

James' vision blurred as he stared at Krystal.

BA-DUMP! BA-DUMP! BA-DUMP!

His heartbeat thumped in his ears as every part of his body pulsed in excruciating pain. He was in agony from his stomach wound's searing heat, while the rest of his body grew numb and cold. The world went dark as he watched Krystal pace toward him.

✦

Machari sprinted around a corner with tears in his eyes. He skidded to a halt as he entered the Archigos' massive chamber. He was filled with ecstasy as he basked in the moment. He admired the stunning arches and the intricate golden etchings carved into every inch of the throne room. He marveled at the massive golden pillars that rose into the darkness above him. He stared across the chamber at the marvelous golden throne at the end of the room. He smiled as he took it all in. *My time has come. All of this is finally about to be…*

"Have you come to gawk?" A rigged voice said.

Machari snapped to attention and drew his blades. Bazek stood before him, choking Gray mercilessly. Gray writhed and clawed as life drained from his eyes. Machari observed Bazek as he prepared for battle. Despite his hunched back, Bazek was taller and more menacing than he anticipated. He had tan skin, a neat crop of grey hair, and he wore a stunning silver robe with golden etchings.

CRASH!

Bazek casually tossed Gray, and he crashed into the wall. Golden restraints pinned him there and he passed out.

Bazek sighed. "This one thought he was clever enough to sneak into my chamber during the chaos. I am filled with genuine surprise that Krystal has failed in her duty twice on this day."

Machari raised his blades. "I've finally found you after all these years! I'm here to end your life and take my rightful place on the throne!"

Bazek burst into hearty laughter. "BA-HA-HA! First a thief and now a jester has broken into my court?! I speak truth when I say to you that I have not heard a jest this outrageous in all my days as Archigos! What right to the throne could a court jester claim to have?"

Machari's blood boiled. "That's for me to know and for you to find out! Maybe you'll see me shitting on your throne from the other side bitch!"

"BA-HA-HA! So, the clown has a temper!" He leaned against the wall. "But your anger is misdirected jester. If you desire to become Archigos, attend the academy and earn high marks. Then, best the Tournament of Champions and pass your Arch Exam like all who have come before. Even if you were to slay me, your rule would not be respected unless you have accomplished these feats." He crossed his arms. "You have wasted your time by coming here in such a foolish manner and additionally you have forfeited your life." He shrugged. "Thus is the way of the jester I suppose."

"Shut up! I will restore this nation to the grand condition it was in before you came here and destroyed everything! Do you know how many people have died, and had their lives ruined because of your terrible leadership?! You should just save me the trouble and kill yourself for being the shittiest Archigos of all time!"

Bazek stared. "I am aware." He glanced at Jerry. "Tell me, is the child to be a part of this conflict as well? Or is he some kind of hostage with which you foolishly assumed you could use to bargain?"

Jerry slipped out of his harness and sprinted into the corner. He trembled as he curled into a ball and covered his face. "PLEASE FORGIVE ME! I HAD NOTHING TO DO WITH THIS! I WAS KIDNAPPED AND..."

"He's with me. And he's my backup plan in case you somehow don't croak in the next five minutes."

Bazek stared with a reserved smile. "I see. On this fateful day, I have been faced with a thief. A coward. And a fool. Yet despite that, your jests in union with the impressive skills displayed by the thief, have set me in a rather, 'agreeable' mood."

Bazek straightened his back and rose to his full height. His muscles bulged and he folded his arms menacingly. His imposing figure caused Machari to tremble in fear.

BOOOOOOOOOOOOOOOOOOOOOOOOOOOOOOOOOM!

A gargantuan surge of Spirit Energy erupted from Bazek's body, shattering the ground around him.

He grinned. "I shall allow the jester who calls himself king to have the first move. And then I shall end your jesting, *for good*."

Machari raised his blades. "You're nothing but a senile old man. And you shall die in your ignorance!"

The impurities in the room's gold ripped from the walls and rushed around the chamber. A massive sandstorm of dirt and metal swirled around the throne room. Jerry sat in the corner and covered his head as he was scratched by the swirling metals.

Bazek stood unmoved in the sandstorm's center. "Nice *trick*. I'm sure it is one they teach Earth Tribe infants during their first training sessions!"

Bazek's bare feet were planted on the golden floor, and he felt the vibrations of each movement occurring in the palace. He sensed Machari's every step amidst the metallic flurry. Suddenly, Bazek's eyes widened as his mind raced. *What is this? I can no longer sense the boy. In fact, I sense more than ten of him!*

Bazek squinted as he struggled to pick out the shifting clones in the sandstorm.

FVOOM!

He sent out a pulse of Spirit Energy that washed through the palace and returned to him. He was shocked as the wave entered his body. *My ability to divine traits is of no use. Each duplicate has the same massive level of malice and murderous intent! This is the pinnacle of Earth Craft!* He smirked. *That jester has much promise.*

A blur approached Bazek from the side and he glanced in its direction.

PUFF!

It instantly exploded in a puff of dust.

SHINK!

Bazek's eyes widened as his robe was cut. An infinitesimally small scratch formed on his calf.

Machari laughed menacingly as his voice reverberated through the sandstorm. "AHAHAHAHAHA! I got you! I bet you didn't expect that! This is my ultimate move that I've prepared for years just to *kill you*! Earth Craft, Progress Art 3, Wicked Sand Battalion!"

The sandy clones rushed Bazek from all angles, each armed with their own daggers.

Machari's mind raced within the storm. *Yes! I got him! I actually got him! But he **is** the Archigos, so I should get in a few more cuts just to be safe. If I could get him in the head somehow, the poison would instantly bind to his neural receptors, and he'd be finished!*

The clones raised their daggers to slice Bazek across his body. Bazek's eyes darted around toward each of them.

PUFF! PUFF! PUFF!

They instantly disintegrated. A flurry of clones rushed him from the right as he dismissively uncrossed his right arm.

PUFF!

The battalion of clones burst into a haze of dust.

SWIPE!

Bazek leaned his neck to the right as he casually avoided a swipe from Machari's blade. He raised his left pointer finger from his crossed arms, and destroyed a group of sand soldiers who were within inches of him. A large group of clones appeared above him and attacked from all angles.

Bazek sighed.

PUFF!

PUFF!

PUFF!

As they approached, each one disintegrated into nothingness.

WHOOSH!

Instantly, more than fifty clones formed within the storm. Bazek eyed them as they weaved their way through the maelstrom.

SLICE!

They suddenly stopped, raised their daggers and blitzed him from every angle.

Bazek yawned. "I've grown tired of this game."

WHOOOOOOOOOSH!

The sandstorm exploded and vanished as Machari froze in midair before him. His dagger was millimeters from piercing Bazek's face. The metal in Machari's dagger rattled as he was suspended in midair.

"Wh...at is this?" Machari trembled.

Bazek grabbed the blade of the dagger in Machari's outstretched hand and ripped off its hilt.

Machari's eyes widened triumphantly. "You idiot! You just touched the tip of my dagger! It's over you…"

Bazek held the dagger's blade to the light as he examined it from all angles. He suddenly scratched his tongue with it and made a sour expression. "Disgusting, is this metallic elephant poison? The formula is exceptionally cheap."

Machari's eyes widened with horror as tears flowed down his face. "NO! WHAT DO YOU MEAN IT'S CHEAP! I SPENT YEARS FORMULATING IT MYSELF TO KILL YOU! I SCRATCHED YOU EARLIER! I KNOW I DID! HOW ARE YOU STILL ALIVE? THIS IS IMPOSSIBLE! I…"

"I sense the poison within that cowardly child as well. Do you believe you are the only one with the ability to remove metallic poison from the body? To make matters worse, your dagger never actually pierced the surface of my skin." He shrugged. "I apologize for calling your work cheap. A more accurate summation would be 'ineffective on a person of my caliber.'"

The silver poison flowed out of Bazek's mouth and splattered onto the ground in front of Machari.

"NO! I HAD IT ALL PLANNED OUT! It can't be…THIS IS IMPOSSIB…GASP…"

SPLAT!

Bazek reached his hand through Machari's stomach.

"A tantrum will get you nowhere, jester."

GUSH!

He ripped out his hand and Machari's blood erupted across the golden floor. His head sagged as life drained from his body.

"P...lease w...ait." Machari muttered as blood dribbled from his mouth.

Bazek chuckled. "Have you set your heart on humoring me with a final jest?"

Machari released his grip and a vial fell to the ground. "If...my...friend survives...please...h...eal...him..."

The bottle levitated toward Bazek. "Your request shall be granted jester."

Bazek turned his attention to Jerry.

He sobbed as he trembled in the corner. "OH MY GOD! NO!"

Bazek's face was filled with disdain. "And as for you *child*. The jester claims you as his accomplice, yet you cowered in the corner and could not even muster up the conviction to assist him. You lead a life of pure shame, and I have no patience for cowardice. The jester possesses my admiration. At least he had the gall to stand and die for what he believed in."

"NO, YOU'VE GOT IT ALL WRONG I SWEA..."

Bazek lowered his hand. "A coward's folly is his cowardice."

CRASH!

Massive golden beams turned Jerry to paste as the roof collapsed and he was crushed by falling rubble.

Back in the grand hall, Krystal walked toward Terrance. She examined the scars and burns across her body as she rubbed her neck. "This sucks! I hate getting burned alive! And I can't believe Kayla's boyfriend actually left a mark on my skin! This will take weeks of treatment to heal!"

Terrance had been stapled to the ground as he watched the battle unfold. As Krystal approached, he lamented. Tears ran down his face as he stared at the still bodies of his friends, laying soaked in pools of their own blood. *Look at what I've gotten them into...My only friends are about to die as a result of my actions. I let them get abused by Machari, while I sat by and did nothing. Because of me, they're criminals of the state, and now I allowed them to be dragged into this ridiculous plot that will probably end up costing them their lives. I was supposed to be their fearless leader...and look at where that's gotten them...*

Krystal raised her blade over his neck. "Do you have any final regards for me to pass on to your family?"

Terrance sobbed. "None. I was a terrible brother and son. I deserve what's coming to me. Please, just take my life and make sure they get to safety. That's what Brooklyn would want too." He gestured toward James.

"She had some kind of relationship with that simp over there. She would be sad to see him die."

Krystal's face was flushed with color as her blade trembled in her grasp. "I'm afraid I can't do that...even for her." She wiped a tear. "Terrance. I'm sorry."

SWIP!

Terrance's head plopped to the ground and his body went limp. She removed the beams that impaled him, and he crumpled to the floor. Tears flooded her face as she stared at his deceased corpse. She covered her mouth and fell to her knees as she was filled with grief.

As Terrance's head hit the floor, he lost consciousness. His mind faded into his memories as his body grew cold. He found himself back as a child in his father's room. There were clear blue skies, and the sun shone brightly over the frozen tundra. Okpa heard the joyful cries of nearby children as they played with a ball of ice outside the window. Terrance sat in his father's lap as he excitedly pointed at a white board.

I need a damn nap... Okpa sighed. "Are you sure you don't want to go play with the other kids Terrance?"

"No! Tell me again daddy! Tell me again how I can be a real man like you and become the best leader this world has ever *seeeeeeeen!*" Terrance giggled.

Okpa smiled as he stroked his son's hair. "It's a Saturday, so I suppose I have time to tell you again. But I bet you have them memorized even better than I do..." He knocked on Terrance's head. "You know what? I think I've forgotten them! Tell me, what is rule one of the Godly Man's Guide to Leadership?"

Terrance pointed to the top line of the white board. "That's easy daddy! Love God with all your mind, all of your heart, all of your soul, and all your strength!"

"Excellent! What's the second rule?"

"Don't be silly daddy! It's Love your neighbor as yourself! It's right there! You can see it!"

Okpa covered his eyes. "I don't see them anywhere! What could the third one possibly be?!"

"Seek the Kingdom above all else! I still don't know what 'Kingdom' means though..."

"That's alright. You'll get it as you get older. What's the fourth rule?"

"Daddy! You know this! The leader is the lead servant!"

The words reverberated within Terrance's mind.

"The leader is the lead servant!", "The leader is the lead servant!", "The leader is the lead servant!", "The leader is the lead servant!", "The leader is the lead servant!", "The leader is the lead servant!", "The leader is the lead servant!"

Terrance's memories shifted and he found himself rushing down a hallway in his father's arms. He sobbed as he clutched his father's shirt. He knew something had gone horribly wrong.

SLAM!

They burst into a hospital room.

Okpa froze in the doorway.

Terrance felt tears dripping into his hair. *Daddy's never cried before...* He looked up and saw his father's expressionless face as sobs rained down. Okpa crumpled into a chair and stared forward silently as doctors consoled him. *What's going on...* Terrance climbed out of his father's lap. He walked over to the bed and ascended the small set of steps to play with his mother. She laid completely still, with a smile on her face.

Terrance's eyes watered. "Mommy! Wake up! Wake up Mommy!"

He pulled on her sleeve and Okpa wailed as he burst into tears.

"Mommy, wake up! I want to laugh too! Please, Mommy! Tell me what's funny! I want to laugh too!"

BEEP! BEEP!

His mother stirred.

Okpa leapt to his feet and ran across the room. "Kierra!"

Kierra's smile widened. She reached out and gently touched Terrance's face. "Oh my sweet Terrance. Take care of your father and grow up to be a man that makes us proud...ok?"

"Alright mommy! I promise!"

Life faded from her eyes. Terrance clutched her hand as it cradled his face.

James's consciousness drifted in a dark void.

I guess this is what it's like to die. I wonder what Semaj will do with my body now...

FLASH!

Suddenly, a bright light appeared before him. He reached out as he floated toward it.

Well at least it's finally over. I won't have to suffer anymore. Tonight, I'll be dining in parad...

A voice called out from the void below. "**But aren't you still, angry?**"

Suddenly, a vision appeared before James. He watched as his family mourned at his funeral. He watched as Kayla went on to marry another man. He watched as files full of his future ambitions were shredded. He watched as his family ring and cross chains were tossed into a blazing fire.

"**WILL YOU LET ALL OF OUR SUFFERING BE IN VAIN?!**"

"NO! It can't be! I won't let it!" James' eyes flashed with red, smoky darkness.

"**IF YOU GIVE UP NOW, WHAT THE HELL DID WE DO ALL OF THAT SACRIFICING FOR? WE NEVER GOT**

LAID, AND WE SUFFERED IMMEASURABLY FOR NO FUCKING REASON! LET ME GIVE YOU A BRIEF REMINDER IN CASE YOU FORGOT!"

James flashed back to his freshman year of college. He shuffled into his dark dorm room after another day of abuse. He trembled as he collapsed onto his bed. His body was wracked with sobs as he wrapped himself under the covers.

He wept. "Am I worthless like they said? Why am I the only one who can't seem to do anything right? I'm giving it my all! I'm doing the best I can!"

FVOOOOOOP! FVOOOOOOP! FVOOOOOOP!

The sound of a whistle reverberated in his mind.

"I don't think I can do this anymore...How can I face my teammates again after the way I was embarrassed today...We did up downs for hours because of me! It's all over! They'll never respect me again!"

A thought crept into James' mind.

He slowly unwrapped himself from the sheet as he stared out the window. He walked over and looked down at the sharp fence below. He shuddered as his fingers pressed against the cool glass. "I can't...I can't do this anymore..."

James reached his arm back to shatter it.

He froze.

Fear gripped his heart. *My parents would feel awful if I did this to them.* He despaired as he envisioned seeing disappointment on God's face firsthand.

He slowly crawled back under the covers. He buried his face in a pillow as his mourning intensified. *I've given up on living. I'll only keep going because I don't want them to be sad and I couldn't imagine how mad God would be when I saw him. I'll give it one more day. But only for their sakes.*

This cycle repeated for months until he became roommates with Micah.

He flashed back to his senior year. He was in the team's meeting room on the last day of preseason practice. The room went silent as his coach began his presentation.

CLICK

A slide with one of his teammates' faces appeared on it.

Energy instantly filled the room.

His coach smiled. "Today, is a very special day. Lenny Kendricks..."

"YEEEEEEEEEEEAAAAAAAAAAAAAAAAAHHHHHH!" His teammates roared as they swarmed and applauded Lenny.

James joined into the raucous crowd as his body was flooded with joy. "I told yall Lenny was cold! I've been SAYING THAT FOR YEARS!" James couldn't stop smiling.

He had coached Lenny every day that summer to help him get stronger. Lenny gained more than thirty pounds of muscle and was in the best shape of his life.

"You are now on scholarship. Congratulations." His coach finished.

The cycle repeated twice more, and each time James' joy multiplied as the anticipation of hearing his name became overwhelming.

"SEBASTIAN IS THE GOAT! HE'S THE BEST O-LINEMEN ON THE TEAM! THAT MAN IS GOING TO THE LEAGUE!" James shouted.

"WHOOOOOOO! IT'S ABOUT DAMN TIME! PETE IS THE GOAT! BEST LINEBACKER TO EVER SET FOOT IN THIS BUILDING!" James hollered.

CLICK

The slideshow faded to black.

James' heart sank.

Tears welled behind his eyes. It took all of his will power to hold them back, but a few cool drops escaped down his face. He sniffled as he wiped his eyes, and his heart was overcome with despair. *Not again! How could this be?! I...I did everything right! I've dominated every practice. I...I've never been late. I...I coach up the younger guys. Even the older guys come to me for advice. I...I'm the strongest on the team...I...I have the playbook memorized. I...*

His coach stared at him and smiled as he addressed the group. "Now! To celebrate a great fall camp, LET'S WATCH THE BIG GAME! We have ice cream, candy, popcorn and drinks outside in the reception area for everyone! Let's enjoy the fruits of our labor!"

The team rushed out of the room filled with ecstasy. James shuffled through the elated crowd like a zombie. He was despondent, and he barely had the strength to put one foot in front of the other. He entered the lobby as his teammates celebrated and devoured treats all around him. James limped forward and made brief eye contact with one of the few upright coaches in the building. The coach looked away with a sad expression and said nothing. James walked into the restroom to cry, but it was already filled with triumphant players. He turned and shuffled back into the meeting room. He sat in his seat and bawled his eyes out, as the players enjoyed the game all around him.

No one said a word to him, and he cried until he had no more tears left to shed.

Something broke in him that day.

James found himself back in the void and a dark figure floated before him.

It pointed and shouted with a heart full of malice. "**I WON'T LET YOU GIVE UP! NOT AFTER WHAT THEY'VE DONE TO US! NOT AFTER WHAT THEY PUT US THROUGH!**" It pleaded. "**WHY?! WHAT WAS IT ALL**

FOR?! WHAT DID DOING THINGS THE RIGHT WAY EVER ACCOMPLISH?! ARE YOU GOING TO LAY DOWN AND LET US DIE LIKE THE SORRY WASTE OF POTENTIAL THAT YOU ARE?!" Its eyes flashed with red fire. **"OR, WILL YOU RISE UP AND SHOW THEM YOUR WRATH?!"** The figure extended its hand. **"TAKE UP YOUR WRATH AND TOGETHER WE SHALL HAVE VENGEANCE!"**

James glanced up at the bright light.

He looked down and gripped the spirit's hand.

Terrance' body stirred.

For my entire life, I've been a sluggard and a fool. A sluggard because I was too lazy to do what was necessary to become the man I wanted to be. A fool because I deluded myself into thinking I already was that man.

James' body stirred.

For my entire life, I've been a failure and a waste of potential. All I've done is suffer...and I have nothing to show for it. Most things in life have come easy to me, and I've always been the best at anything I set my mind to. But I never accomplished anything that matters.

Terrance's limbs began reconnecting.

I spent my entire life living selfishly, not even considering other people's feelings or what they wanted. After my first mother died, I fell into depression. I tried to fill the void I felt inside by any means necessary. I blamed both of my mothers for abandoning me, and as a result, I deemed women as weak and inferior creatures. And yet, their arms were the first I ran to each time I desired a shelter from my pain.

James' blood receded back into his body.

I spent my entire life living selflessly. I always put what everyone else wanted above my own feelings, and I did everything I could to serve them. I suffered and neglected myself of the things I desired to make God and my parents happy. I was willing to sacrifice anything to create a better future for the people I love. Everything I've done was aimed at becoming successful and influential enough to have the resources to affect society on a systemic level. I've killed myself, over and over again, so I could make sure nobody would have to endure the suffering I have in the future.

Terrance's body was restored as new blood coursed through his veins.

I lived in denial regarding my past actions. I always hoped if I ignored my problems long enough, that they would simply go away. I always looked up to my father as the ultimate symbol of manhood and leadership. But despite living under his tutelage for my entire life, I'm nothing like him. I was lazy, and I never worked hard. I skated through life off my status, looks and natural talent. I have nothing to be proud of and nothing to show for my life. I was never a man and now I'll never get a chance to be one.

Heat returned to James' body.

I put my all into everything. I truly believed that if I gave my best effort in life, I would be successful one day. My father was the best person I have ever known, and I always strived to emulate his ways. Since I was a child, I've wanted nothing more than to surpass him, and build a legacy he would be proud of.

Blue mist seeped out of Terrance's wounds as cracks formed across his body.

But I still want to! I desire to be like him more than anything! I crave becoming a man my mother would respect with every fiber of my being! This is my last chance! If this works, I probably won't have long to live, but even if I die, I will sacrifice everything to make sure my friends survive!

The ground trembled as James clenched his fist.

And I will do it! This wicked world has been cruel and unfair to me since the day I was born! My life has been nothing but a cycle of sorrow! But I will not submit! I will have my wife! I will have my legacy! I refuse to die! I refuse to be buried by fate's cruel hand! I will make it home and see my family again and I swear to God I will not perish here. I will survive...by any means necessary!

Terrance's wounds glowed with a blue aura.

I don't remember much about my dad's teachings on God, and I don't know if He's even real. I don't know how to pray...but if you can hear me God...please listen. I'm sorry for wasting the opportunity that was gifted to me and never becoming the man I was supposed to be. If you're out there God, I'm begging for one last shot. Please, give me the strength to save my friends. Just this once...please...give me one a chance to make this right.

Darkness poured out of James' body as a red mist surrounded him.

*God, I don't know why you have dealt me this hand. Why do you allow my enemies to destroy me and for my suffering to continue endlessly without relief? I've faithfully served you for years and all I wanted was a chance to help others and live a good life. I didn't ask to be abused, and I didn't ask to be thrown into a ridiculous new world. I didn't ask for any of this! I just want to go home! I just want a wife who loves you! I just want to make something of myself and leave a legacy! I've been **so** patient! I just want to reap the fruits of my labor after all these years of suffering. Is that an unreasonable request? I don't know why you withhold from me what I've earned...But if you won't give it to me...then it looks like I'll just have to take it. If you won't punish these wicked people, then I will do it for you! If you won't take vengeance for me then I'll take it for myself! I'm tired of waiting. I will have what is owed to me. They shall know my wrath...*

James and Terrance rose to their feet in unison.

Krystal was walking toward the throne room.

She froze as she heard them stir. *What the hell? There's no way...* Gold rushed from the walls into her armor and sword to refine them as she turned and raised her blade.

Terrance and James stood together. Terrance's body was covered in cracks that emitted a constant stream of blue mist. His eyes were brimming with vibrant azure energy as he raised an ornate ax. Darkness enveloped James' entire body like a second skin and his bright red eyes pulsed with rage as he raised a black saber.

"I'll do whatever it takes to save my friends."

"And I have no pity for those who stand against me."

Krystal sighed. "You boys just won't quit."

WHOOSH!

James and Terrance vanished. They rushed her from the left and the right as she readied her blade.

Terrance's mind was calm as he blitzed toward. *Let me use my head for once like James does. That's one area I can admit he's got me beat. She's made of metal...What was that one attack my dad used against those robots in the north that one time? Did he call it OCD or something? I wonder if I could pull it off...*

Terrance pictured the hall becoming a vast ocean. "Ocean Craft, Progress Art 1, Ocean Floor Depths!"

The humidity in the room intensified.

Krystal gasped for air as she struggled to breathe. "How...can you...do that? That's one of the most advanced...Ocean Craft techniques! I've never...seen anyone...but an Archigos..."

"SCREW THE RULES! JUST DIE!" Terrance roared as he wondered the same thing.

Krystal tried to move, but her armor was stiff. She looked down and the gold in her suit was rusting. She tried to force herself forward, but she clutched her neck as she heaved. James pointed his blade and darkness burst out of it.

BOOOM!

The shadows exploded as they blasted Krystal across the hall and disintegrated the armor on the left side of her body.

POW!

Terrance crashed his ax into her right side, shattering her armor as she rag-dolled into the air. James swiftly leapt above Krystal and cocked back his blade.

BOOOOOOOOOOOOOOOOOOOOOOOOM!

He smashed her with his sword and sent her crashing down into the surface in a massive eruption of darkness.

Krystal's naked body was obscured by dust. She laid in a crater unconscious.

James and Terrance nodded at each other.

They ran over to their wounded friends as more cracks formed across Terrance's body. James put a finger to Kayla's neck. Her pulse was extremely faint, and her skin was ice cold. Epios was in a similar condition.

James looked at Terrance with a pained expression. His voice was harsh and distorted. **"Can't you do something about this?!"**

Terrance panicked as he looked back and forth between them. His voice was smooth and calm. "I've never tried this, and I've never been good at the technical side of Ocean Craft. But I *will* save them. This has to work." Terrance cleared his mind and concentrated. He pictured himself storing up his Spirit Energy in a clear, cool spring. "Ocean Craft, Art 1, Progress Depth Command!"

SPLASH!

A transparent wave of Spirit Energy rose behind him and washed over his friends. The wave instantly healed Kayla and Epios' surface level wounds.

SKKKKKKRRRTTT!

When the wave touched James, pain erupted in his body as a sound like scraping metal rang out. Blue sparks bounced off his skin and he writhed in agony as the wave disintegrated.

Terrance winced as he stared at James. "Sorry, I guess I messed up somehow."

James squeezed his eyes closed and gritted his teeth as the pain slowly receded. **"It's fine. Let's see if it worked."**

Heat returned to Kayla's body and her pulse quickened. James' heart was filled with joy, and a measure of the darkness around his body faded. He glanced toward the throne room door and hatred filled his heart.

He stomped forward. "**You stay here. I'm going to go make that bastard pay for his crimes and apologize to Jerry!**"

Terrance walked into his path. "That's not a good idea. We should escape with our lives while we still can." He held out a hand. "But, if you go in there, I'm going too. We need to stop Machari if it's not too late, and help the Archigos put down this rebellion..."

James slapped his hand away. "**I don't give a damn about any of that! Look at what he's caused! He will suffer for what he's done! I will take vengeance for all of the people he's...**"

"James...you sound like Machari. Didn't you come here to reunite the nation? How is making the Archigos suffer going to..."

Darkness flashed in James' eyes. "**Terrance...Get out of my way...Last warning.**"

Terrance raised his ax. "I won't stand by and let my friend make the wrong choice again."

BOOOOOOOOOOOOOOOOOOOOOOOM!

James rushed at Terrance and their blades collided in a massive shockwave that shattered the ground. James dashed into his reflection in the floor, exploded out, and sliced Terrance in the face.

POW!

Terrance crashed his ax into James, and he skidded across the hall. James swung his blade three times, and blades dark of energy soared toward Terrance. Terrance slung his ax at the blades, and it split into three more.

WHOOOSH!

The axes and blades collided, exploding in an icy mist as Terrance swiftly leapt into the air.

CRASH!

He crashed his ax into the ground as massive torrents of ice barreled toward James. James leapt to the side to avoid the first, but he was smashed by the second and third. He was squashed between the torrents and Terrance bounded into the sky to deal the finishing blow.

SLICE! SLICE! **SLICE!**

The pillars erupted in dark energy as James rocketed through toward Terrance.

SHINK!

James impaled him with his blade, and they zoomed through the air across the hall.

BOOOOOOOOOOOOOOOM!

They crashed into the wall and there was a massive eruption of dark energy. James looked down and Terrance's wounds had already healed.

GUSH!

Terrance extended his hand and ice exploded out from it, piercing James in the gut as it burst forth. James was lifted into the air by the ever-growing flurry and Terrance leapt above him as he readied his ax. James rapidly flipped his body with great force, shattered the ice as he spun, deflected Terrance's attack and they crashed down into the golden floor in a blue explosion.

BOOOOOOOOOOOOOOOOM!

All was obscured by the mist. As it receded, James was on top of Terrance with a blade in his chest.

Terrance spread his arms wide.

James glared at him with disdain.

CLAP!

BOOOOOOOOOOOOOOOOOOM!

The ice Terrance formed across the room exploded, and James screamed as he was enveloped in the eruption of blue energy and blown away. "**AAAAAAAAAAHHHH!**'

As the dust settled, Terrance walked out of the crater. James was crouched on a smoldering knee. He was completely still, and smoke rose from his charred flesh.

Suddenly, He slowly rose to his feet and raised his blade once more. He stared at Terrance with eyes full of malice.

Terrance smiled as he clinked his axes. "Fine! I can do this all day!"

POW!

GUSH!

CLANG!

CRASH!

Terrance charged at James and their blades clashed as they engaged in a brutal melee.

21 - The Earth Archigos: Bazek Khalyvas

A S THE BOYS BATTLED, KRYSTAL STARTED REGAINING CONSCIOUSNESS. Her body was weak, and she struggled as she failed to lift herself onto her knees. She grimaced. *Come on Krystal! Remember who you are!* Memories flooded her mind. She curled her fists and gritted her teeth as she steeled her resolve.

I am the oldest of Bazek's 16 daughters. While my other sisters played with dolls, or discussed boys, I wanted to become a warrior like my dad. After my brother died, there were no male heirs remaining in the Khalyvas line. Assassination was common amongst the Archigos in our nation due to the widespread power and influence of the underworld. Who would carry on the family legacy if something happened to our father?

Bazek was a great man, and he did revolutionary things for our nation. In his short time as Archigos, he wiped out a majority of the underworld and turned our tribe into a national superpower. Our tribe had the strongest economy because of our access to the massive temples that laid deep beneath the desert wastes. Within them there was almost an infinite supply of rare and unique metals. Bazek leveraged our massive population and unique access to resources, to transform our desert wasteland into the most powerful tribe, even rivaling the capital.

As a result, my father often neglected his daughters, but I dreamed of supporting him and becoming strong enough to fulfill him in the way that only the son that he longed for could. I knew I could only do that if I was strong enough to become Archigos.

"NO! You are a woman. Focus on your beauty and intelligence! Your only concern should be finding a man of status to marry so you can live a good life outside of my home. I will never allow you to become a warrior!" Bazek shouted as Krystal stormed out of his room in tears.

Our tribe's chief engineer, a brilliant man by the name of Mr. Writing, used his ability to manipulate metals to develop the finest technology the world had ever seen. His genius was only rivaled by Crown Prince Akri of the capitol. I begged him day after day to train me until he finally conceded. I later found out that he did it out of the kindness of his own heart, risking execution by disobeying my father's orders.

"I've never been very good at using Earth Craft to control stone or glass, but I'm the best there is when it comes to manipulating metal!" Mr. Writing said enthusiastically.

"That's fine! Please! I'm desperate to learn anything you can teach me!" Krystal begged.

"Alright, but the training will be grueling and arduous. Though I still believe you can succeed, it will be especially difficult because you don't have the physical strength of a man. It will take many years, and Earth Craft is one of the most difficult techniques to learn. With the other Spirit Arts, you are using your Spirit Energy to generate and manipulate the natural elements as an extension of yourself. With Earth Craft, you must use your Spirit Energy to force the earth to submit to your will. Are you sure you're up for the task?"

"Yes, sir! I will become Archigos one day!" She shouted.

"Archigos Krystal Khalyvas. It has a nice ring to it. Let's get to work Ms. K!"

We spent grueling hours in weight training, combat, conditioning, and practicing Earth Craft. I spent years in the blazing hot forges, smelting blades and armor as I developed my technique. I discovered I had inherited my father's ability to use Spirit Energy to augment his physical capabilities. In my case, I gained great strength and nearly impenetrable skin. I never learned to manipulate the earth, but I became a master at manipulating every metal under the sun. The only thing I lacked was an opportunity to earn my father's approval.

One fateful day, I watched from my room in the palace as my father battled the Slave Master.

Bazek hovered in the sky using magnetism as he gasped for air. He looked down and saw hundreds of slaves that he had sent crashing down to the earth. He looked up and thousands more yellow eyed soldiers stared at him menacingly.

Bazek gripped his hammer. "Damn you Giali! This is a desecration of humanity! I shall have your head for this!"

Jerry's uncle sat high above Bazek on the shoulders of his slaves. "I'm surprised you still came up here to chase me! After the *first* ass whooping I gave you. You're a fool for abandoning the source of your strength. Your words of bravado sound cool and all, but I already told you that you were going to pay for ruining an evening with my son." He spoke with vitriol. "*Don't copy me.*"

FVOOM! FVOOM! FVOOOM!

The slaves soared toward him and fired beams of every element at Bazek.

POW!

He zipped through the lasers and crashed his hammer into a horde of slaves, scattering them.

POW! POW! POW!

A large slave pounded Bazek with three devastating blows that sent shockwaves across the sky.

Bazek spat blood.

POW!

He smashed his hammer into the slaves' skull, spun, and launched him toward the earth.

BOOOOOOM!

He crashed down into the surface in a massive explosion.

GUSH! GUSH! GUSH!

Bazek was suddenly swarmed by slaves, and they ripped and tore at his flesh with metallic teeth and claws.

WHOOOOOOOOOOOSH!

"HUUUUUUUUUUUUAAAAAAAAARG!" Bazek roared as Spirit Energy exploded from his body.

The eruption scattered the slaves and sent many crashing into the ground.

FVOOOOOOOOOOOOOOOM!

Suddenly, a massive beam of energy enveloped Bazek as it blasted him across the sky. He gritted his teeth as he steadied his uncontrolled flight. He fought against the beam and forced himself to fly through it.

He roared as he soared into the laser and it seared his flesh. "HUUUUAAAAAAAAAAAGH!"

POW!

Bazek swiftly gripped his hammer and struck the beam from inside with an uppercut. The laser cascaded upward, tore through the flying horde, and enveloped the Slave Master.

FVOOOOOOOM!

"AAAAAAAAAAH!" He roared as his flesh was seared.

The beam stopped instantly and the Slave Master was dazed as smoke rose from his body.

Bazek felt a damp warmth from his leg. He looked down to see it was dripping blood and had been completely mangled. He steeled his resolve.

WHOOOSH!

He rocketed into the sky as he pounded and dodged slaves on his ascent to the Slave Master.

POW!

Bazek burst through the slaves and rose above the Slave Master.

Spirit Energy erupted from his body as he cocked back his hammer. "Goodbye, Giali!"

The Slave Master snapped back to reality as terror gripped his heart.

"It was me! I killed your son!" He screamed.

"I'LL KILL YOU...GAAAHAAAA!" Bazek roared as his mind was ravaged.

GOOOOOOOONG!

Bazek violently clutched his head as a gong sounded in his skull. He contorted and jerked wildly as he resisted the Slave Master's power.

The Slave Master waved him off. "Just kidding! People are so easy predictable! But anyway, why don't you just crash down into the earth and die for me."

Bazek's body went limp.

He slowly fell through the sky and the entire city stared in horror.

Civilians despaired as they watched his descent. "Oh my God...", "Honey, Bazek...lost.", "The Earth Tribe has fallen."

"DADDY! NO!" Krystal screamed as she reached out her hand. She slowed his descent with magnetism, but it was too late.

BOOOOOOOOOOOOOOOOOOOOOOOOOOOOOOOOM!

He crashed into the earth and the shockwaves destroyed buildings for miles. His body was a bloody mess as he laid in a colossal crater.

Bazek clung to the last wisps of his life. *It's over. My time has...*

SHING!

The sound of metal reverberated throughout the area.

"It's alright father. I'll take care of this." Krystal said as she drew her blade.

Bazek's mind was drifting away, but her voice snapped him back to reality. "Daughter...what...are...you..."

Krystal's beautiful, handcrafted suit of sterling armor shone in the evening light. Lines resembling palm prints ran across her blade forged from the purest silver.

She stared at her father with determination. "It's alright father, you can rest now. If you have no strength,

I will be your strength. If you have no feet, I will be your feet. If you have no hammer, I shall be your hammer. If you have no blade, then I shall be your blade."

"But...you...are...a...woman...Krys..."

WHOOSH!

Krystal rocketed into the sky, sending shockwaves through the air that damaged skyscrapers as she zoomed past. The horde of slaves was slowly escaping toward the desert. A slave heard the noise and turned back.

SHINK!

GUSH!

SHINK!

SPLAT!

GUSH!

SLICE!

Slave after slave was cut down as she tore through the mob. The Slave Master was being treated by and his wounds had almost completely healed.

Another slave floated toward him. "Sir! There has been a disturbance! A woman..."

"A wom..."

SHINK! SHINK!

Krystal sliced through the slave and buried her blade in the Slave Master's throat.

"Let's silence that filthy mouth of yours."

"AGHLALALALAL!" He roared.

WHOOOOSH!

A wave of telekinetic energy blasted her backward and ripped the sword from his throat. He was swarmed by slaves who swiftly used a myriad of abilities to reconstruct his face. Krystal tensed her body and stopped her uncontrolled flight as she raised her blade against the mob.

The Slave Master stared at Krystal. "WHO THE HELL ARE YOU BITCH?! I THOUGHT THERE WAS ONLY ONE ARCHIGOS ALLOWED AT A TIME!"

Krystal felt her emotions rising. *Stay calm girl. He's nothing but an asshole.* She took a deep breath and suppressed them completely. "I am the Blade of the Archigos! And today, I shall end your reign of tyranny against this country, Slave Master!"

He trembled with rage. "I'll kill you! And after I do that, I'm gonna fly to the palace and have my way with every single one of those sisters of yours! Then I'm gonna rip off that armor and..."

WHOOOOSH!

SHINK!

She rocketed through the air and ripped her blade through his neck.

SNATCH!

Her blade had gone halfway through, but a man in a red suit gripped her sword. Krystal strained with everything she had as he effortlessly restrained her. She looked up at him and he was the most beautiful man she had ever seen. His handsome face and bright, amber eyes infatuated her.

He smiled and her heart fluttered.

"Hey there, handsome." Krystal said as she pulled back her blade and swung toward him. It sliced through the air as it neared his head.

He spoke in a gorgeous voice. "Well, hello there beautiful."

CREAK!

He bent the blade and wrenched it from her grasp. He tossed it like a paperweight as his bleeding hand instantly regenerated. She stared at him in shock and then dove through the air for the blade as slaves rushed to the Slave Master's aid.

The man with the golden eyes smiled and admired her form as she plummeted. "I'd hate to interrupt our lovely meeting, but I have other responsibilities this evening! I'd love to chat and get to know you better, but I'll be taking old Benny here back with me if that's alright with you!"

She caught the blade and faced him. "If you think I'm so beautiful then take me out on a date!"

WHOOSH!

She rocketed toward him and cocked back her blade.

He stretched. "I'd love to, but I'll have to take a rain check."

Krystal's eyes widened as he vanished.

SNATCH!

He grabbed Krystal by the neck and she was shocked as he kissed her sensually. He pulled away and gripped her throat tighter as she desperately grasped at his hand.

"I apologize for not being more gentlemanly, but I simply could not help myself from your beauty. Let that be a down payment on our future meeting." He said the mob of slaves escaped in the distance.

She scratched and clawed at his hand as dark spots filled her vision.

He sighed. "I'm sorry, but I do hate putting my hands on women. I'd never want to do anything that could damage your value. I only resort to violence as a last resort. Apologies."

On the ground the crowd cheered. "**That girl did it!**", "**They're retreating!**", "**She saved our nation!**"

As Krystal's consciousness faded, her mind raced as she searched for a solution. *Shit...there's no...metal...* Her vision faded to black.

Suddenly, they stopped hovering.

"Oh dear." The man said.

BOOOOOOOOOOOOOOOOOOOOOOOOOOOOOOOOM!

They crashed into the surface and a massive dust cloud formed around them. The man with the golden eyes was completely unscathed as he dusted off his suit and held Krystal's unconscious body. He erotically kissed her again and grabbed at her waistband.

Krystal jolted awake.

CLANG!

She flipped through the air and kicked the man in the neck. Her leg armor shattered, and she fell to the ground. She quickly leapt up and backflipped away from him. She reached out and her bent sword rushed through the cloud toward her.

He licked his lips. "I apologize. I just couldn't..."

"Ugh! I thought you were supposed to be a gentleman!" She roared in frustration as she zoomed toward him using Polarity.

SLICE!

Krystal sliced and missed, as the man appeared behind her. She swiftly landed and pivoted. She squinted and saw that he was far away at the edge of the dust cloud.

He blew her a kiss as he tapped his earpiece. "Like I said, I *will* have to take a rain check on our first date. Apologizes again for my unscrupulous behavior."

He was swallowed up by the ground.

Krystal stomped around in frustration. "UGHH! I hate men who are handsy! Why are all the beautiful men always so...GRRRAGH! I don't know! Vile!"

The dust cloud slowly dissipated, and it revealed a massive crowd of civilians standing on the crater's edge.

They beamed at Krystal and roared in applause. **"YEEEEEEEEEEEEEEEEEAAAAAAAAAAAAAAAAAHHH!"**

Krystal bowed before them and gave a radiant smile.

As James and Terrance battled, Krystal staggered to her feet.

Despite my father's shortcomings, I still believe that he is truly an exceptional man. Though most have lost hope in him, I never stopped believing that he will overcome his demons and remember who he truly is! On the day he went into seclusion, I promised him that I would defend this nation. I vowed to never fall in battle until he regains himself and returns to his former glory. She rose. *And I intend to keep that promise. I will fight, with every* **ounce** *of strength that I have, until the day I see him smile once more.* She balled her fists. *If my father needs strength! I shall be his strength! If he needs wisdom! I shall be his wisdom! If he needs a blade! I shall be his blade! I will mold and adapt myself. I shall become whatever it takes to keep my people safe!*

"**HUAAAAAAAAAAAAAARGH!**" She roared.

Rusted, golden armor snapped to her body.

James and Terrance pressed their blades against each other as they battled to impose their wills.

"Just give it up James! We're wasting time! We need to get in there and stop Machari!"

"That's what I already said! You just need to get out of my way and...GAAAH!"

CRASH!

A torrent of metal blasted them into the wall. They looked down and saw that they had been hit by a wave of rusted, liquid metal. The metal suddenly hardened and pinned them to the wall.

Krystal stood with her blade drawn as she rode a rising tide of liquid metal. "I've enjoyed meeting you Kayla's boyfriend, but now it's time for you to go!"

SLICE!

James snarled and a wave of dark energy sliced through the metal restraining them.

The boys glanced at each other and nodded.

FWOOOOOOOOOOOOOOOOOOOOOOOOOOOOOSH!

They vanished.

Krystal staggered back in shock as she frantically looked around the ballroom. James and Terrance blitzed away from her in opposite directions. They appeared as black and blue blurs that left colored trails in their wake as they accelerated. They zipped straight up the wall, onto the ceiling, and exploded off the roof as they rocketed toward her from different angles. She swung her arms and torrents of metal barreled toward them.

SLICE!

James sliced through his torrent as Terrance faced his head on. He smashed his axes into the wave, they shattered, and he was sent flying across the hall. James continued his descent and three more torrents raced into the sky to meet him. He flipped to avoid the first, landed on the second in stride, and viciously slashed through the third as he plummeted through the air sending his blade crashing down, inches from Krystal's face.

GUSH!

She extended her hand, and James was impaled through the gut by a golden rod.

CRASH!

Her armor raced off her body to extend the spear as two torrents pounded James and barreled him into the ground.

SMASH!

Another torrent barreled through the air and smashed Terrance into the ground.

The room was silent.

FREEZE!

Suddenly, the torrent's edge froze and shattered. Terrance rolled out of the way as the metal crashed down through the floor. He saw that Krystal was observing the spot where James had been crushed and took a moment to strategize. *Crap! This is bad! We need Ocean Floor Depths again, but I doubt that I have enough Spirit Energy to pull it off! I don't know how this power up works, but I can tell that I have a limit by the way these cracks are spreading.* He analyzed Krystal. *Her gold is already rusty, so she doesn't have much physical mobility or defense. That must be why she's using these waves of metal to keep us at a distance...*

 A new set of rusty armor covered Krystal as she faced Terrance. "I thought you accepted your fate."

"I did, but I'm gonna try becoming a better man instead. For real this time."

Krystal pointed her blade at Terrance. "Tell that to Luna."

WHOOOOOOSH!

A gargantuan torrent of golden metal burst forth, barreling across the hall. Terrance froze his feet to the ground and braced himself. He extended his hands and a massive flurry of ice erupted out of the ground and collided with Krystal's torrent.

RMRMRMRMRMRMRMRMRRMMR!

The entire palace trembled as the elements collided. The torrents pressed against each other, each side fighting to overtake the other. Krystal steeled her resolve and gritted her teeth as her wave started overtaking Terrance's.

"HUUAAAAAAAAAAAAAAAAAAAAAA!" Terrance roared as he strained.

He put everything he had behind his torrent, and it started overcoming Krystal's.

BOOOOOOOOOOOOOOM!

Suddenly, Terrance's wave burst forth and overwhelmed Krystal's as it barreled toward her. She leapt off her platform, narrowly avoiding death as the wave decimated the area behind her. As she fell, she dragged her sword point across the ground and swiped it forward, sending a torrent of metal toward him. Terrance was out of stamina, and he looked down at his frozen feet.

"Shit."

POW!

The torrent of metal barreled into him, blasting him through the wall and over a balcony's edge.

Krystal laid on the ground as she sighed in relief.

WRENCH!

Fuck. Krystal gently pounded her head on the ground in frustration as she heard metal ripping.

SLICE!

James tore through the metal that had crushed him. He was drenched in blood and his red eyes were filled with an animalistic malice.

WHOOSH!

James rushed forward, and she frantically rose away from him on a torrent of metal as his blade hunted her, grazing the skin of her face.

She desperately shouted. "Wire Technique!"

SLICE!

Razor sharp golden wires burst from her suit and impaled James, blasting him into the wall. Krystal rose to her feet on her torrent as James sliced through the wires in his chest. She clawed at him, and golden wires formed from the metal across the room and raced toward him from every direction.

WHOOOSH!

James blitzed forward in a red blur. He front flipped over wires, leapt and spun through cables, and viscously sliced through the clusters of lethal lines as he raced toward Krystal like a madman.

Terrance clung to the edge of the torrent of metal that had knocked him over the balcony's edge. He looked down and the people involved in the chaos below were smaller than ants. He felt dizzy, and his hands trembled as he stared at the ground. He squeezed his eyes shut. *Shit. Even I couldn't come back from a fall like this.* He channeled his Spirit Energy and froze the metal to form hand grips. He climbed on top of the torrent and sighed in relief. He jumped down onto the balcony and observed Krystal and James' battle.

James was fighting recklessly, allowing his body to be torn to shreds by the wires. He was smashed by torrents and each time he sprinted to his feet as his wounds regenerated. He wildly charged toward Krystal like a feral animal. She easily kept her distance and outpaced him as she rode away on her wave of metal. Terrance raced toward them. *Shit! He's not gonna make it!*

As James charged and his body was mutilated, his rage grew exponentially. He picked up speed and his wounds began regenerating even faster. Krystal noticed that James had stopped avoiding her attacks and smiled. *Kayla's boyfriend's power is incredible. His persistence is so hot!* She cracked her knuckles. *But it's time to end this.*

She stopped attacking James and he accelerated toward her.

WHOOOOOOOOSH!

He crouched and launched himself forward wildly. Wires formed on the tips of her fingers, and she swiftly crossed her arms.

SLICE!

The wires crossed, ripped into his flesh, and fileted James as blood exploded from his body.

GUSH!

She uncrossed her arms and James's body was torn to shreds as blood gushed onto the ground. He continued his wild charge and his tongue hung wildly from his mouth, as he stared at her with a primal rage.

Krystal interwove her straightened fingers. "Earth Craft, Art 13, Wire Technique, Executioner's Handbasket!"

Wires burst forth from the walls, floor and ceiling as they wove into a wall before James. *He's finished. The wires will slice through his brain and heart, and he will die. He can't regenerate without a head so...*

GUSH!

James burst through the wire fence as his limbs were severed from his body. He squeezed his head through an opening as his blood congealed and his limbs reattached. Krystal shuddered in frustration as a long, razor-sharp wire formed on her pointer finger. James rocketed toward Krystal and she raised her finger into the air, as the wire snapped back.

Time seemed to stop.

She sighed as James' blade came within inches of her face. *I'll slice him in two. Then this will finally be over.*

She brought the wire down.

SQUISH!

There was a massive eruption of blood that splattered in Krystal's face and obscured her vision. She gasped as she saw Terrance had leapt in the way of the wire. It had split his body in half and severed him all the way down to his waist. James was ducked behind his legs.

He cocked back his blade.

SLICE!

James violently swung his blade, ripped through Terrance's body, decimated her armor and tore into her as blood gushed from her side. Krystal flew across the room and crashed into the ground as her armor skidded across the golden floor until she slid to a halt.

James landed on his feet as Terrance plopped onto the ground. James raced after her as Terrance regenerated. He watched as James wildly bounded toward Krystal and she leapt to her feet with her blade drawn against him.

Terrance watched as James and Krystal clashed. *I want to jump in and take the lead so badly...but I can't. My ice is too fragile to slice through her metal waves. I just have to support James because he's the only one who can actually hurt her right now.*

James raised his blade, but Krystal extended her arm as his body froze.

"You didn't think I forgot about this did you?!" She snarled as James levitated into the air. Rusted gold zipped onto her blade and doubled its reach as she raised her sword above her head. She lined it up to slice James in two and he flailed as he floated. Her blade sliced through the air toward his skull.

BOOOOOOOOM!

The leftover ice around the chamber exploded and Krystal was blasted into the wall. James clattered to the ground as she landed and quickly rose to her feet.

She shouted as she trembled with frustration. "WHY WON'T YOU JUST DIE?!"

Terrance smiled. "If I die, then my family would kill me! Even the butler would be mad!"

James had a revelation and his eyes widened.

Krystal rose on a wave of metal as two more torrents rushed toward him. He zipped into his reflection in the wall and rocketed toward her with his blade extended.

Krystal lined up her blade in the middle of his skull. She glanced at Terrance standing across the hall behind her. *He's too far away and there's no more ice now. James is moving too fast. There's no way he can dodge or avoid this...*

"Freeze." James said.

Krystal and her wave of metal completely stopped.

SHINK!

James' blade pierced her in the gut, and they flew across the hall. As they neared Terrance, James ripped his blade out and back flipped away. Terrance flipped his ax in his hand, smiled, raised it, and crashed it down into Krystal's chest.

BOOOOOOOOOOOOOOOOOOM!

A massive blue explosion rocked the palace.

Krystal laid in a crater soaked in blood.

Terrance sighed as he wiped his brow. "Man we finally..."

CRASH!

Metal erupted around Terrance and blasted him into the wall. Krystal held her stomach as new armor formed, and she rose high into the sky on a torrent of metal. She rose up just below the massive chandelier.

"I WILL NOT FAIL! I WILL KEEP MY PROMISE! I MUST SEE MY DUTY FULFILLED!" Krystal roared as numerous torrents of metal barreled toward James.

He leapt onto the nearest torrent and flipped onto another. He bounded from torrent to torrent as he ascended toward her. Her attacks grew in speed, and he became a red streak, as he dodged, leapt, and sliced his way through them.

Terrance was pinned to the wall, and he looked on in awe.

Until his heart sank. *Oh no.*

The darkness around James started to fade. He gasped for air and his legs grew heavy. Each time he leapt away from a crashing torrent, his escape from death was narrower than the last. *He's not gonna make it! He's running out of steam and he's gonna get smashed before he reaches her. Without that darkness I don't know if he can survive a hit like that!*

Terrance froze and shattered the metal impaling him. His body regenerated and he heard a strange sound as he stepped forward. He looked down and cracks had almost entirely covered his body. Powerful streams of blue mist poured out of them, and dust drifted toward the floor as it fell from his body.

A tear rolled down his face. "It looks like this is it for me. This is probably all I've got." He balled his fists. "Let's make it count."

Terrance placed his hand on the wall as he raced around the hall's perimeter. James ran up a straightaway torrent directly in front of Krystal. He leapt and weaved as he narrowly avoided crashing metal all around him. Krystal had a straight shot to finish James and relief filled her heart as she raised her hand to finish him.

She shivered as the temperature in the hall dropped. NO! *What is he doing!* Krystal frantically looked around for Terrance.

Terrance had almost run a complete lap around the hall when Krystal spotted him. Ice was forming on the floor and walls as the temperature dropped to frigid levels.

CRASH!

She pointed her raised arm at Terrance instead, and a torrent of metal stapled him to the wall. Blood dripped from his mouth as his head sagged. She turned back to James, and he was only a few feet away.

"I'VE GOT YOU RIGHT WHERE I WANT YOU!" She roared.

Suddenly, torrents of silver from the chandelier rocketed toward James from the front, as golden torrents surrounded him from the back and sides.

WHOOSH!

He leapt into the air and raised his blade against Krystal.

Time seemed to stop

There was a moment of silence as he cocked back his blade.

Suddenly, horror gripped James' heart. *I'm too slow. There's no way I can make it before these torrents smash me...*

James closed his eyes as the torrents came within inches of smashing him.

It's over. She got us...

"HEY JAMES! AREN'T YOU DOING THIS FOR YOUR FAMILY! DON'T TELL ME YOU'RE GONNA CHICKEN OUT AND DIE ON THEM NOW!" Terrance roared.

James' ring was enveloped in multicolored energy, and a vision was set before him.

He saw his little sister smiling. "Come on James! You're the best! You can make it out of anything! This girl's attacks are nothing!"

James' younger brother scowled as he appeared before him. "Are you really letting *her* get you this riled up? Pathetic. Get it together before I have to come handle this myself. It would be stupid if you died to someone like her!" He said as he turned away.

James' mother appeared before him with a belt in her hand. "James! What are you doing fooling around with that skanch! Hurry up and get rid of her because she's not good enough for *my baby*! I'm ready for some grandkids, so you need to come home soon so I can pick out your wife like you promised! AND YOU BETTER NOT HAVE BEEN FOOLING AROUND WITH NO HOOCHIES!"

James' father appeared before him.

He wore the widest smile James had ever seen. "I'm so proud of you son."

James' eyes watered as he was overcome with emotion.

FVOOOOOOOOM!

The darkness around James' body and his dark saber exploded as they disappeared.

Krystal's eyes widened in shock. She watched tears roll down James' face as the torrents inched closer. *Where did his sword go?! Is he crying?! I don't know what the hell is going on, but now he's even more defenseless!*

On the ground floor, Terrance was stapled to the wall as he stared up at the scene. Suddenly, a pool of water formed on the ground before him. A liquid version of his father rose from the puddle. Okpa smiled as tears ran down his face. "I knew you could do it son. I've never been happier than I am right now."

Terrance sobbed as he was overwhelmed by emotion. He sniffled and wiped his face. "Th...thanks dad...sometimes people have to learn the h...hard way."

FREEZE!

Terrance pressed his hand into the wall and the entire chamber froze over as Krystal's roaring metal morphed into brittle glass.

Terrance spread his arms.

CLAP!

BOOOOOOOOOOOOOOOOOOOOOOOOOOOOOOOOOM!

The ice around the hall exploded and the torrents barreling toward James exploded into a million fragments.

Krystal's footing shattered. She stared in horror as James descended above her. Tears welled in her eyes. *It's over. I'm sorry I couldn't keep my promise...father...*

A new vision quickly flashed before James' eyes. He saw scenes of a skinny man with short hair slicing through a massive, horned monster with red wings. The man wore crystal armor that radiated with multicolored energy. An entire galaxy seemed to swirl inside his sword as he ripped through the monster.

Those aren't my memories...who is that man.

Something came over James, and a crystalline blade materialized in his hands.

He spoke in a serene calm. "Spirit Craft, Art 2, Reality Burst."

James' blade turned pitch black. Stars shone in the darkness as if there was an entire galaxy inside the blade's crystals. Multicolored energy erupted as James' blade crashed into Krystal's side.

They vanished.

SLICE!

A multicolored line as thin as the horizon rotated and sliced through the entire palace.

James came to and found himself standing on the palace's bottom floor in a crater. He looked up and stared through a gaping hole in dozens of floors, all the way up to the ballroom. His hand was warm, and he raised it to his face to find that his ring pulsed with multicolored energy. He realized that his foot was soaked, and he looked down to find that he was standing over Krystal's body. Her skin was red, and she laid in a large pool of blood at the bottom of the crater. She had been severed in half, and blood poured from her still body. James crouched and felt a faint pulse in her cold neck.

"You are the toughest girl I know. We are the ones in the wrong and I'm so sorry about this." James said as his hand with the ring touched her face.

FVOOOOOOOOOOOOOOOOOOM!

As the ring made contact, her body was enveloped in multicolored energy. Krystal's body reattached as her wounds healed. She remained unconscious and James sighed in relief. *At least I won't be charged with murder today.*

He stood and stared at the ring in confusion. He remembered the vision of his family and stared into the sky. "Thank you guys. I'll be home soon."

James Mirror Dashed up to the top floor. He looked around and Terrance was leaning against the wall near his friends with his arms crossed. He had a warm smile on his face. "Not bad simp. She's almost as strong as an

Archigos. I don't know how you keep doing it, but you never cease to amaze me."

James smiled and spoke humbly. "Thank you Terrance. I lost my head...and I don't even know who I was out there. I couldn't have done it without you."

"Of course..."

POW!

James socked Terrance in the face.

"OUCH! WHAT THE HELL WAS THAT FOR?!"

James smiled. "We're gonna have to work on the nicknames though. Simp was never acceptable."

Kayla stirred and weakly opened her eyes. She smiled as she saw James standing before her.

His heart was filled with joy, and he gave her a thumbs up. "See! I told you that everything would be..."

BADUMP! BADUMP! BADUMP!

James clutched his chest as he collapsed. He laid stiff on his side as his vision blurred, and his body grew weak.

James coughed rancid blood. *What...the...hell...*

His vision was fading, when he heard Terrance collapse. He shifted his head to see Kayla and Epios doubled over, vomiting blood.

BZZZZZZZZZZZZZZZZZZZZZZZZZZZZT!

Terrance mouthed as James' ears started ringing. "P...o...i...s...o...n..."

James lost consciousness as the poison overwhelmed his system.

Back in the throne room, before James and Terrance's battle ensued, Bazek casually walked toward his throne.

He reclined on the bed. "Thieves, Jesters, and cowards...What is this nation coming to?"

Pebbles clattered to the ground in the corner.

He glanced toward the pile that buried Jerry.

Bazek scoffed as he closed his eyes. *It would be impossible for the coward to have survived...*

Suddenly, Bazek started levitating.

"What is this? How can this be!"

CRASH!

A twig-like arm burst through the rubble. The metal and debris rose as Jerry walked out of the rubble.

His eyes glowed with a yellow light.

He stared at Bazek with a heart full of malice.

"How can this be?! Who are you?! Who is your father?!" Bazek said as he slipped out of his robe.

He fell to the ground in his underwear.

ZOOM!

Jerry hovered in his face. "I'm God's child, yo."

POW!

Jerry pounded Bazek with a vicious right hook and he crashed through the throne room wall. He smashed through building after building as he barreled through the city.

CRASH!

He collided with the city's outer wall and the impact knocked over an entire section as the stone fell into the earth. Bazek was badly bruised, and his body was soaked in blood. His ears rang as he laid on the ground in a daze.

"How can this..."

His eyes widened with fear as a skyscraper barreled toward him.

BOOOOOOOOOOOOOOOOOOOOOOOOOOOOOOOM!

The skyscraper exploded in an eruption of fire as it collided with the outer wall. Massive flames rose from the surrounding buildings as they flooded the streets. Bazek walked out of the fire as smoke rose from his body. He was completely naked, and he patted soot off his flesh. A suit of armor made from building materials covered his body. *I would surely have perished if I had not been reinforcing my body with Spirit Energy at a Progress level. Who is this child?*

Jerry wore a suit of golden armor as he levitated toward Bazek from above with an enraged expression.

He pointed menacingly. "The time has come for you to repent of your sins against the Earth Tribe, bro."

Bazek reached out his hand, and a beautiful golden hammer zipped into it.

Bazek covered his face as he tried to hold back his laughter. "BA-HA-HA! The absurdity of this day only increases!" He pointed his weapon at Jerry. "And just who are you to accuse me child?! What do you know of my crimes? If you believe you have the strength to discipline the Archigos, then by all means, come down here and..."

Jerry reached out his hand, and a pair of sunglasses zipped into them.

He slid them onto his face. "I'll take care of this, yo."

SMACK!

Jerry smashed Bazek in the face and he barreled across the city. He crashed through several buildings, until he flipped in the air to stop his momentum.

SNATCH!

Jerry appeared behind him, grabbed him by the hair, and flung him and toward the earth.

POW!

Jerry reappeared on the ground just before Bazek hit the concrete and devastated him with a vicious uppercut that set him soaring back into the sky.

Jerry appeared above him and raised his arm. "Swag Craft, Art 1, Swag Chop!"

SMACK!

BOOOOOOOOOOOOOOOOOOOOOOOOOOOOOOOM!

Bazek crashed into the earth like lightning. Upon impact there was a massive explosion as a dust cloud filled the air. Bazek was in a massive crater as he picked himself up off the ground. He spat blood and shook his head in confusion. "It appears this child is a bit tougher than I..."

Bazek heard a noise, and he looked into the cloud with fear.

Jerry's glowing eyes shone through the dust.

Bazek staggered backward as he looked around. "Where are you? Face me you damn..."

CLANG!

Jerry smashed Bazek in the face with his own hammer, torqued his body and sent him soaring into the stratosphere. Bazek flailed his arms as attempted to control his flight.

Jerry floated toward him and held out Bazek's hammer.

"You dropped this, yo." Jerry said as he released the hammer and it plummeted toward the earth.

"Do not condescend him, bro." Jerry said.

Bazek stared at the falling hammer. *I was using polarity to press that weapon into the metal in my hand...Is his Spirit Energy output higher than mine...*

Bazek balled his fists. "YOU INSOLENT CHILD! HOW DID YOU GET THAT?! YOU COULDN'T POSSIBLY BE STRONG ENOUGH TO..."

Time seemed to slow.

Jerry was in his face with a cocked back fist. "I said...you dropped it, yo."

SMACK!

Jerry smashed his face, ripped back his elbow, and sent Bazek crashing down through the roof of a skyscraper.

BOOM!

BOOM!

BOOM!

BOOM!

BOOM!

Bazek barreled through floor after floor as Jerry raced toward him through the holes Bazek's body created. Bazek swung his arm and a torrent of metal rushed at Jerry. Jerry extended his fingers and the torrent stopped.

He narrowed his eyes at Bazek. "Swag Jerry is unimpressed, yo."

The torrent redirected and raced toward Bazek.

CRASH!

Bazek met the torrent with another, and the metallic flurries crashed against each other. Bazek extended his arms as he crashed through the floors, as he tried to force his torrent to dominate Jerry's.

Jerry casually flicked his hand.

BOOOOOOOOOOOOOOOOOOOOM!

His torrent overcame Bazek's and smashed him down into the surface below.

Bazek rose up in the street from underground. He was furious as his ruined hair fell down into his face. He stared in anger at Jerry as he floated down toward him.

Jerry crossed his arms. "Will you repent and turn back to the Lord, bro?"

"You know nothing of what you speak, *child*." Bazek spat.

WHOOOOOSH!

Bazek rushed Jerry. *This child is so feeble that I shall easily overpower him.*

Bazek tackled him and Jerry folded his legs as he launched him high into the sky.

"Swag Craft, Art 2, Swag Kick!"

POW!

He flipped up, leapt into the air, and blasted Bazek across the city with a devastating kick.

Bazek crashed into a skyscraper and Jerry appeared before him as he cocked back his fist. Bazek avoided his strike and backhanded Jerry down through the floor. Jerry landed on his feet and rocketed toward Bazek. Bazek swung, but Jerry avoided his strike, zipped behind him, and pounded him with two devastating strikes. Bazek swung his elbow at him, and Jerry pounded his face with two more vicious hooks. As Bazek reached out to grab him, Jerry flipped through the air and devastated him with a spinning roundhouse kick to the head that sent him barreling through the building into the surface.

BOOOOOOOOOOOM!

Bazek stood up at the bottom of the ruined building. He raised his hands and hundreds of pipes rushed at his foe. Jerry weaved through the pipes, grabbed one and hurtled it toward Bazek. Bazek's eyes widened, and he sidestepped as he narrowly avoided being impaled. He grabbed the pipe, and it formed into a blade.

WHOOOOOOSH!

He launched himself into the air toward Jerry. An iron spear flew into Jerry's grasp, and they raced at each other.

BOOOOOOOOOOOM!

Bazek swung, but Jerry used the spear point to deflect his slash and impale Bazek as he drove him into the ground.

He stood over Bazek as the spear was lodged in his gut. "Will you submit to my swag, yo?"

"What nonsense *do you speak*, child?"

Bazek flexed his core muscles and the spear popped out of his unpierced flesh.

Bazek reached his arms wide.

CLAP!

BOOOOOOOOOOOOOOOOOOOOOOOOOOOOOOM!

Bazek clapped forcefully and a massive shockwave blasted Jerry through the skyscraper and high into the sky as it shattered the entire building.

CRASH!

Jerry flipped through the air and Bazek blasted him with a torrent of metal. As Jerry was being driven by the torrent, he swung his arm at Bazek, and a skyscraper barreled toward him.

CRASH!

Bazek braced himself as the skyscraper blasted him.

As the skyscraper soared through the air, Bazek raced through it. He avoided sliding furniture and used magnetism to run on the floor as the skyscraper flipped through the air. Jerry burst into the building with his spear, and rushed at Bazek. Jerry stabbed at him with the spear as Bazek deflected his strikes. Bazek reached out, grabbed a printer and formed it into a hammer. He knocked away the tip of Jerry's spear, spun, and crashed the hammer into Jerry's face, sending him through the floor. Bazek leapt through the hole, and they engaged in high-level midair hand to hand combat as the building spiraled around them.

POW! POW!

Bazek pounded Jerry's body with two massive strikes.

POW! POW!

Jerry responded with two ferocious hooks as Bazek was knocked back. Bazek spat blood and looked up as Jerry zoomed away from him.

"Swag Craft, Art 3, Swaggy Retreat!"

"Get back here you coward...."

BOOOOOOOOOOOOOOOOOOOOOOOOOOOOOOM!

The skyscraper crashed into the ground and exploded in an eruption of flames. An entire area of the city had been reduced to a wasteland of ruined buildings as raging fires blazed. Bazek leapt out of the roaring flames and sent torrents of blazing wreckage at Jerry. Jerry was smashed by the rubble, but before he was crushed, he pulled his arm backward and the building rolled over and flattened Bazek.

CRASH!

Bazek burst out of the building and was in midair as Jerry held a stick and a gong.

"Swag Craft, Art 4, Swaggy Gong Beat!"

BAAAAAAAAAAAAAAAAAAAAAANNNNNNNNNNG!

Bazek clutched his head and covered his ears as the sound devastated his skull. The sonic shockwave blew away the building and rubble surrounding them. Jerry reached out his hand and Bazek's hammer soared into it as Bazek writhed on the ground.

POW!

Jerry sprinted, picked up speed, and blasted Bazek across the city. Bazek soared and flipped through the air as he crashed through the palace and landed on the top floor of a nearby skyscraper. Bazek laid on the ground and his body was soaked in blood. He staggered to his feet as he sensed Jerry flying toward him.

He raised his hands. "Earth Craft, Progress Art 2, Shard Storm."

Jerry soared toward Bazek as he zipped through the capital's high-rises. Suddenly, the glass from the nearby buildings exploded and formed a massive hurricane. Jerry zoomed away as a torrential storm of glass chased him through the city. He zipped through buildings, ducked around corners and flew under bridges as the storm of glass steadily gained on him. He zoomed away quickly descended as he dragged his feet into a sandy area.

"Swag Craft, Art 5, Swaggy Temple Throw!"

He pressed his hands forward and a massive temple burst through the sand from below as it rocketed toward the glass storm.

BOOOOOOOOOOOOOOOOOOOOOOOOM!

It shattered the storm and barreled through buildings for miles.

Jerry nervously scratched his head. "Oops. My bad, bros..."

"Jerry, you've grown far too reckless, yo. It is time to end this battle, bro." Jerry said.

Jerry turned toward Bazek and stared at him on the highest floor of a building. He balled his fist and ripped it downward. Bazek's armor shuddered, and he crashed down through the skyscraper.

BOOOOOOOOOOOOOOOOOOOOOOOOOOOOM!

He barreled into the surface and the building erupted in flames as it collapsed on top of him.

Jerry walked forward into the street as Bazek angrily stomped out of the flaming wreckage. Bazek reached out and his hammer soared into his grasp. He stared at Jerry with hatred in his eyes. He looked upon him for the first time and recognized his mop of unkempt hair.

Realization flashed across his face. "Ah, so we have met! You're that inept child who visited me in the hospital after my victory over the Slave Master. It is clear to me that you have only grown more feeble as the years have passed! Is this God's attempt to mock me once more?!"

Jerry dropped into a battle stance. "Come, yo. It is time we ended this, bro."

Bazek glanced at the palace. *This is embarrassing, but I refuse to use my Esoteric weapon to defeat this child! I'll unleash everything I have this time.*

CRASH!

The ground shattered as his Spirit Energy surged. *He won't be walking away from this.*

"Earth Craft, Art 2, Quicksand!" Bazek roared.

Jerry's footing shifted into quicksand, and he was twisted around as he sunk into it. Bazek charged as he swung his hammer, but Jerry blocked the attack and was sent flying through the air.

Jerry reclined as he soared. "Swag Jerry is unbothered, yo."

"Earth Craft, Art 5, Judgment Chains!"

Chains burst through the ground.

BOOOOM!

They grabbed Jerry by the wrist, neck, and ankles as he crashed into the concrete.

Bazek tensed his leg muscles and crouched. "Earth Craft, Art 4, Motherland Bludgeon!"

POW!

Bazek vanished, exploded toward Jerry, and devastated him with his hammer, creating a massive shockwave that decimated several city blocks.

Jerry turned his head to the side and spat blood.

He sighed. "Swag Jerry is unmoved, yo."

Bazek was incensed. "No! I shall unleash every technique in my repertoire until you fall child!"

"EARTH CRAFT, ART 6, SHIFTING DESSERT DANCE!"

"Swag Jerry is unaffected, yo."

"EARTH CRAFT, ART 7, EARTHQUAKE!"

"Swag Jerry is indifferent, yo."

"EARTH CRAFT, ART 8, HAIRLINE EXECUTION! "

"Swag Jerry avoided the attack, yo."

"EARTH CRAFT, ART 9, SWAMP!"

"Swag Jerry can't swim, yo."

"EARTH CRAFT, ART 11, TREMBLE!"

"Swag Jerry's is getting bored, yo."

"EARTH CRAFT, PROGRESS ART 1, NEVER-ENDING DESSERT!"

"Swag Jerry is taking a nap, yo."

An hour later, Bazek had used every single Earth Craft technique to assault Jerry, and he was still unscathed. Bazek huffed and puffed as he leaned on his hammer for support. *How has this child not run out of Spirit Energy?! I have an Esoteric weapon, and even I'm reaching my limit! I have never seen this kind of strength and durability, even from a Spirit Maxed individual!*

Jerry yawned as he dangled his legs on the edge of a building. "Are you done bro? Swag Jerry is really getting tired of this, yo."

Bazek grimaced. *Fine then. He leaves me no choice. I shall have to use my Esoteric weapon.*

Bazek weakly reached out his hand.

Two small stones zipped out of the throne room and into his palm. The stones were engraved with white markings and Bazek held them toward Jerry.

"Your fate is sealed, child! The time has come for me to use my ultimate...!"

Jerry covered his mouth and as he yawned. "Swag Jerry is unimpressed with small pebbles, yo."

"Stop dishonoring the Lord's chosen and treat him with respect, bro." Jerry said.

"Sorry. Please continue, bro." Jerry said.

Bazek stared at the child in confusion and continued. "When I roll these stones, God himself determines my fate! If the stones land face up, then God has given me his favor on this day, and my strength becomes infinite!

Circumstances shall fall in my favor, and in layman's terms, I am guaranteed victory!"

Jerry rubbed his eyes disinterestedly. "And what happens again if they land face down, bro?"

"That has never happened! Though, I haven't utilized them in many years…But regardless! If they were to land face down, then that would mean that the Lord has given me over into your hand on this day, which is impossible!"

Jerry picked at fingernails. "It kind of looks like that's what's already happened, bro. But I'll let you roll your little stones so we can end this, yo."

Bazek held out his hand to drop the stones.

"But wait! Are you telling me that you've had these holy stones for years, and that you can use them to ask God what to do at any moment, but you haven't done it in years, yo?"

Bazek looked away. "Y…Yes that is correct."

"Ok. I was just wondering. Please continue, bro."

Bazek dropped the stones, and they landed face down.

Bazek's eyes grew larger than saucers and his mouth was agape. He crumpled to his knees. "How can this be…The Lord had never judged against me in this way…"

Jerry dropped from his perch and cracked his knuckles. "Swag Jerry has grown tired and is ready to go home, yo." He walked up to Bazek and pressed his face uncomfortably close. "Now it's my turn. *Bro.*"

SNATCH!

Jerry grabbed his face and tossed him into the air.

Jerry leapt and cocked back his fist. "Swag Craft, Art 7, Consecutive Swaggy Punches !"

POW!

POW!

POW!

POW!

POW!

POW!

He unleashed a vicious flurry of blows sending shockwaves that decimated city blocks. He pounded Bazek through building after building as they barreled through the city.

Bazek's mind wandered as he was continuously pounded. *I suppose this is the end for me...Forsaken by the Lord and bested by a lowly child. I suppose this is what I deserve for living such a shameful life.* He stared into Jerry's yellow eyes as his consciousness faded away. *This must be an act of God. Why He has found it humorous to mock me for a third time, is beyond the scope of my comprehension. If God himself has deemed me wicked enough to empower such a feeble boy to deliver His judgment, then I must surely accept it with open arms.*

✦

As Bazek's life drained away, his earliest memories flooded to the surface.

I was raised in affluence and never once knew what it meant to be without. My parents groomed me to become an Archigos from a young age. I never had a free moment to myself, and I resented them for not allowing me to pursue the dreams I held deeply within my heart. Despite their shortcomings, my parents encouraged me to walk in the Lord's ways. I understood that blessing comes from above, and I served The Lord as a means to achieve my desires. As I grew older, I came to enjoy the perks of being an Archigos candidate, and I decided I would give my all to become Archigos so I could bask in the women, riches and fame.

I eventually achieved my goals and spent my early years as Archigos reveling in my achievement. I delegated a council to run the nation as I threw feasts and erected monuments in my own honor. As I grew older, the time came for me to have heirs and secure my family legacy. I felt that my parent's methodology was successful, and I desired to raise up strong male heirs to succeed me as Archigos. My first wife gave birth to daughter after daughter, and I grew frustrated. I secretly married and impregnated woman after woman in hopes of receiving a male heir. Years passed and it was as if a curse had befallen my household. This was the Lord's first mockery against me, and I received female after female until their number reached sixteen.

Finally, God's belly was filled with laughter and his vengeance against me seemed to have been satiated, as one of my wives finally bore a son. He was a beautiful boy, gifted beyond measure. I named him Victor, because surely none would best him for as long as he lived.

After Victor was born, I turned my attention toward the nation he would inherit. I repented of my past deeds, and the Lord guided my hand in creating prosperity for the Earth Tribe. I sought after His voice, and He instructed me in the way I should go. I led the people righteously and spent all of my time attending to their needs. As a result, the people of our nation closely followed the Lord's principles, and in turn we received his blessings for our obedience. Our people crossed the desert and served the other tribes, as we went out and spread the Gospel. Many were brought to know Christ because of our efforts, and we were known as a nation who was blessed by God. In addition, God granted me the wisdom to leverage our tribe's resources and manpower to build the Earth Tribe into a desert utopia. Our splendor was only rivaled by the Capital and the nation founded by Kalarono's warped brat, the Dragon Isles.

Victor was extremely proficient in Earth Craft, and as a child, his ability to augment his body with Spirit Energy *far surpassed even my own. His skin was impenetrable to any blade known to man, and his fists clanged like steel. He was very intelligent, and he had a carefree nature. He loved playing with his sisters, and he had dreams of becoming an artist in the Capital as I did in my youth.*

Unfortunately, I knew that those dreams would be short lived. Despite our nation's prosperity, the Underworld was a constant threat, and Victor would have to reach his potential if he hoped to have the ability to maintain order as my successor. I subjected him to harsh training from a young age, and his skills thrived all the more. He grew to resent me for it, but I knew he would thank me when he received the fruits of his labor, the ability to protect the ones he loves.

Sadly, that day never came. When Victor was around seven years old, he was already sparring against seniors at the Earth Tribe Academy. I stood in the grand hall and watched as he defeated the academy's top student in hand-to-hand combat.

"That's impossible! I keep hitting the child, but I fail to even lay a scratch!" The student complained.

Victor shook his head as he walked out of the hall. "I beat you, so go away, weakling."

I approached Victor and lovingly ran my hand through his hair. "Very good son! Soon you will be ready to…"

SMACK!

He smacked my hand away and stared at me with eyes full of malice. "Get out of my way *father*. You said I could draw after I won my tenth match of the day, and that's exactly what I'm going to do." He stormed away across the hall

I sighed. "Yes, you've earned it. I apoli..."

Suddenly, I felt a disturbance.

"Victor! Come close! Before..."

BOOOOOOOOOOOOOOOOOOOOOOOOOOOOOOOOM!

When I awoke, the entire palace had been decimated by an explosion. I spent weeks searching the ruins, but Victor's body was never recovered.

I flew into a rage. In my passion, I destroyed the entire underworld out of a thirst for vengeance. After my hatred subsided, I no longer desired to live, for how could my legacy be passed down without an heir? I sealed myself away in my chamber for years, as I wallowed in my grief.

"Enough." Jerry said.

Bazek found himself in the middle of a crater in the city's center. His body was weary, and his muscles ached.

Jerry roared as he spoke to himself. "But I hate him! I want to kill him like James said! You know what he did to me! He told me...",

Bazek stared at Jerry in confusion as two distinct voices came from his mouth.

"No, his life is not yours to take on this day. Vengeance is the Lords!" Jerry said.

"But I..."

"That's enough. You have disgraced yourself enough by dishonoring the Lord's anointed with your gifts. It is my time to speak with him." Jerry said as he turned to Bazek.

Bazek bowed before him. "Please, just take my life. I have no more desire to..."

"Stand up. Do not bow before man." Jerry said.

Bazek rose to his knees as tears ran down his face. He sobbed. "I'm sorry, I just wanted my son..."

"Stand up and wipe your face." Jerry said.

Bazek wiped his face and rose to his feet.

Jerry took off his shades, and his yellow eyes took on a white hue. "I have come to speak of what I have heard from the Father. You were appointed as Archigos over this nation by the Lord, and you have failed to steward His provision. He has shown you His grace by allowing you to remain in authority until the day of your approaching death..."

"I welcome it. At least then I will get to be with my..."

"You cry about the loss of one son, but you failed to cherish the seventeen other children the Lord gifted you. To make matters worse, on this very day, you nearly struck down your own seed with your hands."

Bazek looked up. "My own son...what could you..."

Jerry pointed at the palace. "Look and you will discover the truth. Seek and you will find. But as for now, hear me and hear me well. Or the Lord shall surely take this kingdom from you and give it to the boy who stands before you, as this child will one day seek to follow Him with his whole heart."

"What mockery has the Lord sent you to deliver me on this day?"

"Surely the Lord does not mock his children, and these kinds of things should never be said about the Lord of Hosts. The father has sent me to remind you of His goodness and mercy, and to warn you that if you do not steward His people well, He will surely hand you over to your enemies and give the nation over to one who seeks to follow His ways. For everything belongs to the Lord, and it is His to deal with as he pleases."

"Yes, I understand. I cannot ignore a direct command from God, I suppose. But what have you spoken about my son? It cannot be that Victor still lives?!"

"The child I spoke of is the one you struck with your own hand. His life fades as we speak. If you investigate the palace, you shall find what I have said to be true. The son that was born out of your sin lives, and he will live a life full of pain because of your transgressions.

Bazek rose to his feet and grabbed Jerry. "Victor lives?! Tell me! Where can I find..."

"Surely your heart is far from the Lord, and you shall not see Victor again until the day of your death!" Jerry spat.

Tears filled Bazek's eyes. "Why has the Lord judged me so harshly?! I have served him for my entire life and..."

"Truly, I say to you that you have only served yourself since the day you were born. The Lord appointed you over his people and you have used his blessing to enrich yourself and your own family. You have taken many wives, and you have neglected the people He has set under you. Seek the Lord and you will find the truth in what I say to you on this day. Now allow me to complete my message so this child can return home."

Bazek's heart was filled with sorrow. "What you say is true, and I regret each day I have lived apart from the Lord. Complete your message so I may investigate what has become of my son."

"Recall what I have said on this day and treat this young boy and his friends kindly, as this boy will truly desire God's heart. Forgive them of their transgression on this day and provide them with the support they require to go forth on their journey. Thus ends my message from the Lord."

"Fine, I shall do as you say." Bazek said with a remorseful heart.

"You shall do well. Before I depart, I shall begin your work in repairing this damaged nation."

Jerry rose above the city and stared down at it. Several sections of the capital had been completely destroyed, and massive flames raged across the city. Jerry waved his hand and a dust storm raced across the area and smothered the fires. He lifted his fingers, and wreckage rose from the surface until it filled the sky. Jerry had rescued the civilians from their homes on earthen platforms throughout the battle and placed them outside the walls.

They stared up at him in awe.

"THAT MUST BE BAZEK!", "BAZEK RESCUED US FROM THAT CHILD WHO DESTROYED OUR COUNTRY!", "THE ARCHIGOS HAS RETURNED!", "OUR NATION IS SAVED!"

Jerry pointed and waved his arms as metal rushed to the surface and the city was restored. He floated down toward Bazek and curled into a ball. The yellow light faded from his eyes and Jerry fell asleep.

He snored loudly. "SCHOO, PHEW! SCHOO, PHEW!"

Bazek stared at Jerry in awe.

Until he looked away in shame. "It appears that the Lord has not changed. He still uses the meek to shame the proud."

Bazek turned his head toward the palace, and his heart was flooded with hope. He zoomed through the city and barreled into his bedroom. He grabbed Machari and stared into his lifeless eyes. Bazek saw they were the same color as his and he was overcome with grief. He wailed and sobbed as his tears dripped into Machari's hair. "MY SON! WHAT HAVE I DONE?!"

The sun rose on a new day, as Bazek sobbed, holding his long-lost son.

Spirit Warriors Book 3

2027

Acknowledgments

All glory for this novel belongs to my Lord and Savior, Jesus Christ. Thank you to everyone who has picked up a copy of *Spirit Warriors*. I hope this story has been entertaining, and I am grateful for the opportunity God has given me to share this journey with you. My prayer is that these pages reflect His glory and that He uses this story to draw readers closer to Himself.

I am deeply thankful for my parents, friends, and mentors who supported me throughout the development of this series. The period between the release of Book One and Book Two was one of the most challenging seasons of my life, yet God used the people around me to sustain, shape, and prepare me for the calling He has placed on my life beyond collegiate athletics. I would not be here without their love, encouragement, and faithfulness, and I am forever grateful for them.

I am also thankful for the creative team God has brought together for the upcoming comic adaptation of *Spirit Warriors*. Their dedication and incredible talent are a blessing, and I believe this project will serve as another opportunity to bring God further glory. None of what lies ahead would be possible without the continued support of readers like you. Thank you for being part of this journey, and I look forward to what God has in store for the *Spirit Warriors* universe.

About the Author

Caleb James is a former collegiate defensive tackle who played football at Rice University, Baylor University, and University of Mississippi. During his senior year at Ole Miss, his team made a deep postseason run to the Fiesta Bowl, finishing one win away from the national championship. His experiences as a student athlete competing at the highest level deeply inform the themes of ethical leadership, systemic pressures, and Christ-centered identity that shape the Spirit Warriors series.

Spirit Warriors was born out of Caleb's personal journey through faith, ambition, injury, loss, and transition. As his athletic path shifted, he wrestled with questions about his calling past trauma. This ultimately led him to trust God's calling even when it differed from his own plans. Those struggles became the foundation for a story that explores moral compromise, endurance under broken systems, and what it means to follow God in unrewarding situations.

Caleb is a devout follower of Jesus Christ and served with Athletes in Action throughout his college career. He also studied at Truett Seminary, where he gained deeper spiritual insights that he infuses into his stories. Spirit Warriors is both a long-running epic fantasy series, currently projected to span more than fifteen novels, and a ministry expressed through storytelling. A comic adaptation is underway with a planned 2026 release, and long-term hopes of expanding into animation.

When he is not writing, Caleb enjoys anime, sports, video games, reading, and Christian hip-hop. He plans to continue pouring into student athletes as a coach while building stories that challenge, encourage, and point readers toward hope.

www.ingramcontent.com/pod-product-compliance
Lightning Source LLC
Chambersburg PA
CBHW051054030726
47504CB00006B/1619